Two *gardaí*, police-issue pistols in hand, were waiting on the hotel porch. "Máire Ní Flaherty, you are under arrest, pursuant to the offenses against the state—"

Máire flung her pack in his face and launched herself directly at the second *garda*, knocking him backward. "Run, Nuala!"

Nuala barreled into the first *garda*, then kicked at the prone one; his pistol went flying out in front of her. "Stop or we'll shoot!" a man bellowed as she took off after Máire.

Nuala heard two pistols fire, and an instant later plasfire erupted around her. What the hell? she thought wildly. Why aren't they set on stun?

Ahead of her, Máire was dodging the startled people on the sidewalk. Plasfire blazed again, and Máire's back glowed orange for an instant before she fell . . .

D1622170

Look for these Del Rey Discoveries . . .
Because something new is always worth the risk!

THE RISING
OF THE
MOON

Flynn Connolly

A Del Rey Book
BALLANTINE BOOKS • NEW YORK

A Del Rey Book
Published by Ballantine Books

Excerpt from "Backside to the Wind" by Paul Durcan is reprinted with permission from Blackstaff Press.

Library of Congress Catalog Card Number: 93-90180

ISBN 0-345-38289-7

Manufactured in the United States of America

First Edition: September 1993

Acknowledgments

I am grateful for the technical assistance of Dr. John Olerud of the Dermatology Department of the University of Washington Medical Center for his explanation of treating burns. And I would like to thank Ciarán O'Mahony for his help and for making the learning of Irish so much fun. *Go raibh maith agat, a Chiarán!* Thanks to my editor, Ellen Key Harris, for making this process painless; to Lindy Lyons, for reading each chapter as I wrote it, offering encouragement, believing in me, and for being my best friend; and my deepest gratitude to Paula Downing and Tom King, who helped me get a foot in the door, for their endless patience and advice. Thanks, guys.

Finally, I would like to acknowledge Joe Doherty for his inspiration and his courage. If he had not been betrayed by the Reagan-Bush Supreme Court, Joe would be a free man today. Instead, he is a prisoner of war, awaiting the day when Ireland will be truly free. May that day be soon.

Dedicated to freedom fighters and feminists everywhere. *Bua agus saoirse!*

Note to the Reader

In Irish words, the accent is usually on the first syllable unless a vowel is accented in another syllable. Most consonants are pronounced roughly as in English, as are most unaccented vowels. Accented vowels are long (á is pronounced *aw*). Thus Nuala is pronounced NOO-uh-luh; Máire is pronounced MAW-ih-ruh or Moira; Gormfhlaith is pronounced GOR-um-lee; and Éadaoin is pronounced AY-deen. However, Fiona is pronounced Fee-OH-na and Igraine is pronounced Ih-GRAYN. For the curious or the mystified, a more detailed guide to pronunciation and an Irish glossary can be found at the back of the book.

Chapter 1

Aᴄᴛᴇʀ ꜰɪꜰᴛᴇᴇɴ ʏᴇᴀʀꜱ of self-imposed exile, Nuala Dennehy came home.

The walk from the landing bay to the center of the terminal wasn't a long one, but Nuala was in no hurry. She avoided the moving path and did her own walking, the strap of her carryon bag clutched tightly in her hand. The fifteen-minute walk, added to the short hop over from Glasgow, gave her more than enough time to remember the day she had fled Ireland a decade and a half ago.

She had been twenty years old. Twenty going on fifty. It was two days before the graduation ceremony at Trinity, but she had already left campus, left Dublin, because there was no point in staying. They would not be granting her a history degree after all her hard work, because her thesis was not "acceptable" to the Jesuits who had taken over the Protestant university decades before. She had chosen the field of matricentered pre-Christian Ireland, knowing they—the Jesuits and the occasional nun who made up the faculty—wouldn't *like* it, but that there was a slim chance they would grant the degree anyway. It was usually just recent history, especially the last two centuries, that they were so strictly revisionist about. So she had gambled—and lost. It had saddened more than angered her—though she *was* angry—saddened her to see how quickly Ireland was changing. She had been in trouble many times in her life for speaking her mind—since she was six years old and had debated the existence of God with the parish priest, to the humiliation of her mother—but when a free exchange of ideas, a search for knowledge, for the truth, was not allowed even in a university, she knew it was time to leave.

Her sadness was tempered by bitterness: If the people could not see or did not care that the Catholic Church was gaining control over every aspect of Irish society, including the government, then why should *she* care? But she did. Profoundly. Being

1

forced to abandon her beloved country to seek education and opportunities elsewhere inflicted an angry wound that had never healed.

Belfast's travelport was crowded with tourists: Because of the many traditional music festivals, August was a popular time for visiting Ireland. Most of the tourists were speaking English with a variety of accents, but Japanese, Welsh, German, and many other languages could be heard in the din; some Australian students were even attempting to converse in hesitant Tlatejoxan as they waited in line, practicing the clicks and laryngeal stops that were so difficult for human vocal tracts.

Nuala recognized a few of the Tlate phrases. EuroNet had a weekly program on Tlatejoxan culture, and she never missed it, being as curious as anyone else about the first extraterrestrials to make contact with Earth because of the SETI program of the late twentieth century. The powerful NASA radiotelescope had sent a message, and the Tlatejoxans had come in person to answer it. Now the whole world was fascinated with the Tlates and the other extraterrestrials of the Unity. Well, not quite the whole world; countries where religion played a dominant role in politics wanted nothing to do with non-Christian, non-Muslim, or in Ireland's case, non-Catholic strangers from the stars. But Ireland had carried her segregation from outsiders even further. Since its secession from the EEC over fifty years before, reunified Ireland had become more insular and more strictly controlled by the Church. It had become isolated, in spite of continuing dependence on tourism, by restricting outside media contact. Tourists brought out the only real news of life in Ireland these days, and what little news they brought wasn't good. Nuala found it ironic that she knew more of what was happening in space than in the land of her birth, just across the Irish Sea.

She eased her way through the crowd, scanning the signs overhead until she found the one she was looking for: SAORÁNAIGH, it read, and underneath, in slightly smaller letters, CITIZENS.

An exile though she was, she still carried Irish citizenship, so Nuala left the jabbering tourists behind and set off down the corridor under the SAORÁNAIGH sign, her stomach roiling with bitter memories.

She fingered the tiny new ID chip she had been issued at the Irish office in Edinburgh. As she fidgeted with the shiny dogtag, she went over Máire's cryptic instructions in her mind for the hundredth time: Don't attract attention, and say as little as possible to the *gardaí* or anyone in clerical garb. Máire would say no more over the 'phone, and her expression had been, as usual, unreadable, her eyes hooded.

Máire was frequently cryptic, often exasperating, but then she had been ever since Nuala had met her nearly twenty years ago. She wondered why they were friends—or if they really were—but then she always had to remind herself that Máire was the only person from her university days in Dublin who had bothered to keep in touch for the past fifteen years. She was never sure why Máire continued to write and occasionally 'phone, but never having had a surplus of friends, Nuala couldn't just abandon her. In some ways, Máire was one of the remaining tangible links she had with Ireland. And she did write intriguing—if enigmatic—letters about the situation back home. She and Nuala felt the same way about the state of their country, shared the same hopes for Ireland's future. So when Máire hinted strongly that it was time for Nuala to come back, well, she had to come see for herself what was really going on.

Nuala tried, yet again, to decipher Máire's unspoken warning about not attracting attention. What did she mean? Say as little as possible about what? But then she found herself at the end of the short corridor. She fell into the queue of people waiting to pass through the Eye.

"Cuir do thraipisí go léir ar an mbord agus siúil tríd an scanóir." The young female voice repeated in a bored monotone, this time in English, "Place all your personal belongings on the table and step through the scanner." Those instructions had been a recording at the Edinburgh travelport, but in Ireland, where every man and every unmarried woman was guaranteed employment, unnecessary jobs were frequently invented.

As she came closer to the front of the queue, Nuala could see better what awaited her. There was the Eye, looking just like the one at the Glasgow travelport: a black rectangular box tall enough for humans to step through, narrow enough to admit only one at a time, and about a meter long. At its right side was a waist-high table with a smaller Eye for belongings to pass through, and beside it stood a bored Customs Assistant in her forest-green uniform. Beyond the box was another Customs Assistant, and, to Nuala's uneasy surprise, fanning out on either side were four armed *gardaí*: The young blue-uniformed officers held their Armalite plasfire rifles ready, but they looked just as bored as the Customs Assistants.

Even though she carried no weapons or "suspicious

substances"—whatever they were—Nuala's stomach churned
again at the thought of the rumors she had come home to investigate. She told herself to remain calm. She had broken no laws;
she should have nothing to fear.

At the head of the queue, Nuala took the chain off and
handed her ID chip to the Customs Assistant, watched her insert
it into the side of the Eye, then placed her bag on the table and
stepped into the box.

There was a flicker of light as the Eye activated, but Nuala
couldn't see what it was reading; the screens were visible only
to the Customs Assistants on the outside, not to the person in the
Eye. She wondered if every scar, every dental restoration, maybe
even her dozen or so gray hairs and the shape of her spleen were
being noted and added to the sparse information on her new
Irish ID disk. She fought off a wave of claustrophobia, and
sighed in relief when the door slid open.

Stepping out of the box, she glanced at the *gardaí*, but they
were chatting with each other and paying her no mind, so she
reached for her bag as it came sliding out of the smaller Eye and
placed its strap on her shoulder. The second Customs Assistant
slapped the ID chip into her palm and waved her on her way,
saying *"Lean an riabh uaine."*

Green stripe? Oh, there, on the floor, a weathered plastiseal
strip that led past the *gardaí* and on down another corridor.

"Follow the green stripe to the first free Returning Citizens
Interviewer," the Customs Assistant prompted her, raising her
voice at Nuala's hesitation.

"Interviewer?" Máire hadn't said anything about any interview.

"The first open door," the Assistant said, her voice taking on
an edge of annoyance as she waved toward the corridor a second
time.

Nuala moved forward, toward the *gardaí* with their lethal
Armalites, not looking at any of them, wondering why they were
really here. If the Eye had detected any weapons on her or in her
bag, it would have closed, locking her inside until travelport security guards could arrive. At least, that's how it was done in
Scotland. But the *gardaí* were state police, not private security.
Why were they here, in the travelport?

Although she didn't know much about weapons, she knew
enough to recognize a plasfire gun when she saw it. The police
in Scotland carried guns that could only stun; the Irish police
carried Armalites, which could be set on stun or set on plasfire,

to kill. What were they so afraid of that they carried the plasfire weapons in a travelport? Were the IRA up to their old tricks? They were never mentioned on the news in Scotland—but then, *Ireland* was never mentioned on the news.

None of the four men glanced at her as she passed them. Nuala was relieved to leave them behind; she had made it past the first hurdle. She was beginning to wonder just how many more there would be.

Starting down this new corridor, Nuala unbuttoned her sienna linen smock and plucked at her peach-colored cotton T-shirt, pulling it away from damp skin. The first open door? They were all open, at least halfway. They were probably supposed to be closed for privacy, but it was obvious that the air-conditioning was malfunctioning. She almost smiled at that. When she had left Ireland fifteen years ago, the air conditioning had been broken, too. No doubt it had been "fixed" countless times since then by the travelport maintenance men who never had to worry about being out of a job, because they never did that job too well. Remembering before she left Edinburgh for the hop to Glasgow, she had planned her wardrobe accordingly. She was glad she had worn a lightweight cotton skirt and sandals, though she had been stared at for it in the Edinburgh downpour.

Nuala continued down the corridor, looking for the first unoccupied Returning Citizens Interviewer. The lights flickered once and then again; apparently the air-conditioning wasn't the only system on the blink. As she walked, she caught snatches of polite, practiced instruction from the young, female Customs Assistants to their interviewees:

"Oh, no, ma'am, for a stay of less than six months, volunteer charity work is not compulsory. If your husband takes a job in Ireland, however, even a temporary one, that would, of course, change matters."

"You have thirty days to register at the church of your choice, sir. If you haven't decided on a church by then, the closest one in the parish will be chosen for you."

"I'm sorry, but I'm afraid the implant will have to be removed for the duration of your stay, ma'am. Contraceptives are, as you know, quite illegal. But I'm sure it'll be no trouble getting another when you return to England."

"In here, please. *Isteach anseo, le do thoil!*"

With a start, Nuala realized the words were directed at her. A weary young woman with wilted brunette hair waved at her through the wide-open door. "Close the door halfway, please, and take a seat."

Before Nuala had even taken her carryon from her shoulder and sat down, the interviewer's hand was reaching across the circular metal desk. Dropping her bag, Nuala handed her the dogtag, then sat down on the uncomfortable fauxwood chair as the lights flickered once more.

"Welcome home ... Miss Dennehy," the assistant recited as the 3-D computer screen on the corner of her desk lit up.

"Go raibh maith agat," Nuala thanked her politely, telling herself she had no reason to be nervous. She hadn't been here long enough to break any laws, so she should have nothing to fear from an interview. But why the hell hadn't Máire told her what to say? She cleared her throat. "It's nice to be able to speak *Irish* Gaelic again, after so long in Scotland." She winced at the sound of her own babbling.

"Yes," the assistant murmured as she read what little data there was concerning Nuala Maebh Dennehy.

Seeing that the young woman—at least ten years younger than Nuala herself; she couldn't be more than twenty-five—was occupied with the computer, Nuala didn't interrupt. She looked around the cubicle. Just as she had expected, there was the Pope on one wall, an eight-by-ten 3-D glossy of himself in full gaudy splendor, and opposite on the other wall hung another eight-by-ten, this one of the current *Taoiseach*, the Prime Minister of United Ireland. The irreverent joke that declared the two men to be the same person had no truth to it—else how could they appear together in public every year when His Holiness visited Ireland? But there was a certain resemblance, Nuala thought, a sort of weaselish look about the nose and mouth. Perhaps the *Taoiseach* had Lithuanian relatives ...

There was little else to see in the cubicle. No family holos on the meticulous desk, no other pictures, or a plant, or even a window. Nothing to break the monotony of dull celadon walls except those two pompous portraits. How dreadfully bored the poor thing must be to work in here full time, six hours a day, four days a week. Would a friendly overture be the right approach? Máire's instructions had been so ambiguous, Nuala wasn't sure how to act. If she were taciturn, would that provoke suspicion? But suspicion of what? What was the purpose of this interview? Damn Máire for not explaining. Should she—

"I see that this is a new chip, as you've been gone from Ireland for quite some time, Miss Dennehy," the interviewer said, interrupting Nuala's racing and confused thoughts. "I suppose they weren't in use yet before you left. That means there's a great deal of information we'll have to add. Our conversation will be recorded, and the pertinent information will be added to your chip."

"Fine." Nuala glanced at her watch, sighing. It was well past teatime; she wouldn't be getting out of here before Máire got off work. Perhaps a friendly act *would* be her best bet. If only she knew what was expected of her.

Still engrossed in the screen, the interviewer began. "Now then, Miss Dennehy, in the past fifteen years, have you—"

"Who are you?" Nuala forced a phony smile.

The surprise question finally forced the interviewer's eyes from the screen. She blinked. "I beg your—"

"What's your name? You know mine." Nuala's smile felt strained as she pointed to the screen. "And some other things, none of which is anybody's business." No, that wasn't right. Hold the irritation in check. Keep smiling. "I was just wondering whom I was speaking with."

"Oh . . . yes." The assistant flushed, straightening the already-straight lapel of her uniform jacket. "Noreen O'Mahony *is ainm dom*."

"Ah, well then, Ms. O'Mahony—"

"*Miss* O'Mahony."

Nuala raised an eyebrow. "So, Noreen, do you like working here?"

"I—" She blinked in confusion again; the interviewer was not used to being interviewed. "Do I—"

"Well, is it a full-time job? I imagine the pay is pretty dismal, since you're a woman. I doubt *that*'s changed since I've been gone." Nuala glanced around the cubicle. "And you've nothing colorful in here to liven things up even a bit. Or do you hide holos or a novel or something in your desk?" Nuala smiled again; her cheeks were beginning to ache from the forced cheerfulness, and her nerves were already too taut from this tightrope walk between caution and false empathy. How much empathy was going too far? How much honesty was dangerous?

Noreen just stared at her, puzzled. "I think we should get back—"

"If you wish. I was just trying to be friendly. Interviews can be so cold. And so boring for the one asking the questions." She smiled yet again. "I've had bloody boring jobs myself, shop clerk, library tech, and such, so I know how it can be."

A half smile, but still a wary one, finally tugged at a corner of Noreen's mouth. "Yes, it—" She hesitated, glancing at the half-open door, then leaned forward and whispered in a sudden flurry of honesty that surprised Nuala. "If you really want to know, it *is* bloody boring, as well as uncomfortable, asking people questions they don't want to answer for a stranger. But it's all over soon; I'm to be married in three months' time. I'll never have to work again, thank God!"

"You mean for money?"

A startled recognition flitted over Noreen's face, then was gone. The Returning Citizens Interviewer took over again. "Now then, can we get back to this? The sooner we start—"

"The sooner we'll finish, right. Fire away."

"Now then, Miss Dennehy—"

"Call me Nuala. I hate formalities."

"I'm afraid that's not allowed. Now, could we just stick to the questions, please? This will go faster."

"Sure. I don't want to cause you any trouble—or myself, either."

Finally Noreen gave her a genuine smile, though a brief and weary one. "In the past fifteen years, since leaving Ireland, you haven't married?"

"Whatever for?"

Noreen hesitated in surprise, her hands hovering over the keyboard.

Nuala shrugged sheepishly. "Sorry. Uh, no, I haven't."

Noreen typed, watching the screen as the computer added this information. She continued. "Your father is still your nearest male relative, then?"

"He is."

"And does he still reside in Falcarragh?"

"He does."

"And is he still employed by Donegal Renewable Resources, Ltd.?"

"He's not. He retired three years ago, for health reasons. He's not well."

Noreen frowned at this. "Well, if he's not employed, then who—" She stopped, glanced at the screen, then said, "I'm sorry about your father. I hope he's feeling better soon."

Surprised by the gesture, Nuala smiled, and this time the thanks weren't forced. "*Go raibh maith agat, a Noreen.* That's nice of you."

Noreen nodded. "As your father is unemployed, who then is your nearest *employed* male relative?"

Nuala hesitated. "Haven't any."

Noreen stared at her as if she had said something obscene in church. "None?"

"None."

Noreen's frown deepened. "Then who's to be responsible for you while you're in Ireland?"

"I'm an adult, *well* past twenty-one," Nuala replied, an eyebrow raised. "I'm responsible for myself."

"Well, of course, but—" Noreen leaned forward and whispered. Nuala had to strain to hear her. "I have to put something down. You really don't have *any* male relatives?"

"Just my father," Nuala whispered back.

"But he's not employed; I can't use him!"

"Then what shall we do?"

"Well, I—" Noreen was at a loss.

"What do you put down for women with no family at all? Do *they* get to be responsible for themselves?"

"Only as long as they're employed, after that the Church—"

"Why are we whispering?" Nuala interrupted. "Isn't this being recorded?"

Noreen blushed, to Nuala's surprise, and shot a glance at the half-open door. As if in answer to Nuala's question, the lights flickered again, went out completely for a few seconds, then came back on.

"It's not working?" Nuala guessed, suddenly understanding Noreen's previous burst of honesty about her job.

Noreen shrugged, her expression a mixture of guilt and apology. "We're told to lie about it, to make you *think* you're being recorded. But you're right; the spy system's been down for days. They can't seem to get it fixed. *Nothing* works right around here."

"Except the computers?"

Noreen nodded. "The ID computers are working reasonably well—so far. So we can still get the job done."

Nuala saw Noreen's embarrassment at being caught in a lie she hadn't wanted to tell in the first place. "So I won't be dragged off to jail for saying the wrong thing in front of cameras?"

Noreen sighed; she suddenly looked exhausted. "You wouldn't have been arrested, but you might have been followed—and watched."

The two women stared at each other. Nuala wondered if Noreen was thinking the same thing she was: How much honesty can I risk?

"And now?" Nuala said. "Since this isn't being recorded?"

Noreen swallowed and sat up a bit straighter. "You don't have to worry about that from me. I give you my word. Some of us still believe in the right to our own opinions."

Nuala considered that for a moment, then nodded. "Shall we finish this, then?"

"Right." Noreen studied the screen. "Where were—Oh, yes. Well, if you have no employed male relatives, are you going to be seeking employment yourself while in Ireland?"

"I hadn't planned to be here long." Nuala could see that wasn't the answer Noreen was looking for.

"Uh, well, perhaps you might consider that. What is your current occupation in—" She glanced back at the screen. "Edinburgh, is it?"

"It is. I've been living in Edinburgh these ten years past. I was in Aberdeen before that, doing postgraduate work."

"And you've been employed?"

"I have. I'm a professor at the university in Edinburgh, in the Celtic Studies Department."

Noreen's face fell. "But you're not . . . a nun."

"No." Nuala shrugged. "So I suppose I won't be seeking a teaching position in Ireland, will I?"

Noreen thought for a moment, then tried a new tactic. "Do you have any male *friends* in Ireland who could vouch—"

But Nuala was already shaking her head. "Not a one. It's been a long time."

"Perhaps some friend of your father's would be willing—"

"Is it really necessary?" Nuala's jaw clenched in irritation. Perhaps the usual tone of melodrama in Máire's letters hadn't been exaggeration, after all. And the other rumors?

"I'm afraid so. All females must be under the protection of a male relative, or some other suitable adult male, pursuant to the Mother and Child Act of—"

"Why?"

Noreen paused. She had every reason to be angry with Nuala for being difficult, but she didn't seem to be. "Well, it's . . . the law."

"So a female friend, even an employed one, couldn't vouch for my good name and character? Couldn't swear that I wouldn't rob a bank or try to assassinate the Pope or whatever?"

Noreen sighed, shaking her head. She pointed at the screen. "Your ID chip is a legal document, and women can't—That is, women aren't allowed to—"

"Things have really gone to hell in the time I've been gone." Nuala's glare of disgust took in first the *Taoiseach* and then the Pope. "How have the women of Ireland let things get so out of hand?"

Noreen's eyes widened, then she surprised Nuala with a smile that disappeared almost immediately. Noreen cleared her throat. "Uh, perhaps we could try a few of the other questions."

"We can try."

"Good. Then: Where are you planning to stay during your visit to Ireland?"

"I'll be going to Donegal, to Falcarragh, in a few days to see my father. I'll be staying with him."

"How nice. I'm sure he'll be able to think of someone to vouch for you, to fulfill the law ... So you'll be celebrating Mass at St. Finian's, then, where your father is a member of the congregation?"

"Whatever f—" Nuala bit her tongue, then lied. "Of course."

Noreen's expression clearly said she recognized the lie, but she smiled anyway. "You *were* baptized at St. Finian's in Falcarragh—"

"Well, that wasn't *my* fault, was it? I was just a baby at the time."

"There is a Presbyterian church in Letterkenny—"

"No. Not Protestant."

"I don't suppose you're Jewish?"

Nuala returned Noreen's smile. "Atheist, actually."

She knew she had gone too far when Noreen sighed and shook her head. "You *have* been gone a long time, haven't you, Miss Dennehy?"

"Nuala. If we're not being recorded, then there's no need for formalities, right?"

"No. But I have to update your ID. If the *gardaí* stopped you and found you with incomplete or unacceptable records—"

"Why would they stop me if I don't break any laws?"

Noreen stared at her in disbelief. "The *gardaí* can stop anybody, at any time, and frequently do, especially a woman who is not accompanied by a man or a child."

"I can be harassed by the *gardaí* simply for being female?" Nuala forced the words out between clenched teeth.

Noreen shot a glance at the door as a couple passed by. Getting up from behind the desk, she crossed the cubicle and closed the door, then slowly walked back to her seat, frowning. Nuala watched her, cursing her own temper and big mouth. Noreen seemed to be open to honesty, but how far was too far? She was not under the "protection" of any man; she was an atheist; even her profession was unacceptable. If she held foreign citizenship, she might be deported as undesirable, but she was an Irish citizen. What kind of trouble could Noreen cause Nuala if she wished? Had she really meant it about the right to her own opinion? Or would she have her followed, as she had mentioned? Nuala would *have* to be more careful.

Noreen was staring back at her, studying her with a curious expression.

"I'm sorry your father isn't well, Miss—*Nuala*. But my advice to you is to go back to Edinburgh and have him visit you there when he's able. You don't belong in Ireland."

Nuala's eyes widened; her nostrils flared. Her anger made her immediately forget her intention to be cautious. Her voice rasped. "I don't *belong* in Ireland?"

It was a moment before she could continue. "Do you know what I teach in Edinburgh, Noreen? I teach Irish history. Irish history to Scots only a few years younger than yourself. I had to leave Ireland to teach Irish history."

Noreen started to speak, but Nuala continued on, interrupting her. "I memorized Robert Emmett's speech from the dock before I was six years old. I read Wolfe Tone's autobiography—*both* volumes, each almost too heavy for me to carry in hardcopy format—before I was ten. The year the government withdrew all copies of Bernadette Devlin McAliskey's autobiography from the libraries, I *stole* the copy from the Falcarragh branch before they could get to it, and memorized the whole bloody thing, word for word, so that the bastards would never be able to take it from me. By the time I attended university, I had to visit Cardiff and Edinburgh and even—by the gods—bloody *London* to find the Irish history books that were no longer available in Ireland! In those days—little more than a decade and a half ago—travel between Ireland and the bigger island was easy; there were none of these wee interviews to make sure that Irish citizens aren't doing or *thinking* that which is socially unacceptable. I got my education in Irish history from sources that are not as easy for your generation to obtain. I probably know more about *my country*'s history than anybody your age or younger . . . I don't *belong* in Ireland? It appears to me that I've come back just in bloody damn time!"

Noreen was leaning back in her chair, bracing herself against her desk with both hands, her eyes wide. She swallowed, blinked, then spoke. Her voice cracked. "If you're familiar with Irish history, then surely you know of—Mairéad Farrell."

Nuala's anger evaporated, turned to shock. The only Irish people today who would know who Mairéad Farrell had been were—

Nuala stared at Noreen, studying her. It might be a trap. She could be trying to trip her up, to catch her. No. Her instincts about people had never let her down yet. A smile stole over Nuala's face. She leaned forward, looking into Noreen's still-wary eyes, and whispered, "Why, Noreen, you're a rebel!"

Recognition and relief were echoed in Noreen's smile. "Aren't we all, in one way or another?"

They just smiled at each other for a moment. Nuala was relieved that her foolish anger wasn't going to get her into trouble after all and stunned to have stumbled across the truth of one of those rumors. There *were* rebels in Ireland; it wasn't just another of Máire's fevered stories.

Finally Noreen whispered, "What's the *real* reason you've come back?"

Nuala hesitated, then answered, "I don't know yet, really. Just to—see for myself. We don't hear much about Ireland on the outside, just what news tourists bring out. But from what I've heard—I mean, the rumors—" She shrugged. "I had to see for myself just what my country has become."

Noreen nodded as if this were the right answer. "Well, I can tell you that you won't get very far until you learn to curb that tongue of yours."

Perhaps Nuala's blush was from the stifling heat in the tiny room. "I've been told that before." She smiled sheepishly. "I seem to forget it with regularity."

Noreen got up from her desk and went to listen at the closed door for a moment. When she was satisfied, she walked over to the picture of the Pope and took it down. Mystified, Nuala watched as she picked at the edge with her fingernails until she grasped something shiny. Easing the chip out from between the picture and the backing, Noreen whispered, "You never saw this."

"Saw what?"

After replacing the picture on the wall, Noreen hurried over to her desk and inserted the chip into the computer. She pressed the Voice Activator switch. "Computer, transfer information to blank files and reformat."

The whirring sound took perhaps thirty seconds. Noreen beckoned Nuala around to her side, and they both watched as words flew by too fast to read. When the jumble stopped Noreen said, "Computer, scroll readout from screen five."

Nuala stared at the screen as Noreen smiled and said, still whispering, "There. Your father is once again employed, as is your new brother, Séamus Óg, and your uncle Tadhg, all at Donegal Renewable Resources, Ltd. You're engaged to be married to Liam O'Donnell, who also works at Donegal Renewable. Your most recent employment was as a shop clerk. You are still, in spite of your absence, a member of the parish of St. Finian's, where you will be attending Mass regularly from now on. You will be volunteering with St. Finian's Travellers Outreach shortly after your wedding, which is to take place May next."

Nuala was astounded. "How the hell did you—Who is this Liam fellow, and do I like him?"

Noreen laughed, then whispered, "I'm sure you do. As do the other three women I've matched him with. There could be hell to pay if the *gardaí* ever stop all four of you at the same time . . . Now, are you going straight on to Falcarragh from here, or are you staying for a bit in Belfast? If you are, I have to give you a local address."

"I was planning to visit a friend, actually."

"Married?"

"She's not."

"Oh." Noreen frowned. "Well, does she live with her parents, then?"

"She's nearly forty years old! I should hope she doesn't!"

"Sh!" Noreen stared at the door, her knuckles white on the edge of the desk, but there was no sound from the corridor. She swallowed and whispered, "Then what rooming house is she living in, and what's the name of the nun who runs the place?"

"Nun? She lives in a room over a pub."

Noreen stared at her in disbelief. "A single woman living alone? That isn't possible! How can she not live in a church-sponsored rooming house?"

Nuala shrugged. "I haven't any idea. She never mentioned that in her letters. I just know she lives in a room over a pub and when she has to she pretends to be engaged to some fellow in the IRA who's on the run."

"The IRA?" Noreen was even more astonished at this. "She tells the *gardaí* she's engaged to—"

"Of course she doesn't tell *them* that; it's the neighbors she tells. She says it's perfect cover, and they leave her alone for it."

"The neighbors? But where—" Noreen nodded. "She must live in Bandit Country, West Belfast."

"Right, the Falls itself."

"Okay, then, even if your friend doesn't live in a rooming house, I'd better register you in one—at least on your chip. I can list you as staying at one of the houses on the Falls Road. The *gardaí* rarely verify rooming house residencies—I suspect because they don't want to tangle with the nuns. So—Upper Falls or Lower?"

"Better make it Lower."

"Okay, there's one next to Hume Square. I'll put you in that one."

Her fingers danced over the old-fashioned keys, and Nuala watched as the box marked "Current Residence" filled up with an address.

When that was done, Noreen leaned back in her chair and told the computer to scroll the data again. The women watched, reading, as all the pertinent data about Nuala Dennehy, some true, some fiction, trickled by.

"Your sister's a nun?" Noreen turned to Nuala in surprise. "*That* wasn't on my chip."

"That bit's true," Nuala admitted, and shrugged. "Every family has a black sheep."

Noreen just smiled and nodded, then checked the rest of the data. When it stopped scrolling, she copied it to the computer's permanent record, then hit the release. The chip popped out. She clipped the shiny dogtag onto the chain and handed it to Nuala. "Don't lose it. And don't forget to update it when you get to Falcarragh."

"Right."

Nuala stared at the chip before slipping it around her neck. She knew enough to know that that bit of plastisteel could keep her out of jail—or put her in it, if the fraud were discovered.

"Now, then," Noreen said, after she had hidden her precious chip behind the Pope again, "I'll have to confiscate any contraband from your bag, since you have to go through the Eye again on your way out, and they'd catch it there."

"I don't have any contraceptives with me—or *in* me, for that matter," Nuala said as she placed her blue carryon bag on the desk.

"Good, but I have to take any foreign marijuana or alcohol and any printed matter or noninstrumental music chips. Got any of those?" She ripped open the Velcro and carefully dumped the bag's contents on the desk.

"The chips are all *sean nós* music, and I don't drink or smoke, so there's none of that, foreign or domestic."

"I'll have to take these." Noreen held up the news magazine and the paperback copy of *The Grapes of Wrath*.

"But I haven't finished—" Nuala gave up, knowing it was futile.

"Sorry. But if this book is published in Ireland, you can—"

"I'm sure it wouldn't be."

"Oh. Well, I can put them in a bag with your name and ID number at the Reclaim Desk, and you can pick them up when you return to Edinburgh."

"Don't bother. I finished the magazine and I've read the novel many times before ... Say, have you?"

"Have I what?" Noreen was inspecting Nuala's music chips.

"Read *The Grapes of Wrath*? Could you smuggle it home and pass it on when you've done with it?"

"Sure, we do it all the time, every time the spy system goes down. Is it good?"

Nuala smiled. "It's terribly subversive. I recommend it highly."

"In that case ..." The novel disappeared into Noreen's desk.

"Take the magazine, as well. It'd be a nice change, I don't doubt, to read some uncensored news."

"Are there any articles about the Tlatejoxans or the other aliens?" Noreen asked. "We don't hear much—actually, we don't hear *any*thing about them on the official news. We have to rely on tourists or the Guerrilla broadcasters for news about space."

"Yeah, this issue's got a *very* nice historical overview of our last seventy years in space—how the Tlates gave us the technology for interstellar travel and sponsored the Fleet for membership in the Unity. There's an article about the new Chinese space colonies, and it encapsulates brief histories of the other human colonies on all the other worlds. There's even an article about the U.S. Space Corps trying to play catch-up to the Fleet. It's a good issue. That's why I brought it; I knew you didn't get much news over here."

"Great—thank you! I'll try to make copies and pass them on." Noreen didn't hesitate; the magazine disappeared after the novel. She began putting everything back into Nuala's bag. "Okay, then. Everything else looks fine."

When the bag was closed up again, Noreen handed it to Nuala. They stared at each other in awkward silence; then Nuala finally spoke. "Is that it, then? Am I free to go?"

Noreen nodded. "You'll have to show your ID again when you get your suitcase from Inspections, but that won't be a problem. My chip transferred my supervisor's approval to it. So you're ready." She smiled. "Enjoy your stay in Ireland."

Nuala held Noreen's eyes for a moment longer, not knowing how to thank her. "I'm not entirely sure what's going on here, but it's obvious you're taking an awful risk for me, and I don't know why."

Searching for the right words, Noreen paused, but finally gave up, shrugging. "I have a hunch about you." Her tone was as grave as her expression. "I know I won't regret helping you return to Ireland. Like you said, you've come back just in bloody damn time . . . And maybe someday I can brag about it."

"Whatever does *that* mean?"

But Noreen shrugged again. "I don't know. Just a feeling, just—good luck."

"Thank you. *Go raibh míle maith agat.*"

Noreen shrugged and acknowledged Nuala's thanks with a smile and *"Fáilte romhat."*

Not knowing what else to say, Nuala turned to go, then hesitated. "This Liam fellow that I'm engaged to—"

Noreen chuckled. "He doesn't exist. Sorry."

"Oh . . . Ah, it's just as well, then. Divorce is illegal in Ireland."

Noreen was laughing when Nuala left.

Chapter 2

"S*TAD ANSEO*," Nuala said when she saw Máire up ahead on the sidewalk.

The driver, a man named Willie, took her at her word. The electric taxi immediately swerved, sideswiped the curb, and screeched to a halt.

When Nuala had righted herself on the backseat and shaken the dizziness away, she reached for the door handle.

"Here now, I'll be getting that!" Willie leapt from the front seat and almost beat Nuala to the sidewalk. There was a brief tug of war before he got her carryon bag away from her, but she blocked him when he reached into the backseat for her suitcase. She retrieved it herself and set it on the sidewalk, then fished the money from her pocket.

"You're a stubborn wee sort, aren't you?"

No doubt Willie thought his charm irresistible; he flashed a pair of dimples and pushed his cap back to a rakish angle on his fiery red hair. Nuala sighed and handed him the fare.

"Don't be giving him a tip."

Nuala turned at the familiar voice and found Máire glaring at Willie, both hands planted firmly on her hips.

"Well, if it isn't herself," said Willie. "The Terror of the Falls."

"A name that should be given to yourself, the way *you* drive."

"I got her here alive, didn't I? What more could you want?"

"That you don't frighten the life out of her on the way."

"Oh, she doesn't seem the sort to be easily frightened, does she?"

Nuala watched this exchange as if it were a Ping Pong match. Willie was enjoying himself—she could see that in his eyes—but Máire? Máire had always been hard to read. A few years older than Nuala, she had made the overture of friendship back in university because, she had said then, Nuala had expressed a "correct opinion" in an Irish history class—an opinion that had

18

nearly gotten her expelled. Máire approved of Nuala; but whether she actually liked her Nuala had never been able to tell, even after all these years.

Remembering the intense young woman Máire had been then, Nuala noted the changes in her friend: With a great many more gray hairs than when last they had seen each other in Edinburgh several years ago, Máire's hair color could now be called "salt and pepper." Cosmetics, especially hair dye, were widely, almost universally, used by Irish women under sixty these days, but Máire would have none of it. Nuala found the new lines around Máire's eyes, around her mouth. And her clothes were still chosen for their practicality and color—or lack of color. Máire didn't wear trousers, ever; that would only draw attention to herself in Ireland, and, as she instructed Nuala, "A revolutionary needs to blend in until the proper moment." So instead it was always navy-blue skirts with a matching sweater and a white blouse. Or, as today, a black skirt and sweater with a gray blouse. With practical black shoes, of course, and thick woolen socks.

Nuala didn't care for makeup herself, or overly fancy clothes of any kind, but she didn't think a bit of color was improper for a revolutionary. If that's what she was.

Máire reached for Nuala's suitcase, but Willie grabbed for it, too. "Now, what sort of gentleman would I be if I just dropped off a wee girl without helping her with her bags?"

"The sort that wants to father more children in the future?"

Willie obviously thought Máire was kidding; he laughed and relinquished the suitcase, backing away with his hands up in surrender. Seeing the glint in Máire's eyes, Nuala wasn't as certain as Willie that it was a joke.

He started to swing the strap of Nuala's carryon bag up to his shoulder, but she caught it. "We can manage, thanks all the same."

Willie chuckled. "And *wouldn't* the two of you be friends. Same feisty sense of humor in such tiny small packages."

"Go home to your wife and five children, Willie Dunphy, and stop bothering decent women," Máire scolded him.

"And which decent women would that be?" But he laughed as he said it, and headed back around to the right side of his taxi. "If you get tired of this old carbuncle of a woman," he called to Nuala as he opened the door, "remember Willie Dunphy. I'll show you a right good time!"

With a slam of the door, the taxi roared off, expertly dodging the potholes in the Falls Road. With the sideshow gone, Nuala turned back to find Máire studying her soberly.

"So. You made it in."

"I did. But no thanks to yourself. Why didn't you tell me about what I should say and what I shouldn't?"

"You had to see for yourself. And I had to see if you could keep your temper in a difficult situation. This is no game here. So. How much trouble did you have with the Interviewer?"

"I'm here, aren't I? What makes you think I had any trouble?"

Máire just raised both eyebrows, and Nuala flushed. "Well, so I did, then. But I got lucky. She—" Nuala paused as a woman walked by, a string bag of fruit in her hand. She nodded to Máire and smiled at Nuala as she passed. Nuala glanced around, then lowered her voice. "She knew who Mairéad Farrell was."

Máire's eyes widened. She motioned for Nuala to follow and lifted her suitcase. "And what was her name, did she say?"

"She did. Noreen O'Mahony. And what do you mean, you had to see if I could keep my temper? Just how bad *is* it now? What haven't you told me?"

"Noreen O'Mahony," Máire repeated in a whisper, as if she hadn't heard the rest.

Suddenly swerving through the open door of a shop, Máire snapped, *"Gardaí!"*

Nuala darted in after her, her heart racing. Once inside, Máire pretended to inspect a stack of writing tablets on a table near the door. Nuala saw her set down the suitcase and surreptitiously nudge it under the table with her foot. Not sure why they were doing this, Nuala eased her carryon bag to the floor and kicked it under the table, too. When Máire waved her off, she wandered a few feet away and found herself facing an overloaded table: mounds of missals, crucifixes, rosaries, and gaudy, framed 3-Ds of the Sacred Heart. She grimaced, but there was no time to move to another table. A tall, blue silhouette filled the doorway. She picked up a missal and opened it.

Three *gardaí* strutted in, all wearing combat vests and helmets and carrying Armalites. They glanced around the room, the two behind flanking the one in front. From the corner of her eye, Nuala could see that Máire was ignoring them completely, as were the three other women who were intent on inspecting various kinds of merchandise. The man behind the counter eyed them coldly, however, his arms crossed and his chin jutting out defiantly.

The first *garda* brushed by a table piled high with boxes of votive candles and "accidentally" knocked one of the boxes to the floor. The proprietor didn't move from behind the counter, but he cursed quietly in Irish.

Nuala could feel the eyes of the first *garda* as they swung around in her direction. She didn't look up, but pretended to read the missal devoutly. The *garda* started toward her.

"Are you going to pay for that?"

The *garda* turned away from Nuala to face the angry proprietor. "Pay for what?"

"If any of them are broken—"

"You stacked them carelessly, you have to expect a few might be broken." The second *garda*, a young man of no more than twenty, crunched his heavy boot onto the fallen box with a satisfied sneer.

"*That* was no accident!" The proprietor started around the counter, and suddenly there were three Armalites pointed at him. He froze.

One of the customers tried to sneak out the door behind the last *garda*, but he whirled and blocked her path with his rifle.

"And just where would you be going, missus?"

"Home."

Nuala couldn't see her face, but heard the fear in her voice.

"Home, is it?" the *garda* said. "And why aren't you there already, tending to your kids as you should be?"

"I had to come to the shop for some butter; we were all out."

"Butter? Hey, *siopadóir*, you don't sell butter here, do you?"

But the woman answered for him. "Not here. Across the street in Gilhooley's. I just stopped in here for a look."

"In a known republican establishment? Let's have it." The *garda* slung his rifle over his shoulder and thrust his hand at her, snapping his fingers impatiently.

Nuala turned her head just enough to see the woman produce her ID chip.

"What are you peeping at?"

Nuala jumped as the first *garda* spoke in her ear. She turned to face him, dropping the missal back onto the table.

"Are you speaking to me, Officer?"

The *garda* exchanged a grin with the second one at her tone. Across the room she saw Máire shake her head in warning.

"And who do you *think* I'm speaking to, girlie?"

The look on Máire's face made the angry retort die on her lips. She knew she should try to look intimidated, submissive, before this swaggering young man with a rifle over one shoulder, but Nuala hadn't a clue as to how to accomplish this. She had never felt submissive, even as a child.

"What do you want?" She tried to keep her tone polite, but it was a struggle.

The *garda* leaned in and raked a long, slow leer over her from toes to eyes. He was so close she could smell his beard suppressant, could see the outline of a pale scar across his chin.

"What do I want?" The *garda* seemed to find this question amusing. But instead of replying, he answered her question by casually reaching out and squeezing her left breast.

Nuala jerked back in shock, hitting the table behind her. The precarious stack of pictures of the Sacred Heart was knocked over by the blow, and they clattered to the floor. Missals and boxed rosaries came tumbling after.

"Leave the girl alone!" The proprietor had barely taken a step from the counter before the second *garda* rammed his rifle butt into the man's stomach. He hit the counter with his back and slid to the floor, groaning.

"Stop it!" One of the women customers ran to the proprietor, but from behind the counter, so she was out of reach of the *gardaí*. "Éamonn! Has he killed you?" She knelt at his side.

Éamonn managed to shake his head, but moaned again. The woman glared up at the three *gardaí*. "All right, you've had your fun! Now be off with you!"

"We'll move on when we want to." The *garda* who had knocked down Éamonn threatened her by raising the rifle butt again, but she just glared back at him, too angry to be frightened.

"Move on *now*." Máire crossed the room slowly, deliberately not hurrying. She, too, walked behind the counter and came to Éamonn. She stopped between the *garda* and the kneeling woman, who stood up to join her.

The *garda* in front of Nuala turned away from her and pointed his rifle at the two women. "We could take in the two of you for obstructing justice. A few days in the Crum'd change your tune."

The two women standing over Éamonn didn't budge. The *garda* by the door tossed the ID chip back at the woman he had cornered and came to join his two partners. The woman quickly slipped out the door and disappeared. The remaining customer glanced at the door, but then crossed behind the counter to join

Máire and the other woman, the three of them forming a barricade between the *gardaí* and Éamonn.

"We're taking him in for attempting to assault a police officer," the first *garda* said. The three *gardaí* pointed their rifles at the three women, but that provoked no response; the women simply stared at them.

From behind the *gardaí*, Nuala watched the standoff. She could see the fear in the eyes of the blond woman who had joined the barricade last. As usual, she could read nothing in Máire's eyes—nothing but determination. The third woman's face was flushed with anger. She clutched her string shopping bag full of wrapped bundles as if it were a bludgeon. She would go down fighting.

"You've got three seconds to move," the first *garda* said, and all of them hit the safety switch on their guns. There was a brief hum; the Armalites were charged.

"You'll have to be killing us, as well."

The woman who had run out the door a moment before now came back in, and behind her marched a line of other women.

"This is no concern of yours! Get out!" The last *garda* swung his Armalite around, but they ignored him and continued to file into the shop. They crossed behind the counter and came to join the barricade. When the last woman stopped, the barricade was seventeen women strong. They stretched across half the tiny shop, their jaws clenched, their arms crossed or full of bundles. They were teenagers, or middle-age; two were white-haired. None would be moved.

Nuala's heart was racing, her eyes wide. These women could all be killed; the *gardaí* could get away with it, if they claimed they had been attacked by a mob and "hadn't had time" to set their guns on stun. But even knowing this, the women were determined not to let them have Éamonn.

She was ashamed not to be standing with them, but she was afraid to move. The *gardaí* had apparently forgotten her. If she startled them with a sudden move or sound, they might open fire on the women. So she stayed where she was, barely daring to breathe.

After a few tense moments of silence, Éamonn struggled to his feet.

"Hiding behind women's skirts, MacDaid?" the first *garda* jeered. "That's the sort of men you republicans are: no balls."

Though unsteady on his feet, Éamonn grimaced in anger and started to push his way between two of the women. But one of them knocked him back with her shoulder, snapping "Don't be a fool, man! They'll kill you, sure!" The women closed ranks, moving together until their arms touched. Éamonn stood behind them, quivering with rage, glaring at the *gardaí* in open hatred.

Another long moment or two of silence passed, then the first *garda* shouldered his rifle. He smiled at Éamonn.

"It doesn't have to be today, MacDaid; we know where to find you. And find you we will, some time when you're not being protected like a chick by these hens. We'll find you."

He hit the second *garda* on the shoulder, then strutted toward the door. The other two *gardaí* backed toward the door after him, their rifles still covering the human barricade.

When the last *garda* was framed in the doorway, he paused. "You'll be dead before the month is out, MacDaid."

Plasfire shot from the Armalite, and a shelf stacked with boxed stationery exploded behind the counter. Someone cried out, they all ducked, and the *garda* laughed as he disappeared out the door.

Bits of singed paper and cardboard fluttered down all over the counter and the floor in a pink and lavender snowstorm.

"Are you hurt bad, Éamonn?" one of the women said as they all stood up again. "Do you want a taxi, to take you to hospital?"

"I'm all right!" Éamonn snapped, his face still red with fury. He softened a bit when he saw her concern and smiled at her. "I'll survive it, Mary. I have before, haven't I?"

"Will you be wanting some help with this?" another of the women asked, waving a hand at the scattered paper.

"I can manage." Éamonn made a shooing motion with both hands. "The lot of you go on now. You have families who'll be wanting their supper."

The women hesitated, looking at the mess.

"It'd only take a moment—" one began.

"I'll not hear of it," Éamonn interrupted. "It's my shop, and as I've no wife to be doing it for me, I'll clean it up myself. Now go along—and God be with you, all of you."

The gruff blessing was the closest thing to a thank you they would be getting, but none of them seemed to expect more. One by one, the women filed out of the shop. Máire motioned to Nuala and pulled the suitcase out from under the table. By the time Nuala had joined her and had shouldered her carryon, Éamonn was already brushing the bits of paper off the counter into a dustbin. Nuala approached him.

"If I broke anything that I knocked over—"

"It wasn't you, lass. They come in here once or twice a month and do this." Éamonn sighed in anger and disgust. "They destroy merchandise and I file a claim at the station. Sometimes I think they keep doing this just to see how long I'll continue to file claims that are never answered."

"I don't imagine an attorney—"

Éamonn's laugh was bitter. "You're not from hereabout, are you?" But he didn't want a reply; he just went back to sweeping paper.

"That's not what I'm saying, Máire! I thought the lot of you were *terribly* brave today, the way you faced down those bastards. I'm just saying we have the right to defend ourselves!"

Máire refilled Nuala's teacup. They were sitting in the kitchen of Máire's tiny flat above the Four Green Fields. They could hear the low rumble of fifty conversations below and the occasional lilt of *uillean* pipes or a tin whistle.

"Violence would only backfire on us."

Nuala bit her lip until she counted to five. Máire had a brilliant political mind, but sometimes she seemed incapable of understanding the obvious.

"I am not advocating violence, you know that."

"Your adulation of the IRA—"

"I do *not*—" Nuala paused again to get her temper under control. "I do not *idolize* the IRA, or anybody else. You *know* how much I detest violence of all kinds. But you have to admit that, if not for the IRA, we would never have gained Reunification. If not for the IRA, England would have perpetuated its racist laws and gone on pretending to hold talks about talks, accomplishing *nothing*. If not for the IRA, the loyalist fanatics would have continued their policies of apartheid—"

"So IRA violence provoked the English people to force their Time to Go legislation through Parliament, et cetera, et cetera." Máire had that stubborn, you're-wasting-my-time look in her eye again. "I know that part of our history, Nuala. But I know what resulted, too. After Reunification the IRA was again condemned as a terrorist organization, and Sinn Féin was banned as a political party. *That* was when our real troubles began. If Sinn Féin had not been tainted by the stain of violence because of their alleged links to the IRA, they might have survived as an organization. If they had, we might have been able to accomplish a true republic, not the Church-besotted mess of a backlash we suffer today."

"I know, but—" Nuala sighed. Arguing with Máire always exhausted her. The woman should have become an attorney; she was so exasperating she would be excellent at it. But of course she would have to live in another country to do that.

Nuala tried again. "Then what are we to do? Sinn Féin is illegal. Anyone who tries to express republican sentiments is silenced in one way or another. Women are not allowed to run for political office. The schools—the universities especially—are controlled by the Church." She shrugged and ran a weary hand back over her long, dark hair. "You've been living here these fifteen years past, not me. If you think I don't know anything, why did you insist that I return?"

Máire inflicted that searching gaze on her again, that look that had made Nuala's skin crawl since the day they had met. She never knew what it meant, but it always made her feel that Máire knew her better than she knew herself. She hated that; it stripped away all protection.

"You know our past," Máire said, her voice dropping as she leaned in. "The past has always had a grip on the throat of the Irish. It's something we can't ever leave behind. But you *more* than just know it. It's as if you've been there. You *feel* the past living in you. You have the ability to make it come alive for others. And you know—somehow—when somebody's lying to you about it. You can see right through them. I've seen you do that."

Nuala's skin crawled again. The way Máire was staring at her—she had always known that her friend was a bit eccentric. Occasionally, like now, she wondered if Máire was more than just eccentric.

"Next you'll be telling me I'm some sort of witch." Nuala tried to smile, but her heart wasn't in it.

Máire, however, did smile, to Nuala's surprise. Máire didn't do that often. "You can't be both a witch and an atheist, Nuala; make up your mind."

"*My* mind? I thought I knew my mind—before I started this conversation with you."

"Have another scone." Máire pushed the plate of them at her, and Nuala groaned. Incompetent in the kitchen herself, she rarely got to eat homemade scones, so she had already eaten four in the past hour. She grimaced, feeling how snugly the waistband of her skirt fit, but then she sighed and reached for the butter knife.

"What I was saying," Máire said as she pushed the jam over to Nuala, "is that we need a network. A nationwide network of women, first, because we have to win the women of Ireland over before we can begin to convince the men."

"But women have no power," Nuala mumbled through a mouthful of scone.

"No *political* power, exactly. That's why they'll listen. Once we educate them, once we're united, the imbalance of power can change. Unity is the first step—no, *education* is the first step, which will lead to unity. And education is where you enter in."

Nuala suddenly had the feeling that Máire had her entire life all planned out for her. And she was expected to go along with it.

"I'm not a nun. I can't get a teaching position."

"Not in university, no. But I'm talking about educating women, not wee kids who still believe everything they read in a textbook or on a vidscreen."

"And why would they want to listen to me?" Nuala forgot the second half of the scone. Was it indigestion or something else entirely that made her stomach lurch at Máire's second smile of the evening?

"They'll listen. It's not just *Irish* history you know, Nuala. You remember that it was the middle-class women of America and England who started the women's movement in the nineteenth century."

Nuala just nodded warily.

"Poor women often can't afford the luxury of political agitation if they've families to keep from starving. But Ireland's economy is stronger now than it's ever been. Most Irish women are comfortable. More than comfortable, with the necessities of life. I think they're ready."

"Ready?"

"It's when you start losing rights you once had that you get angry enough to do something about it. Irishwomen know what they've lost since our mothers' and grandmothers' time, since Reunification, since the Church took over. They're ready."

"To listen to *me*? Wait a moment, Máire. If you're fancying me as some sort of—of—*leader*, then you're daft. I'm not—"

But Máire didn't seem to hear her. She got up from the table, taking the teacups to the sink, thinking out loud.

"The first thing is to introduce you to the group, so you can see where we stand in our efforts so far."

"Well, of course, now that I know you weren't exaggerating, that there truly *are* rebels, I'll want to meet—"

"Then we organize other groups for you to talk to."

"Máire—"

"You can tell some sort of inspiring story from history, some victory story. I'll leave which one up to you, I suppose, since you're the expert."

"Máire . . . *Máire.*"

Nuala brought the butter and jam over to where Máire was absently washing the teacups, lost in thought.

"Máire." Her friend finally heard her and looked up. "I am not a leader, Máire. I never have been, I never will be. A footsoldier, sure, no problem. But a leader? Not me. That part of your master plan will have to be changed."

"You have more talents than you know, Nuala. The lid's there."

But Nuala would not be distracted; she ignored the jam lid. "I have no intention of becoming a martyr."

"Martyr?" Máire shook her head as she rinsed out the cup. "There you are again with your talk of violence. There doesn't have to be any."

"I know history, remember? Believe me, if we begin a revolution of *any* sort, there *will* be violence. You have to acknowledge that and decide if you're willing to pay that price."

But Máire shook her head, insistent. "No violence. Gandhi achieved—"

"People were killed in that revolution, too, Máire." Nuala sighed. "An oppressed people have the right—and the obligation—to defend themselves. If you want me—for whatever strange reasons of your own—to be involved in this, then you'll get the entire package. I speak my mind."

"Of course. That's why you're here." Máire took the jar of jam from her and screwed on its lid. "Now. You'd better be getting some sleep. Tomorrow night it begins."

Chapter 3

"GARDAI!"

At the whispered warning, Nuala's reflexes took over and she jumped backward, into the shadows of the Falls Road. She pressed up against the jagged brick wall of Dooley's Chemist Shoppe and pulled the balaclava down more snugly into her black turtleneck so no telltale glimmer of white skin would flash between mask and coat.

Most of the street lamps along the Falls Road had been shattered long ago and never repaired; the government saw little reason to throw money down the bottomless pit of rebellious West Belfast, so the moonlit street was full of shadows that could hide her.

There was a wet, broken brick jabbing into her side, but Nuala froze, not breathing, as the patrol approached in the cold drizzle. Had Máire found a hiding place? She couldn't see her anywhere.

Only Nuala's eyes, narrowed into slits, moved as she watched the three men in blue fatigues creep along the edges of the buildings on the opposite side of the deserted street. There was a sudden tinkle of broken glass as one of them stumbled over a bottle. He cursed quietly in Irish, gripping his plasrifle tighter as he shot a nervous glance up at the rooftops and other likely hiding spots for snipers. But nothing happened, no burst of plasfire, no explosion of fire grenades, so the patrol made its way safely through this part of Bandit Country and disappeared into the night.

Nuala silently let out the breath she had been holding, then started when Máire materialized out of thin air.

"They must be out *somewhere* tonight, but where?" Máire's faint whisper was almost lost in the increasing rain. "Where's your bloody IRA when we need them for cover?"

"Must be nearby," Nuala whispered back, "or those three

29

wouldn't be trying to sneak up on them on foot; they'd be safe and dry inside one of their iron pigs."

Máire just nodded and motioned for Nuala to follow. They crept along from shadow to shadow until they came to the intersection. There was no cover here; they had no choice but to walk out into the open. They paused, listening to the night, hearing nothing but the rain and a tomcat's desperate yowl. All of the windows were dark; West Belfast was asleep at 3 A.M.

Nuala helped Máire off with her black overcoat and took her friend's soggy mask, to let her go first, as they had agreed. Máire straightened her lightweight beige slicker, then tied a flowered plastic rain bonnet around her hair, took a deep breath, and stepped out of the shadows. She made it almost to the middle of the street.

"Halt or we'll open fire!"

Nuala melted back against the building and into the shadows, clutching Máire's things, her heart crashing in her ears. She was supposed to flee at the first sign of trouble, Máire had told her, but she couldn't just leave her friend to—

The pig rolled forward on almost noiseless treads over the wet pavement, its hidden driver trying to miss the potholes, but there were simply too many. The *garda* standing up in the turret nearly lost his balance when the right side of the armored vehicle dipped into a hole and then bounced back out again.

"Hold your position!" His command was not necessary, as Máire hadn't moved. Nuala watched from her hiding place, clamping her jaws tight so her teeth wouldn't chatter. The *garda* had spoken English; in this neighborhood that meant he was most likely Protestant. Would Máire choose the right fake ID in the darkness?

The pig jolted to a stop, the *garda* in the turret swaying, but never losing his grip on his rifle or its bead on Máire's forehead. The side door slid aside and two more armed *gardaí* jumped out. One of them holstered his pistol, but the other held his ready, pointed straight at Máire. Nuala couldn't see if it was set on stun as it was supposed to be when the only suspects were female. But he had spoken English, and this was Catholic West Belfast: The government allowed Protestant *gardaí*, who were so like their ancient predecessors, the RUC, to patrol this IRA-friendly part of town with virtual impunity. Nuala doubted that their weapons were set on stun. She held her breath, cold sweat beginning to slide down her sides.

"It's three o'clock in the bloody A.M., missus, a good eight hours after curfew. Just where the hell do you think you're going?"

"Home," Máire replied, her voice wavering a little. "I've just come from tending a sick friend, and I've children to—"

"'A sick friend.'" The *garda* mimicked her with contempt. "You bleeding Taig bitch! You really expect me to believe that!"

"I'm not a Taig." Máire's shoulders straightened. "I may have Catholic friends, but I've been Presbyterian all my life, thank you."

"Prove it."

The pistol in the second *garda*'s hand rose as Máire felt for the chip, then took the chain from around her neck. She handed it with the tiny chip attached to the *garda* in front, who grabbed it from her. From his belt he unclipped the datalink, then slid the chip into its slot. A ghostly yellow and green image from the tiny screen danced across his face.

"Armstrong, Rebecca," he read. "So you *are* Protestant, then."

"As I said."

"Shut up, you!" the second *garda* barked.

"See here," Máire objected indignantly, "you've no call to speak to me in that tone at all. I'm as Protestant as you are."

"We'll speak to you any bloody way we please—"

"If this is truly *your* ID," the first *garda*, still reading the screen, interrupted, "then your home isn't in this heathen part of town at all, it's—"

"Where I was headed, when you interfered," Máire rebuked him. In spite of her fear, Nuala was impressed with her friend's act, but she had no idea how much Protestant outrage Máire could get away with. Protestant solidarity in a Catholic state probably only went so far with men like these; Máire was a woman, after all.

"Now if you'll just give me back my chip, I'd like to get home to bed. As I was saying, I've children to get off to school tomorrow, and it'll take me a good forty minutes to walk home, since your lot don't allow any private vehicles on the Falls."

"Children," said the *garda* who was still reading the screen, in no hurry. "Three, two boys and a girl: William, John, and Elizabeth, ages—"

"*Are* you going to let me get home any time tonight?" Máire's tone was more weary than annoyed now. But was she playing these men correctly, Nuala wondered.

The *garda* eyed her suspiciously, his head tilted. "So, you were tending to a sick Taig friend, were you? How touching. What would this friend's name be, then? And her address."

Máire sighed. "Siobhan Dugan is her name. She lives back down the Falls, next to O'Hanlon's Pub. She and her husband had us over to supper on St. Patrick's. You know, as a gesture for their church. It can be helpful to my husband's career to have Catholic friends, so I thought I should—" She sighed. "You know how it is. Now can I get home, please?"

But the *garda* in front was not sympathetic. "You're out *well* after curfew, for which we could arrest you if we wanted, and there have been rumors of IRA activity planned for tonight—"

"IRA?" Máire's indignation returned. "*That* lot? There's barely a dozen of them left in operation, now that they've got what they wanted, forcing Ulster back under Dublin's thumb! If they have disagreements with the Vatican's influence in the government, what's that to me?" Another nice Orange touch, Nuala thought. But don't push it, Máire. "The bloody Vatican has far too much control over our lives, especially women's lives. Now are you going to give me my chip back or aren't you?"

"You wouldn't be up to some mischief, would you now?" The *garda*'s tone changed as he removed the chip from the datalink. He started to hand it back, then pulled it away, smiling. "You're not one of those females that likes to neglect her family to cluster together in groups and cluck about her misfortunes, are you now?"

The second *garda* chuckled, as did the one in the turret with the rifle. The first *garda* again extended the chip toward Máire, but again pulled it back when she reached for it, taunting her.

A chill went through Nuala, and it had nothing to do with the cold or the rain. Fellow Protestant or no, Máire was a woman first. If they saw her as a threat, they could simply arrest her or even kill her, but obviously they didn't, so . . . It was 3 A.M.; there was no one around to report them.

"I've had just about enough of this!" The waver in Máire's voice told Nuala that her friend was thinking the same thing she was.

The second *garda* holstered his pistol. When he turned back toward the pig, Nuala could see his feral grin in the vehicle's headlights. The *garda* in the turret tilted his rifle up as he leaned back and made himself more comfortable to watch.

"Give me my chip and let me go!" Máire was trying to keep her voice steady, but the attempt was as obvious to the *gardaí* as it was to Nuala.

"You want it, missus?" The first *garda* held it just out of reach, easing toward her. "Maybe we won't run you in for curfew violation, if you're cooperative." He dangled the chip in the air. "Come and get it."

"Come and get it," the second one echoed, giggling. In spite of the drizzle, he started to remove his battle jacket.

Máire took a step back, watching them warily. There was nowhere for her to run, and they all knew it.

"I'll just bet you *are* one of those females," the first *garda* said, unzipping his jacket. "The kind that are always whining about 'freedom' and how 'unfair' life is for you, the kind that encourage disobedience to the government."

For every step Máire took back, he took one closer, not rushing her just yet. The second *garda* giggled again.

Nuala swallowed the bile in her throat, her hands squeezing Máire's coat. If she tried stopping them, three armed men—but she couldn't just stand and watch, she had to *do* something!

"Perhaps you need to be reminded of your responsibilities." The first *garda* took two quick steps toward Máire, trying to spook her into running, but it didn't work. She backed up slowly, steadily, stumbling a little in a pothole but keeping her wary balance.

"You don't have enough to keep you occupied, is what I'm thinking," the first *garda* continued. "Or you don't have a real man to give you what you need, isn't that—"

The distant explosion jolted them all. The *gardaí* whirled around, forgetting Máire, who saw her opportunity and took it: She ran. The *garda* in the turret immediately swung back around and lowered his rifle, aiming it at Máire's back.

Nuala started from the shadows, her only thought to distract them from Máire, but the first *garda* barked, "Leave her! The bitch isn't worth the paperwork. Let's go!"

Nuala jumped back, terrified that the *gardaí* had seen her, but the first *garda* tossed the chip into a puddle and then the two of them piled into the pig. In a moment it had wheeled around, throwing light dangerously close to where Nuala was hiding, and was leaving the Falls, heading toward the sound of distant sirens. When it turned a corner, Nuala ran from her hiding place, scooped up the precious fake ID, and headed at full speed for the spot where Máire had disappeared around a building.

Her friend was waiting for her just out of sight, breathing raggedly.

"Are you all right?" Nuala handed her the coat and balaclava, her own heart still pounding.

Glancing back toward the sound of the sirens, Máire murmured, "Well, thank God for your IRA tonight! Maybe they're worth something, after all."

"Damn it, there was nothing I could do! If I'd had a gun—"

"You'd've taken on three of them? Don't be silly. I told you there were risks."

"Aye, I know there are, but we must *defend* ourselves! We can't just allow them—"

"We're late," Máire interrupted her. "Let's go."

She took off into the night, leaving Nuala with nothing to do but follow.

The brick rowhouse was just as dark as all the others, but Máire hesitated only long enough for a quick glance around, then trotted up the steps. Nuala followed, still writhing with furious impotence over what had almost happened.

Máire tapped furtively twice, paused, then tapped four more times. Immediately the door opened and the two women hurried inside.

"You're late," a female voice said. It was too dark inside to see anything as they pulled off their masks. "They're downstairs."

A glowmatch flared. A middle-age woman in a much-mended housedress lit a candle in a tin holder and raised it to Nuala's face. "Who's this, then?"

"A friend," Máire replied.

"Aye? Well, she better be, hadn't she?"

The candle preceded them across the room, around shabby furniture, and down rickety stairs to a small room where Nuala counted ten more women crowded around a low table on which sat a teapot with cups and biscuits on a tray. None of the women spoke; they all stared at Nuala. She gazed back, flushing a little at the scrutiny.

The youngest woman appeared to be barely in her twenties. The oldest, the one in the housedress who was apparently their host, was probably sixtyish, with nearly white hair; the rest were somewhere in between. All wore black, as they had arrived here as furtively as had Máire and Nuala. One of them reached for a cup on the tray and began to pour tea.

"Who's this, Máire?"

After Máire had taken the last chair, Nuala eased down onto

the only empty spot, the arm of the battered, once-white sofa. The room was piled high with boxes, stacks of *Catholic Family* and other old magazines, a mannequin—looking naked and exposed in the low wattage—and other accumulated junk. The windows were covered with black plastic to hide the furtive light.

"This is Nuala Dennehy," Máire answered the question as she passed a cup to Nuala. "She's just come back from Edinburgh."

"Edinburgh?" someone said.

Máire was taking a sip of her tea, so Nuala spoke for herself. "I was teaching Irish history at the university there—women who aren't nuns are actually allowed to teach in Scotland. As I couldn't very well teach here, I had no choice but to live in exile."

"Then why are you back?"

They were all watching her, studying her, these women who had not left to search for freedom, these women who were proposing to bring that freedom here, to Ireland.

She shrugged. "I'm Irish."

A copper-haired woman in her late thirties smiled at her answer, nodding once. She continued to study Nuala, the smile lingering. Taller than the other women, even sitting down, she sat erect, her shoulders back, not hunching over as so many tall women did. Nuala could see that this woman was comfortable with her height, her thin but strong-looking body. Yes, that's what it was that made her stand out from the others—they were nervous, edgy, fidgeting. But the redhead owned the space she took up, was at ease in it. As she continued to stare back at Nuala, the ghost of the smile still evident, she took a sip of tea. Nuala noticed her hands: Square fingers, bitten-off nails, strong hands enveloped the fragile cup. The woman noticed Nuala's scrutiny and looked down, then back up at Nuala, raising an eyebrow as if to say, "Yeah, so?" Nuala smiled. There was something about this woman that she liked.

"Do you vouch for her, Máire?" a somber-faced brunette with one fake-pearl earring asked. Nuala turned her attention from the redhead.

"I do," Máire replied. "I've known her since my own university days. She believes what we believe. I trust her with my life."

"You're trusting her with ours, too, don't forget," the brunette said. "Any one of us could be disappeared—"

"Tá a fhios agam," Máire said. "I know."

"Right," a woman with black hair said. "Well. Quick introductions—first names only, because she's *your* friend, not ours—then on with it. We've wasted enough time."

Around the room the names went: Eibhlín, Mary, Esther, Mairéad, Nell, Cáit, Patricia, Áine, Elizabeth, and Maeve. The redhead's name was Igraine.

Cáit, a graying blonde in her fifties, turned to Nuala. "If you've been out of the country recently, you've had access to uncensored news. Do you have any idea how valuable that is?"

"Yeah," added Esther, a thirtyish brunette. "You could sell it on the black market."

"Sell it?" Nuala frowned. "Why would I want to do that? I wouldn't want money for just—"

"Good," Cáit interrupted. "Then what can you tell us about the troubles in New Palestine? We can't get much information on that."

"Or about the Hashimite terrorists," Esther said. "The Guerrillas said more of them were arrested in Azerbaijan. Is it true their movement is nearly crushed? We heard that the Muslim Alliance doesn't want anything to do with them—"

"Wait a minute," Nell interrupted. She was about twenty-five, a plain-looking ash blonde. "We don't have much time here tonight. So shouldn't we ask about more pertinent news?"

"Like what?" Esther asked. "It's *all* pertinent, isn't it?"

"Like those rumors about the breakaway denominations trying to pressure the Vatican about ordaining women," Nell replied. "If that ever happens, it could mean real changes in the Church, even here."

"Yeah, what about that?" Cáit asked. Everyone fell silent, staring in anticipation at Nuala.

"Well," Nuala said slowly, "there was a report on EuroNet last week." She paused, trying to remember the details. "The breakaway Catholic churches in France and Lithuania sent a united delegation to the Vatican, but they weren't recognized as being Catholic, and the Pope refused to see them. The same thing happened when the Cuban Catholic Church tried it. The Vatican simply won't negotiate or even listen to any church that forms its own denomination. So even though the breakaways may ordain women, the Vatican doesn't recognize the denominations themselves—much less the validity of their female priests. The report on EuroNet said the number of breakaways is growing, but that the Vatican is still inflexible on it." She shrugged.

"So don't hold your breath waiting for Irish women to become priests."

"Figures," Nell muttered. "Bleeding troglodytes."

"What about Unity news?" Esther asked. "What are the aliens—"

"Hold it," said Maeve, the black-haired woman who had seemed to be leading the meeting. "I'm as interested as all of you in news from the outside, but as Nell said, we haven't much time. So let's take care of business first. Then after, if there's any time at all left, we can ask questions of her. Right?"

There was murmured agreement, then Maeve went on.

"So the picket at the Archbishop's residence is planned for Saturday next. Esther assures us the signs will be ready on time, and the escape routes are set. A simultaneous picket will occur in Dublin in front of the *Dáil*, but that's not our responsibility. We'll be in two groups at each: one with the signs, the other mingling with the onlookers. If the *gardaí* show up—"

"*When* they show up," Mary interrupted.

"—the second group will swarm around the first in a confused jumble, slowing the *gardaí* enough so they can escape. The signs and masks will simply be dropped so we can mingle with the crowd and escape will be easier. Of course, I'd feel a great deal safer if we had a larger group to cover us."

"Few married women want to risk arrest," Nell grumbled. "Their husbands could lose their jobs, and *then* where would their families be? If we could convince more single women to join us, it'd be only themselves they'd be risking, not their husbands and children."

"We can't push our sisters into joining us," Patricia reminded her gently. "They'll come out when they're ready."

"It's been over sixty years since Reunification." Nell waved an emphatic hand, almost hitting Nuala on the crowded sofa. "Three generations! We've all seen the Church taking over more and more control of the *Dáil*, of every department in government! And that bloody Section Thirty-one censoring the airwaves, jamming satellite reception! What's it going to take before they're 'ready'? Do women have to be shot down in the streets for demanding civil rights? Do we have to have another Bloody Sunday?"

"We need more than pickets, that's sure." Igraine's Kerry-accented voice was quiet, resolute. "Pickets and the occasional arrest may get us a wee bit of publicity, but only local. As I've told ye many times before, we've got to be more daring, take

more risks—and *don't* get caught, so word will spread on its
own, censorship be damned. We've got to make a splash, and a
big one." She frowned, her fists clenched. "We've all been
raised to be so bloody obedient, terrified to risk disapproval of
fathers, mothers, husbands, nuns, priests, *gardaí*. Well, it's time
we *provoked* some disapproval and got away with it. Prove to
women that it's possible to dissent and not be slapped down—or
be slapped down, but bounce right back up, stronger and more
determined than before."

"We would be risking too much," Áine argued. "Women getting killed would not bring more support. It would only frighten
off those who might have become involved."

"The executions of 1916 didn't frighten everyone off." Nuala
spoke quietly, unsure if she had a right to speak, since these
women didn't know if they could trust her yet. They paused, all
listening, though Áine was clearly not happy. Nuala pressed on.

"I don't want to see anybody get killed; I've never been involved in any kind of violence in my life, and I'd prefer to keep
it that way, but there's no disguising the historical . . . benefits
. . . that violence brought to the cause of Irish freedom."

"Benefits?" Áine glared at her in disgust. "What in the hell
are you saying?"

"The executions of 1916 angered the people so much that
they fought for and achieved independence for the Twenty-six
counties. The hunger-strike deaths of 1981 inflamed the nationalists of the North. The Enniskillen massacre of 2012—"

"We know our history," Áine cut in.

"Only the version taught by the Church," Nuala countered.

"Let's not forget that it was mostly *men* who were only too
ready to take up arms to fight for freedom," Patricia said. "This
is quite different. In a time when the economy has never been
stronger, to convince women to face down plasfire, prison
terms—"

"If we could coordinate our actions with Sinn Féin," Esther
began, "then we wouldn't be so fragmented. It has the history of
being a viable political party, after all. We could tie in with
that—memory of legitimacy."

Maeve shook her head. "They're still illegal themselves, and
besides, we've talked to the present leaders, and it's the same
tired old story: Their cause first, ours later—maybe. We have to
'secularize society' and resurrect that tired old chestnut, social-
ism, before women start making demands, they say."

"We could get the bloody Church off our backs if women

started *making* demands!" Mairéad hit the table with her fist, nearly upsetting the teapot.

"We're going round in circles again," Eibhlín said, her tone that of someone who had reminded them of this many times before.

"Right," Igraine said, leaning forward, her copper hair glinting in the light of the lamp next to her. "To hell with Sinn Féin. If they're not for us, they're against us. We've waited long enough, and look where it's got us: no rights to contraception or abortion or divorce, no paying jobs for married women, no day care for *anybody*, censorship of *every* bloody thing that comes into Ireland—even the airwaves—mandatory 'charity' work, and now these tax increases for families with less than three kids and those who don't 'voluntarily' tithe to the bloody Church! We've got to *do* something, or we'll lose every right we've ever had!"

"That's why we're here, Igraine." Maeve put up a calming hand. "That's what the picket is for—"

"A picket isn't enough!" Igraine insisted. "You asked for my help, remember? You wanted someone to come to Belfast to help train you in civil disobedience, and I came. I'm here. I'm willing to teach you, but not if you're not willing to take some risks. A picket *isn't* enough." Igraine startled Nuala by shooting a glance in her direction. "We've got to do something bolder: an entire, organized campaign of disruption from one end of this island to the other! We've got to leave no doubt that women have had enough!"

"That could provoke violence," Áine said, her face still puckered in distaste. "We mustn't bring ourselves down to a male level."

Igraine grimaced in irritation. "Whatever it takes." Her nostrils flared, her eyes narrowed. "It's time we stopped the rhetoric and *accomplished* something! If men won't get involved in women's rights, then we'll have to do it without their help. We don't have to *start* the violence; that would only turn people— women—against us, but by gods, we can defend ourselves, force them to take us seriously, to show them we're not afraid of them! That's more than a right; it's our *duty*!"

Nuala glanced at Máire, but Máire avoided her gaze, her lips pressed together. Nuala smiled at Igraine. To hear someone else, a stranger, echo her own thoughts . . .

"Igraine—" Áine began to argue, but Nuala interrupted.

"Organized campaign of disruption?" She forgot the others in the room as Igraine's eyes locked onto hers. "Have you something in mind?"

Igraine's slow smile grew wide; something twinkled in her eyes. "Haven't I, though?"

"Where did you get these?" Nuala asked. "Every port has an Eye to detect smuggled contraband."

Igraine shrugged, blew one last time into the white balloon she was inflating, and tied it off. "I have contacts. I've done this sort of thing before—for almost twenty years, actually. For a while I was part of a wee group in Dublin, but they were too timid for my tastes. So I came north to help train others." She smiled as she picked up a condom and dangled it in the air. "These were stuffed inside mackerel from the North Sea."

"Scotland." Nuala returned her smile. "Well, well. Prods smuggling rubbers to Papists—who would have imagined such a thing? What did you mean, contacts? What kind? Who?"

"It's a long story, and I don't know you very well yet. Perhaps I'll tell you some time." Igraine pushed a handful of prophylactics into a plastic bag. "Have you ever made a water balloon from one of these?" Nuala shook her head. "You'd be amazed how big they'll get. Huge, bloody huge. I suppose we could have used them for the balloons, but that'd be such a waste. But a water balloon or two—"

"We're not here for the sport of it." Máire's dour expression was a rebuke, but Igraine merely grinned.

"Come on, Máire. Who said rebellion can't be fun—at least occasionally?"

" 'If I can't dance, I don't want to be part of your revolution.' " At Máire's confused look, and Igraine's delighted one, Nuala added, "Emma Goldman."

"Good for her." Igraine sealed the last bag and secured it to the last balloon.

"How far do you think the wind will carry them?" Nuala looked around at the attic that was crammed with the fragile plastic globes.

Igraine shrugged. "We can't control the wind."

"We have to be well away before the gardaí—"

"Don't worry, Máire." Igraine held up the tiny remote control. "All I have to do is hit this. The fan goes on"—she pointed to the box fan in the far corner of the clinic's attic—"and begins pushing balloons out the windows. We can mingle with the crowd before the first one hits the ground."

"And they can't tie us to it, anyway." Nuala held up her plastic-gloved hands and waggled her fingers. "No prints. How could they prove anything?"

"Right. I know. It just—it just doesn't seem serious enough."

Igraine sighed as she prodded the white balloons aside on her way to the door. "We could each get five years in Maghaberry for possession of contraceptive devices. Is that serious enough for you?"

"I just hope it does some good."

Máire's gloomy doubt irritated Nuala, but she tried to keep the feeling out of her tone. "Every time a woman avoids an unwanted pregnancy, it defies the Church and the state. *That* does some good, doesn't it? We may not be overthrowing the government with this, but it's a start. It's why I came home. So don't try to discourage me before I've even begun."

Máire startled her with that unfamiliar smile. "*Tá an ceart agat*; you're right. It *is* a start. The first step on the road to freedom. I just never thought the road to freedom would be paved with rubber johnnies." After stepping around them, Máire listened at the door, then crept out into the dark hallway and started down the attic stairs.

As they followed her, Igraine whispered to Nuala, "Well, *I'm* surprised. I didn't think she had a sense of humor."

"I'm not sure she does," Nuala whispered back.

Archbishop Doyle had been droning on for about twenty minutes; it only seemed like half of forever to Nuala. She and Igraine and Máire stood at the back of the crowd that had come to witness his blessing and the dedication of the new community clinic. The *gardaí* were present, but this being Ballymena, not West Belfast, their numbers were few, and their weapons were holstered. There was nothing to fear from the IRA here. They would have no reason to destroy a clinic or try to harm an archbishop; that would only antagonize the community, their fragile base of support. So the *gardaí* were relaxed. If there was no threat from the IRA, then there was no threat. Who else was there?

The Archbishop was calling on Almighty God once again when Igraine slipped inside the shop. The first balloons flew out into the open air, high over Doyle's head, a few moments later. They weren't noticed immediately by the yawning crowd. By the time people began to look up, Igraine emerged, breathless, from the shop opposite the balloon-belching clinic. She, Máire, and Nuala began to ease toward the alley.

Nuala was watching the *gardaí*, who had finally noticed the balloons. They didn't appear alarmed; they probably thought it was just a part of the ceremony. Then some of the balloons sank to within reach, and the words printed on them were discovered at the same time as the contents of the little plastic bags tied underneath.

Archbishop Doyle frowned as some gasps and chuckles rippled through the crowd. He lowered the hands he had raised in supplication to God and motioned for one of his priests to bring him a balloon.

Máire had used a red felt-tip pen, Igraine a blue one, and Nuala green. The red words were: "Get the Church out of our bedrooms." The blue words that caused the chuckling read: "God believes in planned parenthood; He only had one child." The green words on the balloon the ashen-faced priest handed to Doyle read: "Control a woman's body = Control a woman's life."

Even at a distance, Nuala could see Doyle's face turn purple. When he found the condoms, he squeezed the balloon so hard it exploded. The bang made the *gardaí* duck and grab for their pistols, then recover sheepishly. But they sprang into action when one of the priests on the platform barked at them to confiscate all the balloons. Doyle tried to regain control of the crowd, but balloons were popping right and left, sounding like firecrackers, as the people ripped the plastic bags off the balloons, stuffed condoms into their pockets, and scattered in all directions.

As Nuala and her two accomplices turned into the alley, she saw white balloons wafting overhead on the breeze, heading west. She laughed out loud as the three of them ran for the car.

Chapter 4

"THAT'S MY LOT. Got any more?" Nuala asked as she joined Igraine and Máire on the bench.

Around them the park was riotous with the sound of children laughing, fighting, shouting, squealing. Mothers accustomed to the cacophony ignored the noise as they engaged each other in conversation. A few played chess near the swings. Nuala had been amazed, the first time she saw the chess players, at their ability to concentrate amid the pandemonium. Between moves they would call out, without looking up from the board, to young Mary or Liam or Seán to stop that or get down or mind younger brothers or sisters. Nuala was impressed by the mothers' patience and at the same time even more convinced that she never wanted to join their ranks.

"All gone." Igraine had to repeat it to be heard over the childish shrieks from the swings. "I paid a visit to every waiting room in the Medical Building and stuck them in the copies of *Catholic Family* and *Ladies Journal*."

"Fitting." Nuala leaned closer to be heard. "Two of the worst propaganda rags. Wouldn't their publishers be surprised to know they're helping to spread dissension among the slaves?"

"I inserted mine among the produce at Butler's Market." Máire's eyes narrowed in grim satisfaction. "I hope the Church closes him down for it. The bastard's wife and five daughters all work there, but do they ever see a penny?"

Igraine frowned in concern. "A Protestant market? He'll hardly be able to prove to the authorities that he's a loyal Catholic. They might close him down for good!"

"Exactly." Máire's firm nod was merciless. "He won't be making any more money off the women in his family."

"And what will they do to survive if they lose their shop?" Nuala stared at Máire, aghast. "My God, Máire, from what you and Igraine have told me—you *know* what could happen to them! How could you? We are trying to *help* women, not force them out into the street or get them arrested! You've got to go retrieve those pamphlets. We cannot—I *won't*—be responsible for—"

"God Patrol!" Igraine whispered, startling Nuala.

Across the playground three men wearing plain brown monk's robes and rope belts over expensive brown suits meandered in the general direction of the playing children. Though none of the mothers looked over or even seemed to notice, Nuala saw that they were sitting up straighter, their conversations dying; the relaxed, laughing women of but a moment before had been replaced by stiff-shouldered, unsmiling mannequins.

"What—" Nuala began.

"If we walk away together, we'll draw attention to ourselves." Igraine's lips barely moved; Nuala could scarcely make out what she was saying over the noisy children. But then she noticed that the children's squeals and laughter were subsiding, too. One little girl on a motionless swing was staring at the three men as they approached, her eyes wide.

Máire got up from the bench and casually walked over to the swings. She smiled at the little girl and asked how high she could swing.

Distracted by the attention, the child returned her smile. "I can go *very* high. Do you want to see?"

"Show me," Máire said, and the little girl kicked at the ground with both feet, pushing off with an energetic shove. Máire smiled again, encouraging her to go higher still.

"Who are they?" Nuala whispered.

"They mustn't find us together; we're both single. Don't attract attention to yourself." With that, Igraine got up and strode toward the sandbox as if she had business there.

Máire was now pushing the girl on the swing, who shrieked in delight. Igraine joined the three children who had been digging in the sand and borrowed one of their shovels. In a moment she had them racing to see who could fill a pail first, laughing with them as the sand flew.

Nuala had no idea what to do, but the men were coming closer, phony smiles on their smooth faces. She felt vulnerable sitting there by herself, so she got up and started to walk away, with no destination in mind. There was a girl of about twelve sitting in the middle of another bench with a book, and Nuala found herself heading that way. When she came near, the girl, without looking up from her book, scooted over to make room. Nuala sat down.

"If you talk to me, they might leave you alone. Unless they saw you with your friends before." The red-haired girl smiled at Nuala's surprise. "Don't worry, I know what to do." She eased closer to Nuala and held out her book. "We can pretend to be talking about this silly old thing. I carry it with me just in case I run into them."

Nuala didn't understand what the girl was talking about, but she took the book, then glanced over quickly. The three men had surrounded the chess players. Everyone around the chess table was smiling, and not one of those smiles was sincere.

"See?" the girl said. "They always pick the women who

aren't with their kids. It's women talking to women spooks them."

"Who are they?" Nuala kept her voice low, pretending to peruse *Young Person's Lives of the Saints*.

"Christian Brothers," her young ally replied. "But we just call them God Patrols, because they patrol about, sticking their noses into everything, making sure nobody's sinning."

"Sinning? And are those women sinning because they're playing chess?"

The girl grinned up at her. "You're not from hereabout, are you? Where are you from? What's your name?"

"Nuala. And I've been in Scotland for fifteen years."

"Scotland!" The girl's face lit up. "I've always wanted to visit Scotland. It's a Celtic country, too, but it's Protestant. That must be terribly odd." She lowered her voice even further and whispered, "They don't really worship the devil there, do they? The nuns are always telling us that Protestants—especially those outside Ireland—are just fooling themselves when they think they're worshipping God; they're really worshipping Satan, but most of them don't even know it . . . But I don't believe that. It's not true, is it?"

"What? No!" Nuala shot a glance at the men, but they were still "chatting" with the chess players. "Of course it isn't true. Protestants worship the same God the Catholics do, they just do it in a different manner, that's all. It's the same religion underneath, it just looks different."

The girl nodded, satisfied that Nuala had given her the correct answer. "I've known the nuns were full of shit since I was six years old."

A smile broke through Nuala's surprise. "Smart kid. What's your name?"

"Gormfhlaith."

"That's a fine, ancient name."

"I know. And it's spelled the correct way, the Gaelic way, not 'Gormley' with an E-Y like they spell it in England sometimes. They get everything Irish wrong over there, don't they? But you've never seen a God Patrol before?"

"They must not be the same Christian Brothers I remember. You say their job is to see if people are sinning or not? What happens if they are?"

Gormfhlaith's tone was grim. "They say their duty is to encourage people to follow God's chosen path. That's what they call it: 'God's chosen path.' But my sister Fiona says that's just a cover story—their real job is to control people with guilt and fear. All they have to do is ask a woman's name or to see her chip. That's all. Because then they can find out anything they want, and they can make her husband lose his job, or they can make it so her sons can't go to university. They can do anything they want to anybody and everybody knows it, so they don't have to even *look* mean."

"What if you don't have a husband who can lose his job or a son who wants to attend university? What can they do to a woman who's alone?"

Gormfhlaith frowned in confusion. "Well, if she's alone, then she's got a job, right? So they can lose it for her, I suppose. But there's hardly any such thing, is there, as a woman who's really alone? I mean, if you don't have a family, then you become a nun, don't you?"

"What if you don't *want* to be a nun?"

Gormfhlaith grimaced. "*I* sure don't. That's why I'm going to have lots of kids, so there will be somebody to take care of me when I'm old and my husband's dead. *I* don't want to go live in a convent. That wouldn't be any fun. I don't like people telling me what to do. I don't like it at all. Fiona says she won't let them force *her* into a convent when she's fifty and has to quit working. She says she'll fight them."

"Good for her."

Nuala stared over at the brown-robed men, her stomach churning in nausea. Forced into a convent at fifty? That couldn't really happen, could it? Was this something else Máire had neglected to tell her? Or was it just a child's confused interpretation?

"You sure don't know much, for a rebel."

Nuala did a double take and stared at the girl, who smiled innocently back. "It must be because you've been away in Scotland, right?" Gormfhlaith went on before Nuala could reply. "You should meet Fiona. She could teach you a lot. She's been a rebel forever."

After another stunned moment, Nuala found her voice. "If your sister is a rebel, then you shouldn't be speaking about her so freely to strangers. You could cause her trouble—a great deal of trouble, with men like these lot about."

Gormfhlaith frowned, offended. "Do you think I'm stupid? I wouldn't have said anything if I didn't know you were a rebel, too."

"What makes you think—"

The girl took her *Young Person's Lives of the Saints* out of Nuala's hands and opened it, shooting a glance over at the God Patrol on the far side of the park as she did so. She showed Nuala the page she had opened to. Inside the book was a folded pamphlet: the same pamphlet that Nuala, Igraine, and Máire had spent two days writing, printing on bootleg publishing equipment that Igraine had mysteriously obtained—saying she had friends who could locate almost anything—and this morning distributed, leaving them hidden where women would be sure to find them.

Nuala stared at the girl yet again, feeling the flush spread across her cheeks. Here she was, fancying herself some sort of secret warrior, and a girl—a *child*—had already found her out.

"How did you—"

Gormfhlaith grinned, extremely pleased with herself. "I was waiting for my mother to come out of the confessional when I saw you in the back, sneaking something into the hymnals. When you left I went back there and took one. I thought I'd take it home to Fiona. She'll love it; it sounds like the stuff she's forever saying to me whenever Mam or Da aren't about. Did you write it yourself, or did one of your friends?"

"Uh, well, we—"

"Uh-oh."

Nuala followed Gormfhlaith's warning glance and saw that one of the brown-robed men was heading in their direction, a phony smile pasted on his face.

"You better let me do the talking," Gormfhlaith whispered, "since you don't know anything. Just smile a lot. They like that."

Nuala looked from the child to the approaching menace, and did the only thing she could: She smiled.

"Dia duit." Gormfhlaith beamed up at the brown-haired, brown-clothed man.

"Dia is Muire daoibh," he returned the standard greeting. His smile widened, but it was still as phony as Nuala's felt to her.

"It's a beautiful day today, isn't it, Brother?" Gormfhlaith said, and then repeated it in Irish, *"Tá sé go hálainn."*

"Tá," he agreed. *"Tá sé go hálainn. Agus cad is ainm duitse?"*

"Gormfhlaith. Gormfhlaith Maguire. And this is my friend Nuala."

"Friend? You're not a family member of this child's?"

Before Nuala could reply, Gormfhlaith jumped in. "She's a

friend of my sister Fiona. You see"—Gormfhlaith's voice dropped to a whisper as she cast a distinctly sympathetic glance in Nuala's direction—"she can't find a husband, so she doesn't have any kids of her own yet. That's why she likes to come to the park, to be around children. You understand, don't you, Brother?"

It was Nuala's role to look embarrassed, which wasn't difficult under the circumstances, so she cast her eyes down at the Brother's expensive, well-polished synthleather shoes.

"Of course."

Nuala had to grit her teeth when he actually patted her on the shoulder, all the while giving her that insufferably patronizing smile.

"Might I suggest, my dear, that if you want to catch a husband, you should make some effort at beautifying yourself. After all, the fish has to *notice* the bait before it can bite."

It took some effort to smile gratefully and to keep her tone light. "How right you are, Brother. And thank you so much for your advice. I assure you I'll give it all the consideration it merits."

He blinked, frowning in confusion, but Gormfhlaith jumped in again. "I was just asking Nuala about Joan of Arc." She held up her book, and Nuala's eyes widened when she saw a corner of the pamphlet sticking out the end.

"How nice." He didn't notice the pamphlet, to Nuala's relief, because he was paying little attention to Gormfhlaith. He ignored the child and focused on Nuala. Not bothering to sit on the bench beside her—though there was room—he towered over her, forcing her to look up.

"My Brothers and I are quite concerned about an evil influence that has invaded this parish."

"Evil influence?" Nuala exchanged a look of innocence with Gormfhlaith.

"Yes." His expression darkened; gone completely now was the phony smile. "There are certain disturbed people who are attempting to seduce the women of this parish."

"Seduce?" Nuala's eyebrows shot up. "Are you speaking of some sort of sexual predator? Because if you are, Brother, should we be discussing such matters in front of a child?"

Gormfhlaith's eyes widened; her mouth dropped open. Nuala wasn't sure if this was part of the kid's act or if she was genuinely shocked.

"What? No!" The Brother cleared his throat and regained his

composure. "I was speaking of quite another matter entirely." From the deep pocket of his robe he pulled out a familiar pamphlet and thrust it under Nuala's nose. "Have you seen one of these vile documents?"

"What is it?" Nuala reached for it, but he snatched it back.

"Lies," he said. "And printed illegally."

"What sort of lies?" Gormfhlaith asked, reaching for the pamphlet as Nuala had done.

He took a step back, raising the folded paper in the air. "The depraved lies of sick and evil minds, much too evil to be explained to children. It is obvious that there is a nest of vipers in our midst. It is our duty as Servants of the Church to warn the women of this parish about this danger. If you see a pamphlet that resembles this one"—he waved it in the air over their heads—"call the Church *immediately*, and most especially do *not* read it! Do not allow yourselves to be led astray by the sick ramblings of an obviously deranged mind."

"But how will we know what it is if we don't read it?" Gormfhlaith asked.

"If you find one, child," the Brother said, "give it to your father. He will know what to do."

"Who do you suppose would publish something like that, Brother?" Nuala asked.

"It is obvious. Anyone who violates the Word of God as taught by the One True Church"—the Brother thrust the pamphlet back into his pocket—"can only be a Satanist. These men are clever in their evil ways, obedient to the will of their dark master, and eager to seduce gullible women. But we will root them out. We have already closed the market in which the pamphlets were found. We will not tolerate evil to flourish—"

"But I thought you said they were clever," Nuala interrupted. Before he could pick up steam again, she continued. "You said you found that—vile document—in a market? Surely whoever owns the market would not be the author of such a tissue of evil; it would be exceedingly stupid, would it not, to implicate himself by distributing illegal documents in his own place of business? It must have been left by someone else, perhaps in an attempt to incriminate the owner of the market. Does this man— whoever he is—have enemies? A business rival, perhaps? Perhaps the contents of that pamphlet—whatever they may be—are not the true issue here. Perhaps it is merely a clever plot to defame the owner of the market in which it was found. If that is indeed the case, then would not closing the market assist the perpetrator in accomplishing his end: damage to the reputation and business of the owner of the market? And if so, then the Church is aiding and abetting the crime against this innocent man. Surely, Brother, you do not wish to be an accomplice to defamation of character."

Both the Brother and Gormfhlaith were staring at Nuala. Had she gone too far, said too much? Didn't anyone ever speak to a Christian Brother this way? Had that changed, too, in fifteen years? But she couldn't let the family of the man who owned the market be hurt because of Máire's poor judgment.

"Well, of course," the Brother began, "there could be some sort of plot against the owner of this market. But if the man is indeed innocent, then that fact will out. The Church is always fair."

"Of course it is." Nuala smiled against gritted teeth.

"May I ask you a question, Brother?" Gormfhlaith leaned forward eagerly, breaking the stare he was directing at Nuala.

"What? Yes, of course, child."

"Do you know what temporal lobe epilepsy is?"

"Temporal lobe—"

"Yes," Gormfhlaith said. "It's a medical condition I read about in the encyclopedia. It causes people to hear voices, usually just after they hear music. You see, I was just reading about Joan of Arc, and well, she used to hear voices quite often, and usually just after a bell in her village would ring—for vespers or something—and so I was wondering: Do you suppose that perhaps Joan of Arc had temporal lobe epilepsy?"

The Brother stared at her, speechless, then blinked. "Joan of Arc was a saint who heard the Word of God. *Dia is Muire* with you both."

With that he turned and walked away, his gait stiff, his expression confused and unhappy. He cast a suspicious glance back at Nuala, but she smiled innocently at him, her heart pounding. If he asked to see her chip—she really must learn to keep her mouth shut. But fortunately, he was distracted by his fellow Brothers. A few moments later, the God Patrol had finished their rounds of the park, and they left.

Nuala sighed her relief, then turned to the girl with a smile. "Temporal lobe epilepsy? Where did you come up with—"

"You were wonderful!" Gormfhlaith interrupted Nuala. "Defamation of character, aiding and abetting! You sounded just like an attorney. *Are* you an attorney over there in Scotland? I've heard that women are allowed to do things like that in other countries."

"No, actually I'm a professor of Irish history."

"Wow!" Gormfhlaith was goggle-eyed again. "You *must* meet Fiona!"

Igraine and Máire were headed their way as Nuala replied, "If your sister's anything at all like yourself—then I'd like to meet her very much indeed."

"You came!"

Gormfhlaith opened the door wide, stepping back with a big smile. "*Tagaigí isteach!* Come in!"

"Your parents—" Nuala began, hesitating at the threshold.

"I told you, they left to visit Uncle Hugh and Aunt Cáit until Sunday. Come in, come in. Fiona's in the kitchen."

Nuala stepped inside, out of the deepening twilight, followed by Igraine and Máire.

The Maguire home was small and warm, a welcome change from the chilling wind outside. Nuala barely had time to note the portrait of the Pope over the high-resolution 3-D vidscreen before Gormfhlaith was leading them in the direction, presumably, of the kitchen. In the hall they passed a framed copy of the 1916 Proclamation. Nuala smiled, hoping it was a good omen; at least it was a counterbalance to the Pope.

They heard the kettle whistling before the kitchen came into view.

"They're here," Gormfhlaith announced, excited by the importance of her role. She waved the three visitors into the kitchen.

At the stove was an almost plump brunette in a stylishly cut gray skirt, a violet silk blouse, and a cardigan. She turned to face them, the kettle in her hand, and Nuala was surprised to see that Gormfhlaith's sister was in her forties. But then, in a country with no legal contraception, women often had children right up until menopause; Nuala wondered how old their mother was. Fiona studied them for a moment, expressionless, and they stared right back. This woman, who Gormfhlaith claimed had been a rebel "forever," somehow looked too ... *chic* to be a revolutionary. Her clothes were tailored, definitely not off the rack; her brown hair had to be dyed, since it showed not a trace of gray, and it was nicely cut, swept back on the sides. Her synthleather shoes even looked custom-made. Nuala wondered if the woman got facials and pedicures as often as she obviously got manicures: her nails were just the right length, with not one ragged cuticle. But revolutionaries came in all types, Nuala scolded herself.

Fiona's eyes raked them each swiftly, from head to toe and back up again. Then she nodded and brought the kettle to the table, on which sat five cups surrounding a plate of freshly baked scones and a glass butter dish.

"This is my sister Fiona," Gormfhlaith announced with considerable pride.

Fiona smiled. "I believe they know that, *kidín*." She gestured to the table. "Please, off with your coats *agus suigí*."

While they were draping their coats over the backs of their chairs, Fiona looked at her little sister, which Gormfhlaith took as a cue.

"This is Máire," she said, pointing, "and Igraine, and that's Nuala."

"It's an entire pleasure," Fiona said, "to be meeting those responsible for this." From the pocket of her *báinín* cardigan sweater she pulled out the pamphlet and tossed it onto the table next to the scones, then she sat down opposite Nuala. "I've heard that the Special Branch are in a frenzy, trying to round up all of these and not knowing where to look next. And they're looking for myself, too, though of course they don't know it's me they're looking for."

"You?" Igraine asked from the end of the table. "What do you mean?"

Fiona smiled as she poured the tea. "They assume it's the local troublemakers, of which I am the principal phantom. They've no idea as yet that this bit of literary insurrection is the work of imported talent. How distressed they would be to learn that Coleraine has been invaded."

"Poor lads," Igraine murmured.

"You are the leader of the local movement?" Máire almost interrupted Igraine, leaning forward on her elbows and stabbing Fiona with a piercing gaze.

Fiona continued to pour. "It's hardly a 'movement.' There's just a few of us who cause a bit of a ruckus now and again."

"What sort of a ruckus?" Igraine asked, then added, "We could do with more ideas—and help."

"Could you?" Fiona finished pouring and set down the kettle. She searched each of them with her eyes again, lingering for a moment on Nuala, who gazed back, unblinking. Then she spoke to Igraine again. "Why Coleraine? If any of you were from this part of the country, I'd've run into you before now. So, as you're not, why Coleraine?"

"The idea is to keep moving," Igraine replied. "If the *gardaí* don't know where to close in, then they won't catch us."

"And we want to touch base with rebels all over Ireland," Máire said, "so we can form some sort of coherent structure, an organization, a—"

"With yourselves as leaders?" Fiona's challenge was in her eyes, though her tone was friendly enough. Máire began to reply, but Nuala interrupted.

"No. We don't need leaders."

Fiona stared at her, not speaking, and Nuala understood that the woman was taking her measure, as she had every right to do.

"We?" Fiona said.

"Women," Nuala answered.

"Women don't need leaders?"

"That's only Nuala's opinion." Máire's voice held a faint scolding tone as her gaze flitted over Nuala and back to Fiona. "*I* believe very strongly in organization and precise form—"

"While Nuala and myself," Igraine interrupted, "are something of anarchists, to Máire's way of thinking."

"I see," Fiona said. "So you don't represent any group or part of this 'movement' you've referred to?"

"No," Igraine said.

"Yes," Máire said.

Fiona turned to her third guest. "Which is it?"

"I can only speak for myself," Nuala said.

Fiona nodded. "Please do. That's why you've come."

Nuala sighed. "Well, *I* don't believe in hierarchy, in leaders. If a movement depends on leaders, they can be betrayed or killed or arrested and the movement can fall apart."

She paused. She and Fiona were still studying each other. Nuala could see from the corners of her eyes that Igraine was nodding, agreeing with her, while Gormfhlaith was perched on the edge of her chair, fascinated. She could feel Máire's disapproval; she knew that her friend's lips were probably pressed into that tense, bloodless line again.

Fiona was waiting patiently, so Nuala continued. "Mostly I don't approve of leaders because their very existence makes other women think that *they*'ve no right to speak for themselves or act on their own unless they get permission from these so-called leaders, people they've allowed—asked—to usurp the authority that rightfully belongs to *every* woman." She paused, but still Fiona didn't speak, just waited. Nuala sighed again. "If we're ever to be free, we've got to free our*selves*, not wait for somebody else to do it for us."

The smile spread across Fiona's face, deepening the laugh lines at the corners of her eyes. Gormfhlaith grinned. Fiona scooted the plate of scones toward Nuala. "You wouldn't have been in Ballymena on Friday last, would you?"

Nuala blinked in surprise. "How did you know that?"

Fiona chuckled as she lifted the glass cover off the butter dish. "The way I heard it, old Archbishop Doyle—that bleeding toothache of a man—nearly suffered cardiac arrest when he spotted the condoms." She chuckled again. "Brilliant plan. Yours?"

Nuala shook her head, smiling. "I cannot take credit for another woman's perversity." She jabbed a thumb in Igraine's direction.

"Bravo," Fiona said, and passed Igraine a scone. The smile evaporated from her face. "And whose idea was it to leave these pamphlets—wonderful as they are—in Butler's Market yesterday?"

Nuala and Igraine dropped their eyes; Máire flushed.

"Ah," Fiona said, nodding.

"I've been to Coleraine on numerous occasions," Máire began, her voice a bit louder than it needed to be, "and I know about Robert Butler and the manner in which he uses his wife and daughters as virtual slave labor! If the Church closes him down—"

"The Church did close him down," Fiona interrupted quietly, her eyes narrowed and hard. "For which he blamed his daughter Rose—who is a friend of mine and a bit too outspoken in her views for her own safety. Though of course she denied putting the pamphlets in the vegetable bins or even knowing anything about them, he didn't believe her. After the God Patrol paid him their wee visit and closed his doors, he got himself extremely drunk and then proceeded to blacken both her eyes and split her lip for her. He might have done worse, but she got away from him. She's in hiding now. She's been blamed for it officially, so the word from the Church is that Butler's Market will remain closed for a month, then it will be allowed to reopen—if Butler can survive financially until then—but only if Rose Butler is never allowed on the premises again. Her father has disowned her and her mother is afraid to contact her. She is—to all intents and purposes—dead. And who knows what might happen to her once the *gardaí* find her? I don't doubt she'd disappear—and probably for good."

Nuala's stomach clenched itself into a knot. Máire was pale, horrified at what she had caused. Igraine was shaking her head, grimacing: bitter, but not surprised.

"I know someone at the Belfast travelport," Nuala heard herself saying with some surprise. "Perhaps she can help in getting your friend out. To Scotland or Wales—even England."

"Yes!" Máire said, turning to Nuala first, then Fiona. "We'll help her in any way we can. I'll pay for her ticket myself. I never meant for any women to be hurt. I just thought—the pamphlets—"

"The pamphlets are wonderful." Fiona picked up her copy and unfolded it, her anger easing as quickly as it had come. She even smiled grimly as she read aloud. " 'Wives, submit yourselves unto your own husbands as unto the Lord. For the husband is the head of the wife even as Christ is the head of the church . . . Therefore as the church is subject unto Christ, so let the wives be to their own husbands in everything.' " She smiled again as she looked up at Nuala. "Starting off with their own propaganda lies from the Bible was a nice touch." She read on. " 'The Bible tells us that God is male, therefore, it implies, the male is God. Where does that leave us? And who says it has to remain so? Why, the Church does, of course. And who runs the Church? The Pope: a man in a dress. What's wrong with this picture?' "

She chuckled, then her expression saddened as she looked over at Máire. "The pamphlets are marvelous, and leaving them in the offices of the church-medical-government alliance is perfect, but in a market—"

"I know." Máire still sounded defensive, but she didn't argue. "I was wrong and I am more than willing to help your friend, to make it up to her in whatever way I can."

Fiona nodded, but it was Nuala she spoke to. "Getting her out of the country is the only thing to be done—and for the best, anyway; Rose has been wanting to emigrate, but never had the money or the opportunity. Your friend at the travelport—"

"I'll contact her," Nuala readily agreed, wondering how Noreen O'Mahony would react to this new risk for another stranger.

"Good. *Go raibh maith agat.*" Fiona turned to her sister. "Gormfhlaith, the jam, if you please." As the girl got up to fetch it, Fiona smiled at her three guests. "Well, then. Now that I know what to make of you . . . I know Coleraine and the people here. If you want to cause any further mischief—which I'm hoping you do—perhaps I can help."

"What did you mean before," Igraine asked, "about being the 'principal phantom' around these parts?"

Fiona smiled again, deepening the tiny lines at the corners of her eyes once more. A smile seemed to be her natural expression. "Well, it goes back a bit of a way. I broke the law for the first time when I was sixteen."

"When you learned to race!" Gormfhlaith broke in, grinning with pride.

"Right," Fiona agreed, taking the jar from her. "Will you wet more tea for us, Gormfhlaith?"

The girl jumped up again and went to the stove as Fiona went on.

"I got my driver's license at sixteen, and one day I went with my uncle Shane to watch him race at the local track. I begged him to let me have a go at it, but of course he refused, saying I would only get myself killed. But then he made the mistake of saying that I couldn't because girls weren't any good at it; that's why it was illegal for women to use the track: They would endanger the other—meaning the *male*—drivers."

"So how'd you get in?" Igraine asked with a smile.

"My boyfriend's brother was a mechanic, and he had a motorcycle. I stole a pair of his coveralls and one of his helmets. The helmet was the kind that covered most of my face, right? So then I waited until Uncle Shane was gone for a week, and Aunt Rita gave me the keys to his racer and off I went."

"She *gave* you the keys?" said Nuala.

"Oh, yeah." Fiona smiled in fond memory. "Rita was my role model, you might say. A rebel from the day she was born, though a discreet one . . . So anyway, I got in with no trouble. I spun out a few times, nearly rolled the car once, and scared myself witless, but I *loved* it. I was hooked. And that was the beginning of my life of crime."

"You still race?" Nuala asked.

"You bet I do," Fiona replied. "I may have dumped the boyfriend, but I kept his brother's overalls and helmet. And I saved my money. I'm an office manager—well, secretary, of course—so I make almost decent money, and I don't pay rent here, so I squirreled away a bit of it without my father or the bank knowing. Eventually I had enough to buy a car. Later I pretended it was stolen, but really I stashed it in a rented garage and went to work on it. Before too long I'd converted it to a racer."

"You're a mechanic?" Máire asked, sounding skeptical and bored at the same time.

"Don't I *look* like a mechanic?" Fiona smiled. "I race once a month, rain or shine. They know me at the track now—well, they know my car. They wave, I wave, but I make sure they never get too close."

"That's all very interesting," Máire said in a tone that belied her words, "but what has it to do with true rebel activities? You said—"

"So I did," Fiona interrupted, her tone more polite than Máire's. "Through my Aunt Rita—goddess rest her—I met several other women, first in Coleraine, then in Derry City and County, later in Donegal, who were trying to find ways to fight back. We started out small, with pamphlets like your own—though not as well written, I must admit—and other such things. When I took over the bookkeeping and eventually the entire office at the clothing firm I work for, I directed part of the tithe money to women's charities and the like."

The kettle whistled behind Fiona, and Gormfhlaith brought it back to the table. "Rita was not a leader, perhaps," Fiona went on, "but one of the leading instigators, shall we say, and she brought me right along with her, so I met everyone, stuck my finger in every pie. By the time she got sick, I was in on everything, so after her death, I just naturally took her place. I managed to dissuade the few suitors I had—my mother hasn't been well for a great many years, you see, so I avoided marriage by being a dutiful daughter, taking up the slack for her around here and so on. Anyway, being a single woman, I've more free time than the others."

"To do what?" Máire prompted, apparently still not satisfied. Nuala was vaguely embarrassed by Máire's near-rudeness, but Fiona didn't seem to notice—or was too polite to acknowledge it.

"Whatever we can. I do the organizing. For instance, we pick a time, once or twice a month—never the same times each month—to tie up the Church's or the government's local 'phone lines by all calling in at once, hanging up, then calling again immediately and continuing to do so all day. Or we hide women in safe houses, like the one Rose is in now, when they need to get away from abusive husbands for a bit. Unfortunately we don't have the resources to get them out of the country—"

"So your network is really quite small," Máire interrupted.

Nuala wanted to kick her under the table. "But it's a start," she pointed out, "and more than what we've got at our disposal at the moment, since the Belfast group isn't up to taking many risks yet."

"Sounds like a good base to me," Igraine agreed, not even looking in Máire's direction.

"There's little more than a dozen of us scattered throughout Derry and Donegal," Fiona admitted, "but it's enough to give the *gardaí* fits occasionally."

"Perhaps we should stay in Coleraine for a bit," Nuala said to Máire. "I'm sure there's a great deal we could learn from Fiona."

Máire shrugged, indifferent. "If you like. I have to tie up some loose ends in Belfast. I could leave tomorrow and be back in a day or two."

"Fine," Nuala said, then added, as Fiona poured some tea for Igraine, "I'd like to hear more. You have some ideas for creating further mischief, you said?"

Chapter 5

"*Dia duit.*" The nun greeted Nuala with a polite smile through the iron screen.

"*Dia is Muire duit.*" Nuala gave the standard response, ducking her chin into her coat as the rain-soaked wind whipped her long hair. "Nuala Dennehy *is aimn dom*," she identified herself. "I've come to visit my sister Kerry—uh, that is, Sister Bartholomew of the Five Wounds."

"Oh!" The nun's expression wavered between delight and consternation. "But we are allowed visitors only once a week, on Saturdays. And today is Monday."

"Yes, I know; Kerry told me in her letters." Nuala tried her best to appear apologetic. "But I've only just arrived this day from Edinburgh, you see, and it's been so long—nearly fifteen years—since I've seen my little sister. I've no desire to break any rules, I assure you, Sister, but I've missed her so terribly! I—I was hoping—"

"Fifteen years!" The nun's sympathy was genuine. Nuala felt a twinge of guilt. She had been in Ireland since the end of summer, nearly a month; she could have visited sooner, had she wanted to. And she wouldn't be here now, but for Fiona's scheme.

"Oh my, fifteen *years*, is it?"

Nuala nodded, imploring the woman with her eyes. Her involuntary shiver no doubt helped with her attempt to look pitiful; it seemed to decide the nun.

"Please, come in out of the weather. I can go ask the Mother Superior for permission while you wait inside."

The security field flickered off behind the iron screen as the nun opened the door to admit Nuala, who hurried inside, still shivering.

"*Go raibh maith agat*, you're so kind. I'd almost forgotten what Irish weather was like, after the climate-controlled complex I lived in in Edinburgh."

"Oh, it's been nasty for days."

As the nun reached for the security field controls, Nuala spoke up again, distracting her.

"How *is* Kerry—I mean, Sister Bartholomew? I've been so worried about her. It's part of the reason I came home to Ireland."

"Really?" The nun forgot the controls in her surprise, turning to face Nuala. "Why ever were you worried? Is something wrong with Sister Bartholomew?"

"I'm not sure, exactly." Nuala frowned and dropped her voice to confide in the nun. "There was something in the *tone* of her letters. Nothing explicit, you understand, but—" She shrugged helplessly. "I just don't know. You see, I really can't wait until Saturday; I'm so concerned. If you could ask the Mother Superior—"

"Yes, yes, I'll do so immediately. If there is a problem with one of the sisters, she'll want to know straightaway. You wait here, and I'll be back as soon as I can."

Sorry for the lie, Kerry, Nuala thought as the nun bustled off, her traditional black habit almost quivering with concern. As soon as the footsteps died away, Nuala hurried to the edge of the vestibule and looked down the hallway in both directions. Not a nun in sight.

Her damp soles squeaked on the tiled floor as she trotted back to the door. She winced at the creaking of the iron screen and had to grab the door as the wind tried to seize it.

Igraine and Fiona slipped inside, their teeth chattering.

"Are you sure you can get back out again?" Nuala whispered, thinking of what the sentence must be for breaking into a convent.

"If we can make it to the cellar, no problem," Fiona assured her, pulling the rolled-up balaclava off her head and thrusting it into the pocket of her black coat. "It's not long until vespers. Everybody will be in chapel then." At Igraine's dubious expression, Fiona added, "I've done this before; trust me!"

"I just hate it when people say that," Igraine muttered to Nuala, who smiled back, as nervous as her two accomplices.

"This way!" Fiona whispered, a finger to her lips. She led off to the left in an exaggerated tiptoe.

Igraine smothered a chuckle and whispered to Nuala, "Well, she's a lot more *fun* than Máire, isn't she?"

Nuala ignored that, feeling another pang of guilt that they hadn't told Máire about this adventure. After the near disaster of the market, Nuala and Igraine were beginning to doubt Máire's judgment. But even that justification didn't lessen Nuala's uneasiness. Máire was a friend—of sorts. Still, she was glad they had waited until Máire had left for Belfast.

"Good luck. And be careful!" Nuala whispered to Igraine.

"Aren't I always?"

Nuala watched as Igraine crept along after Fiona down the hall, catching up to her at the last doorway. Fiona put her ear to the door, then, satisfied, opened it. They disappeared inside. Nuala released the breath she hadn't realized she had been holding and returned to the vestibule to wait.

There were no chairs, so she was forced to stand for nearly half an hour looking at either an all-too-realistic portrait of the Crucifixion on one wall or a painting of the Sacred Heart on the other. She shuddered in disgust.

"Bloody savage religion," she muttered, and turned away to face the door's iron screen. Was it really designed to keep people out? Who—besides herself and her two partners in crime—would want to break into a convent? Or were the iron screen and security field designed to keep the inmates in? She shuddered again. Kerry's letters were always cheerful; she truly seemed to love her life here, and she didn't sound brainwashed. Nuala shook her head. She never knew what to think about her sister's life or the choices she had made. Were nuns any different from those God Patrol men? Being women, did they have any power at all? Were they a threat? She couldn't picture Kerry spying on people as the men in the park apparently did on a regular basis. What *did* nuns do now, besides teach school or nurse?

"Nuala? Nuala!"

She turned and was immediately enveloped in black cloth. Extricating herself from the bearhug, Nuala held the habit at arm's length and found her sister's overjoyed face in it.

"Is it really yourself?" Kerry grabbed her again, and the cloth seemed to wrap around Nuala's face of its own accord, as if trying to smother her.

"Yeah, *is mise.* If you'd stop trying to strangle me for a moment—"

Kerry released her and backed up to look at her sister, her face still lit up in wondrous disbelief.

"What are you *doing* here?"

"Nice to see you, too, kid."

Kerry shook her head and acres of black fabric swayed. "You *know* how thrilled I am to see you, Nuala; I'm just so *surprised.* You said in your letters that you'd never set *foot* inside a convent, and here you are. I can't believe you've actually come to see my home. Sister Timothy said you just arrived from Edinburgh today?"

"Timothy? The woman's name was Timothy? What is it with you nunnish types and your masculine names? Sister Bartholomew of the Five Wounds? What the hell is that? I have never cared for that one. What do the other nuns call you for short? Bart? Five?"

Kerry laughed, delighted. "Oh, Nuala. You haven't changed a bit."

"Neither have you. Still wearing the latest fashion—from the fourteenth century." Kerry laughed again, and Nuala found herself smiling, too, trying to ignore the guilt. "Well, you certainly seem in a good mood, for all your living in a prison."

"A prison? Don't be silly—but then, you never did understand." She shook her head fondly, still smiling. "But no matter, come in, come in." Kerry linked her arm through Nuala's, pulling her along. "We could sit in the common room—but why don't we go up to my cell for privacy?"

"Your—"

"Now don't start," Kerry interrupted, chuckling. "You know perfectly well that's what our rooms are called. It's just a name."

"Sure it is. Whatever you say, Bart."

Kerry's laugh was drowned out by a loud bell clanging somewhere in the recesses of the convent.

"What the—"

"It's the call to vespers," Kerry explained. "But I've permission to miss chapel because of your visit."

"What would they do to you if you didn't have permission?"

"Don't you know?" Kerry leaned close to whisper as nuns began emerging from doorways to stream down the hall. "They'd lock me in the dungeon."

"What, no horsewhip?"

"Only after the second offense."

"Ah."

As other nuns passed them, most smiled at Nuala. She was surprised that they seemed such a happy bunch; this wasn't at all what she had been expecting. And they were all looking at Kerry's arm linked through hers with great but unspoken curiosity. Finally Nuala glanced down at Kerry's hand on her arm and confided to the nearest nun, "We're just good friends—truly."

Most nuns within hearing range chuckled, but then the laughter died out. A few of the nuns were frowning in clear annoyance as they continued down the hall at a slightly faster rate, deliberately not looking to Nuala's left, so she turned in that direction. She jumped, startled, when she found herself facing the ugliest woman she had ever seen.

The deep furrows in the nun's face reinforced her disapproving frown. Her eyes were narrowed into such tiny slits that their color was undetectable, and her pale and sparse lashes appeared almost nonexistent. Tiny red veins spidered out from her nose, standing out in relief against the fishbelly-white of her face, which glared out from the shroud of her guimpe. Her dry, colorless lips were pressed tightly together, wrinkling her chin. Her age was impossible to guess; her disposition was not.

"Sister Malachi," Kerry said in greeting, her tone polite, but not—Nuala was proud to note—at all intimidated by this glowering creature. "I'd like you to meet my sister, Nuala. She's visiting from Edinburgh."

Sister Malachi's tiny, slitted eyes flicked from Kerry to Nuala, her expression never wavering.

"Nice to meet you, Mal." Nuala smiled and nodded, resisting the impulse to poke a finger into the nun's furrowed brow to see if it was really skin or just a mask.

The eyes flicked back to Kerry. "This is Monday. Visitors are allowed only on Saturdays. You are aware of the rules, are you not, Sister Bartholomew? Perhaps we should review them."

The venom in her tone surprised Nuala with its viciousness. That this creature should speak to her little sister in such a manner made her bristle. But she felt Kerry's gentle squeeze on her arm and said nothing.

"Thank you for offering your assistance, Sister Malachi," Kerry replied, her tone still polite and apparently unaffected by the other nun's animosity. "But that won't be necessary. I know the rules as well as you do, having lived in this particular convent even longer than yourself. Mother gave me permission for Nuala's visit, as I haven't seen her in fifteen years."

"I see." Sister Malachi's eyes flicked to Nuala again and narrowed even further when Nuala raised an eyebrow at her. "And do you also have permission to miss chapel, Sister Bartholomew?"

"As a matter of fact, she does," Nuala interrupted, ignoring Kerry's squeeze. "All this permission being bandied about must play havoc with discipline, eh, Mal?"

The nun's eyes widened only a fraction as she glared at Nuala. "My name is Malachi."

"Right, right." Nuala ignored Kerry's tug on her arm, since it felt halfhearted, at best. "I'm not familiar with that saint, though I suppose he was a martyr, wasn't he? Weren't they all? What happened to him? Did he die of boredom?"

Sister Malachi's eyes glittered briefly, reminding Nuala somehow of a spider advancing on its trapped prey.

"Your sister has a maladjusted sense of decorum." Malachi spit the words at Kerry.

"She most certainly does *not* have a maladjusted sense of decorum," Kerry objected mildly. "She has no sense of decorum whatsoever."

Nuala laughed, surprised and impressed with her sister's boldness. Evidently this sour old woman was no threat; Kerry obviously didn't consider her one.

Malachi's nostrils flared briefly when Nuala turned to smile at her, but again she ignored her, speaking instead to Kerry. "I shall pray for her soul—and for yours, Sister Bartholomew."

"Thank you, Sister," Kerry replied, still polite.

"Yes, you do that, Mal," Nuala said. "I'm sure God's waiting with bated breath."

Sister Malachi's spine stiffened even further as she marched past them down the hall, trailing after the other nuns.

"Better hurry, Mal," Nuala called after her, "or all the seats on the goal line will be taken!"

Sister Malachi never turned around as she disappeared through the door at the end of the corridor.

"Now there was one ghastly bitch," Nuala muttered. She turned to her sister, smiling in approval. "Haven't you the mouth on you, then? Speaking so disrespectfully to a nun—and one yourself. Can't she cause you trouble with your boss—uh, the Mother Superior?"

"Oh, yes," Kerry replied nonchalantly. "She'll try. She always does."

Nuala winced, suddenly worried for her little sister. "Och, I'm sorry, Kerry; maybe I shouldn't have—sometimes I don't think before—"

"If you had done anything else," Kerry said, smiling, "you wouldn't have been the Nuala I remember."

Kerry's smile threw her even farther off-balance. "You seem to be taking it well."

Kerry shook her head. "Don't worry about Malachi; I can handle her. I didn't learn *nothing* from all those years of living in your shadow."

Nuala blinked in surprise, by now thoroughly confused about what to expect in a convent. Kerry just smiled at her, so she tried to cover her confusion. "Well, like I always say: Fuck 'em if they can't take a joke, right?"

Kerry gasped and tried not to laugh, pretending to be shocked at such language.

"Oh, sorry, that's the bad word, isn't it? The one nuns never say, much less do."

"Nuala!" Kerry pulled her toward the stairs, laughing.

"All right, a bit of the truth now, if you think you can manage it."

Kerry gave Nuala the one chair, a straight-backed, wooden chair with no padding, as she sat down on her narrow bed. There was a painting of Jesus on one wall—he was smiling, Nuala noticed with relief; he was not in the process of being crucified, for once—and a Brigid's Cross of rushes on another wall.

"Is that—"

"It is," Kerry replied, smiling. "The one you made for me right before you left for university. Remember the lecture that accompanied it? About how St. Brigid was never a mere saint, but a mighty goddess of Ireland whom the Catholics appropriated and demoted to sainthood. You told me that this cross was not a Christian symbol at all, but a pagan one, signifying the goddess, not the false saint."

Nuala sighed. "I really made you listen to all that before I gave it to you?" Kerry nodded. "I don't remember that, but it sounds like me. You kept it anyway?"

"Of course. It was a gift from my sister."

Nuala shifted her weight on the uncomfortable chair, looking away.

"Why are you really here?"

"I came to see you. Do I need a reason?" That sounded phony even as she said it.

Kerry studied her for a long moment, which only made Nuala more uncomfortable. "Sister Timothy said that you only arrived in Ireland today. But you would have gone to see Da before me, if visiting family was the actual reason for the prodigal's return from exile."

"Prodigal, is it? Could we skip the parables? I'm afraid you have me at a disadvantage in that area."

"No one ever has Nuala Dennehy at a disadvantage—not for long, anyway." When Nuala was unsure how to respond to that, Kerry continued. "Which must mean, then, that you had a different reason for returning to Ireland, or that this *isn't* your first day back. Which is it?"

"You sound like a bloody Jesuit. They could have used you during the Inquisition. When they bring it back, you'll have a job for life."

"This isn't your first day back, is it? That means you lied to Sister Timothy."

"Uh-oh." Nuala tried to look guilty. It wasn't too difficult. "Can I go to hell for lying to a nun?"

"Oh, yes." Kerry smiled, but her arms were crossed, and her eyes were boring right through Nuala.

"How about if the Sister's my sister?"

"*Especially* if the Sister's your sister. So tell me the truth: Why have you come back to Ireland?"

"Well, I did want to see you and Da, of course."

"And?"

Nuala had worried about how much of the truth she would have to keep from her sister. If she only knew Kerry better—but the nearly twelve years' difference in their ages had meant that they hadn't really had a chance to become close before Nuala

left home. Kerry had been just a kid. And after all these years—
now the kid was a *nun.*

"I've been gone a long time," she finally answered. "And so
little *real* news of Ireland ever makes it onto EuroNet. So . . . I
wanted to see what my country had become."

Kerry nodded, still staring at her. "And then what?"

"Then what . . . what?"

"When you see things you don't care for, you're simply going
to turn your back and return to Scotland? That's not the Nuala
I remember. You never walked away from a fight in your life."

"What are you saying? I walked away from the whole bloody
country, didn't I? For fifteen years!"

"That was preparation."

"What?" Nuala stared at her younger sister, suddenly wishing
Fiona had come up with a different plan.

"Nuala, I know you," Kerry began.

"How can you? You were just a kid when I left. You don't
know anything about me."

Kerry smiled and shook her head. "You may not have been
there, Nuala, but you were everywhere I went in Falcarragh.
Everybody in that town told me stories about you: the fights you
had with the nuns at school, or with the librarian over some
book he wouldn't let you read; or the time you publicly chal-
lenged the entire town council about the commemoration of the
Battle of Yellow Ford, saying they'd gotten the historical facts
wrong. I believe you were all of eleven years old at that one,
weren't you? And of course you were right, and made all those
gentlemen appear foolish, and it forced them to change the re-
creation of the battle."

Nuala winced, embarrassed at the memory. "You knew about
that? I'd nearly forgotten it."

Kerry nodded, her smile turning sad. "And of course there
was always Mam and Da."

"Right." Nuala's tone was bitter as she glanced away from
her sister. "I can imagine what *she* told you about me."

"Yes, I'm sure you can," Kerry said, as gently as possible.
"But every one of those battles that she so disapproved of only
made you a grander figure in *my* eyes."

Nuala looked up in surprise and was startled by the expression on her sister's face.

"And Da—well, whenever Mam wasn't about, Da would tell
me about you in a voice nearly bursting with pride. And the fact
that you became a professor of Irish history, well, *that* was the

grandest thing you could have become, of course. He came to visit me when he heard from you about getting your job at university, and he could talk of nothing else but his daughter, the Irish historian, and how you wouldn't be fooled or lied to by revisionists. Oh, no, not his Nuala."

Nuala stood up without really noticing that she had and began pacing around the tiny room, her mind whirling.

"So you see, Nuala, I know you better than you think. I know why you've come back." Kerry sighed, shaking her head when Nuala turned to her in surprise. "I've always been afraid for you. I was relieved that you'd left for Scotland, because I knew it would be safer for you there. But I knew you'd be back someday; you couldn't stay away forever."

Nuala swallowed, her throat suddenly dry. "What are you saying, Kerry? Why should you have been afraid for me?"

"You think, because I chose to serve God, that I'm blind? That I don't see all that is wrong in Ireland—and in the rest of the world?"

Nuala sat down again, staring at Kerry and feeling foolish. She had assumed that she didn't know her sister very well, but she had miscalculated. She didn't know Kerry at all.

"Because I love God," Kerry was saying, "don't you think it hurts me when I see how men have used religion, have twisted God's words, to gain power in Ireland, and in the United States, and in Iran and Afghanistan and Mexico and Chile and so many other places? The world has gone mad with religion and mixed it up with secular laws and governments out of fear of other religions, and all in the name of God! But God is not interested in temporal power; He is concerned with *true* motivation, the *heart* of each person." She started to say something else, but stopped, smiling. "But I forgot, you're an atheist—or so you claim."

Nuala raised an eyebrow but said nothing. Kerry went on, serious again.

"You've always been a fighter, Nuala; you always will be. *That's* why you've come back, isn't it? To fight—somehow—for Ireland." She shook her head, tears coming to her eyes. "And I have to be afraid for you again, because I know you're going to be hurt."

Nuala stared at the tears in Kerry's eyes, ashamed she hadn't taken the time when they were both younger, ashamed that she hadn't written more often in all these years. It was difficult, given the ridiculous outfit Kerry was wearing, but Nuala could see a glimmer, a reflection of the little girl she had told all those stories to on long winter nights, the little girl who had so looked up to her. She sighed, knowing she had lost something she could never regain. It was just too late now. "And since you know whatever it is you think you know about me, what are you going to do about it? Asking you to join me is out of the question, I suppose, so what *are* you going to do?"

Kerry smiled again. "Change is coming—even to the Church in Ireland. And sooner than you think . . . But it isn't spiritual matters that concern you, is it? And patience has never been one of your stronger virtues." She sighed. "Unrest has been simmering in this country for years, and with every new restriction, every unfair law passed, the simmering comes closer to boiling over. The Guerrilla TV has been getting bolder; more and more people are requesting the right to emigrate—even though it's almost never granted—and many are even requesting the right to join space colonies. The Tlatejoxans and the other aliens are a fascination for *every*one, no matter how the Church tries to paint them as inhuman and un-Christian, and therefore evil. Few people believe that. Even with the restricted outside news coverage, everyone knows what the Tlatejoxans have given Earth, and with no strings attached: not just the technology to make faster-than-light travel and colonization possible, but the medical expertise—"

Kerry broke off and shrugged. "Change is in the wind, and no one can stop it, not even the Church or the government. Whether that change can be brought about peacefully or not is another matter." She stared at Nuala, her expression softening, then turning sad. "You may not have known what has been happening in Ireland, but something—I know you won't believe it to be God—something told you that now was the time to come back. And here you are. Just in time to see the spark lit." She studied her sister again, the sadness in her eyes deepening. "Or to help light it yourself, more likely." Kerry sighed again. "What am I going to do? . . . Pray for you, of course. That you succeed—but without getting yourself killed."

It was still raining when Nuala made her way through the oak grove outside the convent walls. There wasn't much moonlight tonight, anyway, and the heavy cloud cover only made it darker. She jumped when Fiona and Igraine materialized from behind a tree.

"Did you get them?"

"Mission accomplished," Igraine said, her teeth chattering.

Fiona held up the plastic-wrapped bundle. "Ours fit and yours should, as well, *Sister* Nuala."

Chapter 6

"GOOD MORNING. YOUR usual teacher is ill today, so I will be taking her place for now. Please find your seats."

Nuala had been fighting a severe case of claustrophobia since putting on the nun's habit. There was so much starch in the guimpe that it had the texture of cardboard, and she had tripped over the long skirt three times on her way over the school grounds. She found it incredible that Kerry trapped herself in this Iron Maiden of a costume every day—willingly!

The teenage girls ambled toward their seats, in no hurry. There were around thirty of them, all dressed in navy and red school uniforms with skirts reaching well below the knee, and every one of them looked bored to death. Little wonder at that, since they were nineteen or nearly so and still in secondary school. When Nuala had been nineteen she had been at university for two years, but the regulations had changed since then. So *much* had changed. Boys could matriculate at seventeen, but girls remained in secondary school for an additional two years, taking more religion and home economics classes. This was to better prepare them to become mothers, as they were expected to do within a few years. If a girl wasn't discouraged from attending university by her family or the parish priest or the low quotas for women students or the entrance exams that emphasized advanced maths—which girls were not encouraged to study—then she was allowed to enroll. But few majors were open to her, as most courses of study weren't considered acceptable for "ladies."

These girls, then, spent all day, as they had the past two years, wasting time. No wonder they were bored.

"What class is this, anyway?"

That woke a few of them up. They blinked in surprise and exchanged puzzled glances.

"Well?"

Finally one girl, a brunette with a precise ponytail from which not one hair strayed, raised her hand.

"Well, speak up, girl. There's no need for this hand-up-asking-for-permission-to-breathe nonsense."

They were staring at her now, most confused, but all wide awake. The brunette awkwardly lowered her hand and spoke. "It's—it's home economics, Sister."

"Is it? How perfectly dreadful."

Girls were looking at each other all over the room, apparently thinking that their neighbors might have an explanation for this odd behavior from a nun.

Nuala walked around the desk and sat down on the edge of it, nearly strangling herself when her hem caught on something. Someone giggled, but most of the girls tried not to smile.

Nuala yanked her skirt away from the desk, muttering "Bloody stupid outfits!" When she seated herself successfully on the desk, she looked up to find the students staring at her.

"Right. Now then. Home economics, you said? Is it really?"

The brunette nodded, her eyes wary.

"Well, not for today it isn't. I don't know a bloody thing about home economics, and it's a stupid thing to waste your time studying, so we won't. I hope no one minds."

This time shock mingled with the confusion in their faces.

"But we're supposed to be—" the brunette began.

"What are we going to study instead, then?" a very pretty girl with long reddish blond hair asked. Nuala noted that her vest wasn't buttoned and her cuffs were rolled back. Punishable offenses, she remembered all too clearly.

Nuala had deliberately rolled back her cuffs every day as a schoolgirl, or turned up her collar or left her vest unbuttoned, or all three. The punishment was always the same in those days: She was not allowed to play *camogie* with the other girls; she was forced to stay inside and study. She hated sports and loved to read, so all she had to do was act sullen and rebellious and she got what she wanted. Her various teachers never seemed to learn that she was manipulating them. It worked all through school, and was a wonderful lesson in how to get her way.

Nuala answered the girl. "What would you like to study—if you were ever given a choice?"

This caused all the girls to exchange still-confused but now bordering on suspicious glances. Nuala noticed, but her gaze never wavered from the blond girl with the rebellious cuffs.

"What difference would that make? We haven't a choice, have we?"

Nuala recognized a kindred and angry spirit when she met one. "Good answer. So you don't." She looked out over the class. "How many of you are planning to try and get into university?"

After some hesitancy, three girls raised their hands.

"I see. And how many of you are planning to marry and have kids soon?"

It was nearly unanimous that time. The blond girl, however, kept her arms rigidly crossed.

"And how many are planning to become nuns?"

That took care of the few holdouts from the last question—except for the blonde. She stared defiantly back at Nuala, her arms still crossed.

"That would seem to leave you in a group by yourself."

"I'm used to that."

The girl wasn't giving an inch. Her expression, her posture, her tone, and especially those cuffs and vest were a defiant challenge to the authority inherent in Nuala's costume. Nuala liked her already. "I can see that. What's your name?"

There were some low snickers from other girls, and the blonde's cheeks flushed. "Heather Lonnegan." Her chin came up as she braced herself for the punishment she obviously expected.

Nuala saw the grim satisfaction on the faces of some of the other girls as they, too, waited. They were probably the ones who never rebelled, who hadn't the courage. So. Heather wasn't liked, was she?

Nuala smiled, startling them all. Yes, this was the one to focus on, to try to reach. Her smile widened as she said, "Give 'em hell, Heather. And don't ever give up."

In the midst of stunned stares, Nuala changed tone abruptly. "Now, then. I've no patience for home economics, a truly silly subject, so that only leaves religion, doesn't it? . . . Doesn't it?"

The brunette with the ponytail had been both shocked and disappointed when Heather was not taken to task, and she was glaring at Nuala in angry suspicion. "Of course, Sister, religion is the other topic we study, but this is a home economics class. We are *supposed* to be learning how to make pork roast almondine today."

"Really." Nuala shrugged. "Well, I suppose then that you kill a pig, cut it up, throw almonds on some portion of it, and toss it in the oven. Is that close enough for you?"

Heather laughed, delighted, and a few of the others chuckled, but most weren't sure how to respond. Except for the shocked brunette.

"May I ask who you are, Sister? I don't recognize you. And I know every Sister in this school personally."

Nuala's smile wasn't kind. "Somehow that doesn't surprise me. My name, if you must know, is Sister . . . Malachi."

"Well, Sister Malachi," the brunette went on, now quite annoyed at this most unnunish behavior, "we are *supposed* to be learning how to make—"

"Oh, put a sock in it, Bernadette." Heather glared at her in disgust. "Who gives a damn about your bloody pork roast almondine anyway, you insufferable arsekisser?"

There were a few snickers at that; it was obvious that Bernadette was not any more popular than Heather.

Before Bernadette could fashion an outraged retort, Nuala spoke again. "Now, then, religion is not really my topic, either, but I am dressed for the part, so let's have a run at it, shall we? Let's see, religion: catechism, confession, communion . . . No, too boring. Ah, I know! Bible stories! Now *there's* a fascinating topic, to be sure."

The girls were watching her warily, not sure whether to appreciate the change in routine or fear it. Bernadette's eyes narrowed, and she shot a glance at the door as if seeking outside intervention. There was a half smile playing about Heather's mouth; she was leaning forward, waiting.

"Do you know the one about the fellow in the Book of Judges who gave his concubine to a crowd of men to be gang-raped to death in order to spare his own life?"

The girls were shocked; Bernadette was outraged. Heather, though surprised, was waiting for Nuala to continue.

"Or the similar story in Genesis where the man who owns the house that two angels are staying in offers the mob who wants these angelic fellows his own two virgin daughters instead, to do with as they wish?"

The girls were now fidgeting in their seats, alarmed and finally aware that something was definitely wrong. Heather was grim, but when Nuala looked into her eyes, she nodded once.

"Or the story of how Absalom raped the concubines of his father, King David, thus besmirching *David's* honor, not the women's, because of course women *have* no honor. So David then, with typical biblical justice, imprisons the *women* for life because they had embarrassed him by being raped. And it's not just his concubines that suffer in this manner, but his many wives, as well." Nuala made herself more comfortable on the edge of the desk, warming to her topic. "Because David arranged the death of Bathsheba's husband so that he could take her as his own possession, the Lord God becomes upset. Not at what David did to Bathsheba, mind you, but at what he did to the husband. So God declares, 'I will raise up evil against thee out of thine own house, and I will take thy wives before thine eyes, and give them unto thy neighbor, and he shall lie with thy wives in the sight of the sun.' "

The girls' eyes were wide. Some were merely confused, but others were clearly frightened; rape was never discussed openly, and certainly not by nuns. What was not discussed could be ignored, but Nuala was making them face it.

"Rape, you see," Nuala went on, "is not considered a crime against a woman, but against whatever man she is considered the property of. And since western civilization is based on Judeo-Christian principles, rape is not treated as severely as it should be. After all, it rarely happens to men, does it? It happens to women, and women don't matter."

"None of our teachers would speak of such things!" Bernadette finally erupted. "I don't know who you are, but this is not a suitable topic—"

"Shut your gob!" Heather turned on her. "How can it not be suitable, when it's *us* it happens to? It's about time we heard a bit of the *truth* in this damned place!"

"Certain things should not be discussed—" Bernadette persisted.

"How can they be stopped if they're never discussed?" Heather hesitated in her anger, looking back up at Nuala. "I mean, *every*thing should be discussed, freely."

Nuala saw the look in the girl's eyes. She was ready to argue the point, if necessary, but she was obviously hoping she had found an unlikely ally. Nuala smiled.

"I agree, Heather. Though the Church, of course, does not. Therefore, neither does the government, since they are the same entity. Do you remember the stories I just mentioned? You must have read the Old Testament when you were young; you couldn't go to a Catholic school and *not* read it."

"Yes, we read the Old Testament in *bunscoil*," Heather replied. Her tone was cautious, but she was obviously curious about this strange nun. Curious enough to play along. "But I don't remember *those* stories being used for homilies."

"Well, they wouldn't be, would they? They're about women." Nuala let them ponder that one, looking straight at Heather.

Heather's expression was grim. "It was forever Joseph and his rainbow coat or Noah and his bloody ark. They stuck to the fanciful, *nice* stories. And then we reached *meánscoil*, and it was strictly New Testament, Jesus and the like. We skipped over the parts you mentioned in school—but I wondered at them, all right. I tried to ask a few times about why God used people so badly, but the nuns always changed the subject back to the Sermon on the Mount or whatever. They always said that, as Christians, it was the words of Jesus we should be concentrating on."

Nuala nodded. "Right. Concentrate on the nicer bits and forget the more unpleasant aspects of the book that Christians claim is the word of God." Before an outraged Bernadette could speak, she hurried on. "How about the story of Jephthah's daughter? You don't remember that one either?"

It wasn't just Heather who shook her head this time. She was gaining their interest, at least.

"Well, you know the one about Abraham being ordered by God to murder his son Isaac, don't you? That's a fairly popular one with priests and their ilk."

Bernadette jumped in. "God in His compassion spared Isaac's life. He never meant for Abraham to kill Isaac, it was just a test of his faith. As the Church teaches us—"

"Just a test of his faith, was it?" Nuala interrupted. She felt Heather's eyes on her. "What a bloody cruel thing to do. Imagine how terrified that poor boy must have been. For his own father to tie him up and raise a knife over him, to almost *murder* the child! What kind of a father would do that? And what sort of a god would ask it?"

"Abraham had to prove his faith," Bernadette insisted, her voice petulant. "Sister Mary Clare says—"

"Why should Abraham or anybody else have to prove *any*thing?" Nuala didn't raise her voice. Though rigid adherence to religion always disgusted her, that emotion was not what was needed here. Heather was watching her closely, waiting to see what she would do.

"And if God was as 'compassionate' as you claim, then why didn't he spare Jephthah's daughter?"

"Who was that?" Heather asked, ignoring Bernadette's splutters behind her.

"Well, I don't *know* who she was, really," Nuala admitted. "The author of the book of Judges doesn't tell us her name. I suppose that, being only a daughter, not a son, she isn't important enough to warrant a name. Anyway, the story goes that Jephthah, who was a mercenary and a very efficient killer, makes a deal with God before a big battle. The deal is that, if God helps him win this particular battle, then whoever comes out of his house to greet him first upon his return will be offered up as a burnt offering to the Lord. Guess who came out first?"

Someone gasped. Several of the girls appeared pale, sick. Heather's expression, however, was silent hatred.

"Yes," Nuala went on. "Her father comes back safe from battle, so she runs out to welcome him home, and what does she get for her devotion: a death sentence. Jephthah feels bad about it, the author says, but he made a promise to God, so it's got to be done. The poor girl is allowed only a two-month reprieve so that she can go on a retreat into the mountains to mourn the fact that she'll die a virgin. After that, her father murders her. Where's your compassionate God and his last-minute stay of execution this time, Bernadette?"

Bernadette's cheeks were bright red in her anger. She pushed herself to her feet. "You're making this up! I don't believe that's in the—"

"Book of Judges, Chapter Eleven, verses thirty through forty. Look it up."

Bernadette tried again. "The Bible is an inspiration to all mankind. It offers us hope—"

"Hope of what? Being treated as less than human just because you're female?"

Nuala wasn't angry; seeing the mixture of rage and confusion on this nineteen-year-old girl's face only made her sad. She spoke gently. "Bernadette, why offer your allegiance or respect to a religion and a government that keeps you enslaved? You deserve better than that. We all do. As James Connolly once said, 'The great only appear great because we are on our knees. Let us rise.' "

Heather was staring at her, her lips parted, her eyes round. Nuala recognized that expression; she had felt that way the first time she stole one of Connolly's books out of the Adult section of the Falcarragh library and experienced the revelation of true words.

"You're not a nun!" Bernadette's accusation came out half

strangled in near hysteria. "You don't belong here! What have you done with Sister Anunciata? Where is she?"

"Calm yourself, girl." Nuala spoke softly, but got to her feet, realizing that her time was up, and far sooner than she had planned. "Your teacher is perfectly fine. I'm sure that tomorrow she'll be happy to teach you how to make pork roast almondine. Now, if you will excuse me, I really must be going."

"I'm getting the Mother Superior!" Bernadette screamed, but she took only two steps before Heather had grabbed her, twisting her arm behind her back.

"You're not going anywhere, Bernie." As she struggled with the furious girl, Heather glanced at Nuala. "You'd best go—and quickly."

The other girls were too dumbfounded to interfere as Nuala headed for the exit in the front. She paused in the doorway, looking back at Heather.

"Keep those cuffs turned up, kid."

Heather smiled. Then Nuala slipped out into the hall and was gone.

"And just *what* did you expect to accomplish with such a masquerade?" Máire was outraged, but Nuala wondered if it was more because she hadn't been told about the convent break-in and the school appearance than because she didn't approve of the tactics.

"Those girls are the next generation," Igraine replied, an edge of irritation coloring her voice, as it usually did when she was speaking to Máire. "If Nuala succeeded in getting them to question the nonsense in the Bible, then they're bound to take it a step further; they'd have to. If we can get those girls—*any* girls—to question the institutions they obey so blindly—"

"And whose idea was it?" Máire's glare raked over Nuala and Igraine and settled on Fiona. "Is *this* the sort of nonsense you indulge in in Coleraine? I don't wonder the movement is so disorganized here."

Fiona crossed her legs and leaned back against the park bench, studying her perfect fingernails, trying to cover her irritation with boredom. The park was deserted—it was almost dinnertime—but still they kept their voices low. "It was my idea, and I stand by it. I certainly don't owe you any explanations or apologies."

Máire's eyes tightened, then she turned abruptly away from

Fiona. "You've been seen in public, Nuala; we can't stay in Coleraine any longer. It's time we moved on, as planned."

"I disagree." Igraine spoke before Nuala could. "We should stay here for a bit longer. There's no hurry to leave Ulster."

"After what the three of you did? Nuala was seen by an entire convent! Someone is bound to connect her visit to the disappearance of three habits. And then the two of you blatantly kidnap a nun—"

"We didn't kidnap her, Máire; don't be so melodramatic." Igraine exchanged a glance with Fiona, smiles creeping about the edges of their lips. "We merely ... waylaid her."

"And accidentally locked her in the school basement." Fiona shrugged. "By the time she found her way out, Nuala had long since left the school grounds. And no one even noticed us; in our habits, we fit right in."

"Tá an ceart aici," Igraine agreed. "It all went according to plan."

Máire's frustration was mounting. Nuala tried to head it off. "Máire, I'm sorry we didn't tell you—"

"That isn't important; I don't care about that!" It was an obvious lie, but none of them pointed it out. "You were *seen*, Nuala! Any of those girls could identify you, habit or no. And after the pamphlets and the convent break-in—I tell you, it's time we got out of Coleraine; it's too dangerous here now."

"We all knew it would be, going in." Igraine got up from her bench, pacing in front of Máire. "For gods' sake, Máire, this is supposed to be a *revolution* we are attempting to foment—it's bound to involve risk. And I say we stay in Coleraine, for two reasons: one, Fiona knows the setup here and who we can trust, and two"—she went on before Máire could interrupt—"there are more Protestants in Ulster, more people dissatisfied with the Church's interference, who might be willing to do something about it. A Protestant base could be helpful."

"You only say that because *you* were raised Protestant." Máire's tone had acquired a pettiness that Nuala winced to hear. Had she always been this way? How much had Nuala overlooked all these years in her letters because Máire had agreed with her politics at a time in her life when no one else had?

"That's enough." Nuala spoke quietly, but her disgust was evident. "We should have told you, Máire, so that you could voice your disapproval, but we did not need your permission to visit the convent or the school. We have no leaders in this fledgling movement of ours, and as you well know, I don't feel that we need them."

"And I disagree with that," Máire scolded her, "as *you* well know. It was a foolish stunt, Nuala, and it put you at unnecessary risk. You are too important to this movement to risk for nothing—"

"I'm no more important than anybody else," Nuala argued. "I don't wish to be. And as for my brief stint at teaching religion, I may not have planned it as well as I could have, but it wasn't entirely in vain. If you had seen the look in Heather's eyes—"

"One girl—"

"We don't know that it was only one," Igraine interrupted. "Just because the others were quiet doesn't mean they didn't hear, or consider what Nuala was telling them about their precious Bible. We can't know yet how many she got through to."

"And even if it was only the one," Fiona added, "a revolution's got to start somewhere."

"Well, I can see that I'm outnumbered." Máire was still angry, refusing to look at any of them.

"When has *that* ever stopped you?" Nuala tried to tease her out of her mood, but Máire would have none of it.

"I am leaving Coleraine as we planned; I'm for Galway. Are you coming with me or not?" Máire was looking only at Nuala; it was obvious she didn't care what Igraine and Fiona planned to do.

"Máire." Nuala shook her head; she had been dreading this moment, but hadn't expected it to come so soon. "Don't put me in this position. Just because we don't always see eye to eye on tactics—"

"You have to choose, Nuala." Máire was adamant. "You can be extremely influential, vital to this movement, because of your knowledge of the many truths that have been denied the rest of us by the Church. This movement needs you, and you need to fulfill your destiny, but—"

"Destiny?" Nuala was on her feet now, too, staring at Máire. "Who in the hell do you think I am, bloody King Arthur? I'm just a history professor, that's all, Máire! Nobody special."

"It is not all." The stubbornness had set into every muscle, every joint. Máire knew what she knew, and would not be dissuaded. "You refuse to recognize your potential. *I* recognized it back in university. I knew that someday you would help change Ireland."

"What? I'm not—"

"You mustn't be distracted by these petty tactics." Máire dismissed Igraine and Fiona with a wave. "You were meant for bigger things, Nuala. You may not believe me, you may think me mad, but I can *see* you changing worlds. You can be the leader you claim is not needed. People will listen to you. They will follow you. I know, with complete certainty, that you will change lives. It's not just your knowledge of history; that's merely a weapon. It's who you are. But if you foolishly follow those who would risk your life, then it is obvious that you have not yet learned whatever lessons you must; you've not yet confronted yourself. I would like to help you with that, but I won't watch you throw your life away, uselessly, on condom balloons and Bible stories. Choose, Nuala. Find your potential, or waste it. I'll be at the inn until tomorrow morning. I'm leaving for Galway at noon. I hope you'll be joining me."

Máire turned abruptly and marched off, not looking back even when Nuala called to her.

The three stared after her as she left the park. Nuala was aghast, Igraine amazed, and Fiona bewildered.

"Has she always been like this?" Fiona asked.

Igraine shrugged. "I haven't known her long myself. I thought she was a bit stiff and uncompromising. I might even have guessed eccentric, if the question was put to me. But this!" She turned to Nuala. "Destiny? Changing worlds and changing lives? What the devil did she mean?"

Nuala shook her head, still stunned. "She was always a bit—well, *mystical*, if that's the word, but—"

"Mystical?" Fiona said. "What's that mean?"

"Well, I never paid much attention to it, but at university she was always on about divination, symbols, ancient pagan beliefs, and the like. She used to blather on about such things to me, but I never really listened to her if she wasn't talking politics. I had assumed, since she never mentioned them in her letters, that she had given up all that. Perhaps I was wrong."

"Maybe whatever they did to her in Castlereagh rattled her," Igraine suggested.

Nuala turned to her in surprise. "Castlereagh? She was arrested? She never mentioned that to me. Not in her letters, not since I've been back. When was this? What did they do to her?"

Igraine shrugged. "I can only repeat what I heard. Apparently, she was picked up four or five years ago. She wasn't charged with anything—you know how that is—but they held her for nearly a month. I don't know what they really wanted." Igraine's tone turned bitter. "Probably just harassment because she's a woman alone who refuses to marry, and without an excuse like Fiona's; they do that. But I can well imagine what they did to her."

"The usual methods they use at Castlereagh," Fiona said, "include frequent strip-searching, sleep deprivation, food that causes you such misery you can't venture far from the stinking toilets they never clean. And rape, of course." She frowned in sympathy and pain. "If she was always, as you say, mystical and given to such things, the horrors she went through in that hell may have pushed her farther into them in search of some manner of comfort."

"And she's seeing Nuala as some sort of—" Igraine began.

"I never knew." Nuala didn't hear Igraine; she was nearly sick with imagining what her friend—yes, friend she was, and of many years—had been through. She looked at Fiona and Igraine: one was tall, thin, wiry, and sardonic; the other was stylish, with a ready smile, using her femininity to hide her surprising skills. As different as they were from each other, they were far more like Nuala herself in temperament, personality than was Máire. If there was truly going to be a revolution, she would much rather be at the side of women such as these, women who had become real friends in such a short time. But Máire, odd as she was, had never given up on their friendship, in spite of distance and time. Nuala had never really understood why, but she respected loyalty, so she always wrote back from Scotland. Why had Máire never mentioned being arrested?

"She never told me. Why didn't she tell me?"

"You're going to Galway with her, aren't you?" said Igraine. "Even though she's half mad."

Nuala sighed; she was suddenly exhausted, and she felt that she had no choice. "She's been a friend for almost twenty years, Igraine. It was reading between the lines of her letters that kept me as informed as I was about the situation here. I can't just abandon her . . . I'll go along to Galway. If nothing else, perhaps I can talk some sense into her."

"Good luck on that." Igraine seemed not at all sure that was possible.

"And yourself?" Fiona asked Igraine.

Igraine hesitated, looking to Nuala. Nuala solved it for her.

"You were right about the reasons for leaving Belfast and for staying in Coleraine. Why don't you? When I—or we—come back through, we can join up again. By then you will no doubt have taught each other a great many things we can use in our alleged revolution."

Igraine smiled. "Perhaps you can pick up Excalibur on your travels."

"What?" Nuala blinked in confusion.

"It's probably buried in another stone somewhere in the west, just waiting for you to come along and pull it out."

Fiona grinned, and Nuala tried to. "Very funny. I do not have a messiah complex. That's all in Máire's fevered imagination—which I will endeavor to rid her of."

"Good luck." Igraine was still doubtful.

"Well, if you're leaving tomorrow, let's have a hooley tonight, then, eh?" Fiona suggested.

"We'd best invite Máire."

Fiona's nose wrinkled, but she gave in to Nuala. "All right, Arthur, you win. Let's go round and collect that bit of baggage. Igraine, are you up for it?"

Igraine shrugged. "Why not?"

The three friends started to leave the park, but Nuala, in the rear, turned back, staring at the bushes. Had she imagined that rustling sound?

"What is it?" Igraine asked.

Nuala didn't answer, listening to the silence that was broken only by the whispering of leaves in the breeze. "I thought there was . . . something," she replied after a moment.

Nothing moved in the shadows. Perhaps it had been just a cat or a dog. Still, they shouldn't have had this conversation in a public place, even a seemingly deserted one.

"Are we after Máire, then?" Fiona asked.

"Right," Nuala said, joining them.

But as they walked away, Nuala cast one more uneasy glance behind her.

Chapter 7

"**W**ELL, I'M CERTAINLY glad you've come to your senses." Máire closed her plastisteel backpack and picked up her sweater, turning to face Nuala as she put it on. "An alliance with Igraine was a mistake from the start. And Fiona is just like her—too frivolous, not nearly serious enough for this business. Becoming closely tied to them would be potentially fatal. We must put as much distance as possible between us—"

"Máire," Nuala interrupted, sighing. She moved the pillows and sat down. "We have to have a chat."

"Plenty of time for that once we're in Galway." Máire was buttoning her light-gray sweater, oblivious to Nuala's expression or tone.

"Plenty of time for it *now*. Because I'm not moving from this spot until I've said a few things to you."

Looking up in surprise, Máire forgot the rest of the buttons and sat down on the foot of the bed. "You're upset."

"You always had a marvelous gift for understatement. Look, Máire, you don't have to agree with Igraine or Fiona—or me, for that matter—but you can't just dismiss them out of hand. You want to unite the women of Ireland, so you say? Well, the women of Ireland are not a monolithic, agreeable lot with no opinions of their own who are just waiting for us to come along and lead them by the hand to freedom."

"I never said—"

"Igraine's or Fiona's opinions are no less valid than your own—or mine. I may have been gone for a while, but I'm not stupid or even especially ignorant, and I'm a quick study. I don't need you to tell me what to believe. And while I have agreed to go on to Galway with you, I fully intend to come back to Coleraine eventually and join up with them again."

Máire frowned, alarmed, but Nuala continued before she could object.

"I don't need your permission or your approval, Máire. I

value your opinion, but I make my own decisions. You should know that by now, eh?"

Máire sighed, shaking her head. "Oh, Nuala. How long must I go on protecting you from yourself?"

"What?"

"I won't be around forever, you know. I've always known I'd die before we achieved our goal. I just hope I can teach you to be less reckless while I still have the opportunity." Máire's eyes drifted to one side, her gaze becoming vacant, and her voice took on a dreamy tone. "I do so wish I could see that day, though. See you in a shelter of shimmering green stones in a land where women are free and proud."

Nuala stared at her friend. Just what *had* those bastards done to her in Castlereagh? And was that why her behavior seemed to be growing stranger every day?

Máire blinked and her gaze focused, fastened on Nuala. "I've seen it, Nuala. I've seen it all. You will make it, but only if you remember that every step you take now is crucial. You cannot take blind risks, and must not go off on your own as you did at the convent and at the school. Unnecessary danger is to be avoided at all costs. It is too early to call attention to yourself. You aren't ready. The women of Ireland aren't ready. Careful, painstaking preparation must pave the way. If you fail now, your death will be forgotten in the span of a few days. It is not your destiny to be a failed martyr. You have much more to do than that. Now then, can we go, or was there more you wanted to say?"

Nuala blinked, unsure how to respond. Would anything she had to say do any good? "What green stones? What was that about?"

But Máire just smiled and stood up, reaching for her backpack and slinging it over one shoulder. "We'll miss the bullet train if we don't hurry." She paused halfway to the door, the smile evaporating. "Every action you take from here on will have enormous consequences that will reach beyond yourself. You must discover your own courage and marry it to the resourcefulness I know you possess. And above all: Avoid violence. Violence could ruin everything."

"Máire—"

But she only called back over her shoulder as she left the room. "Hurry yourself! We don't want to be missing the train."

Nuala threw up her fists in frustration and grabbed for her backpack. She slung it onto her back, putting both arms through the straps. It clunked against the handrail of the stairs as she hurried after Máire, and a corner caught under the rail, pulling her up short. She freed herself with an irritable jerk, wishing she had brought her canvas bag on this trip. This plastisteel pack wasn't heavy, but it was bulky and awkward. Máire had insisted she bring a plastisteel pack like her own—without reason, as usual—and she had acquiesced simply to avoid an argument. She sighed as she trotted down the stairs. Why did she listen to Máire at all?

Máire marched past the checkout desk, not noticing the odd glance the clerk gave her. They had signed out earlier, before packing, so she had no reason to stop at the desk. Nuala wondered why the clerk was so pale, why he couldn't meet her eyes as she passed him. She saw him flick a glance at the door that Máire was about to open, and something icy gripped the back of her neck.

"Máire!"

But it was too late; Máire had already turned the knob and opened the door.

Two *gardaí*, pistols in hand, were waiting on the porch.

"Máire Ní Flaherty, you are under arrest, pursuant to the Offenses against the State—"

Máire dropped her pack from her shoulder to her hand, then flung it in the closest *garda*'s face and launched herself directly at the second one, knocking him backward before he could raise the pistol.

"Run, Nuala!"

Nuala heard heavy, running footsteps behind her and didn't stop to look back. The first *garda*, whose nose was bloody from its encounter with Máire's pack, was recovering his balance when Nuala barreled into him. The force of her blow knocked him off the concrete porch completely. She jumped over the second *garda*, who was getting to his feet. He tried to grab her and she stopped long enough to kick at him. Her foot connected with his right elbow and his pistol went flying out in front of her.

"Stop or we'll shoot!" a man bellowed from behind her.

Máire, far in front of her now, never slowed, kept running in the direction of the park. Nuala, following her, had only taken a step or two when she heard two pistols fire, and an instant later something slammed into her pack and pitched her onto her face. She fell on something, grabbing at it as she scrambled to her feet. She came up with the pistol of the *garda* she'd kicked. She whirled, firing blindly, saw the *gardaí* dive for cover, then she was running again.

Plasfire erupted around her. What the hell? Nuala thought wildly. Why aren't they set on stun? They're trying to kill us!

She heard screams; her peripheral vision caught the sight of people running and—was that someone with a vidcamera?

Máire was dodging the startled people on the sidewalk ahead of her, her childhood skill at *camogie* coming back to help now as she ran all out, zigzagging and managing not to trip. Nuala, instinctively imitating her, darted first right and then left as she tried to outrun the men in pursuit.

Plasfire blazed again and Máire's back glowed orange for an instant before she fell.

"No!" Nuala screamed, and turned. There was no time to fumble with the unfamiliar pistol's setting. She felt the vibration through her palm as she fired. She saw a *garda* fall, aimed at another, and squeezed the trigger. Something hit the side of her plastisteel pack, knocking her off balance. She staggered, twisted, and shot in the direction of two more advancing *gardaí*. They dived for the pavement, rolling, as the shot scorched the pavement between them.

"That way!" someone called. A woman pointed to a shop of some sort. "Through and out the back! Turn right in the alley!"

Whirling in the direction the woman had pointed out, Nuala ran for the shop. Something buzzed past her head and she ducked as she reached the door. She turned to look at Máire, who was sprawled on the sidewalk, her face in the gutter, a pool of blood under it. Her gray sweater was still smoking.

The doorjamb exploded, showering Nuala's face with charred splinters. She ducked inside, found herself in an electronics repair shop. The man at the window merely pointed at the back of the shop. She ran.

A teenage boy opened the back door for her. "Left! They'll expect you to go right, so go left!"

Not pausing to wonder whom to trust or believe, Nuala turned left and ran.

When she reached the end of the alley, she heard loud male voices behind her.

"She had a gun, Officer! We couldn't try to stop her!"

"She seemed to know where she was going. She ran off to the right. I watched her disappear around the corner, there!"

Darting around the edge of the last building, Nuala pressed against the wall, listening. The footsteps were running away, in the opposite direction. The *gardaí* had believed the man and the boy. Why had they helped her? Why—

Máire. The image of Máire's corpse flooded into her mind. Nuala swayed on her feet, gasping in exhaustion and grief. They'd killed Máire. Murdered her oldest friend, her loyal, deluded, mystical, half-mad friend. And her last words to Máire had been so harsh. Nuala moaned, scarcely feeling the rough brick under her cheek. She reached up to brush away tears and her hand came back bloody. She stared at it, confused. Why was she bleeding? But that thought was replaced by another: How had the *gardaí* known where to find them? And if they knew where Máire and herself had been staying, then—

Igraine. Igraine was staying with—Fiona.

She pushed off the brick wall and ran.

Nuala crept behind the hedge, thankful there seemed to be no one about to call the *gardaí* and report a possible prowler. Slowly she raised her head until she could see past the tiny green leaves and across the street.

A *garda* van sat squarely in front of Fiona's house, but the half-dozen men in blue sat, sprawled idly on the porch and the steps, looking bored. The door to the house was closed. What was going on inside?

A soft rustle from behind startled Nuala and she whirled, pistol in hand. She stopped herself an instant before shooting Gormfhlaith.

The girl's eyes were huge at the sight of the weapon. Nuala grabbed her sleeve and pulled her down to the grass beside her. "What are you doing here? Where's Fiona? And Igraine? Are they inside? Did the *gardaí*—"

"No!" Gormfhlaith whispered, though the *gardaí* were too far away to hear anyway. "We saw them coming and got out the back. Fiona told me to hide over here in case you and Máire showed up. Where *is* Máire—You're bleeding! You're hurt!"

She reached out to touch Nuala's face, frowning, but Nuala pulled back. "Where did they go? Fiona and Igraine?"

"A safe place. Where Rose Butler was hiding before she left to meet your friend in Belfast. Where's Máire? If we have to wait for her—"

"We don't. She's not coming." Nuala paused. The girl was so young; she hated to destroy what was left of her childhood. "Máire's dead, Gormfhlaith. They killed her. And they'll kill me, too, if they catch us. Now, can you take me to Fiona and Igraine?"

Gormfhlaith seemed frozen in shock and horror, her face pale. Nuala squeezed her arm gently and lowered her voice.

"Gormfhlaith. I need your help. I don't know Coleraine. I wouldn't be able to find the place on my own, especially with the *gardaí* looking everywhere for me. Will you help me?"

The girl swallowed and nodded. She tried to speak, but had to swallow again first. "I—I'll take you. It's this way."

Keeping low, Gormfhlaith led off and Nuala followed.

"We've got to get out of Coleraine, obviously." Igraine was pale, shaken, as were they all.

"I can arrange that." Fiona spoke softly. "If we can make it to Donegal, I know of several places we can hide, people who'll—wait, that's where you're from, isn't it? Then you might know better—Nuala? Nuala?"

Fiona's face seemed to swim up at her, as if from some great depth. She had heard her name. Was Fiona talking to her?

"Are you all right?" Fiona leaned toward her, frowning in concern. "You're sure you weren't hurt?" Nuala blinked at Igraine. Why were both of them staring at her?

"Yes, Igraine, I'm sure. Just the one cut." She pointed needlessly at the dermaseal strip on her right cheek, where Igraine had removed the remaining splinter that had come from the doorjamb of the shop.

The image of Máire's corpse appeared before her again, stabbing her with pain and grief. She winced. "Máire's shot down in the street, murdered, and all I get is one inconsequential scratch."

"You'd rather have joined her in death?"

Igraine darted a shocked look at Fiona, started to object, then saw her grim expression and let her go on.

"You're alive, Nuala; be thankful for that. And you're not hurt—you're able to fight back, to continue. If Máire's death is to count for something, then you *must* continue. You can't give in to grief or misplaced guilt—"

"Fiona!" Gormfhlaith burst into the attic room, startling them all. Nuala grabbed for the pistol.

"Is it the *gardaí*?" Fiona was already on her feet and halfway across the room.

"No, the *teilifís*. It's on next, come quick!"

Nuala started to put the pistol down, her heart still racing, but then tucked it into her waistband and followed the others.

The small vidscreen in the next room was crowded with the image of *gardaí* running, pistols in hand. The male announcer's voice filled the tiny room, even though the volume was low. His face appeared an instant later.

"What was to be a simple arrest of atheist agitators turned bloody today when the *gardaí* were ambushed by terrorists. One officer is dead this evening, as Micheál É. Houlihan reports."

Film of a *garda* funeral replaced the announcer's face.

"Yes, Seán, another *garda* is dead tonight and his family has been plunged into mourning by the vicious and calculated act of terrorists. The IRA has denied responsibility for the matter, claiming they were not involved, but official sources refute this. A *garda* superintendent, who of course must remain anonymous due to fear of IRA reprisals, told me this evening that the *gardaí* had gone to this inn on Breithiúnas Road on the word of an informant who claimed that atheist agitators had infiltrated St. Brendan's School yesterday, posing as nuns and trying to intimidate the children, and that these depraved women had taken refuge here at Hayden's Inn. The superintendent told me that on the occasions that Coleraine *gardaí* had arrested atheists in the past, there has rarely been violence of any kind. The *gardaí*, therefore, were anticipating little trouble when they walked into the IRA trap."

"IRA trap?" Igraine murmured in disgust, but then the image on the screen changed.

Nuala stared at herself running, pistol in hand. She watched as the Nuala on the screen turned and fired. Two *gardaí* dived for the ground, rolling, as a pistol blast scorched the pavement between them. Then the screen showed five other *gardaí* diving for cover under heavy fire. One of them was caught in the back by pistol fire, and he fell, unmoving, to the ground. The camera lingered on the body, then suddenly cut to another scene of four more *gardaí*—these with rifles—who seemed to be under fire from two directions at once. One of the four was hit in the shoulder, his blue jacket smoking, his face contorted in agony. The camera cut to another shot of Nuala, closing in on her face as she paused in the electronics shop doorway. She had been staring at Máire's body at the time, but the way the tape was edited, it appeared that she was looking back at the *garda* with the rifle who had just been shot. The picture froze on a close-up of her face. The reporter continued with a voice-over.

"This woman was the only terrorist our cameraman was able to get a clear picture of. She has been identified by the informant as the woman who seized control of a classroom at St. Brendan's yesterday, terrifying the children and subjecting them to a vicious stream of anti-Catholic abuse. Unfortunately the *gardaí* were not able to capture her at the scene of the ambush today, due to the heavy fire laid down by her IRA co-conspirators, but the superintendent I spoke with is confident that she will be in custody soon. In the meantime, another brave member of our security forces, Officer Cathal Ryan, has given his life to protect the peace . . . Back to you, Seán."

The announcer's studiously grave visage filled the screen. "Thank you, Micheál. Let us all remember Officer Ryan and his family in our prayers, and may we all continue to pray for peace . . . We'll be back in a moment."

Fiona hit the volume control with her fist, rocking the monitor on its fauxwood stand. "Bloody bastards! Lying through their teeth!"

"They never even mentioned Máire." Igraine was amazed and disgusted. "An unarmed woman is shot in the back—murdered!—and it's not even mentioned."

"I killed someone." Nuala's stomach churned; she had to swallow the bile that was trying to force its way out.

"You had no choice," she heard Igraine say, but she took no notice. She frowned as confusion interfered with the horror.

"Rifles?" Nuala's face contorted with the effort of trying to remember. "There were no rifles. And even though it *seemed* there were *gardaí* everywhere, there couldn't have been that many, not just to arrest two women. I don't remember those four they showed with the rifles. They weren't there."

"Probably not." Igraine sat down on a battered, once-green stuffed chair. "They looked to be under fire from two directions, which is impossible, since there was only yourself. So it must have been stock footage that they edited in."

"Of course they did." Fiona nodded. "Like they did the funeral. If a man died this morning, then they've not had his wake yet, much less his funeral. They edited that in, as well." She shook her head. "I can't believe how blatant they're becoming in their manipulation. Do they really believe we're that stupid?"

"But why would they do that?" Gormfhlaith asked. "Why

would they show *gardaí* who weren't even there? Wasn't it bad enough as it was?"

"Never trust the media, Gormfhlaith," her sister told her. "Especially in this country." Then a puzzled expression crossed Fiona's face. "But why was a camera there in the first place?"

"Informant," Nuala murmured. "The park." What color there was left in her cheeks after the day's ordeal drained away. She raised anguished eyes to Igraine. "Máire was killed because of that stunt I pulled at the school! I—apparently—killed a man, and Máire's dead, too, because I—"

"She's dead because we live under a totalitarian regime that is kept in place by the Church and the Gestapo thugs who call themselves a police force!" Igraine leaned over the arm of the chair and squeezed Nuala's wrist. "It is *not* your fault! And I won't have you punishing yourself for it! Máire knew the risks. I'm sorry she's dead, but the facts are what they are. We have to go on from here."

Nuala gently removed Igraine's strong grip on her wrist, sighing. "I know that, *mo chara*. I have no intention of quitting or even of allowing myself to be distracted from the tasks at hand. But I've *killed* someone. And Máire—she was my friend, and she had no family, no one to mourn her. Only me. If I had only listened to her, done what she—"

"Nuala, you can't change the past." Fiona was sympathetic. In spite of the fact that she hadn't liked Máire at all, the murder had affected her, too. "Mourn her in whatever way you like— once we get the hell out of here."

Nuala looked from Fiona to Igraine. They were both frightened—as they had every right to be—but behind that she could see the concern for her in their eyes.

"You should cut your hair."

The three women turned to Gormfhlaith in surprise.

"As a sort of disguise. You know. They saw you on the *teilifís. Everybody* saw you. You have to look different to escape."

"She's right." Fiona nodded. "You can't exactly grow a beard, can you? So perhaps cutting your hair—"

"Fine. It's more bother than it's worth, anyway." Nuala had to fight off a surprisingly sudden yawn; she had never felt so tired. "Who's going to do it?"

"I can. Have we scissors?" Gormfhlaith got up to look for some, but Fiona stopped her, smiling.

"I think perhaps Igraine or myself—"

"But I know how!" Gormfhlaith protested. "Remember when my friend Bridget and I—"

"I do," Fiona interrupted, chuckling. "You looked a sight, the pair of you."

"Well, I was a kid then; I'm sure I could do it better now." Gormfhlaith was on the verge of pouting. It suddenly struck Nuala just how young the girl was.

"I trust you, *kidín*." The smile felt stiff and awkward to Nuala, like a new pair of shoes she doubted she would ever break in. Not after today. "Why don't you see if there's any scissors about?"

Gormfhlaith smiled in return, though she, too, was feeling the strain. She left the room, intent on her search.

"Why don't you let me do it, Nuala?" Igraine said. "I've had a bit of experience; I have five sisters."

Nuala shrugged; how could she care about something so mundane now? She turned to Fiona.

"Are we taking Gormfhlaith with us? The danger to her could be just as great as to ourselves, and your parents must be—"

"I know." Fiona nodded, shooting a glance toward the door through which her little sister had disappeared. "I can't risk contacting my parents now. They've been questioned by the *gardaí*—probably still are being questioned—and the 'phone is undoubtedly tapped by now. I'd leave her with friends, but even that might be too dangerous for her. I've got to get her out of Coleraine for the time being. Perhaps I can put her on a train in Donegal to my cousin in Ballymena. Once we've gotten away from her—and as long as she doesn't know where we're going—she should be relatively safe after this has cooled down a bit. She *is* still a child; that should afford her some small amount of protection. I just hope my parents are all right."

"I found scissors." Gormfhlaith returned, a tiny pair of fingernail scissors in her hand. She looked down at them dubiously. "This is all there was. But your hair is so thick—"

"Here, why don't I have a try at it, Gormfhlaith? I've done this before."

"Oh, well, okay, then." Gormfhlaith relinquished the tiny scissors to Igraine, frowning at Nuala. "It's such a shame, though. You've beautiful hair—so thick and wavy and long, the kind I wish I had."

"It's just hair," Nuala said. "It'll grow back and look the same as ever."

But moments later, when dark tresses began falling onto the

kitchen floor, Nuala wasn't so sure. How could anything ever be the same again?

Chapter 8

"IT's ON AGAIN!" Igraine whispered, and Nuala instinctively ducked her head, her nose almost buried in the teacup. Igraine and Fiona turned to watch the pub's *teilifís*.

The regular broadcast of a hurling match had been interrupted, provoking curses and groans from the male patrons of the pub—who undoubtedly had money at stake on the match's outcome. The hurling match disappeared, to be replaced with the logo of a wren perched on a vidcamera—the symbol of the Guerrilla TV. The symbol of the Irish Republican Movement a century before had been a wren, the king of birds, according to Irish legend, perched on a rifle. The Guerrilla broadcasters had modified it to represent a more powerful weapon than a gun: the videocamera, the international symbol for exposure of injustice.

After a moment the logo was replaced with videotape: the door to Hayden's Inn in Coleraine. Two *gardaí* stood on the concrete porch, their hands on their pistols as the door opened.

Nuala didn't have to look up over the partition; she had seen the pirated tape several times in the few days since they had made it safely west to Letterkenny, County Donegal. It was silent but complete, an unedited depiction of the *garda* attack on her and Máire: Although a bit jumpy in spots, it clearly showed the unarmed Máire being shot in the back. Unfortunately, it also showed Nuala's face in close-up, as had the official version of the incident.

The Guerrilla TV were pirate broadcasters who occasionally managed—somehow—to break in on regular programming, substituting tapes of their own. Usually a man, his face covered with a balaclava, merely read uncensored news to the camera, letting Ireland know what was really going on in the world and in space, usually with at least a brief mention of the Tlatejoxans or other members of the Unity, since the official newscasts were forbidden by the government to discuss the "un-Christian aliens." Lately the Guerrillas had grown even bolder, breaking in more frequently, showing unedited tapes that they claimed they had stolen from broadcast stations. There were even rumors that they planned to smuggle tapes out of Ireland, to expose to the world the truth behind the government's carefully fostered image of an idyllic, quiet Ireland where everyone lived in peace, freedom, and tranquility.

Nuala admired the pirate broadcasters for their courage and ingenuity, but having her face appear on every *teilifís* in the country made her nervous when she tried to fade into a crowd, even in disguise.

"There, you see!" a male voice said from the bar. "She wasn't even armed until she picked up his pistol. IRA trap, was it? Ha! She was the only one shooting at them and still they couldn't catch her."

"If it was the Provos, more than one of those thugs would've died," another voice added.

"She got off a lucky shot is all," the first man said. "Probably never held a gun in her life."

"If it wasn't the IRA, then who the hell was that girl, and the one they murdered?" a third man asked.

"Atheist agitators, if you believe the media," the publican responded.

"Well, of course I don't believe that lot; do you take me for an entire fool? Atheist agitators are an invention of the Church, and don't we all know that?"

"Whoever she is, the one that escaped," the publican said as the tape ended, "I hope they never catch her. It's a great thing to see somebody escape the bloody bastards."

The hurling match resumed, to the approval of the audience around the bar—until the score came on at the bottom of the screen and it became apparent that they had missed seeing a goal. The swearing that filled the pub was a general indictment: The pirate broadcasters and the *gardaí* both received their share of insults and threats. Nuala was relieved to note that she—and Máire—were not included in the condemnation.

"*I* heard that they were trying to smuggle abortion equipment into the country," a low female voice said from behind Nuala's chair.

"No, rubber johnnies," another female voice corrected her. "Might have been part of the same ring that brought in those rubbers to Ballymena, d'ye remember? Those balloons waving in the Archbishop's face."

The chuckle spread to half of the female section of the pub.

"Wouldn't I have liked to see *that* in person, instead of on the Guerrilla TV?" another woman said, laughing.

"I wish I'd been there." The quiet voice, directly behind Nuala, had no laughter in it. "If I'd gotten my hands on some of those—ah, well, it's too late now."

"Oh, Maureen, no" came the soft reply. "You're not pregnant again?"

There was no answer; perhaps Maureen nodded.

"Christ! You've got eleven now! And the doctor said—"

"The doctor!" Maureen's voice dripped bitterness and disgust. "You know what *his* great medical advice was? To have Declan sleep in another room!" She lowered her voice even further, but Nuala heard it clearly. "He said my only choice was to refuse my husband. As if I *could* do that, even if I wanted to. You can't keep secrets from the devils in brown. If Father McRory heard that I wasn't sleeping with Declan, he'd send one of those blasted God Patrols round to threaten us. Excommunication, unemployment—Declan would never stand for either."

"But you've had three miscarriages already," her worried friend whispered. "What if—"

"Lucky for me the doctor testified on my behalf. If I have another, they might charge me with murder. What if they don't believe the doctor the next time?"

"You could go to Scotland—"

"If I had an abortion in Scotland, I could never come back. They'd know; they'd find out. And we can't all thirteen of us emigrate. There's no money." The woman's sigh was so wretched, so full of despair that Nuala winced. "God willing," Maureen went on, "I'll have this baby and no miscarriage. I don't know how we'll feed another one, but we will. And that's all there is to be done about it . . . Another baby. And Séamie still in nappies."

There was a long pause, then Maureen's friend whispered, "I wonder where those rubbers *did* come from?"

Nuala looked up to find that both Igraine and Fiona were watching her, as if waiting for her to say something.

Sighing, she nodded. "Okay, I've mourned long enough. Let's do it." Igraine and Fiona smiled, and then Fiona got up to make the 'phone call.

* * *

The wind was cold on Nuala's neck, her ears. She had had long, thick hair since she was a girl; her new short haircut made her feel naked, exposed to the cold. And the color. It was a light auburn now, several shades lighter than her natural dark chestnut. That and the scar on her cheek—she didn't recognize herself in the mirror anymore. Even the eyes belonged to someone else, someone much older.

The cold breeze ruffled her hair again, and she shivered. Although Igraine appeared to be engrossed in the corner news kiosk's vidscreen, she murmured, "You okay?"

"I do wish you two would stop asking me that." Nuala kept her voice low so the old man who worked the kiosk wouldn't hear.

Igraine spoke just as quietly. "You're still having those nightmares, aren't you? Seeing your own face in the gutter, instead of Máire's?"

Nuala stiffened as the images flooded back. She didn't reply.

"You don't have to stay, you know. You have a life in Scotland. You could always go back."

After a moment, when she could trust her voice not to quaver with anger and embarrass her, Nuala answered. "Flight would gain me nothing but a shameful safety and the realization of my own failure. There's no guarantee the nightmares would be gone, either. I owe it to Máire—and to myself, if I'm to live with myself—to stay."

The ghost of a smile appeared and then vanished from Igraine's face. "I thought you'd say that."

"Then why did you ask?"

But Igraine didn't answer. "I do wish Fiona would hurry along. I'm freezing my—it's cold for October, isn't it?"

The old man had stepped up to the counter to straighten the stack of magazines. He nodded in silent agreement to Igraine's revised comment.

Nuala half turned away from him. She doubted he would recognize her: Even though the pirate broadcasters had broken in on national programming with the tape many times over the past two weeks, she didn't look much like the woman the authorities were calling a "wanted murderer and known terrorist." Even so, being out in public made her nervous. The new ID chip Igraine had mysteriously acquired—saying only "There are people who owe me"—named her Dara Moran, and it had worked to get her out of Derry and into Donegal, but she was nervous all the same.

A car eased to a stop behind them. Fiona leaned out the driver's side. "Get in."

Igraine tossed a coin to the old man inside the kiosk—a tip because they had watched his vidscreen but hadn't bought anything—and then climbed into the backseat next to Nuala.

"It's all set," Fiona said as she pulled away from the curb. "We have a meeting with the Guerrillas tomorrow night at six."

"You're sure it's not a trap?" Igraine asked.

"As sure as I can be." Fiona stopped to allow a stray dog to wander across the street.

"What did you tell them about us?"

Nuala only half heard Igraine's question; she stared at the dog, watched it approach a man timidly, hesitate when the man ignored it, and then plod off down the street alone. She watched until the car went around a corner and she lost sight of it.

"Only what we agreed. I told them we had information about the incident in Coleraine," Fiona answered Igraine. "That we knew why it really happened. They jumped at it."

"They'll give us air time?"

Fiona shrugged, looking at Igraine in the rearview mirror. "If they like what they hear. They're probably all of them men, you know. At least, the only ones I know of are."

"They'll give us air time," Nuala muttered. "Whether they want to or not."

"Coleraine," Fiona said, and the man nodded. He was perhaps thirty, or a few years younger. His reddish blond hair was shaggy but clean, and it looked as if he hadn't combed it in a while. He wore nondescript faded blue jeans and a chambray shirt. The cuffs were rolled back, which reminded Nuala of something that flitted around the edge of her memory but refused to focus. His gaze raked over Igraine and Nuala. From the look on his face, he didn't trust them, nor was he impressed by what he saw. Nuala raised a scornful eyebrow of her own in reply, and he blinked in surprise, then nodded to Fiona again.

"Follow me."

He led them down an alley and turned right at the corner. Soon they were in another alley. They followed him silently for well over half an hour, turning, doubling back, going forward; they must have visited half the alleys in the neighborhood before he finally knocked at a back door. Two quick raps, a pause, then three more.

"An bhfuil siad leat?" The whispered question was squeezed through the crack in the barely open door.

"Tá, I've got them here," their guide replied.

The door was opened wide and he hurried in, motioning for them to follow.

Wondering again if this was a trap, Nuala brought up the rear. She jumped when the door closed behind her.

They were in someone's kitchen; the smell of baked scones lingered in the air. There was a kettle on the stove, the water cooling down from a boil.

The man at the door stared at them impassively. He was big, probably six feet tall or more, and had the sort of build that boasted of physical labor. His beard and curly hair were a deep red, and his blue eyes were cold.

"They don't look the sort that the *gardaí* recruit for spies." His words were apparently aimed at their blond guide, but Nuala answered him.

"And what sort would that be?"

He did a double take and then squinted at her in surprise. "You look familiar." A gun appeared in his hand as if by magic. He took one step toward her with it. "Now where would I know you from?"

Nuala dismissed the gun with a bored glance. "Perhaps from the tape you've been showing to all of Ireland these two weeks past—and without my bloody permission, I might add. I had no wish to become a celebrity; you've made my life difficult indeed."

"You didn't say it was—" Redbeard said to the blond man.

"I didn't know," he replied, just as surprised. "Perhaps I should—"

"Yes, get him."

Their blond guide edged around them, stared at Nuala for a moment, then left the way they had entered.

"What was that about?" Fiona demanded. "And *will* you put that thing away!"

Redbeard looked down at his gun as if surprised to see it in his hand. "Oh, sorry." He replaced it behind his back, in his belt. "We didn't know it was going to be yourself," he said to Nuala. His cold stare had disappeared, and he surprised her by smiling. "This is quite a coup. An interview with you will have the whole country paying attention to us."

Fiona interrupted before Nuala could reply. "What is going on here? Who did your friend go to fetch?"

"Oh, don't worry. You're quite safe here, with us. Stuart's just gone to get our cameraman. We thought you were just going to supply us with information, but had we known that herself—" He smiled at Nuala again. "Let's go down to the basement, where there's room. The door's right there."

The three women exchanged a glance. Then Fiona shrugged and opened the basement door.

"Whether they want to or not?" Igraine murmured to Nuala as they started down the stairs.

"This will make you look more like you did in the original tape," Redbeard, whose name turned out to be Kevin, said as Igraine helped Nuala straighten the long, dark wig. "And of course it won't ruin your present disguise."

"Keep your left side to me," the new arrival, Daithi, directed Nuala as he sighted through the handheld camera. He was even younger than Stuart, and a small man, barely Nuala's height. He juggled the tiny camera with ease and evident experience. "You didn't have that scar in the original, so we'll keep it hidden."

Stuart and Fiona sat on the couch across the basement, watching. Igraine joined them.

Nuala looked around at Daithi. "Perhaps I should rehearse some—"

"Left side to the camera!" he reminded her.

"Right, right." Nuala turned back, and found herself staring at a pet hamster in a cage, who seemed to be staring back at her. That's the way she felt at the moment: as trapped as that hamster. These men—strangers, every one of them—were going to tape her as she made treasonous, inflammatory statements, then edit the tape any way they chose and broadcast it all over Ireland, whenever they could. She had no control over any part of this situation. Except over what she said. If she had even a remote idea of what that was going to be, she would feel a lot better about all of this.

"How's the backdrop?" Kevin asked.

"Fine," Daithi answered, still looking at Nuala through his camera.

The backdrop was a bedsheet, pale blue in color. The lights were floor lamps brought down, presumably, from the living room. The only illegal piece of equipment in the room was Daithi's vidcamera, and it was only illegal because, he had told them, he had no government license for it. All vidcams purchased for personal use required a license, and a computer record of all tapes purchased as well was kept so that God Patrols could drop by to check the tapes' contents at any time. Daithi's camera and the reused tape in it had been stolen nearly a year ago from the TV station in Coleraine where Stuart worked.

"How long have you been doing this?" Igraine asked Stuart.

"Me? Well, since I got the job at the station, a few years back. I saw what was being taped in the field, then I saw what was done to the tapes, the lies we broadcast. When the Guerrillas contacted me, I was ready to help; I wanted to tell the unedited truth for a change."

"It was you, then, that stole the tape of Máire's murder from the station?" Fiona asked him.

"Yes. Máire? Was that her name? The *gardaí* never told us."

"It was," Nuala answered, ignoring Daithi. "Máire Ní Flaherty. She was *not*, as the *gardaí* would have everyone believe, a member of the IRA. Máire had no use for the Provos at all."

"Save it for the tape," Kevin said, but gently. "So you won't have to repeat yourself."

Nuala nodded and turned to face the hamster again.

"I'm ready when you are," Daithi said.

"Then let's do it," Nuala said, speaking to her one-rodent audience, hoping she would think of something to say beyond the questions Kevin was going to ask.

Kevin's disembodied voice came from behind Nuala; she couldn't turn to look at him. She wondered if she was on camera yet.

"This is Guerrilla TV, the voice of a free Ireland. Over the past two weeks, we have been showing you footage of an outrageous murder committed by the *gardaí* in Coleraine. Two unarmed women were attacked, as you saw on the tape, and one was killed, shot in the back. Her companion has contacted us to tell us—and you, the people of Ireland—what really happened, and why."

He paused, and Nuala wondered if she was supposed to start talking now, but Kevin had said to wait for his questions. Sure enough, after his pause—for dramatic effect?—Kevin resumed speaking.

"You have been identified by the *gardaí* as Nuala Dennehy, an expatriate and now a member of the IRA. Is this true?"

"Which part?" Nuala replied, feeling awkward at speaking to Kevin but looking at the hamster. "My name *is* Nuala Dennehy, and I have recently returned to Ireland after fifteen years in

Scotland—that much is true, yes. But I am not and never have been a member of the IRA or any other organization."

"Why did you leave Ireland and why were you gone for so long? Don't you love your country?"

Nuala frowned in annoyance. What did that have to do with Máire's murder? The hamster stared at her, as if waiting breathlessly for her answer.

"I left because I wanted to teach Irish history. I could not do that in Ireland because only nuns and Brothers are permitted to teach in this country, and the revisionist version of history *they* teach turns my stomach. So I taught true Irish history to young Scots. As for whether or not I love my country, what sort of an asinine question is that? Would I have made Ireland's history my life's work if I cared nothing for her?"

Her irritation was unmistakable. Kevin's polite tone acknowledged it. "So you came back because you love Ireland?"

Nuala hesitated. This wasn't going the way she wanted it to at all. What was important was the fact that Máire had been murdered and that the government was lying about it. Her own feelings didn't matter; they were *her* business, and couldn't be of any interest to anyone else. But she answered the question, hoping his next one would be closer to the subject.

"Yes, that, and because I didn't like the rumors I was hearing about Ireland having changed so much in the few years I'd been gone; that it had become a totalitarian state, where freedom is just a word used by politicians on election day. Or by churchmen who try to convince us that our enslavement is a victory for morality. I came home to see if the rumors were true. And to my horror and revulsion, they *were* true. I am sickened by what my country has become."

"Are you saying that the government should be overthrown, that Ireland needs a revolution?"

Kevin asked the question calmly, as if by his asking it and her answering it he was not convicting them both of treason.

Nuala matched his dispassion. "Henry David Thoreau, a brilliant American of two centuries ago whom I doubt anyone in Ireland has ever heard of, once said, 'All men'—and by that I hope he meant all *people*—'recognize the right to revolution, that is, the right to refuse allegiance to, and to resist, the government when its tyranny or its inefficiency are great and unendurable.' Can anyone, if she is truly honest, disagree that what we are living under is indeed tyranny? When a woman is forced— *forced*—to give birth to twelve or more children, whether she wants to or not, and in doing so risks her life, her health, and her sanity all because the Church says she must: Is this not tyranny? When citizens cannot own a personal computer, a vidcamera, a fax machine, a modem, or even an ancient typewriter without permission and a license from the government lest they produce words or pictures that the government doesn't approve of: Is this not tyranny? When the government jams satellite reception so that Irish citizens can hear no version of world events except through government censorship: Is this not tyranny? When divorce is illegal, so that a woman cannot escape a man who beats and abuses her, and the local priest tells her to go home and submit, uncomplainingly, to her husband's will: Is this not tyranny?"

Nuala paused to take a breath, but Kevin didn't speak. The hamster was now buried in the woodshavings. Only its terrified eyes peered out at her. Nuala sighed.

"I believe—and my friend Máire Ní Flaherty, who was cowardly murdered by the *gardaí*, believed—that the Irish people are weary of tyrants. We threw the British out after nine hundred years, only to succumb to a gutless, spineless, *worthless* government in Dublin that sat back and allowed right-wing Catholic fundamentalists to step in and take over. They have betrayed the memory of 1916 and blasphemed the vision of freedom declared by those who were executed for Ireland's sake. They have stolen Ireland from the Irish people, and I believe it is time that we take Ireland *back*. For ourselves and for our children. That is what Máire believed, too, and they tried to arrest her for it that day in Coleraine. Because she dared to disagree with the government. All of Máire's life she dared to disagree—and they shot her in the back for it."

Nuala's throat felt tight; her voice had suddenly become hoarse.

"So when they attacked you," Kevin said, startling Nuala because he had been silent for so long, "when they attacked you, you grabbed a pistol one of them had dropped, and you fought back."

"Of course I did. I wasn't going to let them kill me as they killed Máire. Or arrest and torture me." She swallowed, groping for the right words. "I would prefer nonviolent change. I believe, along with the great Fenian John Boyle O'Reilly, that 'words can be more devastating weapons than any iron implement in the arsenals of the world.' But if I am attacked, I *will* fight back. The Irish people—women in particular—have been submitting for far too long. I refuse. I will *not* submit to any man, any police force, any church, or any government. If change cannot be wrought by any other means but revolution . . . then let it be so. If we are met with violence and are forced to defend ourselves with violence, then let it be so."

The hamster had disappeared. Nuala swallowed again, trying to ease her dry throat, her hoarse voice. The image of Máire facedown in the gutter flashed before her, and she winced, then clenched her jaw in fury. She turned until she could see Daithi and his camera off to her left. She stared at it, her jaw working, her eyes hard. Her voice came out scratchy and tired and very, very cold.

"Let it be so."

After a few silent moments, Kevin said, "Cut."

Nuala blinked in surprise as Daithi lowered his camera, grinning. "That was a nice touch, staring into the lens. And I didn't see the scar, so you didn't turn too far. Are you sure you didn't rehearse this?"

"What? No, of course not. I didn't—is that all?" Nuala turned in confusion from Daithi to Kevin, who was also smiling. "But I didn't get to say—that is, Máire—What *did* I say?"

"A nice, short, rabble-rousing speech." Kevin came forward and took her hand, shaking it firmly. "Exactly right for our purposes."

"*Your* purposes?" Nuala disengaged her hand and turned to Igraine and Fiona. "Was it all right? Did I say what I should have?"

"Sounded good to me." Igraine nodded in approval. "Well done."

"Good job, Nuala," Fiona agreed smiling. "It's a start."

Stuart was taking down the backdrop, Kevin was unplugging the lamps, and Daithi was packing his camera.

"Is that it?" Fiona asked Kevin. "You don't want to redo any portion of it?"

"Got it all," Daithi answered for him. "I doubt any editing will be necessary." He handed the tape to Stuart, who slipped it into his pocket.

"I'll get this ready for airing," Stuart explained to them, "and you'll be seeing it in a day or two."

"Wait a minute," Nuala objected. "Don't I get to see it *before* you broadcast it? What if I don't like—"

"You'll like it," Daithi assured her. "You were great; don't worry." With that, he scurried up the stairs.

"But—" Nuala began.

"Lonnegan, will you show them back to where you found them?"

Stuart nodded, and Kevin turned to go, a lamp in each hand. "If the response to this one is good, maybe we'll have you do another one, eh? We'll keep in touch. *Slán*." He lumbered up the stairs with the lamps and was gone.

Stuart dropped the folded sheet on the chair Nuala had used. "Shall we?" He motioned toward the stairs.

"Here's your hat, what's your hurry?" Nuala muttered.

"I beg your pardon?" Stuart asked.

"Just an American expression, roughly equivalent to the 'bum's rush.' "

Stuart frowned in confusion, and Igraine said, "Pay no attention. She's forever using quotes that nobody's ever heard of. Part of being an historian, I suppose."

"Ah," said Stuart, still confused, and gestured toward the stairs. Nuala noted once again his rolled-up cuffs. Her eyes widened in sudden memory.

"Lonnegan? Your name is Lonnegan?"

When Stuart nodded, she added, "Do you have a younger sister named Heather?"

Stuart was astonished. "You know Heather? How?"

Nuala smiled. "Yeah, I should have seen the resemblance; you look very much like her. I met her in Coleraine, the day before—uh, I was posing as a nun and commandeered her class."

"That was *Heather's* class?" Stuart shook his head. "I had no idea. I haven't spoken to her in over a month." He smiled in affection. "She's a great kid. Quite the rebel herself."

"So I noticed," Nuala said. "I liked her. I liked her a lot."

"I'll have to tell her I met you," Stuart said as they went up the stairs. "She'll be impressed."

"Will she?" Nuala said. "Whatever for?"

The tape was broadcast, unedited, for the first time the following Tuesday, breaking into the middle of the national news. It was played frequently after that, for the next few weeks. The official response was outrage by the *gardaí* and several newspaper editors. Archbishop Doheny of Clare even used Nuala as the subject of his weekly broadcast sermon. The cleric was all compassion and saddened, bewildered pity, urging his listeners to feel a similar pity for "this poor, deluded girl." He also intimated that perhaps allowing girls to study overly taxing subjects such as history might not be a good idea. It could only confuse them and lead them into tragedy, as it obviously had Nuala.

It was shortly after the first broadcast of the tape that the graffiti started to appear. Nuala, Igraine, and Fiona saw it for the first time in Gortahork, Donegal, but Fiona had reports from her sources in Coleraine that the scrawled message was appearing all over Ireland.

Sprayed in huge black letters along the side of the white-washed post office in Gortahork were the words: LET IT BE SO.

Chapter 9

"THIS IS TOO dangerous. It was a mistake, and I was a fool to think I should—"

"Fiona's contacts have never let us down yet," Igraine reminded Nuala.

They were shivering in a barn near Gortahork, on the northern coast of Donegal less than two miles from Falcarragh, Nuala's hometown. It was just after sundown, and the wind was keening around the corners of the barn as if it were demanding to be let in. But the small, thatch-covered building was snug; the foot-high glowfire lamp kept them plenty warm enough. It was not because her hands were cold that Nuala had burrowed them into the thick fur of the dog that had draped himself across her knee. His eyes drooped in contentment as she methodically stroked the soft fur. She wasn't thinking of the dog; her hands acted automatically, of their own accord. She didn't see the two quiet ponies Igraine was petting in their shadowed stalls, though she was staring in their direction.

"If anything happens to him—"

"It won't," Igraine assured her yet again. "Fiona said—"

"But the *gardaí* know who I am! That means they'll be watching him, just waiting for me to contact him."

"Yes, I know." Igraine was patient, even though they had been over all this a hundred times in the past few days. "But

Fiona's friend Úna in Gweedore has it all arranged; I'm sure everything will come off perfectly."

Nuala's hands continued to stroke the dog, who sighed and dozed off. "I'll never forgive myself if—"

"Did I ever tell you that my family has a stud farm in Kerry?" Igraine interrupted, trying again to change the subject. "I come from a long line of horse people. I was riding nearly before I could walk. It was what I wanted more than anything: to be a horse breeder like my father when I grew up. But of course, being female, that was out of the question."

"I just hope Fiona can get to him safely," Nuala said, not listening.

"Fiona seems to know everyone and her pig," Igraine replied, rubbing one of the ponies behind the ear. "If we hadn't met up with her in Coleraine, we'd still be floundering, trying to decide where to go and what to do next. Now if we can just get all those friends and acquaintances of hers, her wee network, organized somehow with others outside Ulster, perhaps with the few people I know in Dublin, so that there's some simultaneous coordination of effort—"

The barn door opened, startling the two women, who jumped to their feet while groping for their pistols. The dog growled as two people hurried in out of the howling wind and grabbed the door, battling the wind for it and finally latching it shut.

"It's us," Fiona said, but Nuala didn't hear her. She was staring, her pistol still in her hand, at the man behind Fiona.

He approached slowly, staring back at her, his eyes damp. He dragged off his cap and squeezed it tightly in both hands, and his voice cracked with emotion. "And are you going to shoot me then, *cushla*?"

Nuala couldn't speak; tears were beginning to slide down her cheeks. Igraine smiled and gently took Nuala's pistol from her. Nuala didn't notice.

"Don't you have a hug for your old da?" Séamus Dennehy asked as he came to his daughter and opened his arms.

Nuala fell into her father's embrace, grabbing him just as tightly as he held her, her eyes squeezed shut. They stood like that, together, for a long time, trying to make up for eight years apart, since his last visit to Edinburgh. Eventually, over her own and her father's labored breathing, Nuala heard Igraine murmur, "Have you met these ponies, Fiona? They're grand little animals; let me introduce you." When she finally released her father and stepped back, Nuala saw that her two friends had their backs turned, giving her what privacy they could in the small barn.

Nuala studied her father eagerly. It had been so long since she'd seen him! She was dismayed—though she didn't show it—that he seemed to have shrunk; he wasn't as tall as she remembered. He had clearly lost weight; his clothes sagged on his slight frame. But they were clean, just pressed. He was wearing his "Sunday best" coat, the same brown tweed with the chocolate-brown elbow patches that she remembered from all those years ago, and she could smell the aftershave he always saved for extra-special occasions. He had fancified himself, as he called it—for her. That brought fresh tears to her eyes; she was afraid of falling apart completely. He was obviously on the verge of that himself, but cleared his throat and blinked hard.

"What *have* you done to your hair?" He reached out to stroke her new short haircut. "Well, well. My brunette has become a redhead. It's—yes, it's very pretty indeed."

Nuala realized her expression was wavering between joy at seeing him, grief that he had been so ill and lost so much of his burly vitality and size, and worry over the risk he was taking in being here. She planted a smile on her face and lied.

"Da, you look wonderful!"

He smiled as his hand slipped down to her cheek and very gently touched her scar. "Not nearly as grand as yourself. My Fenian warrior." His smile widened as he took her hands and squeezed them. "When Kerry called to tell me you were back, I wondered what you'd do first, how you'd make the tyrants sit up and take notice." He chuckled, which brought on a hacking cough, but he recovered quickly and smiled again. "Posing as a nun and taking over a class! Wouldn't I have liked to have been there! Whatever did you tell those girls?"

Nuala shrugged, embarrassed. "Just some Bible stories. Da, sit down, please. Here, by the lamp."

He sat down slowly, his movements stiff, but his smile immediately returned. " 'The soul of Ireland preached revolution, declared that no blood-letting could be as disastrous as a cowardly acceptance of the rule of the conqueror, nay that the rule of the conqueror would necessarily entail more blood-letting than revolt against the rule.' Who said it?"

Nuala grinned back at him. "James Connolly."

"On the occasion of?"

"The funeral of Jeremiah O'Donovan Rossa."

Fiona and Igraine smiled at each other behind him as Séamus

laughed, delighted. "That's my girl! You haven't forgotten a thing." His smile faded as he clutched at her hand. His eyes narrowed. "That's what they're afraid of, you know: the past. The *tremendous* power of the past, and what a weapon it can be."

"I know, Da."

Séamus's right hand waved in the air, and he sat up straighter; he seemed to grow taller before her eyes as he recited again. " 'They think that they have pacified Ireland. They think that they have purchased half of us and intimidated the other half. They think that they have foreseen everything, think that they have provided against everything; but the fools, the fools, the fools!—They have left us our Fenian dead . . .' " He paused, nodding somberly at his daughter, who finished it for him.

" '. . . and while Ireland holds these graves Ireland unfree shall never be at peace.' "

Séamus's proud smile faded, and he frowned. To Nuala's dismay, he suddenly appeared afraid. "Ah, Nuala. Is this all I've given you, love? Quotes from dead men and a hunger for revolution? What have I done to you? What danger have I led you into?"

"No, Da!" It was her turn to clutch his hand. "While other kids were being brainwashed with the catechism and fairy tales of false saints, you gave me *real* heroes—men *and* women—who spoke the truth, though it sometimes cost them their very lives." She tried to make her smile reassuring. "A harsh truth is better than a pretty lie: You taught me that. And to live a safe life, blind and deaf to the slavery of others, is no life at all. You taught me that, too. You were—are—a tremendous influence on me, yes; parents are that. But in the end, the child makes her own decisions, her own choices. I may not always know what I'm doing—especially these days—but whatever it is, I'm trying to do the right thing. To make my life *count* for something."

She smiled at him again, squeezing his hand, but his smile was so sad it made her ache inside.

"So brave," he said softly. "My little girl, and you've always been so much braver than myself."

"No, you—"

"Ah, yes, it's true. I taught you stories of brave men, men full of courage, because I had none of my own. I told you that the greatest good a person could do is fight for freedom, when I never fought a single battle myself." He looked away, too ashamed to look her in the eye. "Words are all I've ever been good for."

"John Boyle O'Reilly."

"Hm?" He looked back at her, and she smiled.

"Have you seen my infamous tape on the Guerrilla TV? I quoted John Boyle O'Reilly."

She got a smile out of him then. "Ah, yes. 'Words can be more devastating weapons than any iron implement in the arsenals of the world.' " His smile faded. "He was a hero, a grand man. Whereas myself—"

"You are, too!" She was irritated now; how dare he belittle himself before her! "It was *you* taught me those words. That's what words *are*, Da—weapons that are passed from one person to another, growing stronger with each repetition. You taught them to me; that's putting weapons into my hands, making *two* fighters, where before there was only yourself. And I went on the Guerrilla TV and passed them on to who *knows* how many people. So you see, it started with you, only yourself, and now there are—I don't know *how* many people angry with the government. That graffiti—'Let it be so'—have you seen it? It's all over Ireland now! Four wee words, but the *gardaí* are furious! And the Church." She smiled grimly, with great satisfaction. "Those four words are a symbol of the anger of the people. I'll bet those Church fellows—all of them—are pissing their pants, they're so scared at the thought of people actually saying 'No! I disagree.' "

Séamus grinned then, and suddenly he looked like the man Nuala had known as a little girl. "You haven't been to Falcarragh without my knowing?" When she shook her head, he chuckled. "It's all over town. And guess who painted it there?"

"Yourself?" Nuala's surprise turned to delight when he nodded, still grinning.

"Four o'clock in the bloody A.M., I did! On the side of Feeney's pub, on the front of Dolan's chemist shop, even on the shaggin' *garda* barracks itself!"

She laughed with pride as well as joy. Fiona and Igraine joined in.

"You're Nuala's father, all right," Igraine said.

"We wondered where she got it," Fiona added, grinning.

Séamus waved them over, and they sat down on the bales of hay. "Yes, I'm her father," he said, beaming with pride. "And she's my daughter. And aren't we a pair?"

"Nuala's told us some of the stories you taught her," Igraine said.

"Yeah," Fiona said. "Stories neither of us ever got to hear in school when we were kids. My Aunt Rita used to tell me some, of course, but you must have told Nuala every story there ever was! Like the bards of old."

"I especially liked the one about how Red Hugh O'Donnell escaped from the dungeon of Dublin Castle in the dead of winter," Igraine said. "Exciting stuff, that one."

"Oh, aye, that's Nuala's favorite," Séamus said, smiling at his daughter. "We're descended from Red Hugh himself, you know. For all that it may have been on the other side of the blanket, so our name isn't O'Donnell, still, we are."

Nuala nodded, happy that the horrible self-doubt seemed to have left him, for now. "If you want to hear about an escape! Tell them, Da, how Dev escaped from Lincoln Prison."

"Ah, no." Séamus shook his head. "When they've got yourself to be telling them stories, they'll not be wanting to hear some old man—"

"Of course we do, and you're not old; you're only, what? Sixty? Sixty-five? That's not old." Igraine's tone scolded him for even implying such a thing.

"Certainly not," Fiona agreed, nodding firmly. "A handsome figure of a man in his prime, and if we were staying longer, I'd have a go at you myself."

Séamus laughed, flattered by her blarney.

"Go on, Da; it's a great story."

"Oh, well . . ." He hesitated, but the look on Nuala's face made him smile. "Just the one story, eh? We have time for that." Nuala nodded, encouraging him. He took a deep breath, a painful wheeze, and Nuala winced at the sound. But then he cleared his throat and smiled again.

"After the Easter Rising in 1916," he began, as Nuala petted the dog who had once again placed his head on her knee, "most of the leaders were executed by the British. But Dev—Éamonn de Valera, of course—was saved from execution by having the good fortune of being born an American citizen."

"He was?" Igraine said. "I never heard that."

Séamus sighed and shook his head in disgust. "Very little is told children about our past anymore."

"Go on," Fiona urged him, making herself comfortable on the hay.

"Right. Well, instead of murdering Dev, the bastards locked him up. He was eventually put in Lincoln Prison in 1918, over in Britain. Back home—here—Michael Collins was more or less in charge of the spreading unrest and organizing the fight for independence." Séamus smiled. "Now *there* was a grand lad, Michael Collins. The Big Fellow, he was called—but that's another story. Anyway, Dev used to attend Mass in the prison, and help out with it and all. And he noticed that the priest had a key to the prison, but that he didn't bring it to the altar with him; he always left it in the sacristy. So this gave Dev an idea, and he turned his idea into a plan." Séamus reached out to pet the dog himself before going on.

"As he was tidying up the altar, Dev would collect wax from the candles, and he continued to do this until he had enough for what he had in mind. So then, one Sunday, while Mass was being said, Dev got into the sacristy and found the key. He rubbed all the wax he had together in his two hands to soften it up." Séamus demonstrated, and Nuala remembered the nights of her childhood when he had told this story in front of the fire, with the wind howling outside as it was now.

"When it was good and soft, he pressed the key into the wax to make an impression of it. He couldn't steal the key, of course, because it would be missed, so he made an imprint of it. But of course just an impression wouldn't unlock any doors, now, would it? So he gave the wax imprint to another prisoner, an artistic fellow, who drew a Christmas card, as it was that time of year, with a picture of a prisoner trying to unlock his prison door with a *very* large key. And guess what shape was on the key? Aye, exactly the notches that were in the wax impression."

"Clever, these Irish," said Igraine.

"Of course," Séamus agreed. "So the card was sent home to Ireland, and given to Michael Collins."

"The Big Fellow?" said Fiona.

"Himself." Séamus nodded solemnly. "So Collins organized the escape attempt. He had a copy of the key made and baked it inside of a cake, which was sent to Dev over in Britain."

"A cake with a key in it?" Igraine evidently thought Séamus was having them on. "That's the oldest trick in the world!"

"Ah, but," Séamus said, shrugging, "this was almost two hundred years ago. So perhaps it wasn't such an old trick at the time."

"And it worked?" Igraine still didn't believe it.

"Not the first time." Séamus had to pause when another coughing fit seized him. Nuala took his hand, feeling helpless and terrified for him. But again it passed, and he patted her hand as if it had been nothing.

"Not the first time," he repeated. "Or the second. At each

failure, Dev sent word, and Collins sent another cake with another key. Finally Dev asked that Collins send unnotched keys and files in the cake, so that they could try to make their own keys."

"And the guards didn't find either the keys *or* the files?" Igraine shook her head in amazement.

"They did not," Séamus replied. "Perhaps they weren't such bright lads: They *were* British, you know."

The women laughed at his little joke, and he went happily on. Nuala smiled to see him so happy, telling one of his stories again. She wondered if he had anyone in Falcarragh who would listen to them now.

"So they filed their own keys on the third try. But it still didn't work. So Dev sent word yet again, and Collins sent another cake, with more unnotched keys hidden inside. And this time, success was on Dev. He followed his wax imprint *very* carefully, and—" He paused for effect, then smiled. "The key worked! It opened his door and the doors for two other prisoners, and the three of them made their way out to the prison yard in the middle of the night. But they weren't out yet! The corner gate of the prison they unlocked, only to find—that it was a double gate! And in the lock of the second gate was a broken-off key. If they tried to smash the lock, the guards would hear them, so Dev—very carefully—eased his own key into the lock and jiggled and tapped and pushed and finally—the broken half of the key fell out onto the ground outside. So Dev used his key to unlock the last gate of the prison and—who do you suppose was outside, waiting for them with a getaway car?"

Igraine guessed it. "The Big Fellow!"

"Aye," Séamus said, smiling. "Michael Collins himself was there, and he spirited the future Prime Minister and his two companions off into the night and to freedom."

His audience applauded, and Séamus pretended to bow, pleased with the attention and their appreciation. His smile softened as he looked at his daughter.

"So. What are you on to next, my wee band of Fenians? And how can I help?"

"You're not going to try and talk me out of this, are you." It wasn't a question; Nuala already knew the answer.

Séamus chuckled. "It's *my* daughter you are, isn't it? Don't I know you too well to even try?" He frowned and squeezed her hand. "I'm terrified for you; you know that already. It would kill me entirely if you were hurt." He took a ragged breath. "If I were younger and had even half my health back, I'd be out there with you. By God, I wouldn't let my fear hold me back any longer." He sighed. "But I'm a sick man with little time left— now, don't look that way, *cushla*; it's the truth of it, and I've accepted it. So I'll have to let you, my own brave daughter, fight this fight for me. But can't I help? Somehow?"

Before Nuala could think of an answer, Igraine jumped in. "Those stories you know. Do you tell them to anybody? To the kids in Falcarragh?"

He shook his head in disgust. "They're only interested in the football and the hurling. They don't want to listen to stories."

"Are you sure?" Fiona asked. "I should think stories of rebellion would be perfect for teenagers. Aren't they forever rebelling against *something*?"

"Right," Igraine agreed. "And don't they hate the puerile stories they're force-fed in school? I'm sure they'd love a bit of the truth."

"Yeah," Nuala said. "You should have seen the faces on those girls in the class I took over. Especially this one—Heather was her name. She was *aching* for the truth."

"I can't think of any better way for you to aid the present revolution than to tell people about the rebellions of the past," Fiona suggested.

"Well, of course I *would*," Séamus said, "illegal or not. But they're watching me, the bastards. How could I—"

"Hedge schools," Nuala said. "Remember, Da? During the time of the Penal Laws, when Catholics were forbidden to attend school, the teachers would meet with them secretly, behind hedges, or in barns like this one, wherever they could. And they were so eager for education, they came."

"That's it!" Igraine beamed at Séamus. "You could start a hedge school. The more knowledge people are armed with, the better able they'll be to resist."

"Perhaps the Guerrilla TV could have a hand in something like this," Fiona said, frowning in concentration. "It could be national, then."

"Maybe," Nuala said. "But even if it doesn't get on TV, it could still work. Hedge schools could spring up everywhere, starting in Falcarragh, with the best teacher I ever had." She squeezed her father's hand again. "Teach them, Da. Tell them about the ancient heroes, the people who fought for freedom. And don't leave out the women. Girls have to know that this is *their* fight, too, that they deserve freedom every bit as much as men do. Tell them, Da."

Séamus looked uncertain. "Do you really think they'd listen? I'd do it in a minute; I'd find a way to evade the bloody surveillance, if I thought I could get them to listen."

"Of course they'll listen, just as I did." Nuala's smile swelled with pride. "Éamonn de Valera, Michael Collins, even Red Hugh himself—they've got nothing on Séamus Dennehy. He's as big as they are, every bit, because he knows how to dream. They'll listen, as I did, because they *need* to. They'll want to." She took his hand in both of her own. "You taught me to dream, Da. You can teach others. You can."

"And it's a lot healthier than breathing paint fumes from spraying graffiti," Igraine added.

They all laughed at that, and then Séamus nodded. "By God, the Dennehy family *will* make a difference. I thought that my one contribution to Irish freedom was yourself, but if I could—" He smiled, determined. "I'll do it. If I have to waylay the kids on their way home from hurling practice, I'll get to them. We'll make it a game, evading the *garda* spies. Kids love games, especially rebellious games, eh? And *some* of them are bound to care, to want to know, like that girl you mentioned."

"Right." Nuala smiled, ignoring the wetness that slipped past her eyelashes. "That's my da." She wagged a finger at him. "And *don't forget the girls*! This revolution is going to be different from all the others, because no longer are women going to be pushed to the back. This is our fight! So you tell *that* to the girls of Falcarragh."

"I will," Séamus promised. "Constance Markievicz, Maud Gonne McBride, Bernadette Devlin McAliskey, Mairéad Farrell—even the pirate queen, Grace O'Malley! I'll tell them." He nodded. "I'll tell them all."

"With *two* Dennehys on our side," Igraine teased, "God help the government."

"God can *have* the shaggin' government," Séamus said. "Because soon enough those politicians will be seeking other employment, if I have anything to say about it. And I bloody well do."

"Da," Nuala said, smiling, "tell the story of the Retaking of the Boyne."

"What, that?" he said. "Everybody knows that one; it was the most decisive battle of Reunification."

"Igraine and Fiona probably only know the version they learned in school. Tell them the *true* story."

"Please," said Fiona. "Tell us."

"We have a few hours still," Igraine added.

"Well . . . all right." Séamus's face lit up again, as Nuala had hoped it would. "It was 2023. The war had been going on since the Enniskillen Massacre eleven years before, and the IRA were not about to give up . . ."

He told his stories all night. His voice grew tired as it labored and wheezed, but Nuala could see that he was the happiest he probably had been in years.

"I hope we're doing the right thing, trusting this young Lonnegan to get us out of Donegal." Igraine's knee was bouncing, her right hand keeping time with it, as she watched the Gortahork traffic through the window. She wasn't aware of the twitch of either hand or knee.

"You don't distrust the lad merely because he's male, now, do you?"

At Nuala's tone, Igraine's nervous bouncing stopped. She raised an eyebrow at the faint smile on Nuala's face. "And that is supposed to mean?"

Nuala shrugged and the smile disappeared. "Oh, I was just thinking."

"Uh-oh."

Nuala ignored this and continued. "Máire was convinced that men would be of no help to us—or worse, that they would work against us, try to stop us, keep us in our place."

"And you don't share that opinion?"

"Do you?"

"I asked you first."

Nuala paused before answering. "Some would—will—be against us, yes; I don't doubt that. It's unfortunate, but true. But the majority—" She shook her head. "I don't know. After all, we're advocating freedom for everybody; we're trying to free our country, not just the female half of it. All men with true republican sentiment—"

"Will be willing to give up their privileged rank, their 'right' to female servants who bear the title of 'wife' or 'daughter'?"

Nuala sighed. "Perhaps it's just seeing my father, or meeting the lads from the Guerrilla TV, I don't know. But I want to believe that the Church has not been entirely successful in its divide-and-conquer tactics. If women and men could work together—"

"The men would take over and try to tell us what to do." Igraine's frown was bitter. "It's always been that way. They accept our help when it suits them or their cause, then push us out at the first opportunity. You're the historian—surely you know that."

Igraine's anger stopped Nuala from disagreeing. The bitterness in her friend's tone suggested that perhaps mentioning how women and men had sometimes worked together in the long struggle for Reunification would not be a good idea at the moment. She wondered again where Igraine's anger really came from, what had made her so bitter. It was something more than the way men in general treated women in general; it was very personal with Igraine. But whenever she asked personal questions, Igraine deflected them casually, changing the subject. Nuala was reminded, yet again, that she really didn't know her at all.

"Well, as for accepting Stuart's help," Nuala said, "we really don't have much choice, since Fiona's friend in Letterkenny was arrested."

"Yeah." Igraine turned her attention back to the window of the safehouse. "If they torture her, we can't trust that she won't talk. If she names names—"

"Right. So we've got to look elsewhere, outside Fiona's network, for safe transportation. And your acquaintances in Dublin have disappeared, so we really have no other alternative. The Guerrilla Broadcasters have people all over; they can arrange to get us away from Donegal. And the farther we get from my father, the safer it'll be for him as well as ourselves. He's taking enough of a risk as it is, with the hedge school he's started."

"There's Fiona!"

Fiona was trotting across the street from the pub. Nuala and Igraine hurried downstairs to meet her.

"He's coming up the street," Fiona said as she slipped inside and quickly shut the door against the cold.

"Alone?" Igraine asked.

Fiona shook her head. "He's being followed." Pistols materialized in Igraine's and Nuala's hands. "Relax, she's just a kid; I doubt she's a *garda* spy."

The three of them jumped at the knock on the door. Fiona stepped out of the way of the pistols, then leaned toward the door. *"Cé atá ann?"*

"Lonnegan."

Stuart blinked in surprise at the two pistols aimed at his chest. "Hey, it's just myself."

"And who's your young friend?" Igraine asked.

"Friend?" Stuart looked around at the three of them, baffled. "What friend? I'm alone."

"I was watching you from the pub," said Fiona. "I saw a blond girl following you down the street, big as life."

Stuart grimaced in irritation. "Damn it!" He disappeared out the door again, and a few moments later returned, dragging a disgruntled teenager by the arm.

"Let me go, Stuart, or I'll kick your bloody arse!"

"How dare you put us all at risk!" Stuart was furious, but he released the girl's arm and even backed up a step, evidently believing her threat. "I *told* you, you're going home! And as soon as possible!"

"I'm not!"

"Uh, excuse me," Fiona said. "What precisely is going on here?"

"This brat," Stuart answered her, his cheeks pink and his ears beginning to take on the same hue, "is my youngest sister—"

"Heather," Nuala interrupted, smiling. "Nice to see you again, *kidín*, though the circumstances might have been better. We're in a bit of a hurry just now."

Heather was staring at Nuala, but then her face lit up. "I knew it! When I saw your interview on the Guerrilla TV, I just *knew* Stuart would know where to find you, even if he denied it."

"Indeed?" Igraine didn't like this at all. Her glare made him turn even pinker. "If *she* knew you could find us, who else might know—"

"Don't blame Stuart!" Heather stepped toward her brother, frowning at Igraine. "It's not his fault I followed him. I've left home, you see, and when I called his TV station to find him, because he wasn't at his flat, they said they'd sent him on assignment to Donegal, and of course I know he's with the Guerrillas, and the last time they—the TV station, I mean—sent him on assignment to Donegal, it was to Letterkenny, and while he was there the Guerrillas broadcast something, so I figured he must be in Letterkenny this time, too, because of that interview tape being broadcast while he was on assignment to Donegal, so I went to Letterkenny, but they said he was in Gortahork doing some silly report on a hog festival or other, so I came here and found him, and when he said he had to work and that I couldn't come, I knew it had to be Guerrilla work, because why wouldn't he let me come to a hog festival?—so I said okay, I understood, but then when he left, I followed him, because I knew he'd lead me to you, and I've come to join you. So you see, it isn't Stuart's fault at all, so you mustn't blame him, right?"

The four adults were staring at her, stunned by the gush of words. She looked around at them, puzzled by their expressions. "What? Did I say something wrong?"

"Yes!" Stuart recovered with a blink. "You said something wrong, right enough. You are *not* staying here or joining anybody; you're going home!"

"I'm not." Heather didn't raise her voice, but her eyes narrowed, and she crossed her arms as she stared down her brother. "I am *never* going back to Coleraine. As I tried to tell you before you went rushing off, Da said he was going to put me in a convent, and he meant it. I would rather die than—"

"He didn't mean it, Heather." Stuart blushed again, embarrassed that the three women were listening with great interest. "He's threatened it before, and he hasn't done it, has he? And he won't this time, either."

"He *called* the convent," Heather said, the icy calm of her voice belying the fury in her expression. "Right in front of me. He made the arrangements. I was to be shipped off to them the next day."

Stuart was so shocked he couldn't speak for a moment. "What did you do that set him off this time?" he finally asked. "It must have been a whopper."

"I defended her." To Nuala's surprise, Heather pointed at her. "After her interview. I told him what she'd said at school, and that she was right, that the Church did nothing but brainwash people. And that women have always been abused by the Church and the government, and that it was time we fought back, just like she said. And that I wanted to fight back, too."

"You said *that*?" Stuart couldn't believe his ears. "To *Da*? What *were* you thinking, girl? I've told you, the best way to handle him is to pretend to agree with him but ignore everything he says. You can't—"

"What I can't do is pretend any longer." Heather's voice dropped a notch or two. It was deeper, more adult, and completely determined. "It's easy for you to say 'just pretend,' Stuart, because you don't have to live there with him. You're a man, so you can go off and get your own flat. But I can't, because I'm female. It's either live with him for the rest of my life, which I *will* not do, enter a convent—and I'd rather die than do that—or marry some pimply-faced, whiskey-smelling oaf who'd turn me into a baby-making machine and sexual slave."

Stuart was again speechless. He stared at his little sister as if he didn't recognize her. Heather saw this, and smiled. "I know you think I'm just a kid, Stuart, but I know what's what. I'm not blind and I'm not stupid, and I will *not* be a slave. You fight in your own way, with the Guerrilla TV, and let me fight in mine."

She turned away from him then and faced Nuala. "I'm not just a worthless kid. I can help if you just tell me how. Let me join you."

Stuart started to speak, but Nuala raised her hand to stop him. "She seems to have made up her mind, Stuart. And can you find fault with anything she said?"

"But she's just—"

"A kid?" Nuala interrupted. "You're what? Eighteen? Nineteen?"

"Almost nineteen," Heather answered.

"Almost nineteen." Nuala smiled. "When I was almost nineteen, I'd already been suspended from university twice for daring to tell Jesuit professors they were wrong, that what they were teaching was lies. *I* was fighting back at almost nineteen."

"It's different now," Stuart protested. "And you know it! She could be arrested, tortured, murdered like your friend Máire."

Nuala winced, but Heather spoke up before she could say anything. "I know all that, Stuart; do you think I don't? I saw that tape of her being killed. But you said"—she turned to Nuala—" 'the great only appear great because we are on our knees. Let us rise.' Remember? Well, I'm not on my knees anymore. If I have to die, then I'll do it on my feet, not on my knees—or on my back, giving birth to the fifteenth kid I didn't want."

Nuala stared at this impassioned girl—no, young woman was what she was. How could she argue with her to protect her, when she agreed with every word? But if Heather was hurt or killed because she had listened to Nuala, how could she live with that, with herself?

"I have nowhere else to go," Heather said. The pleading that she was trying so hard to keep out of her voice betrayed itself in her eyes. "If I go back to Coleraine, he'll lock me up for life in a bloody convent. If I try to live alone, to get a job, I'll be found out by a God Patrol and sent back anyway. I have no choice. None."

"Any one of us could be killed at any time," Nuala said. "As Máire was."

"I know." Heather swallowed, managed to keep her voice steady. "I don't want to die. Or be locked up, or tortured. I *know* it's no game. But I don't have a choice. I have to fight back. It's either with you or alone. And alone I don't stand much of a chance."

"You could emigrate," Nuala argued. "We could get you out."

"And go where? America? You can't get into America unless you're one of those fundamentalist Protestants. I can't go there. And they still hate the Irish in England, so I can't go there."

"Scotland, as I did, or Wales. Or Australia, if you're afraid of extradition. I've heard Australia is a good place if you want to disappear."

Heather frowned at Nuala. "You're testing me, aren't you?"

"What? No, I—"

"Aye, you want to see how determined I am." Heather's chin rose. "I'm Irish and I'm a woman. I'm staying to fight. With you or without you."

Nuala struggled not to smile, but gave up. How could she not like this girl who was so like herself? She looked to Fiona and Igraine. "Does anybody want to try to tell her she can't come with us?"

Fiona smiled, too. "Gormfhlaith'll be just like her in a few years. How can we turn her away?"

"This is bloody dangerous, you know. *Very* dangerous," Igraine said to Heather. "You've got to learn to watch your back. One slip-up, one moment of carelessness—"

"You watch my back, I'll watch yours," Heather interrupted, flushing with excitement. "I'm in then, right?"

"Now wait a minute—"

"Oh, stuff it, Stuart!" Heather stared him down, toe to toe. "I'm through taking orders from men, and that includes you! You're my brother, and I love you dearly, but don't get in my way."

Stuart's mouth worked as he tried to think of a response. He looked around at the other three women and was flustered to see smiles on their faces. "You—I—" Finally he threw up his hands in disgust. "Women!"

"And what's *that* mean, then?" Igraine was no longer smiling.

"I'm sure he meant no disrespect, Igraine." Nuala was still smiling, but now at Stuart's discomfort. "Did you, Stuart?"

"No, I—That is—"

"Oh, don't be a silly ass, Stuart." Heather patted his cheek. "There's a good lad."

"Since your sister is coming with us," said Igraine, "you'll be twice as motivated to get us out safely, won't you now?"

Stuart looked from Igraine to Heather, frowning. Finally he sighed. "Have I a choice?" He sighed again, and his shoulders slumped. "Okay, you can leave tonight. I can get you safely south to our people in Kerry or Cork, whichever you want." He put his hand on his little sister's cheek, much as she had to his a moment ago. The fear and worry were plain on his face, but he didn't try again to object.

"Kerry?" said Fiona, turning to Igraine. "That's your neck of the woods, isn't it? Do you know people there who could—"

"No." Igraine looked away at nothing. "Cork would be preferable."

Fiona and Nuala exchanged puzzled glances, but Igraine didn't elaborate.

"Right," Nuala said, after an awkward silence. "I've always wanted to visit Rebel Cork. Michael Collins country, you know."

"Who?" Heather asked.

Nuala smiled. "Have I got some stories to tell you, D'Artagnan."

Heather was completely confused now. "Art who?"

"Stuart," Fiona said, "make your arrangements. It's on to Cork."

Chapter 10

"**T**HERE HAVE BEEN SO many arrests." Fiona took the cup of tea from Heather and slumped back onto the sofa in the room she had rented for them in Rathcoole, County Cork, in the south of Ireland. Her three fellow fugitives gathered round her.

"No one answered the 'phone at Ailís's house, and a machine answered with a stranger's voice at Tríona's."

"Did you leave a message?" Heather blushed at her own words. "Of course you didn't, that was a stupid question. Sorry."

Fiona went on as if she hadn't heard. "I don't dare try to contact anybody else. It would be as dangerous for them as for ourselves."

"You think somebody talked," Igraine said. It wasn't a question.

Fiona sighed, staring into her teacup. "I can't blame anyone for not being able to bear up under torture. I just hope it wasn't someone who knew everyone else."

"We have to assume it was, with all the arrests, and the fact that you haven't been able to reach anyone," Nuala said.

Fiona nodded, frowning. "We had barely a skeleton of a network, only a few contacts and safe houses around Ulster." She sighed again, in exhaustion. "Now we'll have to start over."

"Perhaps not," Igraine said, looking at Nuala. "We haven't heard of any arrests in Belfast. Perhaps our original group there—"

"Just because it hasn't been on the Guerrilla TV doesn't mean it hasn't happened," Nuala reminded her.

"I know," Igraine agreed. "But four people do not a revolution make. We need numbers—and a unity of purpose."

"Maybe we could contact Stuart," Heather suggested. "You could make another tape, Nuala; do another interview. The graffiti from the last one is still showing up in new places all the time. Your last interview had a tremendous impact, a new one could—"

"Get more people arrested on suspicion?" Guilt made Nuala irritable; she spoke more sharply to the girl than she had intended. She sighed, and tried again. "I don't want anybody getting hurt because of something I said."

"You didn't force anybody to do anything!" Igraine snapped. She was on edge, too; they all were. "People make their own choices, their own decisions."

"Painting graffiti is now a jail offense," Nuala argued. "The *Dáil* has rushed legislation through before, but this! There was no debate on it at all. Anybody who has purchased paint in the last six months can be brought in for questioning! And all because I—"

"Told the truth." Fiona set her cup down on the coffeetable, her eyes boring into Nuala's. "That's all you did. It's the truth that they're trying to fight, not just the one who tells it. So it's no good blaming yourself. If they were to take you out tomorrow, the truth wouldn't go out *with* you, you know. It has a way of popping right back up again, like a weed that refuses to be eradicated."

"We'd be here to tell it." Heather squeezed Nuala's clenched fist. "*I'd* tell it. And if they got me, Igraine would tell it. And if they got Igraine—"

"Fiona would tell it; I get the picture, *kidín*." Nuala smiled at the earnest girl.

"Right," Heather said. "And if they got Fiona, somebody else would take her place, and somebody else, and somebody else. It's our job to be the messengers, but it's the message that's important, right? Not who says it." She blushed again, a frequent habit that Nuala found somehow endearing. "At least, that's how I see it."

"You see it quite clearly," Igraine told her, then turned to Nuala. "She's right about doing another tape. The arrests have people frightened, but they're angry, too. We need to take advantage of that."

"Yeah," Fiona agreed. "Now is not the time to disappear. The people you reached before will think you've—we've—been frightened off. We have to show defiance. It will give people courage."

"Right." Heather nodded emphatically. The way Heather was looking at her made Nuala uneasy. It had become apparent over the weeks since leaving Ulster that the girl looked up to her, admired her far more than Nuala felt she deserved. Heather seemed to think she could do no wrong. Nuala hated to disillusion her; she wondered how the girl would react when she finally saw the feet of clay.

"Well, if the three of you think I should—"

The knock at the door startled them all. The four women scrambled to their feet, grabbing for their pistols. As they had rehearsed, Fiona and Igraine crossed to the door, one on each side, pistols up, safety off, while Nuala and Heather waited in the bedroom doorway, ready to head for the fire escape.

"*Cé atá ann?*" Fiona said to the closed door.

"*Bean agus cara*" came a soft female voice.

Igraine and Fiona exchanged puzzled glances, then Fiona motioned Nuala and Heather toward the fire escape. She reached for the doorknob.

Nuala and Heather backed into the bedroom, pistols in hand.

Heather ran to the window and looked out, then shook her head at Nuala. No danger in sight.

Nuala frowned. Was a strange voice at the door that proclaimed its owner to be "a woman and a friend" sufficient cause to run? Even though the fire escape was in an alley, the sight and sound of two women rushing down it in the absence of a fire was bound to attract someone's attention. In the second or two that it took Nuala to decide not to flee, Fiona had opened the door.

A stout, raven-haired woman of around thirty smiled at Fiona. She was wearing a heavy corduroy coat of charcoal gray over a black-and-gray plaid skirt, with thick black stockings and rubber-soled black shoes. Though ungloved, her hands were not in her pockets, but in plain sight. If she had a gun, it was not visible.

Fiona held her pistol behind the door. Igraine stood back on the other side, out of sight.

"Yes?" Fiona said.

"*Bandia duit,*" the visitor said.

That brought Nuala out of the bedroom. The standard greeting was "*Dia duit,*" or "God with you." To substitute "Goddess" was unorthodox at best, blasphemous at worst—in the eyes of the Church, that is. Fiona was cautious enough not to return the greeting. She merely raised an eyebrow and waited.

"My name is Sorcha, and I am a friend, though we haven't yet met. If you'd allow me to come in, you may search me, if you like, for weapons or listening devices."

After a surprised moment, Fiona said, "The alley?"

It was an instant before Nuala realized the question was directed at her. "Clear—so far," she answered.

"Very well," Fiona said, and opened the door wider, her hand with the pistol going behind her back. "Won't you come in?"

Sorcha entered, nodding politely to Igraine, not at all surprised to see her lurking beside the door. When she spotted Nuala, and Heather behind her, her smile grew. "Ah, good. You're all here."

Heather eased up behind Nuala, but Nuala put out a hand to keep her back. If a squad of *gardaí* were to come bursting through the door in this woman's wake—

"Not to worry," Sorcha said, at Nuala's protective gesture. "I really am a friend, and no one followed me. You're quite safe."

"You'll understand if we don't take your word for it." Igraine motioned with her pistol, ease and familiarity with the weapon making it seem an extension of her body.

"Of course," Sorcha replied, unperturbed, and unbuttoned her coat. Fiona took it from her, and Sorcha raised her hands. Fiona searched the coat quickly as Igraine patted down their visitor. When the two women were satisfied, they put their pistols away. Sorcha lowered her hands, then spotted Fiona's teacup.

"Ah, tea! What a lovely idea. It's beastly cold out. Would you mind?" She made herself comfortable on the sofa next to her coat while the four women exchanged more puzzled glances.

Finally Fiona shrugged and said to Heather, "Please get our guest a cup, will you?"

The other three women took seats around Sorcha, none of them too close, and none with her back to the door.

"You look much prettier with short hair," Sorcha said, to Nuala's surprise. "But then that was a wig you were wearing on the tape, wasn't it? Wigs are never very flattering. Thank you, my dear."

"*Fáilte,*" Heather murmured, and sat down next to Nuala.

"Who the hell are you?" Nuala's hand wandered behind her, closer to the gun in her waistband.

The visitor took a nonchalant sip of the tea Heather had given her, then smiled in appreciation. "Lovely. So good on a cold day." She took a second sip, then lowered the cup, warming her fingers around it.

"My name is Sorcha, as I said, and I've come because we decided it was time someone contacted you. You four are something of a loose cannon, which can be dangerous—or extremely useful, depending on how it's handled."

"What—" Fiona began.

"Who's 'we'?" Igraine asked.

"What do you mean, 'handled'?" Nuala demanded. Heather said nothing, but eased closer to Nuala.

Sorcha smiled again and took another sip of tea. Her complacency was beginning to get on Nuala's nerves.

"Answer the question," Nuala insisted.

"My goodness, which one?" Sorcha raised a hand before Nuala could reply. "You roused the people with that insurrectionary interview of yours, my dear, and that's all to the good. Action on more than one front confuses and divides the energies of our enemies. The resulting arrests of graffiti artists and other 'traitors' have further aroused the people. It is obvious that they—some of them, at any rate—are ready for a larger-scale rebellion. You can be useful in that, which is why we have decided to contact you. Your roaming around Rathcoole so very much at large is bound to be noticed eventually, even by the myopic misanthropes of the *gardaí*, so it has become imperative that we give you some sort of shelter before they find you. We have much for you to accomplish, and your getting arrested now would simply not do."

Nuala leaned forward, a dangerous smile playing about her lips. "Who—are—you? Explain yourself—now. Patience is not one of my virtues."

"No, I can see that it isn't. But I'm sure that your others are legion, aren't they?" Sorcha smiled that annoying smile again. "We are—to put it concisely—rebels. Though there are many throughout Ireland who claim that appellation, from the IRA to the Baptists, we have the singular distinction of being completely unknown to the authorities. As far as we can tell, they don't have any idea that we even exist. And that has been to our advantage. The network we have organized takes many guises—some of which we have allowed the *gardaí* and the Church to gain an uncertain knowledge of, because it camouflages our true purpose."

"Which is?" Fiona prompted.

Sorcha raised her eyebrows in surprise. "Why, the same as yours, my dear: treason. A complete and utter overthrow of the current regime, replacing it with one more to our liking."

"And that would be?" Fiona again asked.

Sorcha's smile was now patient. "A secular, egalitarian, feminist republic, of the Irish people, for the Irish people. A republic where the Church has nothing to say about anything, and women have unfettered control over our own lives. That is what you yourselves want, isn't it? That was the clear message of that interview."

"Are you one of the leaders?" Heather asked.

Sorcha smiled yet again, but it was obviously a practiced gesture, and a patronizing one. Nuala gritted her teeth in distaste. "Oh, no, Heather. I'm not a leader, I'm merely a humble emissary."

"Humble hardly seems applicable in your case," Nuala muttered.

Sorcha chuckled. "Oh, dear. I have been accused of pomposity in the past. Am I doing it again?" Nuala raised an eloquent eyebrow and Sorcha laughed. "Sorry. But, you know, my initial impressions of people are invariably correct, and I would venture a guess that you and I have a great deal in common, Nuala. I do hope we get to work together."

Nuala blinked. Had she just been called pompous?

"How did you know my name?" Heather asked. "You knew Nuala's from the interview, of course. But how did you know mine?"

"Heather Lonnegan of Coleraine, Derry. You're a runaway, my dear. Your father notified the *gardaí* of your disappearance, and I don't doubt that every *garda* office in Ireland has your picture on its telenet. I'm surprised you haven't been picked up before now. Fortunately, we are blessed, in Rathcoole, with a remarkably incompetent *garda* force. That is, no doubt, what has protected you so far."

"You didn't answer her question," Nuala pointed out, the irritation in her voice kept barely in check. "How did you know her name?"

"I was coming to that," Sorcha said. "We enjoy an unparalleled information system. We have rebels in nearly every city, and in most occupations—those that women are allowed in, that is, or those that women have access to through husbands or brothers or sons. We have also trained our people in the use of the most sophisticated technology, and then secured them jobs in strategic locations—a janitor in a Security Office, say, or secretary to a government Minister. In short, we have infiltrated a surprising variety of the strongholds of the enemy."

Though astonished by such news, Nuala was tired of this performance, and wouldn't give the woman the satisfaction. "Well, then you don't need our help, do you?" She leaned back in the overstuffed chair and put her feet up on the coffeetable. "Sounds to me like the government's on its knees and we should be free any day now. So why trouble yourself with this wee band of malcontents?"

Sorcha's poise finally slipped; a shadow of surprise crossed her face. But it was only momentary. She smiled at Nuala again, but there was a different quality in the smile now, a tiny measure of respect.

"Yes, you're exactly as she said you would be." Before anyone could pursue this, Sorcha went on. "We are perhaps not as omnipotent as I have a tendency to paint us, I'm afraid. Pervading caution and secrecy are imperative, which is why we have been at this business for so many years with so few concrete victories to show for it. We must protect ourselves, so that we can continue. Freedom won't be gained in a day, but from years of prudent and painstaking planning. At that, we have been quite successful, but it has been obvious for some time that a public gesture, a voice, is needed that would arouse the people, to nudge them or even to lead them, if possible, in the right direction. When the time comes, we hope to have people in place to create the new structure that will be needed, but we are a long way from that time. And it won't happen without that voice I mentioned. A male voice would be more successful initially, because, after all, who listens to women? So we were considering a few male possibilities—unbeknownst to themselves, of course. But then you gave that interview on the Guerrilla TV—a perfect venue, by the way, as it enjoys more viewers than all of the sanctioned stations combined—and 'Let it be so' began appearing all over Ireland. We realized we had found our voice, and we were both astonished and delighted that it was a female one."

Nuala caught the glance Fiona exchanged with Igraine and sat up straight. "Now wait a moment—"

"You do need our help, then, is that it?" Fiona said to Sorcha.

Sorcha nodded with a shrug, but hadn't the chance to reply before Igraine jumped in. "At what price? At what price to Nuala? Just how expendable do you think we are?"

"Expend—" Heather began, alarmed. She grabbed for Nuala's arm.

"We will protect you to the best of our abilities," Sorcha assured them. "And our abilities are considerable. As for your being expendable . . ." She smiled at Heather. "You needn't worry about Nuala, my dear. In the harsh reality of our present situation, nearly everyone is expendable . . . What a harsh word, that. But that doesn't mean that we would throw her to the wolves. We will protect her."

"Will you, now?" Nuala freed her arm gently from Heather's grasp. "You intend to use me. And to protect me as long as it suits your purpose. When it no longer does . . ." She shrugged, spreading her hands. "Why the hell should I trust you?"

"Trust me?" Sorcha said. "I didn't for a moment expect that you would. As I said before, Nuala, you and I no doubt have a great deal in common. We are both pragmatic people. I have a cause, you have a cause. It is but coincidence that the two are one and the same. We look out for ourselves, you and I, always. But our cause, our goal . . ." She paused, then smiled. "This is why you came back from Scotland, isn't it?"

Nuala said nothing, merely staring at Sorcha, studying her.

The truth in the woman's words didn't make Nuala like her any better. Sorcha was unperturbed by Nuala's scrutiny. She sipped her tea and waited.

"You have leaders, I suppose," Nuala said. "I'll want to meet them."

Sorcha shook her head. "I'm afraid that's neither possible nor prudent. Our network is extensive, our numbers many, yet few have ever met those that you would call 'in charge.' We protect them by this. If no one knows who they are, then no one can betray them under torture, as your paltry but well-intentioned network was betrayed."

Fiona flushed at Sorcha's pointed remark but said nothing. Igraine glared at Sorcha, her hand moving almost imperceptibly nearer her pistol. Nuala could feel her friends' anger like static electricity or ions in the air. What Sorcha had said was true, perhaps, but spoken far too cavalierly.

Nuala's eyes narrowed. "I don't like you. You're arrogant, smug, unfeeling, and patronizing. And I would never trust you as far as I could throw a cow by the tail." She saw Sorcha's jaw clench, even though the woman's expression never changed. Nuala took a small measure of satisfaction from that clenched jaw. "We have the same goal, aye. And that is the only reason that I *may* agree to work with your network or organization or whatever the hell you call it. But only if I meet those in charge. If they're anything like yourself, then I'm not interested. If they don't agree to meet me, then to hell with the lot of you. If they do agree, I'll talk to them myself, without any more sorry go-betweens such as yourself. So you go back to them and tell them that. And tell them this, too: I don't take orders from anybody. I listen to reason and I decide to go along or not go along, but I don't follow *anybody's* orders blindly. Never have, never will."

Sorcha took a last sip of tea, her face wooden, then set down her cup and got to her feet. The others stood up also. She studied Nuala as Nuala had studied her, then finally smiled. "I will relay the message and let you know their decision." She walked to the door, but no one accompanied her. With her hand on the doorknob, she turned back. "You're wrong about me, you know; I must have simply made a bad first impression. But then we don't have to like each other to work together. And I do admire your loyalty to your friends and their feelings." Her gaze flicked to Fiona and then back. "I think you'll be a very valuable member of our team, Nuala."

"It remains to be seen whether I'll be a part of *any*body's team, other than this one right here," Nuala replied. "You heard my conditions. If you want me to be your 'voice crying in the wilderness,' I'll want to meet your mysterious leaders, face to face. Then I'll decide."

Sorcha smiled again. "I wouldn't have thought you'd quote the Bible."

Nuala shrugged. "It suited the occasion."

Chuckling, Sorcha nodded. "This is going to be an interesting collaboration. I'll see you soon." With that, she let herself out.

The four women sat down, one by one, frowning.

"Well," Igraine said, "we wanted to make contact with other rebels. It seems we have. Or them with us."

"That's good," Heather said. "Isn't it?"

"I didn't care for her assumption that we'd jump at the chance to join them," Fiona said. "Just who are they? I've never heard anything about them."

"And why did they contact us *now*, not three weeks ago, when we got here?" Nuala ran a hand back over her short hair. "It's as if they waited for us to discover we were alone, that all your contacts have disappeared. How did they know? Who *are* they?"

Chapter 11

"**Y**OU'LL BE EXPECTED to cook, of course," Sorcha said as she led the four fugitives down the school hallway. "You do know how, I presume?"

"You should never presume anything," Nuala replied, her nerves on edge from a half hour spent in Sorcha's supercilious company. "You will be invariably disappointed."

"You can't?" It was obvious from the tone in those two words that Sorcha herself could probably whip up a seven-course gourmet dinner in her sleep. Nuala resisted the urge to trip her as they went down the stairs.

"I manage to boil water for tea, and I know my way around a tin opener. It's kept me from starvation so far."

"Why do we have to cook?" Heather asked. "I thought it was all for show."

"In case a God Patrol drops in, which they always do, every week," Sorcha explained. "It must look real. It must *be* real. Since we spend every Saturday afternoon doing this, we thought we might as well actually be learning to cook new recipes, rather than just pretending to do so, and our extra creations we sell to raise money for charity—and for our own needs. Here we are."

Sorcha had led them to the Home Economics kitchen of St. Gobnait's *Meánscoil.* She pushed open the double doors and led the way into a large room filled with women, who glanced up in curiosity as they passed, then went right back to mixing or rolling out dough.

"You said your leaders would be here," Nuala whispered at Sorcha's elbow.

"And so they are" came the murmured response.

"But you also said that few people had actually met them."

"Did I? Perhaps I wasn't quite—"

"Honest?"

"Concise." Sorcha hissed the word, the only evidence of any annoyance. "Of course many people have *met* them, I simply meant that not many are aware of who actually leads our organization. The leaders don't say any more than any of us at these weekly get-togethers."

"Then how do they lead?" Heather whispered. "If nobody knows—"

"Brigid," Sorcha said, stopping abruptly at a table where a graying brunette in her mid-sixties was crimping the edge of the dough in a pie tin.

Brigid looked up and smiled at them, tiny lines at the corners of her blue eyes deepening. "Sorcha. I was beginning to wonder if you weren't coming this week."

"Oh, wouldn't miss it. My husband is looking forward to the sour-cream peach pie I promised him this evening. Let me introduce you. This is Nuala, Heather, Igraine, and Fiona."

Nuala felt the eyes of every woman in the room. Sorcha was certainly not trying to hide their identities. What kind of secrecy was this? Could *all* of these women be trusted not to run to the *gardaí*?

Brigid nodded to them in greeting. "We've been looking forward to meeting you. Welcome to Rathcoole, and to our cooking class. I'm afraid you missed the first bit, about preparing the peaches, but you can copy the others. Sorcha, why don't you introduce them to Dana and Éadaoin; they can watch how it's done."

"Right, see you later. This way." Sorcha started off, the four women following, but Brigid plucked at Nuala's sleeve with flour-covered fingers.

"Why don't you stay and help me, instead of getting bunched up with the others?"

Nuala shrugged and joined the older woman as her friends were led off. Sorcha never looked back.

"You could roll out more dough for the second pie," Brigid suggested. "But you'll want to take off your coat first, and put on an apron."

Nuala hung her coat next to Brigid's, on a peg at the side of the tiny individual "kitchen," and took the extra apron that hung there. She glanced over to see that Fiona and Heather had been matched up with a red-haired woman of about thirty-five.

"My daughter, Éadaoin," Brigid said. "And that's Dana Sheehan that Igraine's with. She should get on well with Dana. They're much alike, I should think; Dana's late husband was a horse trainer."

"And how would you know what Igraine's like?" Nuala kept her voice low, as Brigid had.

Brigid smiled as she finished crimping the dough and looked into Nuala's eyes. "You've guessed that by now, surely."

"That you're the one we came to meet."

"Myself," Brigid said, nodding, "and Éadaoin and Dana."

"A holy trinity?"

Brigid chuckled. "Oh, we're not very holy, I'm afraid. We're merely the ones who began it all, back when my Éadaoin was little older than your Heather is now."

"She's not *my* Heather." Nuala was studying Brigid, trying to figure out what to make of this woman who appeared so . . . content.

"But she'd like to be. She's young, at just the beginning of her adulthood, and her hero worship of you is also at its beginning. Treat her gently in it, and it and she will mature on to something else when she's ready."

"Is that how you 'lead'?" Nuala asked. "By giving motherly advice?"

But Brigid just continued to smile. "Why don't you roll out that dough now?"

"Because I'd botch it," Nuala admitted. "The few times I

tried it as a kid, I tore great holes in the dough, over and over, until my mother, in her exasperation, did it herself."

Brigid nodded as if Nuala had just explained something of great significance. "That's lack of patience, that is."

"On my mother's part?"

"Well, yes, but I was referring to yourself. There are some things—many things—that you simply have to keep trying until you learn to do them right."

"As I told Sorcha, patience is not one of my strengths."

"I believe you used the word 'virtues' with Sorcha."

Nuala stared at Brigid's placid smile. "Did she memorize the entire conversation, then?"

"Oh, no. She has many talents, but that isn't one of them. I know you find her a bit abrasive, but Sorcha's heart is in the right place."

"It's just her brain that's out to lunch, then?"

Brigid laughed and reached for the rolling pin. Nuala's eyes widened in sudden realization. If Sorcha hadn't reported the conversation word for word, and they had found no listening device on her, then—

"You bugged the room!"

"Please keep your voice down, dear; not everyone knows why it's myself that's meeting you," Brigid murmured. "They think I'm just giving you the once-over, as it were . . . Of course we bugged your room. We had to determine whether you were safe to approach, so—"

"When?"

Brigid took a mound of dough out of the mixing bowl and dropped it onto the counter, sending up small white puffs of flour. "The day after your arrival. I apologize for the invasion of your privacy, but it was a necessary precaution. There is only one in each room, in the electrical outlets. You can remove them now."

"Really? Why?"

Brigid looked up in mild surprise. "Because we have decided that we can trust you. We don't spy on our friends."

"You trust us already?"

"After what we have heard, yes. And you would hardly be here if we didn't, would you now?"

Nuala sat down on the stool across the table from Brigid. "Okay, why *are* we here? Sorcha—as you well know—gave us a tantalizing but brief glimpse of your organization. We know very little about it, but if anything she said was true—"

"Oh, it was all true. Sorcha wouldn't lie to you."

"Then you're really—" Nuala hesitated, wanting desperately to believe it. "You're really organized all over Ireland? You've infiltrated the government?"

Brigid's rhythmic rolling of the dough stopped, and she looked up at Nuala as she nodded. "You're not alone in your dream of freedom, Nuala. And you aren't alone in your attempt to do something about it."

"Who *are* you people?" Nuala leaned closer, nearly putting her arm in the bowl of peach mix. "How did you get into this? If you want me to join you—"

Brigid nodded. "Yes, you have to know enough to make up your mind, don't you? Well, then. How I got into this?" She seemed to ponder the question, her hands continuing to work with dough as if of their own accord. "Well, I suppose I've *always* been 'in it,' thanks to my mother Roisín and her mother and hers and so on. The women in our family have always been fighters, in one way or another. To do or be anything else is quite unthinkable. And we choose our men well. My Conor was a *garda*, but a good man in spite of it, and he never interfered in how I raised Éadaoin. If we had had sons, that might have been a different matter, of course—but as Éadaoin was the only child we were blessed with, Conor doted on her and didn't object when I allowed her to sit in on the gatherings that Mother and later myself had in our home."

"Gatherings?"

"Discussion groups. Always disguised as sewing circles or some such, which is what gave us the idea for expanding into this format. So I was merely carrying on the family tradition of providing a forum for women to meet and discuss anything they wanted to, including politics. And then when Éadaoin married Piaras, she brought up the idea of expanding even further. You see, Piaras designs and sells software—government-approved software, naturally—and he travels around quite a bit, installing what he sells and training companies to use it. So it was Éadaoin's idea to travel with him and get to know women in these other communities. She single-handedly spread our network beyond Rathcoole, by finding one or two women in each community who would help organize. She never revealed herself to too many in any one place, of course. Quite persuasive, my daughter, but much better one on one—and prudently cautious."

Nuala glanced behind her for a moment and watched

Éadaoin, deep in discussion with Fiona, with Heather hanging on every word, her eyes round.

"I know I sound like a typically proud mother," Brigid went on, "but that's because I am. My Éadaoin has surpassed the meager attempts of her mother, grandmother, or great-grandmother. Her determination to earn a university degree in political science—which, as you well know, *very* few women in the last fifty years have accomplished without being discouraged from doing so—made people in Rathcoole sit up and take notice. So now when she talks about what women can accomplish, they listen."

"Wasn't that rather conspicuous of her?" Nuala asked. "This is a secret organization—"

"Right," Brigid readily agreed. "But she—with a modest bit of input from myself—planned it very carefully. She got her degree, then immediately married Piaras, 'retreated' into the home, and soon thereafter produced two children, thereby becoming what every woman in Ireland is supposed to be: a wife and mother. And therefore quite helpless and under control—in the eyes of the law. She does nothing overt that the authorities can be alarmed at. She travels with her husband, because that's a wife's duty, isn't it? Her present life is a perfect cover, and it has the added and genuine benefit of demonstrating to other women that she understands their situation, their problems—because isn't she a wife and mother, just like themselves?"

Nuala nodded. "And her husband doesn't interfere?"

Brigid smiled again; it was apparently a habit with her. "I told you, the women in my family choose our men well. Piaras is a feminist himself, and very supportive of our efforts. He even helps us from time to time with computers. He's as proud of Éadaoin's organizing skills as I am."

Nuala cast another speculative glance at Éadaoin, who was now listening intently to Fiona, nodding emphatically from time to time. When she turned back, she found Brigid watching her.

"And Dana—Sheehan, was it? What does she do?"

"Dana was my mother's closest friend," Brigid explained. "And a second grandmother to Éadaoin. She does several clever things with computers herself, which I'll let her explain to you. But she also serves as a—link, if you will—to the older women of Rathcoole. Shows them that there is indeed a role for 'little old ladies' in rebellion."

Nuala smiled at the image. "Yeah, I like that. All women are underestimated, but older women are written off as useless. I've always thought there was a huge, untapped source of energy there."

"You and I think alike on a great many things, Nuala." Brigid was smiling yet again. "I look forward to working with you, if you decide you wish to do so. We could certainly use your special talents."

Before Nuala could reply to that, a voice called out from across the room: "My nephew, Feidhlimidh O'Turlough, just got a new position in the Justice Department, in the Office of Corrections. He'll be making twice what he was before. We're all so proud of him."

Congratulations came from all sides. A moment later another voice called from somewhere behind Nuala: "And my daughter Clodagh also has a new position: She's with a travel agency in Dublin now. So she can let me know about low fares to Scotland or Wales—or anywhere else, I suppose. So if you're looking to take a holiday, let me know, and I'll call her."

Amid the new round of congratulations, it dawned on Nuala. She leaned over to whisper to Brigid. "Sorcha said you'd contacts in nearly every occupation. This is how you pass information on that, isn't it? But is that safe? Suppose you couldn't trust me, I could go to the *gardaí*—"

"And tell them what? That Dervla's nephew has a new job? Or Esther's daughter? There's nothing in that, is there?"

Another voice precluded Nuala's reply: "Could you call her, then, about a fare to Scotland? Mary Frances Doheny's eighth child, Pádraig, is just out of nappies, and I've been thinking that Mary Frances could use a bit of a holiday. Of course they've no money for it, but if we could take a wee collection—"

"Of course we can!" someone else called. "Mary Frances is one of the finest women God ever made. And doesn't she deserve a rest in the Highlands? Her sister May could mind the kids and feed her husband while she's gone."

"We could make dinners to take round to them, too," someone called out.

Nuala was watching Brigid, who continued with her second pie crust, apparently oblivious. Nuala leaned in. "Is this what it sounds? Or more?"

Brigid's reply was so soft Nuala could barely hear her above the other voices. "Mary Frances is obviously pregnant. Her doctor does not yet know, nor her husband, or he would be going with her to Scotland. But Mary Frances knows. And she told Séarlait, who has just told us. We change travel agencies as often as we can, to avoid suspicion of so many trips to Scotland or Wales. That's why Esther told us of her daughter's new position. Her daughter will make the travel arrangements, and we will raise the fare—probably from the selling of these pies. Once in Scotland, our contacts there will arrange a disguise for Mary Frances and a complicated series of buses, taxis, and the like—in case anyone has followed her to Scotland—and we will get her to a clinic. Someone else will take scenic photographs of the local tourist attractions to give to Mary Frances to show about once she returns here." Brigid glanced up at Nuala. "If you make information as public as possible, then you can't be caught in a secret or a lie, can you? There's nothing we say here that the God Patrol or anyone else can make anything of. It's worked quite well for years."

Nuala looked around at all the women who were busy making pies and chatting about the details of their lives. She smiled. "It's like the Underground Railroad."

"Pardon?"

"That's what it was called in America. It was a group of people, a network, who helped slaves escape north to freedom. Only here, you're helping women escape unwanted pregnancy by getting them out to Scotland, where they can get an abortion."

Brigid smiled. "Underground Railway. That has a nice sound to it." She studied Nuala before returning to her pie crust. "So what do you think, Nuala? Is our quiet revolution the sort you'd want to be party to?"

"It was my understanding from Sorcha that you want me to help make it more . . . unquiet?"

Brigid chuckled. "In a manner of speaking. We need you to inflame those that are not part of our organization into revolt. We could remain—as you called it—underground, and ready to help. But not open ourselves up to exposure and attack from—"

"God Patrol!" someone called.

"We will discuss this later," Brigid murmured, and slipped a hand into the pocket of her apron. She handed Nuala an ID chip. "Updated. You're still Dara Moran, but now you're recently widowed and visiting your aunt Brigid."

Nuala stared at the chip in surprise until Brigid whispered, "Put it on, dear."

"Right." As she exchanged her old dogtag for the new one, Nuala glanced over at her friends. She was relieved to see them putting on new ID dogtags, too. She smiled at Brigid in new respect, then turned to look as three Christian Brothers in brown robes paraded in.

"It's best to ignore them," Brigid murmured. "Here. You can do the crimping while I peel more peaches."

Nuala reluctantly pulled the pie tin toward herself. On the first try, she shoved her thumb through the crust, tearing a jagged hole in it. Cursing herself silently in disgust, she attempted to mend the hole by patting the dough with her fingers. She pretended to be engrossed in the pie crust, head down, but she watched the three men patrol the room, the patronizing smiles she had come to expect from such as these on their faces. When they started in Heather's direction, Nuala glanced toward her coat, gauging the distance between herself and the pistol in her coat pocket.

"Don't worry," Brigid whispered. "They aren't *gardaí*. They won't know she's a runaway. They'll believe she's Fiona's daughter, as it says on her chip, if they ask to see it. And that they're visiting Fiona's sister and her family."

"And Igraine?"

"Dana's daughter, visiting from Kerry. She really does have a daughter there."

"How did you—"

"I'll explain later."

Continuing to fumble with the pie crust, Nuala glanced around the room. She was surprised to see that none of the women appeared at all afraid at the presence of the Brothers. They continued to work on their pies, chatting, even laughing with each other.

As if reading her mind, Brigid spoke. "If you fear your enemies, you grant them power over you. What you do not fear or respect cannot control you."

"Makes sense," Nuala replied. "For all it sounds like a fortune cookie."

Brigid laughed. "I'm so glad you came to Rathcoole." She shot a glance at the Brothers. They were still far on the other side of the room, but she lowered her voice anyway. "It's time we escalated our—project—to a new phase. And you're just the person to help us with that."

"Fine. I'll do my bit. As long as I don't have to make any more bloody pies!" Nuala shoved the pie tin with the shredded-edged dough toward Brigid and grabbed a leftover peach. "Here, let me do this. The worst damage I'll do is cut off a finger. You finish the shaggin' dough."

Brigid passed her the knife, smiling, and set about trying to transform Nuala's disaster into some semblance of a pie crust. Out of the corner of her eye, Nuala saw the God Patrol leave Heather and Fiona, bypass Igraine, and start in her own direction.

"Good afternoon, Brothers." Brigid's friendly greeting sounded so genuine that Nuala smiled in admiration. "It's a lovely Saturday, isn't it?"

"*Buíochas le Dia,*" intoned the Brother in front, a bearded man with jowls and a paunch.

"Yes, God be thanked, indeed," Brigid agreed. "Have you seen how many pies we're making? God bless that generous man, Antoine Harrigan, for donating so many peaches from his hothouse orchard. These should bring in quite a bit of money for charity, don't you think?"

"You and all the fine ladies in this room are to be commended for such an unselfish Christian spirit, my child," said the second one, a blond fellow not half the age of the woman he had just called "child."

"Oh, we do what we can," Brigid murmured modestly. "It is God's law, isn't it?"

"Which we as Christians are honored to obey," the jowly fellow declared.

"And who would this be?" asked the third Brother, a tall, thin fellow with black hair and a permanent squint that somehow gave him the appearance of a snake.

"Let me introduce you," Brigid said, her voice taking on both affection and a certain sadness. "This is my niece Dara, from Donegal. She's just recently lost her husband, poor dear, and has come to me to help her begin her life anew. Perhaps you could remember her in your prayers, Brothers? And say a novena for the soul of her beloved Liam?"

Nuala tried to look grief-stricken, keeping her eyes down and her face turned away.

"My dear child," the snake said, patting her on the back. "We grieve with you in your loss. Do you have children to grant you solace?"

Children? Brigid hadn't said anything about children. What did it say on her new chip? What if they asked to see it? They had no reason to, but they did have the legal right.

Nuala dropped the knife with a clatter and buried her face in her sticky hands. "I can't—talk—about it!"

"Oh, there now." Brigid put her arms around Nuala, pushing

Nuala's face into her shoulder until she couldn't breathe. "Please, Brothers, as you can see—"

"Of course," one of them said, discomfort in his voice. Nuala couldn't see them; she continued with her fake sobs. "We'll pray for you, my child, that God will mend your shattered heart."

Someone patted her on the head with a heavy and clumsy hand, and the three of them exchanged awkward good-byes with Brigid. Nuala continued to sob until, after an interminable, suffocating interval, someone called out, "All clear!"

Brigid released her and Nuala leaned back, gasping for air. "Well, *that* was bloody inconvenient!"

Brigid laughed. "You were wonderful!"

"Self-righteous arseholes," a woman behind Nuala said, and then someone made a deliberately loud, rude noise. Everyone laughed, and Nuala glanced over at her three friends, then around at the laughing, defiant women. She smiled. For the first time in months, she was beginning to feel that they really had a chance of succeeding.

Chapter 12

"ARE YOU SURE it's safe for me to be walking about in the open like this?" Nuala glanced over her shoulder again, but still found no squad of *gardaí* ready to swoop down on her.

"Furtive actions only attract attention," Brigid replied. She stopped to examine a basket of apples set up in front of Bradigan's Market. "You're my niece; it would look a bit odd for you to lock yourself up at home, never venturing out into the light of day. The neighbors would begin to wonder."

"I suppose you're right—again." Nuala watched Brigid select four apples carefully, rejecting most of the ones on the top and burrowing down into the basket. In the week she had lived in Brigid's house, she had come to respect the older woman's wisdom and marvel at her quiet, unflappable courage. And Nuala never knew what she was going to do next.

"But someone is bound to recognize me sooner or later. Especially if—when—I do another—"

"*Dia duit, a Bhrigid,*" said the tall, aproned man who hefted a second basket of apples out onto the sidewalk and set it down next to the other one.

"*Dia is Muire duit, a Fhiacra.* Have you met my niece, Dara?"

"I haven't." He wiped his hand on his apron, then extended it to Nuala in greeting. "Fiacra Bradigan," he said, smiling. He was a blond bear of a man, his shoulders and arms huge, his hair and beard coarse. He had clipped the beard short, but apparently had left his hair to its own devices: It stuck up in unruly tufts at odd angles, matched in its wildness by the irregular thickets of his eyebrows.

"A pleasure to meet you," he said, and from his friendly tone, he obviously meant it. His hand surrounded Nuala's and swallowed it up in a firm but gentle shake. She didn't doubt he could crush her hand easily if he wanted. In spite of his genuine smile, she was relieved when he released her. His smile disappeared. "I'm sorry for your loss."

"Thank you." Nuala was no longer surprised at meeting strangers who already knew of the death of her mythical husband.

Fiacra's smile reappeared. "And how are you finding Rathcoole? It's a long way from the untamed wilds of Ulster, especially Donegal, which is the back of beyond, isn't it?"

Nuala smiled at the gentle teasing. "I'm finding Rathcoole very much to my liking, thank you. Cork's a decent enough place—or it would be, but for all the Corkmen."

Fiacra's laugh boomed out, startling Nuala with its volume and vehemence. She took a step back, afraid he might slap her on the back and knock her off the sidewalk. But the roar ebbed to a chuckle. "Ah, you're related to Brigid, all right."

Two girls in denim jumpers and sporting ponytails raced out of the shop. They hadn't made it very far from the door when Fiacra yelled at them to wait: "*Fanaigí go fóill!*" That brought them to a halt, and they turned back, their expressions so innocent it was obvious they were guilty of something. They were identical twins, about eight years old, and both blonde, like Fiacra; their hair was not as coarse as his, but every bit as thick. Their eyes were robin's-egg blue, and their noses were sprinkled with light ginger freckles. Their smiles faltered under Fiacra's stern and suspicious gaze, and when he held out his hand, palm up, they sighed in unison, blushed, and dug into their pockets.

Into his hand they each placed three pieces of fire-red candy wrapped in cellophane, their eyes on the sidewalk in embarrassment.

"Three pieces!" Fiacra rumbled. "If your ma knew, it's myself she'd murder entirely. You know how she feels about too many sweets, don't you, now?"

"Yes, Da," they murmured, not daring to look up.

"And you know she blames me for not putting locks on the candy bins, don't you?"

"Yes, Da."

"I've put her off that idea so far, because I'm afraid she'd keep the only key, but if you two keep this up, we'll all three of us be out of sweets for the rest of our lives."

"Yes, Da."

"All right, off with you." But before they could flee, he said, *"Fanaigí!"* and they turned back, obviously expecting more scolding. Instead he held out the candy, saying "Only *one*, now." Smiles lit up their faces as they snatched one piece each, saying "Thank you, *Daidi!*" He had to bend a long way down for their kisses before they scampered off. He chuckled, unwrapping a piece of candy and popping it in his mouth. He offered the candy to Brigid, who took one, and Nuala, who declined.

"Well, if you're finished picking over my apples, woman, come along inside."

The inside of the shop smelled of vanilla and cinnamon, fresh fruit and fresh bread. Nuala breathed it all in and smiled in appreciation. She followed Brigid over to the counter.

Fiacra opened the five-liter glass canister on the counter and dropped the two pieces of fire candy inside with the others. He lowered his voice to confide to Nuala. "I wasn't joking about my wife murdering me over these sweets. She's a tongue on her that'd clip a hedge, she has." He sighed. "Still, she's a wonderful woman, for all that."

Not knowing what to say to this, Nuala just nodded. Brigid placed the four apples on the counter and Fiacra took them. He put them under the counter and then put four apples back on the counter in front of Brigid, who was fishing coins out of her bag. Nuala watched this transaction in puzzled silence. Those weren't the same four apples that Brigid had so carefully selected, but why? . . . She said nothing; she had learned to ask Brigid her questions in private.

"Is there nothing else for you ladies today, then?" Fiacra asked as he gave Brigid her change.

"No, not today, Fiacra, thank you." Brigid gently placed the four apples, one by one, into her string bag. "But I'm sure there will be tomorrow."

"Ah, I'm expecting a shipment of apricots in tomorrow, bushels and bushels of them. You be sure to come round for some of those. I expect to sell quite a bit to those wanting to make jam."

"Sounds lovely. I'll be here."

"See you tomorrow, then. And it was nice meeting you, Dara. Stop in any time."

"*Go raibh maith agat.* I will."

As they were stepping outside, Brigid called back. "My regards to Sorcha."

Nuala stumbled on the last step. "Sorcha?" She stared at Brigid's smile. "You're not telling me that *he*'s married to—"

"Your favorite person in Rathcoole, yes." Brigid chuckled, amused at Nuala's surprise. "You did know she was married."

"Well, yes, but—" The startling image of supercilious Sorcha in the arms of a massive teddy bear like Fiacra dissolved when Nuala remembered the apples.

"What—" But she had to stop when first two passing women, then three teenage girls, another woman, and finally a white-haired couple greeted Brigid and exchanged pleasantries before continuing on their way.

"Do you know *every*one in this town?"

Brigid didn't reply, because she stopped to admire a little boy's fox terrier. Half a block and several more greetings later, she answered Nuala. "Well, yes, actually I do, or nearly so. I make a point—though not too obvious a one, of course—of meeting everyone who comes here to live. Which is why no one thought anything of it when Sorcha brought you to me at the cooking class, remember? Everyone knows that Brigid Moynihan has her finger in every pie, so to speak. The local priest and his henchmen believe it to be because I'm such a good Christian woman that I organize half the charities in town, and the *gardaí* aren't suspicious of me because my late husband was a *garda*, and I still bring them pastries and such on a regular basis. It pays to know people, Nuala, and to be on good terms with them, especially your enemies. Remember, a soft word never broke a tooth yet."

"You ought to write a book," Nuala said as they turned into Brigid's backyard. "An anthology of Brigid Moynihan's Pithy Sayings."

"Mother's being pithy again, is she?" Éadaoin looked up from the compost heap, to which she was adding potato scrapings.

Nuala nodded. "Ever and always."

"Part of her charm." Éadaoin kissed her mother's cheek and the three women went inside. Heather and Fiona were sitting at the kitchen table, chopping vegetables for the stewpot. Heather's face lit up when she saw Nuala, but she blushed and said nothing.

"Did you sweep the house when you came in?" Brigid asked her daughter, out of long habit.

Éadaoin nodded as she took her mother's string bag. "All clear."

"Doesn't it make you paranoid," Heather asked as she dropped potato cubes into the pot, "to have to check for listening devices or vidbugs every single time you come into your own house?"

"Better safe than sorry," Brigid replied, then grinned at the look Nuala threw at her. "An ounce of prevention—"

"Is worth a pound of manure," Nuala finished for her.

"What?" Fiona looked up, startled.

"I'm afraid my 'pithy sayings' are beginning to bother Nuala," Brigid explained. "She has an aversion to epigrams."

"Only when somebody else says them," Fiona corrected her. "Nuala's full of it—uh, them—herself."

Nuala sneered at her friend, then pointed at the apples Éadaoin had just taken from Brigid's bag. "What's the story with those? I *know* those aren't the four you picked out. He substituted those from behind the counter. Why?"

Éadaoin handed one of the apples to Nuala. "Pull out the stem."

"What?" But she tried it without waiting for an answer. It took a few tries, but finally the stem came out—along with the part of the apple that had formed a plug for the hollow core. Nuala peered inside, then reached in with thumb and forefinger and pulled out a small plastic sack filled with about a dozen tiny green pills.

"Contraceptives from France," Éadaoin explained. "By way of our Celtic cousins in Brittany. That's a year's supply in your hand."

"And a five-year prison term," Fiona added.

"Are they for you?" Heather asked Éadaoin. "All of them?"

Éadaoin shook her head as she joined them at the table. She took the apple from Nuala and replaced the pills and then the apple plug. "After my two wee ones were born, I stocked up several years' supply, which are safely hidden away. These are for others who need them. We supply these and occasionally abortion pills—which are much harder to come by and very risky to use—to women in our network all over Ireland. Though of course not to as many as need them. We do what we can."

"If contraceptives are readily available in one place—in Rathcoole, for instance," Fiona said, "wouldn't the Church notice the drop in the birth rate?"

"They've been concerned about it for some time," Brigid replied as she washed her hands at the sink. "It's one of the reasons a Brother is required to be in the room with a gynecologist for every patient, because they were afraid doctors were illegally supplying women with contraceptives. And it's a frequent sermon topic, of course: the 'need' for larger families."

"So far," Éadaoin said, "women haven't been forced to use fertility drugs to correct the 'problem.' But you never know."

"We get the contraceptives from various places on the Continent," Brigid explained as she dried her hands, "smuggled in using different means, and then put them in local fruit, as we don't import much these days. We've arrangements with every greenhouse in the area: We give the growers free contraceptives and they insert others in the fruit they sell to people like Fiacra—our suppliers. We generally save the apples for those women who already have one child or more, and give apricots or peaches, which are cheaper and more plentiful but not as effective, to childless women."

"Apricots?" Fiona asked. "And what's in them?"

"Condoms," Éadaoin answered. "Where the stones should be."

"Fiacra said he was expecting bushels of apricots to be in tomorrow," Nuala recalled, smiling.

"Our most effective recruiting weapon," Éadaoin told her.

"Yes." Brigid nodded solemnly, then smiled. "The phrase 'making jam' has acquired a whole new meaning in Rathcoole."

"I have a license because I produce church-sanctioned recipe booklets and I write daily-meditation pamphlets," Dana was saying as she showed them her computer setup. She was about seventy, her hair nearly white and pulled back in a bun. She pointed to the monitor. "Because of my age, I got government permission to buy a large-screen monitor." She smiled at Nuala. "I have excellent vision, but I lied about it to the government doctor, putting on my 'frail, wee granny' act, so I got permission for this monster. It has much higher resolution; it makes it easier to do quality graphics—and the printer! Ah, that's my pride and joy! I can make documents so clean, the *gardaí* can't tell which are their own and which are mine. And I can make ID chips and passports, too."

"Passports?" Nuala asked, as Igraine, who had been staying with Dana, carried the tea tray into the tiny, book-crowded study. Dana's cat padded after her, never letting Igraine out of her sight. Heather got up to help pour the tea, and Fiona took the plate of biscuits, passing it to Dana, who took one of the small sugar-coated cakes.

"Oh, yes," the older woman answered Nuala. "My specialty." She nibbled on the sugar cake, then elaborated. "One of our people managed to supply us with a broken chip producer. Piaras fixed it, and now I can make ID chips. I can also produce passports of professional caliber, and my son is an amateur photographer—he specializes in birds—so he has registered equipment. It's really a simple matter to transfer photos onto chips. Of course the government can do it much more quickly, with their elaborate and expensive equipment. In spite of their rhetoric, they buy Tlate-produced computers from England. But I can achieve the same results with my own cobbled-together gizmos. I've supplied over fifty passports, and not one of them has been spotted yet."

"Who do you make them for?" Heather asked as she passed Dana a cup of tea.

"All sorts of people who want to emigrate. Since entire families are almost never allowed to travel abroad together—for fear they'll not come back—I create new identities for them, usually Scottish or Welsh, and they leave separately, then meet up again when they get where they're going."

"Tell them about the girl last month," Igraine said, leaning forward in her chair and stroking the purring cat, who lolled blissfully on her lap.

Dana smiled and finished her sugar cake, brushing the crumbs off her skirt. "Now *that* one was a pleasure." She focused on Heather as she explained. "It was a girl about your age, perhaps a year younger. Since she was a child, Aisling had always had one ambition: to join the Fleet when she grew up."

"Irish girls can't," Heather interrupted. "We can't even consider it." The bitterness in her voice made Nuala wonder if Heather had ever had the same dream.

"Precisely." Dana nodded. "But Aisling refused to give up. She didn't mention it to anyone outside her own family after she got old enough to understand the way things are in this country, but she took every science and maths class offered to girls, and excelled in all of them. She sought out as much of the background for such a career as was available to an Irish girl, and she dreamed of finding a way to escape Ireland, escape to the stars."

"She told me," Dana went on, speaking now only to Heather, who hung on every word, "that when she first heard about the Tlatejoxans, how they had made First Contact with us, she swore to herself, promised herself, that she would make it to space. Nothing would stop her from joining the Fleet."

"And she made it?" Heather asked. Nuala heard the emotion in her voice. Heather had never said anything about her own dreams, her own ambitions. Nuala suddenly felt a bit guilty that she had never asked.

Dana smiled in triumph. "She knew of the network, of course, because her mother is one of ours, and she came to the cooking class one Saturday, with Eithne, her mother. Eithne told us that Aisling was going to apply to university, and Aisling said how much she hoped for a foreign scholarship—though of course those never go to girls—so she could go abroad to study. Well, I knew what that meant; I remembered Aisling from when she was a wee thing, with her dreams of the stars, and I knew— Rathcoole is a small town, after all—that she had always got her best marks in science. So I spoke to Brigid and Éadaoin, who agreed with me, and I dropped by Eithne's house one afternoon. When Aisling came home from school, I made her a proposal: I would get her out of Ireland, and in exchange, she would do whatever she could to help us on the outside."

Dana sighed, no longer smiling. "Even though it had always been her dream, it was a very hard decision. It would mean never returning to Ireland and possibly never seeing her family again. And the repercussions on her family if the government ever found out her true reason for leaving could be severe, so Aisling had to consider carefully what she wanted."

"But she went, didn't she." It was not a question; Heather was certain of the answer. "She *had* to go."

Dana's smile returned. "She went. She practiced a Scottish accent at home for weeks, and memorized all the information I gave her about her fictional family in Aberdeen, then she said good-bye to her real family, got her new Scottish passport from me, and left to meet our contact in Dublin. Last week I got word that Aisling is now attending Fleet University in Geneva. She's in the Officer Training Program."

Nuala saw the sheen of tears in Heather's eyes when she smiled. "She made it. And she'll make it to space."

"And her family?" Fiona asked.

Dana frowned in both sadness and anger. "They had to publicly denounce her in Church for running away. The true reason she left or how she managed it was never let out, of course, both to protect her family and us, and because it would have made it that much harder for girls to study science. Her parents merely said that she had left a note saying she wanted to 'see the world' and so she went, without their permission, and to their great sorrow, as they feared what would happen to her soul. A prayer was said for her, and the priest urged the other parents to exercise greater control over their children, lest they too be 'lost.' So Aisling's parents now pretend to be humiliated at her disobedience, while secretly they're thrilled with her success."

"Will she ever see them again?" Heather asked.

Dana shrugged. "We could probably arrange for them to leave Ireland to meet her somewhere, but it could be dangerous for them; they have other children, so they might not want to take that risk."

"She must miss them terribly," Heather said. "But I know she's not sorry she went. The chance to go to space! She's so lucky. I'd give anything—" She stopped, blushing. "I didn't mean that. What I'm doing now is more important." The look she turned on Nuala showed such an evident need for approval that Nuala tried to make her smile reassuring.

"Just what *are* we doing now?" Fiona said, with an edge of impatience. "We've been hiding in Rathcoole for weeks, doing nothing. We're making invaluable contacts, I know, and we're all extremely impressed with your network, Dana, but if we don't contribute something soon—"

"Right," Igraine agreed, scratching the cat gently under the chin. "I thought the idea was for Nuala—and the rest of us, in some way—to stir up trouble. So let's start stirring."

Dana smiled. "Ah, the impatience of youth."

Igraine, who was nearing forty, and Fiona, a few years past it, exchanged a bemused glance.

Dana went to the bookcase and removed a volume of St. Thomas Aquinas. She opened it and removed a folded paper. "Remember this?" She handed it to Igraine. Nuala recognized the pamphlet she and Igraine and Máire had distributed in Coleraine on that day that seemed so long ago.

"How did you—" Igraine began.

"Our network is extensive," Dana reminded them. "A copy was brought to us. And we'd like you to write another one."

Heather, who had never seen the pamphlet, took it and began reading avidly. Dana went on. "We thought it best not to make copies and distribute them here, because that might alert the Church that you had fled to Cork. But if you were to write another, different one, we could distribute it through our network all over Ireland, and the authorities couldn't be sure it was the same author, or just where to look. What do you say?"

"You wanted to do something, Igraine?" Nuala smiled at her friend. "You wrote a great part of that one yourself. Think what you and Fiona together could turn out."

Igraine looked at Fiona, Fiona looked at Igraine, and they both grinned.

"What about me?" Heather said. "I could never write something like this."

"It doesn't have to be like that one," Dana told her. "We need to reach young people. You could write how you feel, being a young woman in Ireland today."

"Well . . ." Heather looked doubtful.

"Just put down what you think," Nuala told her. "Write it like you'd say it to a friend. Don't worry about grammar or punctuation, if that's what's stopping you. We can help you with that after you're done."

"Sure," Fiona agreed. "Think of it as giving girls like yourself all over Ireland a chance to read the truth, for a change. Write what you'd want to read, if you were them."

Heather looked up at Nuala. "Do you think I could do a good job?"

"I know you can."

Nuala's certainty made up Heather's mind. "Okay, I'll try it."

"Good," Nuala said. "Now as for me—"

There was a knock at the back door, downstairs. Several hurried raps, then barely a pause before several more.

"Relax," Dana said when her visitors sprang to their feet. "The God Patrols don't knock like that, nor do the *gardaí*; they nearly pound the door in. That's somebody needing help. Wait here."

Dana closed the study door after her, but Igraine reopened it a crack after she had gone down the stairs and the four women crowded around to listen.

"Aoife! Jesus, Mary, and Joseph, what has he done to you?"

"You have to help me, Dana! I can't take it any longer. He did this to me last night, then he left. God knows what he'll do when he comes home!"

"Perhaps nothing, dear. He rarely beats you two days together."

"No, you don't understand. It's not just myself now, it's Mary Kate! The way he's been looking at her lately. The things he's said about his own daughter!"

The women listening winced at both the implications and Aoife's dissolving into tears. Nuala saw that Igraine was furious, her expression deadly. Nuala felt that way herself.

"She's only a child!" Aoife gasped out between sobs. "Eleven years old! I know what he wants. It's when I caught him sneaking into her room last night that he did this to me. He threatened to kill me and to keep Mary Kate for himself. And he'd do it, too. I know he would! I have to stop him! I have to—"

Aoife broke down again, and for several minutes there was only the sound of muffled weeping. Nuala squeezed the pistol in her pocket, her jaw clenched in fury.

"All right, Aoife. All right. Have a sip of this . . . There. You know I'll help."

"What am I going to do, Dana? The *gardaí* won't help. And even if I were to escape with the children, they'd return us to him; no matter where we went, we'd never be safe! We'll never be free! I have to stop him somehow. I have to protect Mary Kate! Even if I have to kill him—"

"Now, now, calm yourself, dear. Getting yourself put in prison will be no help to your children, will it? I'll take care of everything. Don't you worry about it at all."

"But he'll—"

"No, he won't. I promise you. Is he at work at the recycling plant?"

"Yes, but—"

"Good, that will give us some time. Now I want you to go into hiding; it shouldn't be for more than a day or two—"

"My children!"

"Every one of them will be collected and sent to you, as soon as they're out of school this afternoon. Where's the baby? Where's Christy?"

"With Kathleen."

"Good. You'll go straight from here to a safe house—"

"Not without Christy!"

"Kathleen will bring him to you tonight. You're not to go near home, lest Cormac come home early and surprise you. You'll go now, as soon as I make a 'phone call. Don't worry about the children at all; we'll see to them and get them safely to you."

"He'll find us! I know he will!"

"He won't have the chance, Aoife. I promise you. Now you drink your tea and I'll make that call."

After a moment, in which the women upstairs listened to Aoife's continued weeping, they heard Dana's voice again.

"It's myself. Aoife finally needs us to help in redecorating her house . . . Yes, everything is to be changed, top to bottom. If you know anyone with skill in this area—ah, good . . . Well, as soon as possible; she's ready for a change right now. Are you free tonight? I don't think it should wait until tomorrow . . . Wonderful . . . Yes, the children's rooms, too. The baby is next door, with Kathleen. I'm sure she won't mind looking after him until— . . . Yes, what a good idea . . . Right. See you tonight, then. *Slán.*

"Now, Aoife, everything's set in motion. You don't have to worry about a thing. Everything's going to be all right."

"I loved him once. He was a good man when I married him."

"They all are, at first. Have more tea, dear."

Fifteen minutes later the listeners upstairs heard a familiar voice as Éadaoin came into the kitchen. After several minutes Aoife left with her, and Dana returned to the study upstairs. Her expression was grim and determined.

"Would you like to see how I make passports?"

It was twilight. Nuala shivered and pulled the balaclava down farther into her black turtleneck. She heard rustling among the trees but saw no one. The forest clearing was empty, and the trees grew thick enough around it to hide anyone.

"Do you think this will work?" Heather whispered. Nuala merely shrugged in reply, saying nothing. Neither did Fiona, Igraine, or Éadaoin. They continued to wait, silently, for almost an hour.

Finally a low whistle, resembling a birdcall, drifted through the trees. Éadaoin nodded to her companions, and they moved, as noiselessly as possible, through the trees to the edge of the clearing. From all around the clearing, from behind nearly every tree, faceless people emerged: both men and women, but all wearing balaclavas. They eased up to the edge of the clearing and circled it, leaving only an opening at one end.

Nuala heard something large crashing through the underbrush. A heavy man less than two meters tall, quite naked except for a gag, a blindfold, and the rope that bound his hands behind him, stumbled into the clearing, propelled forward by the shove from behind. The opening closed behind him, the faceless people surrounded him. Nuala's eyes widened when she saw who had brought him here. Fiacra Bradigan was wearing a balaclava too, but there was no mistaking his size. He dwarfed the naked man, who was making terrified sounds behind the gag. The other two men with Fiacra grabbed the man's arms and Fiacra ripped off the blindfold.

Immediately, powerful flashlights were switched on, held by every other person all around the circle, illuminating the terror-stricken man. Fiacra and his two assistants stepped back and took their places at the edge of the clearing. The naked man whirled in a frantic circle, wincing at the bright light, and saw that he was surrounded. He pulled at his bonds, but they held him fast. He took a step, but as soon as he did, those holding flashlights aimed the beams down, away from his eyes, so that he could see the people who stepped forward, raising shillelaghs over their heads, brandishing the wooden clubs. He stepped back and they slowly lowered the clubs. No one spoke; they all continued to glare accusingly at him through the eyeholes in the black balaclavas. After a few moments of this, the man slumped to his knees, tears of terror shining in the beams of light on his face. His breath rasped; his shoulders heaved.

Finally a voice rang out, and the man jumped as if he'd been shot. The voice was female and seemed to echo in the crisp stillness of the autumn night. Nuala didn't know the voice, but its tone was cold rage.

"Cormac Scanlon, you have been accused of vicious assaults on your wife, consisting of numerous beatings and rapes, and of attempting to molest your eleven-year-old daughter. As the state does not allow wives to testify against husbands or children against their fathers, you cannot be brought up on charges in an official court. But you have been tried by *this* court, by the people of your community. We do not tolerate the injustices that the Church and the government encourage. We recognize a higher law than that of the state, a higher law than that of the Church. We have our own law: the law of morality."

The faceless woman raised her implacable voice. "People of Rathcoole, what say you? How do you find Cormac Scanlon?"

One by one, all around the circle and without hesitation, the masked people pronounced the same word: "Guilty." By the time the last voice had spoken, Scanlon had fallen forward, his forehead on the ground as he wept.

"Cormac Scanlon," the woman acting as judge continued, "you have been found guilty of assault and attempted child abuse. We consider you extremely dangerous and a threat to us, your community. Get on your feet while I pronounce sentence."

But Scanlon continued to huddle on the ground, shivering violently and weeping, so Fiacra and another man stepped forward and grabbed his arms, jerking him upright. They had to hold him up, or he would have collapsed.

"You should be grateful to your wife, Scanlon," the judge began again. "If she had not stopped you from molesting her child—your daughter—then your mandatory sentence would have been death. She asked us to show you mercy, because she loved you once, and because, in spite of all the atrocities you have committed against her, she yet retains that humanity that you have long since abandoned any pretense of. We bow to her wishes and will not execute you. Instead, your sentence is exile. Exile from your family, exile from your community, exile from your country."

The judge walked forward, into the light. She carried a bundle, which she dropped at Scanlon's feet. Even slumped as he was in the grip of the men who held him, Scanlon was still almost a head taller than the woman who passed sentence on him. She pointed at the bundle.

"Clothes, a small amount of money, and a passport in a new name. You have twenty-four hours to use these to leave Ireland forever. We will be watching. If you do not leave the country within the time allowed, or if you try to contact the authorities, we will come for you. You will be buried here, in this ancient forest where druids once executed criminals, and no one will ever find your body. You will go or you will die. Those are your only choices. Your wife and children will remain in Rathcoole, surrounded by those who will watch over them. If you ever contact them in any way again, we will find you. We are everywhere, not just in Rathcoole. Look over your shoulder, no matter where you go, and you may find one of us watching you. If you bother Aoife ever again, you will never be safe from us, not even on the farthest space colony. We will find you."

She paused, watching him shiver uncontrollably. No expression was visible because of the balaclava, but the disgust was obvious in her voice.

"No doubt you do not believe me. But remember Éamonn Mulgrew? His drowning was no accident. He, too, beat his wife and threatened to kill her. She was not as merciful as Aoife."

Scanlon's eyes widened; he began to breathe faster, glancing around wildly. The judge went on, her voice even colder now, even more angry.

"And Tadhg MacCarthy, remember him? Slipped and fell in his own bath. And Will Moloney. Heart attack, the *gardaí* thought."

Scanlon moaned in terror, but the woman showed him no mercy, spitting the words at him in repulsion. "They thought they could terrorize women, and their families, and get away with it. But not here. We don't allow that in Rathcoole. Now be gone from our midst, rapist. Take nothing from Aoife's house; take only this bundle, no more. And never return. Or you will fertilize this ground."

With that she turned her back on him and walked away, out of the circle, and disappeared into the forest. The flashlight beams wavered over the ground, the people, and the trees, as the circle of people melted back into the forest. Nuala looked back to see Fiacra untie Scanlon's hands.

"Twenty-four hours," she heard him say. "We'll be watching."

When the other man released him, Scanlon dropped to his knees again, clutching at the bundle, his hands shaking with cold and fear as he grabbed at the clothes. Nuala turned away.

"Will he stay away?" Nuala asked. She and Éadaoin huddled near the fire, shivering as they sipped the tea Brigid had brought them from the kitchen.

"Yes," Brigid told her as she took a seat on the sofa and passed the plate of sandwiches to Piaras, Éadaoin's husband, a gentle, intellectual man who had helped Fiacra control Scanlon in the woods. He took one, then unbuttoned his coat, sticking the balaclava in his pocket.

"He knows we meant it," Piaras said. He took another bite, his black mustache quivering as he chewed. "He knows what will happen to him if he comes back."

"He won't go to the *gardaí*?" Nuala asked.

"And tell them what?" Éadaoin countered. "They'd never believe such a story, and he can't positively identify anyone. He could guess at identities, but he'd have no proof. And everyone there tonight made sure they had an alibi for their whereabouts. So it'd just be his word against theirs. And even if the *gardaí* did believe him, they wouldn't protect him twenty-four hours a day for the rest of his life. Besides, they'd just arrest him for possessing a false passport. He'll use it, and leave."

"Then Aoife and her kids will be all right?" Nuala asked.

"Well, she can never marry again, of course," Brigid replied. "Unless we hear that Cormac is dead and we can prove it. We could supply false documents to 'prove' his death, but that's too risky for Aoife and for us, in case he ever does show up again. But she can apply for Abandoned Wife status, and the government will support her. After five years they'll give her legal claim to the house—or to her nearest male relative, I should say. And we'll look after her. We take care of our own."

"Obviously," Nuala said, smiling. "Does the Church have any idea that you do things like this? I mean, will they suspect that Scanlon was chased off?"

Éadaoin shook her head. "They won't have a clue, Nuala. You see, they think they run our lives. We let them think that, because it makes it easier on us if we don't arouse suspicion. But the important thing is, *we* know who has the real power in Rathcoole. And we use it cautiously."

"And we will continue to use it cautiously," Brigid added, "until all the people of Ireland have learned to reclaim power for themselves, to stop giving it away."

"Reclaim our own power," Nuala murmured, and smiled.

Chapter 13

"It's all arranged." Fiona stood back, out of the way, as the two-person camera crew, Dana and her son Árdal, set up the backdrop and lights. Nuala sat in Dana's basement, in the middle of all the activity, tugging the wig into place. Fiona went on.

"As soon as we're finished here, we move east, to Kilkenny.

Éadaoin's spoken with her people there, and we'll be provided with places to stay."

"New identities again?" Igraine asked. Dana's cat was in her lap again.

Fiona nodded. "Right. Heather's still my daughter, and the two of us are visiting my aunt Teresa. You and Nuala are sisters, visiting your cousin Máda. We'll stay for a week or so, then move farther east, to Wexford. As long as we keep moving, we'll be less likely to arouse suspicion. And I've memorized all the names and 'phone numbers of the contacts we'll need."

"Are the pamphlets still going out on schedule?" Igraine asked.

"Next Tuesday," Fiona confirmed.

"Mine, too?" Heather still looked nervous; she had worried over the content of her pamphlet since Nuala had finally gotten it away from her after seven rewrites.

"Yours, too." Fiona smiled at the girl. "Will you stop fretting over it? We've told you and told you: It's good. *Really.*"

"Okay, let's get this done." Árdal looked up from the vidcamera, which they had acquired from someone in the Network. "Are you ready, Nuala?"

"We can redo this, right? In case I—"

"Sure," he told her for the fourth time. "But you want to be on your way before nightfall, don't you? So try to get it the first time."

"Right. No pressure," Nuala muttered.

"Do you want to go over your notes again?" Heather asked her.

Nuala shook her head. "They don't say much anyway. I'll be making this up as I go along. So let's do it."

"Okay, everybody quiet!" Árdal said unnecessarily. Fiona, Igraine, and Heather had moved back to the stairs, where Dana had gone to sit, out of the way. None of them said a word.

"The Guerrillas will insert their logo," Árdal said, looking through the vidcamera at Nuala, "and their voice-over will say, 'This is Guerrilla TV, the voice of a free Ireland,' then—you're on."

Nuala took a breath, then half turned to look at the camera, keeping the scar on her cheek hidden.

"I am Nuala Dennehy. Some of you will remember me from the last time, the interview I did after my unarmed friend, Máire Ní Flaherty, and I were attacked by the *gardaí*, and she was murdered. I did that interview to correct the lies the authorities were telling about the two of us and why we were attacked. Because I told you the truth, the *gardaí* want very much to get their hands on me, to shut me up. Well, they haven't found me yet. And so here I am again." Nuala paused long enough to sigh. She could feel the eyes of the five people in the room on her, as well as the unblinking lens of the camera. She had to get this right.

"After that last tape I had to flee Ulster. I am sure now that my family is being watched, by the stormtroopers who call themselves *gardaí*. They're not safe, my father and my sister, because I dared to speak the truth. There is a bounty on my head, I've heard, and anyone who offers me shelter could be arrested as an enemy of the state. And all because I spoke the truth. The truth, you see, is not welcome in Ireland. And anyone who dares speak it or even seek it is committing an illegal act. As I am doing at this moment." She sat up a bit straighter. "And I'm proud to do so. For as long as the truth is illegal, then I will take pride in being a criminal; I will revel in rebellion. As our great hero, Patrick Pearse, once said, 'As long as Ireland is unfree the only honourable attitude for Irish men and Irish women is an attitude of revolt.' I agree and I stand with Pearse. As did the women I want to tell you about."

Nuala paused again, wishing she could turn and look at Fiona.

"When my friends and I fled Coleraine, we were aided by women I didn't know, women I didn't even meet, women who were courageous enough to risk everything to help us escape. And now those women have disappeared. We tried contacting them, but first strange voices answered their 'phones, and then there was no answer at all. Now we know that the 'phones have either been disconnected, or they are tapped and the other members of the families cannot speak freely. As for the women . . . even their own families don't know where they are. Some of them were taken from their houses by the *gardaí*—arrested. Some simply disappeared—they didn't come home one afternoon. The ones who were openly arrested have been held incommunicado; their families have not been allowed to see them. The attorneys representing them—well, I don't have to tell you how that works, do I? The attorneys are only allowed to tell the families that the prisoners are in good health, nothing more, and that may or may not be the truth. It has been over a month now since the arrests and disappearances, and there have been no trials. Not one. No charges have been filed; the *gardaí* won't even admit that they are *holding* some of these women!"

Nuala paused, trying to keep her growing anger under control, then suddenly shook off the attempt. Why the hell shouldn't she be angry? She glared at the camera lens.

"Where is Tríona Rafferty? She was seen last on 14 September, leaving a shop on Díreach Street in Gortahork, Donegal. She never came home that afternoon, and she has not been seen since. The *gardaí* claim no knowledge of her whereabouts; instead, they suggested that the *IRA* may be responsible for her disappearance. The IRA? Please! Must *everything* be blamed on the IRA? Whom do the *gardaí* think is stupid enough to believe such a story, that the IRA would kidnap a wife and mother, a woman who has nothing to do with their struggle, and for no apparent reason? There has been no ransom note; further, the IRA have denied knowing anything about Tríona Rafferty. And why would they?" Nuala shook her head, disgusted now, as well as angry. "No. No! It is the *gardaí* who took her, and no one else. That is obvious to anyone with more than half a brain—which would exclude the *gardaí*, all government officials, and the Church. Tríona Rafferty is a political prisoner, just the same as Ailís O'Hara."

Nuala slid to the edge of her chair, forgetting the women behind her, forgetting the camera operator. The long hair of the wig swept down off her shoulders, and she shoved it back irritably.

"Ailís O'Hara didn't just disappear, like Tríona Rafferty. She was arrested at two-thirty A.M. in Coleraine, two days after Tríona Rafferty disappeared in Gortahork. Without any warning or notice, the *gardaí* kicked in the front door of the O'Hara residence, ran up the stairs with their rifles in their hands, shouting obscenities, and rousted out Ailís, her husband Dennis, and their six children, the youngest of whom is barely out of nappies. They kept Ailís and her husband separated from their children, so they couldn't protect them, and then proceeded to terrorize the entire family. Dennis was kicked in the stomach and beaten repeatedly, the children were slapped, the girls with an open hand, the boys with a fist. Ailís herself was pushed back onto her bed and molested, and when Dennis tried to come to her aid, he was hit in the head with a rifle butt and knocked unconscious."

Nuala was spitting out the words in fury, as angry as if she had been there herself and had not merely heard this second-hand.

"All the while this was going on, other *gardaí* were downstairs, destroying the O'Haras' possessions. A family album was ripped to bits, the piano was toppled and destroyed by sledge-hammers, the kitchen cabinets were torn from the walls, their contents smashed, the floorboards were completely ripped up—the bastards even allowed their two Alsatian dogs to urinate on and chew up the furniture!"

Nuala, in her anger, didn't notice that she had gotten to her feet and had clenched her fists.

"This sort of behavior was common in the last century, before Reunification, when the accursed RUC would routinely terrorize nationalists in the Six Counties. And of course we all know how the *gardaí* treat those they suspect of IRA membership. But Ailís O'Hara? Ailís has *never* been a member of the IRA or even a Sinn Féin sympathizer. The only thing Ailís O'Hara ever did was to dream of an Ireland where the truth could be told, where women and men could live in freedom and peace, safe from the terror of the *gardaí*, the tyranny of the Church. And because she dared to dream, and to talk to other women who shared the same dream, her home was destroyed, her husband put in hospital, and she herself was dragged away from her screaming, terrified children to be locked away somewhere where her tormentors can do to her whatever they like, with no one to see or stop them. It has been over a month, and no member of her family, no friend, no one has been allowed to see her, except her attorney, who reports she is 'well' and that there are no visible bruises. Even if he is telling the truth about the bruises, what the hell does that prove? There are countless varieties of torture that leave no bruises on the face or arms. And make no mistake about it: Ailís O'Hara and Tríona Rafferty—wherever she is—are being tortured."

Nuala took a breath, and it seemed to shudder its way in and back out again.

"I know that because of all the other arrests. A dozen women have been arrested or disappeared since I fled Ulster. Women I didn't know, but who were friends of my friends, women who helped us escape, and women who had nothing to do with us except that they knew some of the same women we knew. Someone talked, you see, under torture, and who can blame them? She or they were forced to name names, and now twelve women and their families are paying the price."

Nuala had to pause again to swallow the bile in her throat.

"Why is this happening? Why are the *gardaí* and other minions of the Church-infested government getting away with such atrocities? . . . Perhaps because we are allowing it."

Nuala started to pace, but then remembered she wasn't to turn and show her scar, so she stopped, crossing her arms.

"The Church and the government's power exists only because we grant it to them. We give our own power away—to the very people who are oppressing us. We believe the lies the priests tell us. We obey immoral laws; we curtail our own rights— voluntarily. Because we are afraid. We are afraid of the power of the authorities—but they wouldn't have any power if we didn't give it to them! We are in collusion with our own tormentors, and it is time we changed that. It is time we took our own power back, away from them. It's *our* power; let's reclaim it. I have begun to do that for myself, because when they made me a criminal, they set me free. The *gardaí*, the Church—*no* one has the right to tell me what to believe or what to say or how to live my life anymore, because I will no longer *give* anyone that right. I dare the Church, the bloody Pope himself to do his worst, to excommunicate me. I do not give a good goddamn what any priest has to say. If I wish to seek a deity, I will do it on my own; I don't need some shaggin' pontificator telling me what God's opinions are. I'll make up my own mind, and you can, too, every one of ye that's listening. Don't go to Mass next Sunday, and just see how free you feel. Take *back* your own power. If you need faith in something, have faith in yourself and your own strength, your own intelligence. When you take back your own power, it will increase in proportion to your faith in it. You have to believe in yourself first, in your own power, and it will grow. It will increase in strength, and so will you."

She paused, then smiled sardonically. "Ah, I can already hear the uproar this tape will cause. Cardinal Daly will trip over his skirts hurrying to the cameras to denounce me. He'll tell you that what I've just said is proof that I am an 'atheist agitator'— whatever that is—trying to lead all of you—especially women, of course, whom he considers to be particularly gullible and stupid—to stray from the path of righteousness. After all, he'll say, anyone who tells you to believe in yourself rather than in the servants of God—and here he'll no doubt shudder and put a hand to his heart—and who tells you to *stay away from Mass*— can be only—horror of horrors!—a *Satanist*!"

Nuala chuckled, shaking her head. "I've no doubt he'll call me both an atheist and a Satanist, because Irish people have been carefully trained to tremble with fear at those words. Of course an atheistic Satanist is a contradiction in terms, but then, since when has logic ever had anything to do with Church theory? What fools they take us for!

"But Cardinal Daly is unimportant. His opinions are unimportant, and his official decrees are immaterial. Ignore him and he will lose his power. Ignore the *gardaí*, and they will lose *their* power. Defy them by not fearing them. What you do not fear cannot control you." She took another deep breath.

"Doing nothing can sometimes be a weapon. But there is a time and a place for action, too. And the lives of twelve women might depend on your actions now. I want to know where these twelve innocent women are—those who were seized because they dared help me and my friends—and when they'll be released. Don't you? Then demand to know! 'Phone the Justice Department in Dublin—the number is 07653—and demand the release of Tríona Rafferty, Ailís O'Hara, and the other ten women who disappeared last month. The Justice Department may pretend that they don't know who you're speaking of, but they bloody well do know. Demand the immediate release of these women, and then hang up. Don't stay on the line for more than fifteen seconds or so, because that will allow them to trace your call. And of course cover your face. There's no sense in getting yourself arrested, too. Make your feelings known, hang up, then call back immediately and say it again. And then call again. And again. Call from a pay 'phone, if you want to leave a message longer than fifteen seconds. If enough people call—even brief calls such as these—the Justice Department's 'phone lines could be tied up for days. And don't just call *them*, call your local *garda* barracks, call the mayor of your own village, call the Lord Mayor of Dublin, and that pustulant pontificator, Cardinal Daly himself, and tell them you want these women released. Call every single person of any authority in Ireland and demand freedom for the September Dozen. The lives of these brave, innocent women are in your hands. And if the authorities think they can dispel our anger, defuse the threat of our protest, our awakening to a sense of our own power, by disposing of these women—by murdering them—then they had better think again! History has proven, time and again, that martyrs can fuel Ireland's fight for freedom more potently than any other weapon. As Patrick Pearse said, 'Life springs from death, and from the graves of patriot men and women spring living nations.' Well, Ireland has not been a living nation—a true success of a nation—in a very, *very* long time. But it is time now to change that. The first step is in demanding justice. For the September Dozen and for every Irish woman, man, and child. Show the authorities that we will no longer be obedient sheep. Demand freedom for the September Dozen and tie up the 'phone lines today, and tomorrow, and for as long as it takes to free them. You have the power to paralyze the 'phone links of every official in Ireland. Do it! You have nothing to lose but your shackles."

Nuala paused again, shaking her head, dissatisfied by the rambling way the tape had turned out. But then she saw Árdal, his face still hidden behind the camera, raise an emphatic thumb in encouragement. Had it been all right, then? What else should she add? Her mind raced; then the quote suddenly clicked into place.

"One of the greatest of all rebels was an American, Thomas Paine. In the eighteenth century he said something that is just as important today. He said: 'Ye that dare oppose, not only the tyranny, but the tyrant, stand forth!' It is time for us, for all freedom-loving people, to stand forth. We have allowed ourselves to be enslaved for too long. No more! Stand forth, all of ye! Demand freedom for the September Dozen and for yourselves. Stand forth and resist."

After a moment of silence, Nuala spread her hands and shrugged. "Was that enough?"

The red light on the vidcam went out, and Árdal's face reappeared from behind the machine. He was grinning. "I think the bounty on your head just doubled."

Nuala attempted to smile. "Now there's a cheery thought."

Her friends left their perch on the stairs and surrounded her, smiling.

"Stand forth!" Dana said, raising a defiant fist with a grin. "Succinct and to the point. I approve."

"I rambled too much," Nuala worried as she pulled off the wig. "I got sidetracked and then went off on a tangent—"

"No, it was fine," Igraine assured her. "Public defiance is just what this country needs, and you've instigated it. Good work."

"I hate to cut this short," Fiona interrupted, "but we have a lorry to catch. Just in case any Rathcoole *garda* recognizes your face when this tape airs, we should be gone before then."

"You're sure you and Brigid won't be in any danger because of us?" Nuala asked Dana, still worried over their safety in spite of Brigid's final reassurances. "If the local *gardaí* do recognize—"

"They won't be able to prove a thing," Dana said. "It will

merely be a startling resemblance. Brigid's niece Dara has returned to Donegal, and if the *gardaí* check on that, they'll find her there. And our friend looks enough like you to assuage them, don't worry. Now, then. Your bags are waiting, and I've packed you some food for your trip. You'd best be on your way. *Sinn féin abú!*"

"Ourselves to victory, indeed," Fiona agreed, smiling. "We'll do our best on our end, and we know that your lot will be busy here, and all over Ireland. We'll keep in touch. Thanks for everything." Fiona gave Dana a hug, as did Heather. Igraine reluctantly handed the cat over to Dana, then turned away without an embrace for the woman whose home she had shared. But Dana seemed to understand; she just smiled.

Árdal joined them as they made for the stairs. He had the tape in his hand.

"How soon—" Igraine started to ask him.

"It'll be in the Guerrillas' hands by tomorrow night," he told her. "An anonymous present. Once they play it for themselves and see that it's Nuala, I'm sure they'll air it straightaway. Then we'll see what sort of an impact it makes."

They had been in Kilkenny for only a day and a half when the tape first aired. The next day they spotted the new grafitti. Painted in blazing red on a concrete traffic barrier in the middle of the busiest street in town were the words: STAND FORTH!! By the next day it was all over town, and, according to Éadaoin's network of contacts, all over Ireland.

Nuala tried calling the Justice Department in Dublin the day after the tape was first aired. The line was busy. It was busy all that day, and the next, and the next. Every time she heard the busy signal, she smiled.

Chapter 14

"I WISH I'D run away *years* ago!" Heather kept her voice down, though she and Nuala were alone in the alley, hiding behind some quaint, old-fashioned recycling bins.

Even though she had been back in Ireland for a few months now, sometimes it still struck Nuala how backward the country was technologically. Scotland, like the other countries of the Terran Economic Alliance—those nations that had no religious or political objections to trading with extraterrestrials—had incorporated alien technology into nearly every aspect of modern life. Nuala had grown accustomed to recycling right in her own flat, for instance, merely depositing used containers, all kinds of paper, articles of clothing—almost anything—in the recycling chute in the kitchen. A Tlate biotech reprocessor in the basement reduced the items to their constituent materials, sorted them, and credited to her account their current resale value. Such a system—like so much else—was unheard of in Ireland. Coming back here after only fifteen years had been like entering a time warp. It still threw her off at times.

"I mean it," Heather went on. "This is the first time in my life that I haven't had someone telling me what to do every moment. And I've learned so much! All those stories you tell me—I would never have heard about *any* of those people if I hadn't left home and come with you. And I've seen parts of the country I would never have seen!"

It was twilight, but Nuala could still see the girl's smile. It made her look all of thirteen, which reminded Nuala again of Kerry and all the years she had missed with her sister. She returned Heather's smile, but with a sad wistfulness Heather didn't notice. "So all in all, you think it was a *good* decision to leave home?"

Heather started to answer with her usual fervor, then saw that Nuala was teasing her. She blushed and ducked her head, grinning.

The cold breeze made Nuala shiver suddenly. She tugged her forest-green scarf tighter around her neck. Heather shivered, too, and pulled the knit hat down over her ears. It was less than a week after Samhain, but November seemed even colder this year than usual. Nuala wished she were indoors next to a fire with a cup of tea, instead of standing in this cold and windy alley waiting for Fiona and Igraine. They never stayed anywhere more than a few days, lest a God Patrol or the *gardaí* become suspicious—as had almost happened at the last house, when a God Patrol had taken too much interest in visiting relatives. They had had to leave quickly and hide. Since it was Nuala and the runaway Heather that the *gardaí* were actively looking for, it was Igraine and Fiona who always sought out the contacts and safe houses Éadaoin had supplied, and moved in their sparse luggage. Nuala and Heather always met them in a prearranged place and then followed them to safety after dark.

Nuala shivered again, trying not to think about her cozy flat in Edinburgh, so near the campus she could walk to work. She used to start and end her day with a cup of Irish tea, in front of her wee fireplace. But that life was gone now; there was no use remembering and missing—

"Leave me alone, please! I've done nothing!"

The woman's frantic voice shattered Nuala's sad reverie. It had come from the other end of the alley, though there was no one in sight.

"Stand still! I didn't say you could leave."

A man, his voice cold and imperious. A *garda*? Or any man who thought he had the right to control and bully this woman?

"Please! Let me go! I have to—"

The voice was cut off by a slap. Nuala started at the sound, then whispered, "Stay here!" and headed down the alley, walking as silently and quickly as she could, keeping to the shadows.

When she reached the end of the alley, she stopped. The woman was weeping now, and the man had lowered his voice, but Nuala heard him clearly; he was no more than a meter or two away, still out of sight around the corner.

"Shut up! You give me what I want, and I won't run you in."

"But I haven't done—"

"Shut up, bitch!" Another slap, and more weeping. "If you make me arrest you, there'll be more than just myself taking his pleasure with you. Or is that what you're wanting?"

Nuala had her pistol in her hand. There was only one male voice, but *gardaí* usually traveled in twos or threes. Where were his partners? Was this a trap? Nuala hesitated, the woman's desperate weeping making her hand tighten around the pistol. She had to be cautious; it was too risky. She couldn't just—

"Excuse me, Officer. But I really think you should let that woman go."

What the—Heather? The *garda* was apparently as surprised as Nuala. It was a moment before he managed to speak. "What do you think you're—get away from here, this is official business!"

Nuala had no choice now; caution be damned. She stepped around the corner, the pistol up, the safety off.

The *garda* had his back to her; he was staring at Heather. There were no other *gardaí* in sight. His pistol was in its holster; he obviously didn't consider Heather a threat. The woman he had assaulted, a young brunette in her twenties, had stopped weeping at Heather's sudden appearance. She was backed up against the wall of the building, a string bag of vegetables spilled at her feet. She stared at Heather, too, but movement caught her eye and she turned her head. At the sight of Nuala easing closer, pistol in hand, the woman's mouth opened as if to cry out, then snapped shut. Her terrified gaze darted from Nuala to the *garda* and back.

The man, oblivious to the threat behind him, took a step toward Heather. "Did you hear me, you little bitch? Or maybe you'd like some of the same for yourself?"

Heather was frightened, that was plain enough from her pale face and wide eyes, but her voice didn't waver.

"Certainly not. I have better taste than that."

With a muttered oath that sounded incredulous and furious at once, the *garda* started toward Heather.

"Move!" Nuala barked to Heather, both hands on the pistol. The officer whirled, Heather jumped aside, and Nuala pulled the trigger. She felt the vibration in her palm, and the gun kicked slightly. But it was over in a second. The *garda* crumpled, a look of astonishment on his face.

Nuala was frozen only for an instant. Then she lowered the pistol, automatically hitting the safety and scanning the empty windows opposite them. Heather took a cautious step toward the unconscious man.

"Is he—"

"Only stunned," Nuala answered, tucking the gun into her waistband, where it would be easy to reach. "And not for long.

We have to get out of here. His partners have to be somewhere close."

"Right." Heather knelt next to the *garda* and plucked his pistol from its holster, then grabbed his prodstick-baton and yanked it free of his belt.

"Are you all right?" Nuala grabbed the string bag as she spoke, stuffing the bruised vegetables back inside. The woman was staring at her. Was she in shock? "Are you all right? Are you hurt?"

Nuala put the bag's handle in the woman's hand, then took her arm. "Are you hurt? Do you need a doctor? Answer me!"

Still staring, finally the woman spoke. "Aren't you—you're that woman on the Guerrilla TV! Nuala something. I recognize your voice. I've watched your tapes a dozen times."

Shocked, Nuala tried to think of a reply. "I'm sure I don't know what you mean." She ducked her head. "Did he see your chip?" But the woman only continued to stare at her. Losing patience, and afraid the other *gardaí* would show up at any moment, Nuala grabbed the woman's shoulders. "Your ID chip! Did he see your chip! Does he know who you are?"

"No, he—" The woman blinked, stared down at the *garda*, then back up at Nuala. "He didn't even ask to see it. I didn't break any laws, he was just—he wanted to—"

"I know what he wanted." Nuala released her grip, tried to sound reassuring. "It's okay, he can't hurt you now. And since he doesn't know who you are, he won't come looking for you." She hoped that was the truth. "But you should go home now; he'll be waking up soon."

"You *are* her, aren't you? In spite of the hair. I'd know that voice anywhere."

"Look, just go, will you? Before his friends show up."

The woman nodded but didn't budge. Instead, she grabbed Nuala's arm, startling her. "You saved me from—I won't forget this, I won't."

"Yeah, right. Uh, you're welcome." Nuala tried to back up, but the woman wouldn't let go.

"Those things you said, on the tapes? I agreed with all of it. But I was afraid. I was afraid to do anything, to resist, like you said. I didn't think women could. I mean, we're not as strong as they are; we can't fight back. I thought—" She shot a dazed glance toward the unconscious *garda*. "But I was wrong." She looked back at Nuala. "I know that now. I was wrong. We can fight them."

"Yes, we can," Nuala agreed, nodding firmly, and tugged her arm free from the woman's grasp. "But there is a time to fight and a time to run. And at the moment—"

"Do you need a place to hide? I could hide you!"

"No, we have to meet someone—"

"Well, if you do, my name is Rita Boyle. I live at 1237 Sackett. It's that way. On the corner of Sackett and Garritty." She waved in the direction of north. "Only a few blocks from here. I could hide you in my basement, if you wanted. My husband rarely goes down there, so he wouldn't know—"

"Thank you," Nuala broke in. "If we need your help, I'll find you. Now you've got to go!"

"Okay." Rita took a few steps, then looked back. "I won't forget this. And I'll tell every woman I know that we *can* fight back. We have to."

"Good, you do that. Now go, Rita, quickly!"

Rita nodded, stared at her another moment, then turned and ran. Sighing with relief, Nuala turned, then stopped in shock. "What in the—"

Heather was just tugging the second leg of his blue trousers off the unconscious *garda*. When the pants were free, she wadded them into a ball and threw them up as high as she could. They caught on the fire escape above her, next to his shirt and coat, and hung, one leg up and the other dangling.

"What are you doing?"

"Help me with—"

"Heather!"

The girl let go of the elastic band in the man's boxer shorts and looked up.

"Leave him!" Nuala snapped. "We have to go. Now!"

"Right." Heather kicked his shoes into the shadows, then grabbed his belt from the ground. It still had his datalink and radio attached to it. She slung the belt over her shoulder and tossed the baton to Nuala, who caught it by reflex. She was still staring at Heather and the nearly naked *garda* in amazement.

"Well, let's go." Heather headed back down the alley.

Nuala followed, shaking her head. "I told you to stay put!"

"Well, I couldn't do that; you might have been hurt. So I circled the building."

"I could have been hurt? *I* was the one with the gun!"

"You needed me to distract him."

"I did not!"

"Of course you did. And it worked. We make a great team, don't we? This datalink will come in handy, I should think."

"What in the hell did you think you were doing? This is not a game!"

"Maybe not, but it was fun."

"Fun? Oh, God."

Nuala and Heather picked a different alley and waited nervously for their friends, who appeared seconds before the *garda* van did. The four women scurried off into the night.

The *gardaí* had roadblocks everywhere. They were checking every vehicle entering or leaving Wexford, and of course there was a swarm of them at the train station. But it wasn't Nuala they were searching for—apparently the *garda* hadn't gotten a good look at her before she shot him. It was Heather they were after. Although the bustle of *garda* activity certainly looked intimidating, Nuala and her friends weren't too concerned. It had been dark in that alley, and Heather's hair had been tucked up inside her knit cap, so the *garda*'s description was nearly useless. They knew this because they had been listening to *garda* chatter on the radio Heather had lifted. The *gardaí* hadn't a clue as to where to look for the two "possible IRA terrorists" who had assaulted an officer "in the performance of his duty."

So the four women stayed inside, sipping tea, watching the occasional blue-uniformed men parade on the street below in the steady downpour. There was little worry of a knock at the door, as they were staying in an attic room where the only entrance was a door hidden behind a bookcase. It was a perfect—if cramped—hiding place. The woman who owned the building—well, her husband owned it, of course—was part of the Network, as the four travelers had come to call Brigid, Éadaoin, and Dana's organization. This woman, Bébhinn Casey, supplied them with food and shelter and could serve, if they needed it, as a contact to Éadaoin. Bébhinn's husband knew they had fugitive houseguests but preferred not to know who they were. So, in the two days they had been there, Bébhinn was the only person they had seen.

"It's a bit of overkill, isn't it?" Nuala said, peering through the crack in the curtains. "You'd think there was no crime at all in this town, to be wasting so many men on a wild goose chase." She turned away from the window and came to sit on the sofa's arm, near where the other three were playing yet another round of gin rummy in yet another safe house.

It was Fiona's turn. Nuala suddenly noticed the gray in Fiona's hair. Her friend had had an opportunity to get her hair done professionally while they were in Rathcoole, but she had declined, saying it was "a silly thing to be concerned about," and that she didn't "need to be something I'm not anymore. How liberating."

Gone too were the colorful tailored outfits she had worn at her job in Coleraine. Fiona now dressed as they all did: nondescript skirts, blouses, sweaters or coats that did not attract attention. Fiona had kept her custom-made shoes, though, and Nuala smiled as she remembered how, over lunch one day in another safe house, Fiona had explained that this was for "practical reasons."

"You never know," Fiona had said, "when we might have to go tearing off on foot somewhere, and blisters would slow me down. I'll never have that problem with these wonders. And besides, we can't all carry off the 'horsy' look, like our Igraine."

Igraine had been startled at the remark. When Fiona pointed, still smiling, Igraine looked down at her boots. They were feminine enough not to look incongruous with a long skirt, but definitely sturdy, no-nonsense footwear with barely a heel at all. They reflected Igraine's character perfectly; Nuala couldn't imagine Igraine in high heels any more than she could imagine *herself* in the impossible things.

"Some of us have the sense not to waste time," Igraine had replied, one eyebrow raised, "on flimsy, foofy footwear that affords no defense for festering furuncles."

They had all laughed at that, surprised and delighted at Igraine's alliteration. Nuala smiled again at the memory. If she had to be on the run, she was glad that it was in the company of these women.

"Oh, the *gardaí* will give up looking for us here as soon as there's something else to distract them," said Fiona, discarding a seven of clubs.

"Too bad the IRA are so quiet in this part of the country," Igraine said, picking up the discarded seven. "They're always good for a distraction."

Where's your bloody IRA when we need them for cover? Máire had asked that night in Belfast. Máire. Nuala felt a twinge of guilt. She hadn't even thought of Máire in days—no, weeks. What would Máire think of present circumstances? She would have been thrilled to know of the Network's existence. And she would probably have approved of making tapes for the Guerrilla

TV. But taking the outrageous risk of attacking a *garda* . . . Oh, no, Máire wouldn't have liked that at all.

Nuala sighed. She hoped her slightly mad friend had found peace somewhere. Perhaps in that land of shimmering green stones she had mentioned only moments before her death. *A land where women are free and proud*, she had said. Did such a place exist, outside of Máire's troubled mind?

There was a soft rap at the door: tap, tap, tap—pause—tap—pause—tap. The fugitives relaxed as they recognized Bébhinn's code. Heather laid her cards facedown on the table, then hurried across the room. She pushed the heavy recliner away from the door and Bébhinn came in, pulling the bookcase shut again behind her. She was a youngish woman, perhaps thirty, and she wore her long black hair pulled back in a single heavy braid. Still thin, even after five children, she could no longer afford the fashionable clothes of her youth, before the children's arrival had strained her husband's paycheck. So she made do, never complaining about the lack of money, and added her own touches to her cheap clothes: a bit of lace sewn to her collar, a bright handkerchief sticking out of a pocket, sometimes even a feather stuck in the tie of her braid. Nuala admired—but couldn't quite comprehend—the woman's innate optimism.

"I brought sandwiches," Bébhinn said unnecessarily. The plate in her hand was piled with them.

"We're eating you out of house and home," Fiona said as Heather took the plate and brought it to the table. "And we have no money to—"

"Nonsense." Bébhinn waved the idea of payment away. "Brigid will send money when she can, from one of their bake sales. And even if she can't, it won't matter." She smiled, looking from Heather to Nuala. "You risked your lives and your freedom to save Rita Boyle from the *garda*. There's not a woman in town who doesn't know about that by now. I'm just proud that it's myself who's sheltering you."

Heather blushed in pleased embarrassment. Nuala looked away, uneasy. She still wasn't entirely sure she would have risked facing a possible trio of armed men if Heather hadn't forced her hand.

"So don't ye worry yourselves at all about money," Bébhinn went on, taking a seat. "It's glad I am that I can do it."

"We're very grateful," Igraine replied, "but what was that you were saying? Every woman in town knows about Nuala's taking down that *garda*? Do they know it was herself that did it?"

"Oh, yes." Bébhinn raised her hands as if to soothe Nuala's panicked expression. "But the word was spread that you escaped from town that same day, before the *gardaí* sealed us all in with their silly roadblocks. So no one thinks you're still here, not even Rita Boyle herself. The *gardaí* are just trying to make themselves look good, to ease their embarrassment."

Nuala sighed, but she was only partially relieved. "The sooner we get out of Wexford, the better."

"Absolutely." Igraine passed Fiona a sandwich. "Any rumors about when the roadblocks will be down?" she asked Bébhinn.

Bébhinn shook her head. "But I'd guess tomorrow or the next day at the latest. We made sure that the rumor of your having escaped town reached the ears of the *gardaí*. They have no reason not to believe it, as they've had no sign of you, and they're pleasingly predictable. They'll give up soon."

"And then we can go on, north to Wicklow?" Heather asked around a mouthful of sandwich.

Bébhinn spoke before anyone could reply. "I was hoping that, before you go, you might do something for us." She was looking directly at Nuala.

"Me? If I can, certainly," Nuala said. "After all you've done for us, I'd be glad to do what I can. What is it you're wanting?"

"Well, you see," Bébhinn said, leaning forward and gazing intently at Nuala, persuasion loading every word. "We have this . . . group. It's not part of the Network yet; Éadaoin and I don't think they're quite ready, so I haven't told them of it. It's called the Ladies Auxiliary of the St. Columbanus Society, and naturally we do the usual charitable things that the Church expects, but it's also a sort of a discussion group. We talk about our problems, both individually and collectively, as women in Irish society today. I'm not sure we actually solve anything, but it gives them the chance to talk to other women, to support each other. And when no God Patrol sticks their noses in, we can speak honestly. We've known each other for years, after all; we're friends. And I think they just need a bit of a push."

"Push? You want me to . . ." Nuala was sure she knew what Bébhinn was going to say, and winced in anticipation.

"Make a surprise visit to the first meeting after the roadblocks and curfew are finished—probably this Thursday."

"A meeting?" Igraine nearly choked on her sandwich. "In public?"

"Everyone thinks she's gone," Bébhinn hurried to explain. "Wexford is the last place anyone would expect her to turn up, even the *gardaí*. And we'd have a car waiting in the back, to get you out of town immediately after."

"Suppose a God Patrol drops in?" Fiona objected.

"Or someone leaves the meeting and 'phones the *gardaí*," Igraine said, just as alarmed. "There is a price on her head, remember. That would be awfully tempting, especially to a woman with several kids and little money."

"Not one of the St. Columbanus group would dare." Bébhinn was adamant. "They may not have convinced themselves of their own courage just yet, but even so, they know what you did for Rita and they've all seen your tapes. To turn you in would guarantee ostracism by every other woman in town, at the very least. None of them would risk that—money or no. I can promise you that." Bébhinn saw the look on Nuala's face and rushed on. "We need you, Nuala. They're on the verge, I know it. But we need *you*. If anyone else said the exact same words, they'd just be words, theory, that's all. But you live what you urge others to do. And women need to see that, face to face, so the words won't be abstract and dismissable. We've seen the tape of your fighting back when your friend was killed and your own life was in danger. And everyone has heard Rita Boyle—again and again—telling how you appeared out of nowhere to save her. You're not just a theory, you see. You're real. They need to see you, to believe they can—and must—fight back. I think they're almost there. You could push them that last step. They'd join us. I know it."

"It's too dangerous." Igraine dismissed the idea with a shake of her head.

"*Much* too dangerous, appearing in public," Fiona agreed. "Out of the question."

"But isn't this what we're *supposed* to be doing?" Heather met her friends' surprise with only a faint blush. She stood her ground, addressing her words to Nuala. "We're the ones who are supposed to be taking the risks and making the noise. It's Éadaoin and Brigid and Dana and their Network who have to stay underground, out of sight, while we stir up trouble and keep attention off them. Right? How can we stir up trouble if we stay in hiding all the time?"

"How can we accomplish anything if we're in jail—or dead?"

But Nuala didn't look at Fiona. Or Heather. She got up and went to the window again, peering out at the twilight through the slit in the closed curtains.

"It's too dangerous, Nuala. Forget it," Igraine urged.

"If these women are ready to join the Network, with just a little push," Heather said, "then aren't we obligated to give them that encouragement? Isn't that what we're here for?"

"You could make a tape specifically for the women of Wexford," Fiona suggested. "It could be shown at one of their meetings. It'd be the same thing."

"No, it would merely be better than nothing," Bébhinn disagreed. "It would not be the same. They need to be encouraged—inspired—to take their own risks, to make their own difference. If they saw that you were willing to take a risk for them, it would mean something, make a *big* impression." Nuala heard Bébhinn cross the room and stop behind her. "I don't want to put you in danger, Nuala, honestly. But for the first time, the women in this neighborhood—in this entire town—are excited about standing up for themselves, the way you did for Rita. No one has ever done that before—defy and humiliate a *garda* like that, *shoot* him! I want to take advantage of that now, before this tentative courage has the chance to dissipate. The women of Wexford are just as important—and can learn to be just as brave—as any women anywhere. If you didn't believe Rita was worth helping, then why did you bother?"

Because Heather forced my hand, Nuala thought. But she wasn't sure that was actually the case. Would she have turned that corner if Heather hadn't endangered herself? Maybe. Probably.

Máire was back again, her image floating before Nuala's mind. *You can be the leader you claim is not needed. You have more talents than you know.*

Nuala sighed, exhausted and more than a little frightened. Why hadn't she stayed in Scotland? But she knew the answer to that. Staying safely in Scotland forever was simply not an option. It never had been. She turned, slowly, and saw that the four women were all watching her, waiting. She looked at Bébhinn, this good and brave woman who risked prison by sheltering them. The bright-orange handkerchief sticking out of her black sweater pocket was so like the woman herself: a defiant splash of color in a monochromatic world. Nuala sighed again.

"The security must be airtight. We have to be ready to leave straight from there, with a direct route out of town already worked out, as well as alternative routes, and I can't stay long."

Bébhinn's face lit up with a tremendous smile, and she grabbed Nuala's hand. Before she could speak, Fiona jumped to her feet.

"Nuala, you can't! It's too—"

"It's been decided!" Nuala hadn't meant to snap at her; she was surprised at her own vehemence. She took a calming breath. "I have to, Fiona. Heather's right, and it's what I came home to do—whether I knew that at the time Máire recruited me, or not. It's what I'm here for; it's my job. You three can go on ahead—"

"I'm not leaving you!" Heather insisted. The stubborn look in her eye brooked no argument.

Nuala braced herself for Fiona's protest, and Igraine's, from the look on their faces. She raised her chin and stared back at both of them. To her surprise, their adamant and outraged expressions faltered. First Igraine sighed and nodded; then Fiona started to raise her hands in an exasperated gesture, but let them fall. She, too, sighed in surrender.

"I don't like it one bit," Fiona said, "but if it's what you want, all right. But leaving you vulnerable is out of the question . . . and you'll need me to do the driving, in any case."

"Of course I'm coming, too, to stand watch—as crazy as I think this is—because I have experience with this sort of thing, and you lot don't," Igraine said.

Nuala was moved by their loyalty, but didn't know how to say it. She merely nodded.

Fiona turned to Bébhinn. "We'll need to work out *every detail* in advance; there can be *no* slipups."

"Of course," Bébhinn agreed eagerly. She glanced back at Nuala, the "thank you" in her eyes, then joined Fiona and Igraine on the couch, already spinning plans aloud.

Heather was beaming at Nuala, who was startled by the—pride, it looked like—in the girl's eyes, her smile. She tried to smile back, then gave up and turned back to the window. She watched a *garda* patrol the sidewalk across the street. Wouldn't he love to get his hands on her? But she paid him little attention. She was remembering how Fiona and Igraine had backed down from their vehement objections, had acceded to her wishes so easily and were so ready to risk their lives to stand with her. Why?

You can be the leader you claim is not needed, Máire repeated in her mind.

Nuala shivered, though the room was warm.

Chapter 15

"**Y**OU SAID FORTY women—at most!" Igraine was outraged; she glared at Bébhinn.

Bébhinn was just as surprised as the others. They watched from the alley as the steady stream of women filed into the church basement. The parking lot was rapidly filling, and each vehicle carried at least two women, some as many as four or five.

"I don't under—" Bébhinn began, keeping her voice down as they peered around the corner of the building. "The word must have spread; this obviously isn't just the St. Columbanus women."

"Even if the *gardaí* don't know about this yet," Fiona said, "someone's bound to notice a full parking lot at a church on a Thursday evening. This is enemy territory, Nuala; your walking in there would be suicide!"

Fiona was right. Igraine was right. But Nuala saw the expressions on the faces of the women who were still arriving: excited, nervous, determined. They had come to see her. That was a concept she still could not quite comprehend. But they had. Would Máire have been surprised?

"And if I don't show? What will they think? That I only believe what I preach when it's convenient? That I'm not willing to take the risks I urge them to—"

"Getting arrested or killed wouldn't—" Igraine began, but Nuala interrupted her.

"You're right, of course, Igraine. To show myself here would be suicidally stupid." Nuala saw the disappointment in Heather's and Bébhinn's eyes. "But I'm going in anyway."

"Nuala!"

"Heather," Nuala went on, before Igraine could add her outrage to Fiona's, "just as we planned, you watch the front. Igraine, you're on the back. Fiona, you stay behind the wheel. Bébhinn, you're inside with me. If a God Patrol or a priest or

any of that ilk shows, Heather or Igraine will signal us inside,
I'll disappear into the crowd, and you'll take over, pretending
it's your usual meeting or anything you think plausible—
whatever the other women will go along with to cover our exit."

"Nuala—" Fiona began, but again Nuala interrupted.

"Well, of course I know they won't believe it's the usual
meeting, with so many women, but if they don't spot me—"

"If," Igraine said.

"—then all they'll have is suspicion, no proof, right?" Nuala
finished.

Fiona sighed. "Okay, remember: If the *gardaí* come at both
the back and the front, the window in the bathroom will get you
out on the north side. The backup van is—"

"I know where it is." Nuala nodded. "The key is under the
mat."

"It's almost time," Bébhinn said, looking at her watch. "And
there's not many left in the parking lot."

"The sooner we start this madness, the sooner it'll be over."
Fiona shook her head, sighing. "I'm for the lorry. If I spot any
garda vans, I'll lean on the horn." She suddenly gripped Nuala's
shoulder. "Good luck." She trotted back to the end of the alley,
where the truck waited.

"You keep out of sight," Nuala told Heather, who grinned.

"Knock 'em dead." She disappeared around the corner of the
building. Without saying a word, Igraine headed for the other
end of the alley; she and Fiona would watch both directions
while Heather watched the front. Every angle was covered—or
so they hoped.

"Okay," Nuala said to Bébhinn. "I'm ready."

The small basement room was packed; there had to be at least
three hundred women crammed into a space that was built to
hold one hundred at most. The chairs were folded in a corner;
unfolded, they took up too much room. So the women stood in
a solid mass, waiting. The buzz of their voices reverberated,
making so much noise Bébhinn had to whistle twice, her fingers
in her mouth, before she got their attention and was able to
move through to the front, Nuala behind her.

Nuala had spoken to crowds this size back at the university in
Scotland, in lecture halls with desks—speaking to silent students
who were usually bent over scribbling notes, hoping only to get
a good mark in the class. This was hardly the same thing.

At the sight of her, the women fell silent, their eyes widening.

In back some stood on tiptoe to see better, squinting and frowning. There was some polite jostling for position, but not a word, not a whisper. Just three hundred pairs of eyes, staring.

A small table had been pressed up against the blackboard on the wall. It wasn't foldable, so there it remained. Bébhinn clambered up onto it to address the crowd.

"I won't waste any time," she began, "as obviously you know why you're here. I just wanted to point out what a risk Nuala is taking by coming here to talk to you. She believes the women of Wexford are important enough to take that risk, so if the *gardaí* do show up, it is our duty to hinder them in any way we can, to stop them from taking her. If you are not prepared to do that—to take the same risk for her that she is taking for you—then leave now and tell *no* one where you have been."

She paused, but no one moved, no sound broke the silence. Bébhinn was smiling proudly as she climbed down from the table. Nuala took her place.

She looked down at the upturned faces, saw the excited eyes, felt the palpable tension in the room. What expectations did they have of her, and what could she say that wouldn't disappoint them?

"Hello, Nuala!" someone called from the crowd, and a hand waved.

"Rita," Nuala said, smiling. "Good to see you again. Had no more trouble with the *garda*, I hope?"

"Haven't seen the bastard," Rita called back. "And I'd better not, for his sake. I had my brother check out a disk on karate from the library, and I've been practicing. Nobody's going to intimidate Rita Boyle so easily again!"

A chuckle rippled through the crowd, but there were many determined nods, too. Nuala smiled. Here was her opening.

"Men have always underestimated women's anger and our strength. And we have underestimated it, too. But can you imagine how different the world would be if we *stopped* underestimating ourselves? What would happen if all women everywhere learned to defend ourselves, as Rita is learning to do? If we all said, *No*, I will not let you bully me, I will not let you hurt me. Can you imagine a world like that? I can. I can see it. If every woman refused to be intimidated, then they could enslave us no longer. We would be free! Imagine saying to your husband, 'I've learned karate, darling. So the next time you come home drunk and try to hit me or the kids, I'll flatten you. Don't even think of trying it ever again, dear.' "

There were some nervous chuckles at that, but murmurs of "Right!" too.

"Can you imagine that?" Nuala went on. "I can. And the *gardaí*. Yes, I know they carry weapons and they can throw people in jail. That may happen to me all too soon. But what would happen if all women said, 'You can kill me, you can imprison me, but you can't get us all. There will always be another woman to take my place. Always. So you can't win, Mr. Swaggering *Garda* who thinks he can attack any woman he likes. You can kill me or imprison me, but you can't impress me, and you can't frighten me. I will not be intimidated any longer. You are *nothing*.'"

The "Yeah!"s were louder this time, the nods more numerous. Almost imperceptibly the women inched closer to Nuala.

"Imagine a world where every woman said, 'I will have as many or as few children as I want, not however many the Church tells me I have to. And then, after I've raised them lovingly, taught them to be true to themselves and to fear nothing, I'll send them off on their own. And after I've done that, I want my own life back! I want to use my own talents and skills and interests for *myself*, not just to serve my children and grandchildren and my husband and the Church, but to do whatever the hell *I* want to do with my life. If I want to become a doctor, so women don't have to spread their legs for male gynecologists, then by god, I'll go to medical school and become one! And if everyone tells me I can't, I'll ignore them and study abroad, if I have to, but I will do it! I'll be a doctor, or join the Fleet and go to space, or be an engineer, or an author, or any bloody thing I choose to be. No one has the right to tell me I can't. No one.'"

"Ceart go leor!" Right enough, someone yelled, adding to the general agreement.

"Can you imagine such a world?" Nuala asked. "Can you imagine a world in which women are free? Can you? Well, can you?"

"Yes!" was the resounding reply; some fists pounded the air and smiles surrounded Nuala, but then a moment later someone in the back said, "No." Nuala didn't see the woman who spoke, but she heard the emotion in the voice, the tears choking that one word. The other women were shocked into silence, looking around to see who had spoken.

"I can understand that," Nuala said quickly. "After all, we've never seen freedom, so it may be difficult to imagine. But let's talk about faith for a moment. You all know about faith. We're taught to believe in its power practically from the moment we're born. Have faith in God, we're told, and He will provide. Well, what would happen if we stopped giving our faith away to some unseen entity and gave it back to ourselves instead? Have faith in yourself, and *you* will provide." She paused. "That's hard to imagine, too, isn't it? We're taught *not* to have faith in ourselves, but in God, the Church, the government, our fathers, our husbands—everyone *but* ourselves! That's no accident, you know. No one wants us to have faith in ourselves, because they know what that would mean. *They* can imagine the trouble that would cause them, so we've got to learn to imagine it too. We've got to. James Connolly once— Do you know who James Connolly was? I'm sure you remember his name from your history classes, because Connolly was one of the leaders of the 1916 Easter Uprising. He and all the other martyrs of that Uprising have been safely made into saints now, so we can be told that they did something vaguely heroic once, but that the details are no longer important. Well, James Connolly was a truly grand fellow—for all he was a man—and he said many brilliant and insightful things that no one wants you to hear today. Things like: 'No nation is conquered until it accepts defeat' and 'Timidity in the slave induces audacity in the tyrant.'

"Women were nearly conquered thousands of years ago when they accepted defeat at the hands of men with their patriarchal religion and their love of violence. I say 'nearly' conquered, because there has always been that flicker of a memory—call it genetic memory, if you like—of a time when women were free. Some of us were born with that memory, with an instinctive refusal to accept defeat. Some of us were born with it, some have to learn it. And it can be learned. You can learn to imagine freedom; you can learn to have faith in yourself and in other women. You can. All you need is the desire to. That's all. The desire grows into a need, a need to be free, a need to stop being timid. Connolly was right about so many things; he was right about the slave's timidity inducing audacity in the tyrant. Do you think your husband would bully you so much if you ceased to be timid? If you refused to be afraid of him, stopped respecting his nonexistent authority? He has no right to treat you badly, to bully or beat or rape you. None at all, the Church be damned. He has *no* right. No more right than the Church or the government has to enslave us. No right. All we have to do is realize that, believe it, and we can stop the tyranny. A great South African rebel of the twentieth century, Stephen Biko, said, 'The most potent weapon in the hands of the oppressor is the mind of the oppressed.' If we go along with the oppressor, if we consent to being oppressed, then we will never be free. Isn't it time we stopped participating in our own enslavement? Isn't it time we reclaimed our freedom? Isn't it time?"

Nuala paused. She felt she had been going on and on, randomly. But no one was bored. The women had pushed forward by inches; the ones in front were pressed against the table, their heads tilted back as far as possible to see her. She could have touched them just by reaching out. A few of them were staring at her with a fervent look—adulation, almost—that made her uncomfortable. But there were many faces in the crowd that were frightened, too. All this talk of demanding freedom was great in the abstract, but . . .

"All this talk of demanding freedom is great in the abstract, isn't it?" Nuala went on. "But in real life, you may have a husband who's bigger than you are who's been beating you for years, and the *gardaí*—well, they do carry guns, don't they? I know you want to be free; who doesn't? But you want peace, too, right? Well, unfortunately, until freedom is gained—for us all—then it will be necessary to choose between a 'peaceful' enslavement and a frightening and dangerous fight for freedom. We're not the first people to be forced to make that choice, and we won't be the last. An American rebel of the eighteenth century, Patrick Henry, understood that when he said, 'Is life so dear, or peace so sweet, as to be purchased at the price of chains and slavery?' How long will you go on choosing slavery because it's 'safer'? I know that a known evil is easier than facing the unknown of revolution—but isn't the risk worth it? Isn't it necessary? Remember, it's not just yourself and your own daughters you're choosing for, it's for every woman in Ireland. We all have to stand together, because none of us can be free until we are all free."

The nods were spreading across the room. Nuala was startled to see tears in the eyes of some women. She smiled at one of them, a woman in her seventies, it appeared. The woman didn't bother to wipe away the tear that slid down her cheek.

"I know you're afraid," Nuala said to her, but she was speaking to every woman in the room. "I am, too. I don't want to be killed, and I don't want to go to prison. But I want to be free. I want to be able to teach Irish history in an Irish university without censorship, without fear. And if I ever have a daughter, I want her to be free to live her life in peace and safety, free from the fear of rape, the fear of the *gardaí*'s knock at the door. And if I have a son, I want him to be free, too. Free of the Church's brainwashing him into being a tyrant in his own home, and having sole responsibility for his family. I know some of you have fathers, husbands, or sons who aren't happy with the present system; they're good men. Like my own father. Well then, use your influence with them, their love for you to get them to join us in this fight. Because don't we all want to be free? I want to be free, so I have made the only choice I can: I choose to fight. Because I know that I *cannot* be enslaved if I consider death less hateful than bondage."

The white-haired woman was still crying, but she smiled at Nuala, nodding. And so were other women, even the ones who still looked frightened.

"When Rita Boyle was attacked last week," Nuala went on, "I didn't have time to stop and consider the political ramifications of my interference in the matter. A man—an armed man— was assaulting an unarmed woman. So I shot him. It was all over in an instant, but I'll be honest with you: It felt good." She smiled, and they smiled with her. "It felt good—no, actually it felt *great* to be saying by pulling that trigger, 'No more. I will not allow you to harm this woman. I don't give a damn who or what you are. You are just a man, and I do not fear or respect you. No more. From now on, no matter the consequences to myself, I choose the fight. I will be free.' "

"Yes. Yes!" It was not a shout, but the word rippled through the room, repeated by hundreds of women; it echoed and hung in the air.

Nuala smiled again. "I read an account once of a woman named Diana Norman who, in the late twentieth century, was speaking at a feminist conference—yes, they actually had those in Ireland back then—about the role of Constance Markievicz in the 1916 Uprising. Countess Markievicz—she was called that, if you remember, because she married a Polish count, but she was quite Irish herself—was one of the leaders of the Uprising. One of the *leaders*, mind you, and herself a woman! She carried a gun and she commanded a squad of soldiers, *men* who obeyed her orders. Imagine! Anyway, Diana Norman said of this, 'Anyone with a gun is frightening, but for men a woman with her finger 'round the trigger of a gun has a terrifying Freudian significance.' " Nuala smiled again. "Do you see? They're afraid of us! Men are afraid of us. Why do you suppose they try so hard to keep us enslaved? Because *they* realize our power, even if we don't. They—"

The front door suddenly burst open, hitting a few of the women nearby, and Heather rushed in as far as she could.

"*Gardaí!* Two vans headed this way!"

Someone cried out and the crowd immediately began to churn, but Nuala yelled and got their attention.

"Stop! Listen!"

They turned back, terror on their faces.

"Let Heather through, quickly!"

In moments a narrow path was cleared, women bumping back into each other. Heather hurried forward. Nuala continued.

"If they don't see me, then you're just here for a Ladies Auxiliary meeting; that's not illegal. So remain calm. Remember, they are just men. They have no real authority—"

"Nuala, come on!" Heather grabbed her hand and pulled her off the table. Bébhinn immediately took her place.

"Clear a path to the back door for them," she called out, "and block the front door, but leave it open. We are doing nothing secret here. This is the weekly meeting of the Ladies Auxiliary of the St. Columbanus Society. Why don't we conclude this meeting by singing a hymn?"

Nuala and Heather eased their way through the crowd, who were moving aside for them, jostling each other to make room. They were all frightened, but many of them smiled.

"Good luck, Nuala!"

"We won't let the bastards through!"

"We'll choose the fight!"

The voices came from all sides. As Nuala and Heather ran out into the alley, three hundred voices joined in on "Onward Christian Soldiers." The singing was loud, defiant, frightened, and joyous all at once.

"Igraine!" Heather shouted as she and Nuala headed for Fiona and the truck. Igraine heard somehow over the singing, and raced after them.

Fiona had seen them, and the engine was already running. Nuala and Heather piled in. A few tense moments later, Igraine reached the truck. Nuala and Heather grabbed her and pulled her in. She almost fell out again as Fiona took off, but then they got the door closed. Heather climbed into the back, watching behind them.

A squad car turned down the opposite end of the alley. Nuala just caught a glimpse of it as Fiona careened around the corner and sped off, then rounded another corner, scattering pedestrians from a crosswalk.

The squad car appeared again, a half block behind. Fiona floored the truck's accelerator, jumped the truck onto the sidewalk to avoid traffic, and screeched around the nearest corner, then the next and the next. By the time they roared through the open doors of the half-empty warehouse, they could still hear the siren, but it was several blocks back.

After piling out of the truck, not saying a word, Fiona and Nuala ran for the waiting van, while Igraine and Heather raced back to the warehouse doors and hit the switches that would close them, then headed for the van. One of the warehouse doors stopped, half open. Cursing in Irish, Igraine turned back, then Heather ran after her. Together they grabbed the door and pulled. At first it wouldn't budge. The siren was getting closer. Finally the door jerked, came unstuck, and began to move. Igraine and Heather hurried it along, pushing as hard as they could.

"Come on!" Fiona yelled. The siren was almost on them.

Heather and Igraine ran for the van again. The squad car sped past the almost-closed door behind them, its siren screaming, and kept going.

Fiona took off before Igraine and Heather were seated, knocking them into each other. Nuala pulled the van door closed behind them.

At the other end of the block-long warehouse, Fiona slowed and eased the van nonchalantly out onto the street. The other three women huddled in the back, keeping their heads down. The squad car was nowhere to be seen; its siren was growing fainter by the moment.

Keeping carefully to the speed limit, Fiona followed the planned escape route. They beat the new roadblocks by listening to the *gardaí* on Heather's stolen radio and made it safely out of Wexford. They were five miles out of town and on their way north to Wicklow before Nuala took a deep breath.

Early the next morning, in the safe house Fiona had found for them in Wicklow, they were still trying to relax from the adrenaline rush of their escape. None of them had been able to sleep, so they sat, drinking tea. Neither Fiona nor Igraine had so far castigated Nuala about their near capture; neither had said "I told you it was too dangerous. Don't ever do something that crazy again." They didn't say it, but Nuala knew they must be thinking it.

Still shaken, the older three were in no mood to talk. Heather, on the other hand, was exhilarated. She tried, once or twice, to say how exciting the escape had been, but the only responses were dirty looks, so she gave up. She flitted around the room for a while, too keyed up to sit, but finally—to the other women's relief—she began to wind down. At last she sat in front of the *teilifís* and turned it on.

After twenty minutes of inane chatter, the most popular morning show in Ireland was interrupted. The screen filled with static, then the familiar logo of a wren perched on a vidcamera appeared.

"The Guerrillas!" Heather said, and the others hurried over.

"This is Guerrilla TV, the voice of a free Ireland, with news from Wexford."

The logo disappeared, replaced with a tape of two *garda* vans disgorging officers in battle gear in front of the St. Columbanus church. The camera followed the officers as they trotted toward the basement steps. The strains of "Onward Christian Soldiers" nearly drowned out the barked commands of the *garda* in charge.

The RTE cameraman was behind the first three *gardaí*, so he got a mostly clear shot of the room packed with women. The men tried to force their way into the room, but there seemed to be nowhere for the women to move to get out of their way. One *garda* raised the butt of his rifle to threaten the woman blocking his way, but she just gazed back at him impassively as she continued to sing. Then the *garda* saw that the camera was on him and hurriedly lowered his rifle.

The women went on singing, ignoring the police completely, not moving an inch in spite of commands to do so. There were just too many women in the room; the *gardaí*'s passage was completely blocked. After a few frustrated moments a male voice shouted, "Around back! Someone's escaping!"

The camera followed the *gardaí* as they backed out of the crowded, music-filled room and began to run around the building. But when they got there, it was all over. The alley was deserted. A *garda* radio began to squawk.

"In pursuit of a black lorry, license 475 Xavier Francis 3. Occupants unknown, but driving at high speed, heading north on—now heading west on O'Connell ... couldn't be the women we're looking for—women don't drive like that. Perhaps they're IRA after all ... now heading north on Linnet. Continuing pursuit."

The camera swerved to a *garda* who had walked up to the officer in command.

"Shall we take them in, sir?"

"Who?"

"The women inside."

"For what, singing off-key? Christ, we don't have any proof—" The commanding officer noticed the camera. "Shut that fucking thing off, there's no story here!"

The *teilifís* went black and then a man in a balaclava appeared in front of a bedsheet backdrop.

"That was the uncensored scene last night in Wexford. The *gardaí* had received a tip from a Church source that something unusual was going on at St. Columbanus, a crowd of women was gathering. As assembling in unauthorized large groups without the presence of clergy—or politicians—is considered subversive and suspicious in this country, a single squad car was to be sent in to catch the women at whatever they were doing. However, rumors reached the *gardaí* that Nuala Dennehy, who has appeared on our broadcasts and has inspired a sleeping nation to awaken, was to be present at this meeting, so the troops were increased. Unsubstantiated rumors say that she did in fact appear before this crowd of women to urge them to choose the fight for freedom. As I said, the rumors are unsubstantiated; the women who were questioned at the scene denied that she had been there, and in many cases they went so far as to scold the *gardaí* for so rudely interrupting their meeting of the Ladies Auxiliary of the St. Columbanus Society. When asked if they were *all* members of the Columbanus Auxiliary, one woman is reported to have said, 'We are now. And it's about time, isn't it?' When asked what she meant by that, the woman merely smiled and walked away. As there is no proof that Nuala Dennehy, who is presently at the top of the *gardaí*'s Most Wanted list, was present last night, the *gardaí* can take no further action. Whatever the women were actually up to in that Church basement, they cannot be charged with anything.

"In a perhaps related story, more unsubstantiated rumors have it that a Wexford *garda* was shot and stunned last week while attempting to assault an innocent woman. The *gardaí* deny this, of course, but the rumors say that the would-be rapist was stopped by none other than our ubiquitous Nuala Dennehy and an accomplice. The identity of the woman they rescued is unknown. Whether this rescue is related to the women's meeting in the church or not, this reporter cannot say. But we at Guerrilla

TV hope these rumors are all true. If the women of Wexford have risen to the challenge of fighting for freedom, we say *Fáilte*. Welcome. And what will it take to shame the *men* of Wexford into joining you?

"And to Nuala Dennehy, if you're listening: If only half the exploits attributed to you are true, then good work. Keep up the fight. We could use ten thousand more like you. *Bua agus saoirse*—Victory and freedom.

"And finally, to close this report of Rebel Wexford, we bring you the latest graffiti update. This morning, all over Wexford, a new graffito is appearing. It says simply, 'I choose the fight.' Congratulations, Wexford. And welcome to the struggle. And now on to the international and universal news. At a Unity meeting on Telos IV—"

Heather switched off the *teilifís*, then turned to Nuala, grinning. "Did you hear that? They called me an accomplice! Isn't it wonderful?"

Nuala couldn't resist her enthusiasm; she smiled back. "And is that a worthy goal to aspire to?"

"Absolutely!"

"They scolded the *gardaí*," Fiona said, surprised but happy. "Those women stood up to the *gardaí*!"

"And you know what she meant when that woman said they were now members of the Auxiliary," Igraine said. She studied Nuala for a moment, then nodded. "All right, okay. I guess we did the right thing by going there last night. But next time, let's try not to make it such a close call, eh? You took ten years off my life."

"Fiona got us away," Nuala replied. "We owe our survival to her."

Fiona shrugged modestly. "We make a good team. But hanging about with you is no picnic. Next time we plan even more carefully and be sure to pick a place where we *can't* be cut off."

"So what *are* we doing next?" Heather asked.

All three women looked to Nuala, awaiting her answer.

Chapter 16

"They're all over town!" Igraine slipped inside and took off her trench coat, shaking it before hanging it on the peg on the back of the door. Heather picked up the string bag of groceries.

"Who are?" Nuala asked as she poured her damp friend a steaming cup of tea.

"These." Igraine pulled a folded paper from the pocket of her skirt and thrust it at Nuala. Heather came to look over Nuala's shoulder as she unfolded the stiff white sheet.

REWARD, it said at the top in big black letters, and then in smaller type: "£50,000 reward for information leading to the arrest of Nuala Dennehy, known terrorist and murderer." In the center was a photo, reproduced from the carefully edited tape that had made it look as if Nuala and her "IRA accomplices" had ambushed a squad of *gardaí*, of Nuala in the electronics shop doorway, taken when she had been staring at Máire's dead body. But what was more alarming than this photo—which had been aired extensively on the *teilifís*—were the other, computer-enhanced photos underneath. These showed Nuala with a variety of hairstyles and disguises. One of them could have been a photo taken of her yesterday: The picture was in color, and the hair was short and red. No one, seeing the photo and then seeing her, could have mistaken her for anyone but Nuala Dennehy.

"Wanted posters are redundant, what with my picture on the *teilifís* nearly every night," Nuala said, frowning. "But these other pictures are a nuisance."

"They're all over town?" Heather asked.

Igraine shrugged. "I saw four just between here and the shop. I assume they're all over."

"Why here?" Heather went on. "Do they suspect we're in Wicklow?"

"They could be all over the country, for all we know," Nuala pointed out. "Perhaps Éadaoin will tell Fiona."

"From now on," Igraine said to Nuala, "you'd best not go out at *all* during the day, not even the little bit you do now. It'd be too risky."

Nuala nodded. "Perhaps I should reread Bram Stoker."

"Who?" Heather asked.

"*Dracula,*" Nuala replied, then added in a lousy Transylvanian accent, "I seem to have become a creature of the night."

Heather groaned, but smiled. While Igraine was sipping her tea and warming her fingers around the cup, Nuala idly drew a mustache on the photo that looked most like her.

"I've never wanted to be a man, but maybe I should try it."

"With those hips?" Igraine's tone was innocent, but Nuala glared at her anyway.

"And what is that supposed to mean?"

But Igraine only had time to shrug before the door opened again and Fiona hurried in, shaking rain from her umbrella. She dumped it in the stand near the door and shed her coat and hat.

Nuala held up the flier and Fiona nodded. "I've seen it. And so has everybody else in the country. Éadaoin says they're everywhere. She suggested we make contact with a friend of hers who's with a theater group. She'll have access to false beards and the like."

"So from now on, I'm a man." Nuala shot a warning glance at Igraine, who merely raised her eyebrows.

"Stay in whenever possible, of course," Fiona said, taking a seat across from Nuala. "But then pretend to be a man when we travel." She smiled. "Think you could do that?"

Nuala frowned. "You mean, get drunk, swagger, curse, make rude noises, and order the three of you about? I don't know, it'd be a bit of a stretch. But I could try."

Fiona's smile faded after a moment. "There's more news from Éadaoin. Her sources in Armagh say there's going to be a new Church proclamation soon. Very soon. Concerning the 'low' birth rate."

"Oh, no," Nuala muttered. "What now?"

Fiona sighed in disgust. "A five-hundred-pound incentive will be offered to every father who marries off a daughter." Before the others could do more than grimace, she hurried on. "And five hundred pounds to every man who marries, and another five hundred pounds to the father at the birth of a child."

"What?" Igraine was outraged.

"And where the hell's this money to come from?" Nuala asked.

"Oh, I'm sure we'll see a coincidental rise in taxes," Fiona replied. "You don't think the *Church* would actually shell out any money."

"So even more pressure will be placed on women to marry and have kids." Heather looked sick. "Fathers like mine will insist; there'll be no choice about it. It'll be marriage or the convent, I don't doubt."

"And local parishes will be instructed to increase the number of *céilis* and other social functions expressly for singles," Fiona added. "Young people are to be 'encouraged' to attend these events at least once a week."

"Encouraged!" Heather spat out the word, bitterness twisting her expression. "Yeah, I know what that's like. My father 'encouraged' me to go the youth *céilis* at the chapel every Sunday afternoon, by beating me if I slipped away to meet friends—female friends, anyway—instead. A lot of girls I knew had fathers like that, fathers who wanted to be rid of us as soon as possible. Some of my friends married just to escape their fathers. But that's just trading one misery for another. When is it going to stop?" She turned to Nuala, pleading in her eyes. "You've got to do another tape, denounce this. Girls shouldn't be forced to—"

"I know." Nuala nodded. "And I'm sure I won't be the only one; the Guerrillas might beat me to it. But it would be a good idea to try to get it on the air before the pronouncement comes down. If we beat the Church to the airwaves, they might modify the plan. If we can show it for what it is—just another attempt to turn women into broodmares—it might take the wind out of their sails a bit."

"I've been thinking about the Guerrilla TV," Igraine said. "Your doing tapes is great, but it can't always be yourself, can it? You can't do it all. Other women—Éadaoin would know who—could do tapes on a regular basis, instructional tapes on how to avoid pregnancy, how to do a safe abortion at home, menstrual extraction and the like."

"And self-defense for women," Fiona suggested.

"Aye," Igraine agreed. "A variety of things."

"And a lot more international news," Nuala said. "To show how women live in other countries, or if they're citizens of the Fleet, on the space colonies, or if they're women—I mean, female members—of the alien races. To show that it doesn't have

to be this way; there are alternatives that are working right
now."

"I know Stuart would be interested," Heather said. "If we
could contact him—"

"Right," Nuala said. "If the Church is stepping up their campaign against us, then we've got to do the same back at them.
Fiona, I know the weather is horrible, but would you mind going
back out again, to contact Stuart? And Igraine, contact this
friend of Éadaoin's in the theater." She held up the photo with
the penciled-in mustache. "I'm about to find out how the other
half lives."

The number of people in the gathering crowd in Limerick had
to be more than five hundred, and there had been no recent winning football or hurling matches, so the very existence of this assembly was unusual. There were no priests or other clergy
visibly present to sanction the gathering, and the *gardaí* were
nowhere in sight. Many of the people carried signs, but the signs
were still upside down, unreadable, so the other people already
in the park—the mothers and their children, the few retired
people—had no clue as to what was going on.

The mood of the people who were all headed for the same
spot was tense, nervous, and in some cases—mostly women—
angry. They glanced over their shoulders as they walked toward
the children's stage at the edge of the trees. It was still drizzling
softly as a man around forty in a black raincoat and Donegal
tweed cap climbed up on the stage. He raised his voice, and as
the tense crowd was already silent, he could be heard clearly.

"We are here today to make a public stand against the new
Church policies that would turn husbands against wives, fathers
against daughters. The five-hundred-pound bounty to sell a
daughter to the first man who would agree to marry her—and
thereby collect *his* five hundred pounds—is not, as the Church
claims, to 'promote family life.' It is a blatant method of turning
young women and girls into a commodity, making them worth
a thousand pounds a head—or rather, a womb. The fact that the
government is the one paying these bounties makes the government, once again, a collaborator with the Church in interfering
in our private lives. And to tell a husband that getting his wife
pregnant is the only sure way of curing her dissatisfaction in the
marriage—and promising yet another five-hundred-pound
bounty for each child born—is blatant interference in a *very* private arena. Those of us who truly love our wives and daughters

do not *wish* to sell them or turn them into broodmares, and we refuse to do so!"

Finally the crowd made a noise: A rumble of agreement began, some of it nervous and cautious, with much glancing over shoulders, but most of it loud and angry. At last some of the signs were held up; most at shoulder-level, a few high and defiant. The signs bore slogans like "WOMEN ARE NOT BROODMARES" and "MY DAUGHER IS NOT A SLAVE." The man in the cap continued, his baritone loud enough to reach every corner of the small park.

"As husbands and fathers, we do not need to be told how to treat our wives and daughters. The relationship within a family is a personal, private matter, and we will not be dictated to about this. As the spiritual head of the household, it is our duty to consider the well-being of the family as a unit, and as individuals. We know how to do this: with prayer as our guideline, and faith as our support. For priests to suddenly tell us that these bounties are a gift from God to inspire us is suspicious at best, even for the most devout among us."

The agreement was a bit louder this time; men were finally raising their voices. The women in the crowd, who slightly outnumbered the men, were not as vocal, though they carried more signs.

At the front of the crowd, to the left of the stage, was a short, mustachioed man in a long overlarge coat, a cap, and a scarf wrapped twice around his neck. The November day was cold as well as damp, and he seemed to huddle in the bulky clothes. He was shaking his head at the speaker's words, not in disagreement as much as disappointment. As the man on stage continued to speak of God and a man's responsibilities as head of the household, the short man with the bushy red mustache began unbuttoning his coat. He unwrapped the long scarf and handed it to the young blond woman standing next to him, who was whispering and smiling at him. He shrugged his way out of the voluminous tweed coat, and a red-haired woman next to him took it as she scanned the edges of the park. He doffed his cap, which the blonde also took from him. He ducked his head, and when he looked up again, the mustache had disappeared. Nuala walked up the steps of the stage, her hands in the pockets of the baggy corduroy trousers, and finally stopped behind the man who was still speaking. She tapped him on the shoulder, startling him into silence. He turned in surprise.

"Excuse me," she said. "Mind if I have a word?"

"I—" The man recognized her and stared, astonished. She smiled politely.

"Would you mind? There's a good lad."

He backed up a few steps, still staring. Nuala faced the crowd. "I agree with much of what this gentleman has said." Nuala waved in his direction as he climbed down from the stage. "And I am very pleased to see men here today protesting this latest scheme of the Church to further enslave women. It is the moral duty of every man in Ireland to refuse to go along with the Church in its efforts to put women in 'their place,' as it were. And it is the duty of every citizen to protest totalitarian acts. So I'm glad you've come out today."

The crowd had begun to buzz as soon as Nuala began speaking. Those close enough to recognize her passed along who she was, and within moments, all five hundred of them knew. Eyes widened, and the people in back stood on tiptoe.

"It is only right for men to refuse to go along," Nuala said, "and we're happy to have your support. But men's response is only half the answer, the response to this insult by the Church. The other half—the more important half—is the response of women. After all, we are the targets of this attack."

She looked out over the still-growing crowd and saw the women standing up a bit straighter, holding their signs higher.

"Many of you came here with your husbands or even your fathers, and that's wonderful. If we are united, women along with men, there can be no stopping us. We need unity, for in unity there is strength. Solidarity will bring victory. But I suspect that there are women here today who came without husbands or fathers, women who came alone or with other women. Perhaps some of you even came in defiance of husbands or fathers. And it is yourselves and your presence here that makes me proud to be an Irish woman. For it is you who are learning what it is to say no to a man, to stand up for yourselves, to refuse to be slapped back into your 'place.' It is you who will save Ireland and make her the country she can be."

The women in the crowd were smiling now, and some of them began moving forward, easing between the men in front of them.

"I know that most of you could use the five hundred pounds that you—or rather, your husband—would get for another baby. But is five hundred pounds enough to pay for raising that child? Is five hundred pounds enough to buy food and clothing for eighteen years? Is it enough to pay for the discomfort of pregnancy, the agony of childbirth? Will it make up for the months of lost sleep—especially if you've other wee ones at home? Will it pay for the fear you would feel if that child should take sick or be injured? Is it enough to make up for your grief if that child should die? And what if you should die in childbirth? Will that pittance replace you? Is that what you or a child is worth? Five hundred pounds? And those of you who aren't married and have no wish to be: Is that how much your life is worth? Five hundred pounds in exchange for whatever dreams you'd be forced to give up? Is that all you're worth?"

"No!" someone yelled. It was an angry, female yell, and Nuala smiled. Some of the men began to glance around at the determined women who continued to move forward.

"Well, the Church thinks it is," Nuala went on. "The Church has decided that a woman is worth five hundred pounds. Five hundred pounds to sell one, and a five-hundred-pound reward to the man who buys one, and another five hundred pounds to rent her womb. That is what the Church believes. Do you agree?"

"No!" The answer came from all sides. A few male voices joined in, but they were drowned out by the anger and volume of the women.

"And if your father tries to insist you get married when you don't want to, tries to threaten or bully you into it—are you going to consent, to surrender your life and your dreams?"

"No!"

"And if your husband tries to persuade you to have another child you don't want, if he follows the Church's recommendation and tries to take your temperature every night to see when you're most fertile—are you going to allow it, to let him turn you into a broodmare?"

"No!"

"And if he threatens to force you into it, to rape you in order to get you pregnant—are you going to allow that?"

"No!" It was a roar this time, the fury palpable; the park rang with the sound. Nuala looked down at the women who had surged to the front, and the men who now stood mostly at the back. The men were frowning, nervous and uncomfortable. They had undoubtedly never seen female anger on such a large scale before.

"Then you'd best learn how to fight back, hadn't ye?" Nuala said. The crowd was silent, waiting.

"It may be a bit frightening at first," she went on, "but it can be done. If a man—your husband, say—threatens you, then threaten him right back! He probably won't believe you the first time unless you're angry enough or holding a weapon of some sort: a rolling pin, an iron, even a bottle or a broom. Anything handy that you are absolutely determined to use. Remember: Don't pick it up unless you are fully prepared to use it. You can practice at home, when he's off to work and the kids are at school. I'm sure you've seen the self-defense lessons the Guerrilla TV has begun. Pay attention to them, practice it. Those lessons might save your life one day.

"But even more important than defending yourself by yourself is defending *each other*. I once read of a tribe in Africa who used to do that. No doubt they've been 'civilized' out of common sense by this time. But in the old days, whenever a woman was attacked or harassed by a man—any man—she'd begin to scream, and *every single woman in the village* would drop whatever she was doing and immediately run to her aid. Every woman in the village would join in, and they would surround the woman being attacked, protect her from the man with their own bodies, all the while screaming at him. And since he was only one man, how could he fight every woman in the village? So he was chased off, and the woman was protected. And the women in that village knew they had nothing to fear, because they knew they had the protection of their sisters, their friends, their neighbors. They were safe. Safe in their homes, safe in their village.

"Can't we do that, too? Can't we protect each other? If you suspect a woman is being abused, don't ignore it. Go to her. Ask her, offer her your help and protection. Oh, I know, we're taught to believe that what goes on between a husband and wife is nobody else's business. Well, why the hell not? If he's beating her, raping her—why shouldn't it be your business? And more than just your business, shouldn't it be your *duty* to do something? To help her? I shot a *garda* in Wexford, as you've heard, because he was attacking a woman. It took no great amount of courage; I simply pulled the trigger and stunned him. We—my partner and I—we stopped him. Because it was the right thing to do. To stop a woman from being harmed is the right thing to do, whether you are a woman or a man. To stop the Church from turning women into broodmares is the right thing to do, whether you are a woman or a man. To defy the Church's attempts to subjugate us further is the right thing to do, whether you are a woman or a man. To join together to protect yourselves and each other is the *right thing to do*."

The crowd, men as well as women, caught her rhythm and emphasis and began to chant along with the words "right thing to do."

"To join together to free ourselves, to free our country, is the *right thing to do*. To push the Church out of government completely is the *right thing to do*. To insist that women be granted the same opportunities as men is the *right thing to do*. To limit the number of children to whatever number a *woman* wants is the *right thing to do*. To end censorship and to receive news broadcasts from other countries is the *right thing—*"

Nuala was interrupted by the sight and sound of three squad cars and a *garda* van barreling through the park toward the crowd. She jumped off the stage and ran full out for the trees, Igraine and Heather on her heels. She heard screams and shouts behind her as the crowd scattered.

The vehicles were forced to stop near the stage because of the thickness of the trees beyond it. Nuala heard the whine of plasfire and instinctively dodged. A tree branch exploded to her right.

"On stun!" she heard a man bellow. "We want her alive!"

The three women continued to run, but when she heard running behind her, Nuala glanced back to see how close the *gardaí* were. What she saw made her stumble in surprise.

It was women who were running after her, zigzagging back and forth between her and the *gardaí*, who were trying to get a bead on her. One *garda* fired, and a woman running in front of him went down. Two other women immediately grabbed her and pulled her out of the way. Another woman, then three more, threw their signs at the approaching *gardaí*, tripping two of them.

"Come on!" Heather yelled, pulling her along. Nuala turned away from the women who were protecting her and ran.

At the edge of the park a car roared up onto the grass toward them and swerved to a stop. They scrambled into the backseat, and Fiona took off. A blast of plasfire hit the rear window, but Fiona never slowed.

A mile away they dumped the car for the *gardaí* to find and escaped in the waiting van.

"I cannot stress enough that Nuala Dennehy is a threat to the security of every community in Ireland." Lieutenant Commander Hugh Cassidy of the *Garda* Public Relations Office frowned into the camera. Nuala could feel his animosity as if he were in the Galway safe house with her.

"Four women are in hospital this evening because they were foolish enough to join in an illegal assembly and they stayed to listen to this terrorist, Nuala Dennehy, when she suddenly appeared and unleashed her usual treacherous tirade of treason."

"Alliteration," Nuala murmured. "Why, Hugh."

"Fortunately, these women will recover from being accidentally stunned by the officers who were merely—"

The screen went blank, then the familiar logo appeared. The four women applauded the Guerrilla introduction.

A man in a balaclava whom Nuala thought looked to be at least the size of Kevin, the Guerrilla she had met at her first taping, appeared before the usual bedsheet backdrop. His voice confirmed it; it was Kevin.

"That was Lieutenant Commander Hugh Cassidy, mouthpiece and fatuous *garda* idiot, whom I so rudely interrupted," Kevin said, to the appreciation of the four women. "As usual, Hugh was lying. Only two women, not four, were shot and stunned by the *gardaí* in Limerick yesterday, and neither was taken to hospital. They are both home and quite well by now. The people of Limerick are to be commended for daring to meet together in public to protest recent Church and government policies. The right of free speech cannot be granted; it must be seized. Congratulations, Limerick, for doing so.

"Now, to combat censorship and to spread truth, here is the international and universal news." Kevin picked up a stack of typewritten pages. "The citizens of the Chinese colony on Chiang Xiao have finally—officially—declared independence from Beijing. You will recall that Beijing stopped all support of the colony three years ago when they tried to relocate the colonists to a planet farther from Ghizhbassan space, complaining about the 'alien influence' on the Chinese colonists, and the subsequent refusal of the colonists to leave their adopted world or to break off relations with the Ghizhbassans, a people devoted to free expression. Cutting the colonists off only hardened their resolve, and now they have voted unanimously to sever all political ties with Beijing. Under interstellar law, Beijing has lost all rights to oppose Chiang Xiao's secession because they willfully abandoned the colony. Chiang Xiao has formally adopted a new Constitution that calls for, among other things, that very freedom of expression they had been denied as Chinese citizens. They have applied for Fleet membership, with Ghizhbassan sponsorship . . . Closer to home, an historic first and a blow for freedom: A compilation of some of our recent broadcasts has been smuggled out successfully to Wales, from where it was transmitted via EuroNet to all of Europe. At a rally of the Children of the Irish Diaspora in London, support for our struggle was pledged in the form of twelve thousand pounds. A special collection was taken by Irish-English feminists in the name of Nuala Dennehy. This special collection of fifteen hundred pounds is to be spent on contraceptives, which will be smuggled into Ireland. We have a clip of the rally."

Trafalgar Square appeared on the screen. A crowd of several thousand people swarmed over and around the famous lions. Huge banners were held or hung everywhere: IRELAND WILL BE FREE, BUA AGUS SAOIRSE, IRISH WOMEN ARE NOT BROODMARES, ERIN GO BRAGH, VICTORY IN IRELAND, FREE THE SEPTEMBER DOZEN, and, to Nuala's astonishment, NUALA DENNEHY FOR TAOISEACH.

A woman with a British accent stood in the center of the crowd and spoke into a microphone. "The brutal murder of Máire Ní Flaherty will not be forgotten. Nor will the courage of Nuala Dennehy."

The crowd roared and applauded. Nuala stared, mouth open, at the screen. Her three friends were just as stunned.

"In this day," the British woman continued, "when total equality for women is enshrined in the Fleet Charter and is standard operating procedure on all Fleet space colonies, when the Tlates—even *aliens*—treat their female citizens with equality and respect, it is painful to realize that there are far too many places here on Earth where freedom for women is but a dream and a bitter struggle. In a country like Ireland, so beloved by the descendants of those who left her generations ago, that struggle has become a war, a war in which there are many unnamed casualties. But we do know the names of some of those casualties. Names like Máire Ní Flaherty, shot in the back by a murderous policeman. And Tríona Rafferty, who disappeared and is still missing. And the rest of the September Dozen. No doubt the Irish authorities would prefer the world to forget these women, the ones they've murdered and the ones they have imprisoned without trial. But one Irish woman had the courage to speak out, to tell her country about these women. And because Nuala Dennehy told Ireland, she has now told the world. And the world will not forget. The world will never forget. To Nuala Dennehy we say: Remain strong, sister, we are with you in the struggle. And to the authorities in Ireland we say: You murdered

Máire Ní Flaherty, and for that you will pay. Free the September Dozen *now*, or the price you will pay for their lives will be more than you can bear. Free the September Dozen *now!*"

The crowd roared again, waving their signs and their banners. Then they began to chant: "Free the September Dozen! Free the September Dozen!"

After a moment, the London scene disappeared, and Kevin returned to read some news of the latest peace talks in Somalia and progress on building the new Fleet colony on Alpha VI. Nuala scarcely heard him, nor did her three friends. They were still stunned.

"All of Europe?" Igraine murmured.

"You're famous, Nuala!" Heather said.

"They're listening," Fiona said. "The world—or at least all of Europe—they're listening to us."

"Do you think it'll do any good?" Heather asked.

"Can't hurt," Fiona replied, shrugging.

"Can't it?" Nuala wasn't so sure. "Publicity is good, of course; we need as much as we can get, to embarrass the government. But it might provoke them, too. And who will they take it out on?"

Two days later, they got the answer. The body of Tríona Rafferty was discovered in a ditch in Gortahork.

Chapter 17

"IF MY DAUGHTER had not become involved with terrorists, she'd be alive today."

The father of Tríona Rafferty, Peadar Sloane, had been interviewed by the RTE, the state *teilifís* network, the day of Tríona's funeral, and the tape—especially this portion of it—had been aired countless times in the two days since.

"There is no doubt in my mind that it was the IRA who took her," Mr. Sloane continued, his eyes red and his voice thick with grief and anger. "She sympathized too much with those who did nothing but complain about the government. I told her—and I told her husband—that it wasn't her place to worry about politics. Her duty was to her husband and her children—her family. But she wouldn't listen to me. She thought she was too old to listen to her father. And her husband—that worthless republican—he couldn't control her, didn't even try." He had to stop to blow his nose before continuing. "Tríona never listened to me or to the priests, that was her trouble. She wouldn't listen to those who knew better. I'm not surprised she got mixed up with the IRA. But she was a good girl at heart, for all that. I don't doubt she finally came to her senses and tried to get out. That's why they killed her, to protect themselves. But did they have to beat her like that?" He choked up, and his last few words were difficult to understand. "Why did they have to make her suffer so? My little girl."

It was always those last words that made Nuala cringe. She had never met Tríona Rafferty. Never would now. And yet she felt responsible for the woman's death. If Tríona hadn't helped her escape Derry, if someone hadn't talked under torture, if . . . If.

Tríona Rafferty was dead, beaten to death by the *gardaí*.

"Turn that fucking thing down!" Igraine snapped, her head in her hands. Heather complied, leaving the *teilifís* on, waiting for the Guerrillas to appear with the truth. They had been curiously silent since the discovery of the body.

Nuala glanced at Fiona, who stood at the window, her back to them. She had been silent, too. She had known Tríona, known her well. But she said nothing. She seemed incapable of putting her grief and her anger into words. So she stood apart from her friends, her arms crossed tightly, hunched over as if her stomach pained her. And she said nothing.

Nuala glanced at the screen. There was Hugh Cassidy again, *garda* mouthpiece. He had made a tape, too, after the funeral. Nuala knew nearly every word of it by heart now, especially the lies he had made sound so plausible—at least they would to those who believed his point of view, people like Tríona Rafferty's father. It was Hugh Cassidy's—and therefore the government's—contention that Tríona and the other eleven "gullible" women, the so-called September Dozen, had been led astray by the IRA, most particularly by the terrorists' "spokesman," Nuala Dennehy. As Hugh's lips formed her name, Nuala saw, once again, the famous photo of herself appear on the left side of the screen. She was familiar enough with his text by now to read his lips as he called her a "propagandist for the forces of evil." He was about to go into the part where he called on all decent citizens who might have seen her to 'phone the *gardaí* when the screen went blank and the long-awaited logo appeared.

"It's them!" Heather lunged for the volume control.

"—voice of a free Ireland."

Though the black balaclava hid the man's features, his mood was easy to read. His voice matched it: grim, mournful, angry.

"As the entire country—and thanks to us, all of Europe—knows, Tríona Rafferty, one of the September Dozen, is dead. She was brutally murdered, and her body was callously dumped in a muddy ditch outside her hometown, Gortahork, Donegal. As you have no doubt heard, the government—and her grief-stricken father, to whom our heartfelt sympathy is extended—would have you believe that it was the IRA who kidnapped and murdered Mrs. Rafferty. We have made contact with the IRA—with whom, I shall repeat, we are *not* affiliated—and they have informed us that they know nothing of Tríona Rafferty. She was never recruited by them, she was never a Volunteer, they did not kidnap her—none of their Volunteers has ever met her—and they most certainly did not kill her. They offer their condolences to her husband and children. I repeat, the IRA claim they have never had any connection to, or involvement with, Tríona Rafferty.

"We at Guerrilla TV have spent the last few days trying to find out just what group—if any—Tríona Rafferty was allied with."

Nuala looked behind her. Fiona had turned away from the window; she was listening intently.

"But we found no group," the Guerrilla continued. "We can only conclude that Tríona Rafferty and the other eleven women whom Nuala Dennehy has named the September Dozen are not members of any organization, no matter what the government claims. It is our belief that these women are merely citizens who recognize what is wrong with this country and who dared to try, individually, to do something about it. The fact that twelve women were arrested or disappeared *seems* to indicate a network of some sort, but it appears to us that this was not an *organized* network, but merely twelve women who happened to know each other."

Fiona sighed. Nuala shared her relief. Since Fiona's Ulster group had been small and not connected to Brigid and Éadaoin's at all, they were still safe. It was a shame that Éadaoin's people couldn't join with the Guerrillas and reveal the existence of a real network—more than just a few people with illegal vidcameras and the black market for foreign news—but it was safer if the Guerrillas had no real confirmation of their existence.

"Their only affiliation," the Guerrilla went on, "was a common concern for their country and for free speech, which is why some of them aided Nuala Dennehy in her escape from Derry. This concern cost them their freedom and, in Tríona Rafferty's case, her life. These women—the eleven who are still alive—are prisoners of conscience in the truest sense. They are being held against their will, in violation of all moral laws, because they believe in freedom."

He paused and looked at someone off-camera who must have signaled him, because he nodded. "We have received confirmation of the information we have been seeking. We at Guerrilla TV have learned that all eleven of these women, the September Dozen, are being held in Maghaberry Prison."

Fiona came nearer the *teilifís*, staring at the calm man in the balaclava. Her expression was unreadable, but she looked very pale.

"And we have learned," the Guerrilla went on, his voice never wavering, but now taking on a hard edge, "that it was Maghaberry Prison where Tríona Rafferty was held, and from where her body was taken and transported all the way back to Gortahork to be dumped in a ditch. We have proof that Tríona Rafferty was in fact in the clutches of the government, all the while they were blaming the IRA for her disappearance."

"Proof?" Igraine whispered, incredulous. "They have someone on the inside?"

The Guerrilla was handed something from off-camera. He glanced at the paper, and Nuala could see him go rigid with anger. Stepping toward the camera, he held up a photo.

Heather gasped and put her head down, squeezing her eyes shut.

The woman's face was battered nearly beyond recognition; her eyes were swollen and purple, her lips split and bloody; her nose had been broken. Her blouse was torn, revealing angry purple bruises on her shoulders and down both arms. She was sprawled on the ground, her bloody legs apart, her skirt twisted around her waist. She had no underwear, no shoes, no socks. She was dead, her head resting almost on the toe of a black boot. A boot that looked like standard *garda* issue.

Igraine glanced at Fiona, grimacing in pain and anger. "Is it herself?"

Fiona nodded once, tears spilling down her cheeks. She was clutching her stomach with her crossed arms. Nuala wanted to do something to help her, but what could she do? She gave Fiona her privacy by looking away.

"This," the Guerrilla said, sounding nauseated and enraged at the same time, "is the body of Tríona Rafferty. And this was Tríona Rafferty three weeks ago." He took another photograph from someone off-camera and held it up next to that of Tríona's corpse. The second photo showed Tríona, in the same torn clothes, being "escorted" down from a *garda* van by two male *gardaí*, one on each side of her, gripping her already bruised arms. Her face was not as badly beaten; her lower lip was swollen and one eye was blackened, but it wasn't the injuries that sickened the women watching—it was her expression. Tríona was terrified.

"Oh, god." Heather moaned. "That poor—"

"Tríona Rafferty," the Guerrilla continued, fury making his voice finally waver a bit, "was not kidnapped by the IRA. She was in *garda* custody the entire time, as you can see. And it was the *gardaí* who beat this woman to death."

He didn't lower the photos; if anything, he held them a bit closer to the camera.

"The authorities will no doubt attempt to explain this by claiming that these photos are fakes, that we somehow added the *gardaí* in by some clever process. The only people who will believe that will be those who refuse to face the truth. These photos are genuine. We at Guerrilla TV have always told you the truth. Our very existence serves one purpose only: to tell the truth that the authorities don't want you to know. These photos are real. Look closely at the truth. *This* is what the government does to those who dare to disagree with it."

He held the photos silently for several long moments. Nuala was unable to look away. In the midst of her guilt and grief over what had happened to Tríona Rafferty, one other thought intruded: When her turn came, she hoped she would be able to hide her fear from them.

Finally he lowered the photos.

"There are eleven other women who are in immediate danger of this same fate. We know that they are in Maghaberry Prison, as Tríona Rafferty was. The authorities may try to deny their presence or even to move them, after this broadcast, but that won't change what we know. We know they are in the hands of the prison officials, of the *gardaí*, and we demand their release.

You may help in this, all of you who are watching. The day after tomorrow at noon, come to Maghaberry. Come from all over Ireland. Gather outside the prison gates and demand the release of the September Dozen. There are only eleven of them now, so come day after tomorrow, before there are only ten or nine. Come Saturday at noon. The authorities will be expecting you, and the *gardaí* will be out in force. Come anyway. You will have no freedom until you demand freedom. The world will be watching—we have already sent these photographs to our contacts in Wales, so the true fate of Tríona Rafferty is a secret no longer. Come day after tomorrow and defy the government. Come and demand freedom. For them and for yourselves. The lives of eleven women depend on you. Come for them. Come for yourselves. Saturday at noon. Maghaberry Prison."

The Guerrilla logo appeared; then regular programming returned. Heather turned down the volume, then turned to Nuala. "We're going, aren't we? No matter how dangerous?"

Nuala caught Fiona's eye and just nodded.

The photos of Tríona had succeeded: The crowd outside Maghaberry on Saturday numbered in the thousands, despite the steady drizzle. As Nuala, in her male disguise, wandered nearer the center of the milling people, she was both amazed and exhilarated. This was the largest unauthorized political gathering in recent years, perhaps the largest in a generation, and the people present realized it. They were nervous, excited, on edge, and frightened. At least half of them were wearing balaclavas or had wrapped scarves around their faces. They had reason to be frightened: Guards lined the inside of the charged fence, rifles in hand. *Garda* vans sat at the back of the crowd, outside the fenced compound, and *gardaí* in battle gear swarmed around them, watching and waiting. Theoretically, every person here could be arrested for participating in an unauthorized rally. And though the *gardaí*'s rifles were supposed to be set on stun when their lives were not in danger, who knew if they really were? All things considered, outside the gates of Maghaberry was a dangerous place to be.

Her three friends stuck to Nuala's side, trying to keep watch in all directions at once. Though it was doubtful she would be recognized behind the bushy red mustache and the cap pulled low over her eyes, there was always the possibility. So they intended to stay in the center of the crowd, as far away as possible from either guards or *gardaí*.

If there were to be speakers, they must have had the same plan: There was no stage of any kind either near the fence or at the rear of the crowd. But Nuala saw two men carrying plastifoam crates, which, upended, could serve as a quickly assembled platform. With a crowd this size, it would take the *gardaí* awhile to reach any speaker, by which time the person could have disappeared into the jumble of people.

A chant began off to Nuala's right, and quickly spread: "Free the September Dozen!" The four women joined in, scanning the line of guards and darting a glance back at the *gardaí* to gauge their reaction. Not one of the armed men moved, except the occasional shifting from one foot to the other. They had probably been ordered not to take action until—until what?

The chant grew louder when the crowd saw that the armed men would do nothing to stop them. A note of defiance and anger was added, and signs started to bob rhythmically in the air. A disembodied male voice shouted above the din: "Louder! So they can hear us inside! Let them know we're here for them!" The crowd obliged, the shouted chant reverberating in the air under the low clouds. Nuala wondered if Ailís O'Hara and the other ten women were still alive, were still there, or if they had been spirited away in the night.

A man eased his way in front of Nuala, his sign to the side of his face. When he passed her, she saw that the sign was intentionally obscuring what was in his other hand: a tiny vidcamera, scanning the crowd. Was he RTE, infiltrating the protestors to take their pictures so they could be arrested later? She considered tripping him and accidentally smashing his camera. But then she saw the red-bearded giant of a man behind him: Kevin of the Guerrilla TV. He moved forward and lowered a sign to the shorter man's eye level, blocking the sight of the camera from the other side. It would limit the camera's maneuverability, but it was better than nothing. She smiled, admiring their audacity. They obviously wanted to get their own tape this time, not steal it from the RTE.

After about ten minutes of impassioned chanting, during which the *gardaí* continued to observe, expressionless, Nuala watched the two men with the three crates pile them on the ground: two stacked, and one next to them to serve as a step. One of the two men, a tall, thin blond with a downy beard, slipped a balaclava over his head before climbing up on his platform.

"Listen!" It took a moment or two before the crowd noticed

him and the chant died out. Nuala shot a glance at both guards and *gardaí*. Still no reaction from them, but they were no longer chatting with each other: They, too, listened as the speaker began.

"You all saw the Guerrilla TV last night," he said, turning sideways so his back was to neither group of armed men. "Tríona Rafferty was beaten—tortured—to death, and apparently by men the likes of whom are attempting to intimidate us with their armed presence here today. It was not the IRA, or so say the Guerrillas, but perhaps the *gardaí* themselves! Men whose salaries we pay with our taxes! A woman has been murdered. A woman whose only crime was that she helped someone else slip through the fingers of the government. She committed no violence. She was not a criminal, she was only a woman. A wife and mother, not a warrior. It is one thing for the *gardaí* to shoot or arrest terrorists, but it is quite another when their weapons or their fists are turned against innocent citizens—helpless women. And there are eleven other helpless women locked away, perhaps inside this hateful place. Eleven women who are no more criminals than Tríona Rafferty was. You heard the Guerrillas say that there is no network, no conspiracy to overthrow the government. If that is true, then these eleven women are innocent! They are someone's wife or daughter or sister or mother. They are not warriors, they are merely women. And if the authorities do in fact have them, we have the right to know that. We demand to know, one way or the other, for the authorities have no right to imprison them! They are innocent!"

Finally the crowd burst into applause and shouts of encouragement. Nuala eyed the *gardaí*, but still there was no response. What were they waiting for? The man in the balaclava began again.

"Most of us are law-abiding citizens who believe that if improvements are needed in government, they must come from within the system. We do not approve of radical revolutionaries who would topple generations of work into the dust."

"What?" Igraine muttered in surprise as scattered applause agreed with the speaker.

"We believe that good, honest men have been and will be elected to bring about a better standard of living for us all, that subversive activities are not necessary to improve an already democratic system."

The crowd began to mutter at this; some catcalls and boos answered him.

"Who the hell is this jerk?" Fiona was incredulous. She turned to Nuala. "Who—"

In reply, Nuala nodded in the direction of the *gardaí*, who were leaning against their vans, relaxed and once again chatting with each other.

"Don't seem too interested, do they? Or surprised."

"Maybe he's not just an idiot." Fiona looked back at the speaker. "You think he's a plant?"

"But we must draw the line," the speaker continued, "when innocent women, whose only crime is in listening to the wrong people, are brutally beaten. If the women erred in some way, and if they *are* being held in this prison, then allow them the chance to make up for their mistakes. Restore them to their families now! We will not tolerate any more beatings or torture of any innocent women! If you have the September Dozen, then release them now!"

He stepped down to much applause and renewed chanting of "Free the September Dozen!"

"He hedges his bets," Igraine said, frowning. "He keeps saying 'if' they're being held by the authorities, then he praises the 'democratic' system. He's either crazy, blind, or—"

"Look!" someone called. "The gates!"

The gates of Maghaberry were opening, but the line of armed guards didn't move. Instead, a man in an expensive black trench coat and hat marched to the edge of the crowd, followed closely by two guards. He took a microphone from his pocket and addressed the assembly in confident, ringing tones.

"I am Superintendent Sweeney. The death of Mrs. Tríona Rafferty is a tragedy, one which all of Ireland regrets deeply, but I can assure you in all confidence that the *gardaí* were not responsible."

The crowd began to rumble ominously, but he ignored them and continued on, unperturbed. "The photographs you saw on the illegal, so-called Guerrilla TV broadcast were fakes. The experts on such matters have studied them thoroughly, and I can confidently assure you—"

"Liar!" a deep voice bellowed, and hundreds of people echoed the word. Nuala saw that the *gardaí* were alert now, gripping their rifles in readiness.

"Furthermore," Sweeney went on, "the *gardaí* have been searching all over Ireland for the missing eleven women—"

"Why don't you look behind you?" a woman called. "In those cells?"

A roar of agreement went up, and Nuala saw some of the *gardaí* move forward, only to be ordered back with a wave from another *garda*, the commanding officer, apparently.

"The missing women are *not* in police custody," Sweeney continued, raising his voice, as he was almost drowned out by the boos and catcalls, even with the microphone. "But we have found the possible location of some of the kidnapped women. We are not certain yet, but the Special Branch is moving in even as I am speaking to you. We have every hope that some of the women will be free shortly."

The crowd buzzed in confusion; this development had shaken their angry confidence.

"He's lying!" Fiona yelled, startling Nuala. "It's a smoke-screen to cover their tracks. If they release a few of the women, they hope to convince and pacify us. But it's a lie! They're holding all eleven women in *there!*" She jabbed a finger toward the prison. "It's the government who has them and only the government can release them, not some mythical kidnappers!"

Before much of the crowd could agree, the first speaker had reclaimed his platform. "Wait a moment! Wait!" The crowd shifted their confused attention to him. "If the photos were faked, then show us the proof!"

"Yeah!" and "Proof!" and "Show us!" rang out on the moist air. Sweeney raised his hand to silence them.

"Tonight at six o'clock on RTE1, our experts will show you how it was done. The evidence is quite conclusive, as you will see. I can understand how you were led to believe what you saw, but I'm afraid that you have been manipulated and used by those terrorists for their own ends. Perhaps—once you see the proof—you will think twice before believing Nuala Dennehy again."

"Liar!" someone yelled, but the agreement was scattered and weak; he had managed to insinuate doubt in their minds.

"Well, I'm willing to wait until I've seen the proof," the man on the crates called out. "It's only fair—"

"Fair?" Nuala deepened her voice as best she could, but she knew she still didn't sound like the man she appeared to be. She moved through the crowd until she was standing directly in front of the crates, looking up at the man in the balaclava. "Is what the *gardaí* did to Tríona Rafferty fair? Was the *gardaí* dragging Ailís O'Hara away from her terrorized, screaming children after they destroyed her house and all her possessions *fair?*"

"We don't know for sure—" he began, but Nuala cut him off.

"The hell we don't! I've talked to an eyewitness, a neighbor of Ailís O'Hara!"

"The kidnappers could have been posing as—"

"There are no kidnappers!" Nuala yelled at him, furious but controlled. "And *you* are a bloody *garda* plant. That balaclava is just for show! The entire time you were speaking, the *gardaí* were leaning against their vans, bored stiff! They weren't about to arrest you or even try to. Because you're on their payroll!"

The crowd began to murmur at that, looking from the suddenly uncomfortable man in the balaclava to the *gardaí*, who were darting glances at their commanding officer, obviously waiting for his signal.

"That's not true, I—"

"It is true, and you know it, you bloody quisling! All your talk of 'good, honest' politicians and our wonderful 'democratic' system! Who the bloody hell do you think you're fooling?"

Fiona began to ease toward the edge of the crowd. Igraine and Heather moved closer to Nuala as she stepped up on the crate that served as a step, shoved the man in the balaclava off his perch, and took his place. He nearly landed on two men, who grabbed him. One of them ripped the balaclava off him. But the man made no move to cover his face; he seemed interested only in getting away. The two men released him with a disgusted shove.

The *gardaí* were tensed, straining at the invisible leash that their commanding officer held them with. Nuala knew now what he was waiting for. But it was too soon; Fiona wasn't to the car yet.

Nuala waved in the direction of Sweeney, who had moved back inside the now-closed gates and was watching her, eyes narrowed and hard. "He claims that we have been manipulated and used by the Guerrillas. Well, he should know all about manipulation; he's just tried to do it himself! The Guerrillas warned you they would try this, try to tell you that the photos were faked, and here he's done just that. They *have* to make that claim; what else can they do? They don't want you believing the truth, that they really do have all eleven women locked up inside that concrete hell! Well, who are you going to believe? The Guerrillas, who have never lied to you about anything? Or the government, a bunch of cowardly, power-mad men who would do anything to protect their position? I believe the Guerrillas, because I have no reason not to! And every reason not to trust the government!"

Most of the crowd had forgotten Sweeney, though a few people closest to him were glaring at him. He glanced over at the *garda* commanding officer and jabbed a finger at Nuala, but the officer just shook his head. So the ineffectual prison official turned and stomped off, his two guards trailing him.

"See!" Nuala called out, pointing after Sweeney. "He's given up. He couldn't fool you, so he's running away. I hope—fervently—that the women he mentioned are released tonight. The *gardaí* could play it up to their own advantage, make themselves look like heroes by 'rescuing' them, but we'd all know the truth. The important thing is that they'd be free. I hope it happens, for the sake of whichever of the women are freed. But I can't count on it, and neither should you. And even if it does happen, what about the others? There are *eleven* women left of the September Dozen. Eleven! We will not—cannot—be satisfied until the *gardaí* have released *all eleven*!"

A roar of approval went up; signs began to wave again. Nuala had them back. She wondered if they would listen long enough.

"That fellow that was up here a moment ago," Nuala went on, "the one that's at the back of the crowd now and about to slip into the waiting arms of his *garda* comrades—" She pointed, and heads turned. The blond man and his companion, who had helped him carry the crates, began to trot toward the *gardaí*. People at the edge of the crowd yelled a few insults but made no move toward them. After a few moments they scrambled inside one of the vans.

"That fellow said that the only crime the September Dozen committed was to listen to the wrong people. What wrong people?" Nuala scanned the crowd. She wondered if there were any other *garda* plants out there. Armed ones, perhaps. How convincing was her disguise? "People who tell the truth? People who aren't afraid to question the tactics of the government and the Church?"

She tried to keep one eye on the *gardaí*, who still hadn't moved, and to look, at the same time, in the other direction. Out of the corner of her eye, she spotted the maroon four-door wagon. Fiona was in position.

"Or perhaps the September Dozen didn't listen to anyone at all, except their own consciences. Perhaps they had simply had enough of the lies, the intimidation, the denial of basic human rights. Perhaps they said 'Enough! I must do something to right these wrongs, no matter the cost to myself.' Well, if that is the case, and I have reason to believe it is, then the September Dozen are not criminals but heroes!"

The crowd agreed, yelling and waving their signs.

"I wish they could hear me inside," Nuala said, and the words were barely out of her mouth when something poked her in the knee. She looked down and found Kevin holding up a microphone. His partner had the vidcamera pointed straight at her. Nuala took the microphone, and Kevin smiled and winked in recognition. Nuala smiled back.

"Well, let's try this again, shall we? Is this loud enough? Can you boys in blue hear me in the back?" The *gardaí* didn't respond, but a chuckle rippled through the crowd.

"I hope that the September Dozen can hear me now." The tiny device was powerful; some of the people in front winced. "Because I want to tell you to keep your courage up, that you are not forgotten. We are here because we haven't forgotten, because we care, and we will not give up until you are free."

The crowd roared again, and Nuala held the microphone out over the heads of the nearest people.

"Did you hear that, Ailís O'Hara? There are thousands of people here who want you to know that you are not forgotten, and that we will hold the *gardaí*, the prison officials, the government, and the *Taoiseach* himself responsible for every bruise, every threat, every sleepless night you and the other ten suffer in this place."

The crowd yelled again, applauding like thunder. Nuala saw the commanding officer issue some order. The *gardaí* moved closer, then stopped. A dozen or more of them had slung their rifles over their shoulders and taken their batons from their belts. The *gardaí* flanking them held their rifles ready. But still they waited. Surely they were positive by now.

"And I want to tell you, Ailís and the others, about Bobby Sands." Nuala communicated with a glance and cock of the head to Igraine and Heather, who nodded. They were ready.

"Bobby Sands was a poet, a soldier, a patriot, and finally, a martyr. He was the first of ten men to die on hunger strike in Long Kesh prison in 1981. He died for Ireland, courageous to the last. He left a legacy of poems and other writings behind him. And among them I found this: 'If they aren't able to destroy the desire for freedom, they won't break you ... They won't break me because the desire for freedom and the freedom of the Irish people is in my heart. The day will dawn when all the people of Ireland will have the desire for freedom to show.

It is then we'll see the rising of the moon.' I want you to remember that, Ailís, and the rest of you. They can't break you as long as you want to be free. And they can't break us!" She gestured to the crowd. "They can't break us if we refuse to let them. They bandy the word terrorist about, but what they're really afraid of is not a few people with bombs. What they fear is a nation that refuses to be intimidated any longer. A nation of warriors, the Fianna come back to life."

Igraine was moving back through the crowd, her hands in the ample pockets of her bulky overcoat. Heather didn't budge from Nuala's side, but her hand was in her pocket, gripping the pistol hidden there. She was pale, her jaw set.

"In spite of what the quisling said," Nuala went on, "women can be warriors. We are all a nation of warriors. A nation of warriors that has been asleep too long. But a nation that is finally waking up—waking up to the truth. The truth that the gardaí murdered Tríona Rafferty in cold blood, beat her viciously until she was dead. We have awakened to that truth, and to the fact that we cannot go on averting our eyes from the ugliness around us. We will ignore it no longer. And hear this, you murderous bastards in blue: From now on, if we are attacked, we will defend ourselves! You will not find us so easily terrorized any longer!"

The crowd yelled their defiance and their agreement. Nuala watched Igraine's progress. She had stopped near the back row but had not left herself exposed; there were a few irregular rows of people between her and the gardaí.

"They tried to manipulate us here today," Nuala continued, unwrapping her scarf, "with lies. No doubt their little demonstration on the teilifís tonight will convince some of the more easily swayed. But don't be fooled! The photo of Tríona with the gardaí was real. It was genuine. They murdered her and you know it! And they allowed this protest to go on today for only two reasons: to appear to be 'reasonable,' that they had nothing to hide, and because they were hoping to flush someone out, someone they want very much to silence."

Nuala removed her cap, then carefully tugged off her mustache. "It wasn't much of a disguise, lads. You should be embarrassed that you were so easily fooled."

Several people in the front gasped, and Nuala heard her name spread through the crowd before they started to applaud. There were even some cheers, but she called out, using the microphone so they could hear her, "Look to your backs! They're coming!"

The *gardaí* finally began their charge, batons high. At their first movement, Igraine pulled something from both pockets and threw. Nuala couldn't hear the popping sound from the front, but before she jumped off the crate she saw smoke beginning to spread and billow. She grabbed Heather's arm so she wouldn't lose her in the melee, and they ran as Igraine threw a few more smoke bombs.

At first glance, it seemed a total rout. People were screaming and running in all directions. The *gardaí* clubbed a few people, who staggered back or fell, but the smoke quickly became so thick that the *gardaí* ended up clubbing each other, so they were forced to lower their batons and simply try to run forward, shoving anyone, including each other, out of the way.

Nuala glanced back on her way to Fiona and the car, trying to spot Igraine, and saw, to her grim satisfaction, that more than a few *gardaí* were going down. Batons and rifles were being ripped from their hands and used as clubs by an enraged crowd. Many people were being stunned or knocked aside in the smoky confusion, but they were fighting back. For the first time in recent memory, they were fighting back.

Nuala and Heather reached the car. As Nuala was scrambling inside, plasfire buzzed behind her. But it wasn't *garda* fire; it was Heather. She was standing, feet planted firmly, knees bent, her left hand steadying her gun hand as she fired, eyes wide. She hit nearly every *garda* she aimed at, and the rest dived, rolling, out of the way. Another indistinct figure loomed in the smoke, and Heather would have fired if Nuala hadn't yelled "It's Igraine!"

As soon as the three of them were in the car, Fiona hit the accelerator and they began a wild ride in reverse through the maze of parked cars. They spotted a *garda* van off to their left, but something was apparently wrong with two of its tires.

"Who—" Nuala began.

"Kevin, perhaps," Igraine replied. "Or some other Guerrilla. There were probably more of them here than we saw."

"I wonder if Stuart was—" The rest of Heather's words were cut off when Fiona whipped the car around, threw it in gear, and started forward. Heather ended up in Nuala's lap.

"To the right!" Igraine shouted.

"I see him," Fiona replied, deadly calm and focused. She turned and headed straight for the approaching squad car, the accelerator floored.

"What are you doing?" Heather yelled, gripping the edge of the seat in a stranglehold.

But Fiona didn't reply, just bore down on the squad car. At almost the last minute, the squad car swerved and turned sideways to block them, but Fiona merely turned the wheel a few degrees and never slowed. They sideswiped the fender of the squad car, but got around it. Before any others behind could catch up, they had escaped across three parking lots and a field.

The "evidence" presented that night on RTE that the photo of Tríona had been faked was almost convincing. It was a glum trio that watched it in the safe house in Fermanagh. Fiona came in just as the program was ending.

"Well?" Heather demanded.

"No one was killed," Fiona replied as she took off her coat. The others sighed in relief. "But there were several injuries, some serious. Éadaoin says there were also a lot of arrests."

Nuala winced. "I should have just kept my mouth shut."

"If you had," Igraine told her, "the crowd might have believed that Sweeney fellow; they might have given up."

"But if people are injured or hurt because I—"

"Éadaoin also said," Fiona interrupted, "that Ailís O'Hara's husband has been contacted by the gardaí. She may be released soon, and perhaps the others. The government wants this problem gone. Kevin and his cohorts have already sent today's embarrassing coverage over to Wales—it was shown on EuroNet an hour ago. The women and their families won't be able to talk about being imprisoned, for fear of reprisals, but everyone will know the truth anyway. They already do."

"You didn't see their 'evidence,'" Igraine said, pointing to the teilifís.

"Doesn't matter," Fiona insisted. "The battle has been joined. Every person in that crowd today will know that their actions forced the release of those women. They'll know, and when the Guerrillas show their tape, the rest of the country will—"

"There they are." Heather turned up the volume as the Guerrilla logo disappeared.

A man in a balaclava was smiling as he said, "The courageous protestors at Maghaberry have won a major victory tonight. The gardaí announced moments ago that the September Dozen have been 'rescued from their kidnappers.' The eleven women have surfaced at last. Their families have been summoned to St. Brigid Hospital in Belfast, where the women are, at this moment, being treated for numerous contusions and other non–life-threatening injuries received 'at the hands of their kidnappers,' the *gardaí* would have us believe. It is understood that the women will be going home shortly and that there will be only one interview with them, a week from now, on RTE2. A week should be sufficient time for them to learn the lines the authorities have no doubt already prepared for them."

The Guerrilla paused. "The government may issue any statement it likes, and the women and their families may back up that version to protect themselves—that is understandable. But make no mistake about it, these women will be free shortly for one reason and one reason only: because the Irish people *demanded* it. A risen, united people can accomplish anything. Congratulations to each and every person who was present outside Maghaberry today. *You* gained freedom for the September Dozen. Now you can learn to demand it for yourselves. *Beir bua!* Seize victory."

The logo reappeared, and then regular programming was back. Heather turned down the volume. "We did it!"

Nuala and Igraine tried to return Heather's smile, but Nuala was thinking of all the people arrested today. Had they merely taken the place of the eleven women?

"Pity this victory should come at the cost of Tríona's life," Fiona said, and turned away.

After a moment, Nuala looked at Igraine. "We'd better make some more of those smoke bombs. I don't doubt we'll be needing them soon."

Chapter 18

"WHAT YOU'VE BEEN doing is wonderful," Nuala said, looking into the camera. "It makes me proud to be Irish when I witness your courage and your determination."

She was so familiar with the process of being taped by now that Nuala forgot about the Guerrilla behind the camera. She paid no more attention to the fact that her three friends and two other Guerrillas were also present in the Monaghan safe house, watching. She concentrated on what she had to say.

"I've heard that more and more of you are refusing to go to your unpaid and involuntary 'volunteer' work. Well, good for you! Don't allow yourselves to be exploited and used that way. If the government wants your labor, and your time, it can bloody well *pay* you for it! And until it does, don't cooperate—don't do the work. I'm very proud that you're not knuckling under and giving in to their threats of firing your husbands from their jobs if you won't go back. All workers—paid and unpaid—have the absolute right to go out on strike if working conditions are unfair and intolerable. Let's see *more* of you exercise that right! Volunteers: Stop volunteering. And paid employees—men and single women—you go out on strike, too. It is the workers who keep this country going. If you stop working, the government will have no choice but to listen to us."

Nuala smiled, thinking of the news Éadaoin had told them last week. "And to those of you who are refusing to be maids, cooks, laundresses, servants, and prostitutes in your own homes: *Molaim sibh*, I commend you. I'm proud of *you*, too. You've been brainwashed since birth to obey first fathers and then husbands, and some of you are finally saying 'Enough! I am a free woman.' *Molaim sibh!*"

She paused for a moment, her smile dying. "And yes, I have heard of the bravest among you: those women who have been learning to fight back against physical abuse. I know about Shannon MacGreevy, who was arrested for 'assaulting her husband.' Of course it wasn't assault; it was clearly self-defense. The bruises—both new and old—on Shannon's face and body are testimony to the fact that the bastard had been using her as a punching bag. She was arrested as an attempt to intimidate other women, to frighten them into doing nothing. Well, it won't work. Because Shannon MacGreevy's neighbors won't allow her to be railroaded into prison. They have stepped forward, bless them, demanding to testify on her behalf that MacGreevy had been abusing her for years and was attempting to do it again when she stopped him. The trial is coming up in a month or so. I urge all of you in the vicinity of Navan to strengthen her neighbors' protests. Picket the courthouse every day, demanding justice, and pack the courtroom for the trial. Support Shannon MacGreevy and the right of all women to fight back. Show the authorities that we do not fear them. If we all join together, there's *nothing* we can't accomplish.

"And that's why I'm making this tape. To urge you to turn out in great numbers on Saturday next in a demonstration of solidarity, to *demand* freedom for Shannon MacGreevy and for all of Ireland. If the entire country joins together, we *will* achieve freedom. There are not enough jails to hold us all; the *gardaí* can't kill us all. We have the power—when we are united—to accomplish anything and everything. We can take back control of our country from the professional politicians who serve as mouthpieces for the Vatican. We can abolish the God Patrols, we can import and disseminate free contraceptives to all who want them. We can establish day-care centers, train *women* to be gynecologists, make divorce and abortion legal. We can do *anything*—if we are united. It's no longer enough to privately hope or pray for change. It is time to speak out publicly, to take action. It is time to take to the streets. The demonstration in Belfast on Saturday next will begin at ten A.M. in front of City Hall itself. Bring your signs, your banners, your tricolors, and yourselves. If there are enough of us, they cannot stop us. We *can* stand up to them. We will. But we need all of you. Shannon MacGreevy needs all of you. Come to City Hall, ten A.M., Belfast, Saturday next. Come and demand freedom." She paused for a moment. "I'll see you there."

The red light went out, and the Guerrilla lowered the camera. Nuala stood up and stretched.

"When will it air?"

"Probably tomorrow," said Ciarán, one of the other Guerrillas. "It's short, so we can tack it on after our international news report."

"Speaking of international news," Fiona said, dodging the pole lamps the other two Guerrillas were already moving back to the other room, "is it true that some of your tapes have made it to the U.S.?"

Ciarán grinned, his blond mustache stretching. "Yeah. We got some into Canada, and they smuggled them across the border. Copies are being sent all over America." He turned to smile at Nuala. "Your fame is spreading."

Nuala didn't reply; she just nodded and walked away, moving off into the back bedroom of the small house, and closed the door.

A few moments later there was a soft tap, and Heather came in. She was frowning as she sat on the other bed. "You okay?"

Nuala sighed. "Why wouldn't I be? You heard the man: My fame is spreading."

"You look less than thrilled." When Nuala didn't answer, Heather just waited, watching her with the same concerned expression she had been wearing for days.

Nuala tried to smile, but failed. "Don't worry about me, *kidín*. I'm all right."

"No, you're not. And don't tell me not to worry. I'll worry about you as much as I like." Before Nuala, in her surprise, could reply, Heather went on. "You are not all right. *Gardaí* all over the country would love to get their hands on you, the government wants you silenced, the Church no doubt wants to burn you at the stake, we never *really* know who we can trust what with the betrayals and the arrests that have been happening, you're worried about your father and your sister, and you seem to insist on feeling guilty and responsible every time someone gets hurt for joining the struggle. Did I leave anything out?"

Nuala's attempt at a chuckle was weak. "Yes, you completely overlooked the crisis in China, the civil war in Paraguay, and Israeli aggression against New Palestine. Don't forget those. The world is in a sorry state."

"You're taking responsibility for that, too, now?" Heather's smile was patient and so full of affection that Nuala was startled. "Nuala, go easy on yourself. Do you blame Pearse and Connolly for the deaths of those who joined them in 1916?"

"I am hardly to be mentioned in the same league as P—"

"And why not?" Heather interrupted Nuala's protest. "They led by example and inspiring words, and so are you doing the very same."

"I am not a—"

"Leader? Of course you are. I don't know why you don't just accept that."

Nuala writhed under Heather's confident gaze. Where did the girl get such ideas?

Heather suddenly smiled and, leaning toward the other bed, squeezed Nuala's hand. "Like I said, go easy on yourself. You're doing Ireland—and who knows what other countries—a great service in speaking the truth. What the people do with that truth is up to them. It's not your fault if people get hurt for demanding freedom. If James Connolly was alive today, he'd be doing the same, just as he did before, wouldn't he?"

Reluctantly Nuala nodded. "I suppose he would, at that."

"Of course he would. It was his duty, and he performed it well, as you've told me many times." Heather squeezed her hand again, then stood up. "Why don't you get some rest? You

look exhausted. I'll see nobody disturbs you." She stopped at the
door. "Don't worry so much. You're doing the right thing. Just
like Connolly. Now get some rest."

"Yes, Mother," Nuala replied, raising an eyebrow. Heather
chuckled, her cheeks turning a faint pink. Then she left, closing
the door behind her.

Nuala lay back on the pillow, sighing. Heather was right; she
was exhausted, had been for days, ever since Éadaoin had sent
word of the arrests in Tralee, the work of an infiltrator who had
betrayed the local, separate underground. Éadaoin, Brigid, and
Dana's Network had not been implicated, but the betrayals had
put them all on edge. But they had to continue. And Heather
was right too about speaking the truth: What people did with
that truth was up to them. Still, if people died or were arrested
because of something Nuala said . . . What would Connolly do?
Well, that was obvious, of course. Connolly would continue
on, letting nothing stop him. But then, Connolly had been a
hero, larger than life, and strong enough to shoulder whatever
guilt he might have felt over those who followed him being hurt.
She was no James Connolly.

Nuala eventually dropped off to sleep, only to dream of
Connolly's execution. He had been so badly wounded in the
1916 Uprising that he couldn't stand before the firing squad.
The British tied him to a chair to face death. Nuala jerked awake
as the bullets struck her.

The newest tape was aired for the first time on Monday, then
repeated several times over the next few days. By Thursday almost everyone in Ireland had seen it or heard about it. And they
had heard the government's response. Several politicians and
clergy had appeared to warn people not to join the protest in
Belfast, as there was danger of violence by "the extremists." The
concern of the government was for the "safety of the Irish people." Government spokesmen warned the public that Nuala
Dennehy was dangerously deluded, psychologically unstable,
and they reminded them of the other, recent disturbances outside
Maghaberry Prison and in Wexford, where there had been violence, due—they claimed—to Nuala's presence and her "provoc-
ative influence over the extremist fringe." The authorities could
not guarantee the safety of any citizens who were foolish
enough to deliberately put themselves in harm's way.

On Thursday, after a morning of going over the various escape strategies planned for Saturday, Nuala was trying to con-

centrate on reading a school textbook on Irish history, wincing at the inaccuracies and blatant lies. Heather and Igraine were playing the inevitable gin rummy; Heather was ahead by a few hundred points. Fiona had gone out to meet a contact.

A rap at the door startled them until they recognized Fiona's all-clear signal. Heather put down the pistol she had grabbed and went to unlock the door. Nuala lowered her pistol, hiding it behind her book.

Fiona wasn't alone; Éadaoin hurried in out of the cold after her.

"Éadaoin! What are you doing here?"

"Hello, Heather, how are you?" Éadaoin's mouth turned up when she saw the pistol as Nuala put it aside. "Expecting trouble?"

"Always," Nuala replied. "Now what brings yourself so far north? Not a social call, I'll wager."

"I'm afraid not. Have you any tea? It's beastly cold out."

"I'll get some—but don't say anything until I get back!" Heather hurried off to the kitchen as Éadaoin took off her coat. Fiona took it and hung her own alongside it on the back of the door.

"We've got worries about Saturday," Éadaoin told them as she took a seat on the sofa. "You may have to call it off—if it's not too late."

"Why?" Igraine demanded. "What's happened?"

"Wait for Heather," Nuala said. "She's part of this team."

"Right, right." Igraine nodded impatiently.

"How are Brigid and Dana?" Nuala asked Éadaoin. "And how are things in Rathcoole?"

"Fine." But Éadaoin's smile wasn't very convincing. She made small talk about the people of Rathcoole until Heather scurried back in carrying the tea things.

Igraine waited until Éadaoin had taken one sip, then leaned forward. "Well? What's going on?"

Éadaoin took a second sip, then warmed her fingers around the cup. Her frown and her tone were both grim. "Our sources in Belfast report an influx of *gardaí* this week; they're coming in from all over. But even more alarming is the weapons stockpile next to the *garda* barracks in Andersontown."

"Weapons stockpile?" Igraine said. "What sort—"

"All manner of small arms," Éadaoin explained. "Plasfire pistols and rifles, jabbers, fire grenades—no sonic stun grenades, mind you. *Fire* grenades. They're not looking to just disperse or arrest this time. They're looking to kill."

"Oh, god," Heather murmured, her face ashen.

"Bastards!" Igraine muttered the word with such hatred that Nuala glanced her way. Igraine's fists were clenched, the knuckles white.

"Perhaps you can get on the air in time," Éadaoin said. "Call it off, so no one will be killed. We could contact the Guerrillas today, this afternoon, and you could—"

"And the bastards'll know they can scare us off with the threat of deadly force," Igraine interrupted. "We knew this would happen sooner or later. If they stop us now, then they'll just stop us again the next time, and the next. We *can't* back down."

"But people will be killed!" Heather protested. "Surely you can't want—"

"We have to stand up to them!" Igraine was adamant.

"We're outnumbered," Fiona said, "and certainly outgunned."

"We can't know how many will show up on Saturday," Igraine argued. "The numbers have been growing, the protests spreading. You heard the Guerrilla news earlier: three hundred in Galway, seven hundred in Cobh, over a thousand in Dun Laoghaire—"

"But we have no weapons!" Fiona threw up her hands. "It'd be suicide! And what do any of us know about fighting, about violence? We can't—"

"Near the *garda* barracks in Andersontown, you said?" Nuala interrupted, looking at Éadaoin, who nodded. "It's well guarded, I would imagine."

"Of course." Éadaoin's eyes narrowed. "What are you thinking of?"

Nuala shrugged. "Well, if they were deprived of their weapons, then they couldn't use them against us, could they now?"

"Oh, no," Fiona muttered, but Igraine smiled.

"We can't—I mean, how—steal them?" Heather asked. "That's impossible—isn't it?"

"Yes, I suppose it probably is." Nuala nodded. "But a few well-placed grenades—"

"Even if we succeeded without getting ourselves killed," Fiona interrupted, "which I sincerely doubt is possible, it wouldn't destroy every weapon in Ireland, you know. Not all their weapons are kept there. They'd still have more than enough—"

"Right," Nuala said. "I know. But if we destroy most of the ones they have readily on hand, that would delay them a bit—and if we could steal a few, we could surprise them by fighting back and cover the retreat of the others."

"I still think it's suicide," Fiona insisted. "We are not an army. We're not even the IRA, who at least have some training at this sort of thing. If we fail—"

"We won't," Igraine said. "Not if we plan it carefully enough."

"Need I remind you," Fiona argued, "that the demonstration is less than forty-eight hours from now? We can't possibly—"

"As long as we think we can't, then we won't!" Igraine was just as determined. "We have some degree of momentum going now, Fiona. If we allow ourselves to be scared off, it could all collapse. We have to show the people that we are a match for the bloody storm troopers. We have to make them believe that we can win, or they'll give up trying."

"But—" Fiona began.

"Have your people been watching the area?" Nuala said to Éadaoin.

"Oh, yes. It's been under surveillance for days, and they've been making note of the delivery schedule. But it's not terribly regular."

Nuala's eyes stared off at nothing, lost in thought. When she spoke, she sounded preoccupied. "I'll need to talk to one of your surveillance people."

"Fine, no problem," Éadaoin said. "But do you really think this is such a good idea? The violence—"

"By destroying their weapons, perhaps we can *prevent* some violence," Nuala replied. "I don't want to see anybody killed, but if they insist on making it them or us, I'd prefer it were *them*." No one had a reply to that, though Igraine nodded grimly. "We'll have to contact the Guerrillas," Nuala went on. "They'll want a tape of the arms being delivered, to counter the certain lies afterward."

"I'll contact them," Fiona offered, but she didn't sound happy about it.

"And the IRA," Nuala said. "We'll have to talk—"

"What?" Éadaoin's vehemence startled Nuala from her thoughts. "We've never had anything to do with—"

"I know that," Nuala replied. "And for good reasons, considering some of the things they've done. But Fiona was right: We have no military training, and they do. We need their help."

"Asking assistance from that lot could make everything backfire on us," Éadaoin argued. "We can't trust them not to use us
for their own ends."

"Unless we use them first," Nuala countered. "Look, we've
got less than forty-eight hours to find a way to prevent a massacre, but without stopping the movement dead in its tracks. As
I see it, we either give up and wait for another day, which could
prove a severe blow to our momentum as well as our credibility
if it's believed we've been scared off—or we fight back with the
element of surprise."

"The best defense is a good offense!" The other women
turned to look at Heather and she blushed. "I read that somewhere once."

Nuala smiled. "And it's exactly right. The *gardaí* won't be
expecting us to do anything of the sort. After all, most of us are
women; what could *we* possibly do?"

"We'll show them what we can do!" Heather was on the edge
of her seat. "If they think they can frighten us into giving up and
just accepting slavery—"

"What about the IRA?" Fiona interrupted. "Why would they
help us?"

Nuala shrugged. "Why wouldn't they? Many—most—of our
goals are the same as theirs. And any chance for them to steal
or destroy government weapons—you think they wouldn't jump
at that?"

"Maybe," Fiona conceded. "But they'll try to take over, make
us mere accomplices to *their* plans."

"Let me worry about that," Nuala said. "I think I know what
to say to them, to convince them that it would be in their own
best interests. Provided we can make contact in time." She
looked to Éadaoin, who was frowning.

"I don't like this, but other than calling it off, I don't see what
we can do. And if we call it off now, it might make it that much
harder to get people moving again the next time." She sighed.
"I'll see if I can contact the IRA, but I can't promise you—"

"I'll do it." They turned to Igraine in surprise. Her jaw was
clenched in determination and some other emotion; her expression was grim. "I still know a few 'phone numbers. And besides, the bastards owe me."

Chapter 19

"W̲E̲ ̲W̲A̲I̲T̲ ̲H̲E̲R̲E̲ for the signal," Igraine said.

"It would be helpful to know what the signal *is*," Nuala muttered.

"We'll know."

Igraine's assurance wasn't very reassuring. Nuala studied her friend, trying to read her, to decipher what had been left unspoken between them since they had met in that darkened basement in Belfast. She knew little of Igraine's past: only that she was from Kerry, that she had some mysterious reason for not wanting to return there, that she had "contacts," that she had been fighting back one way or another for half her life, and—apparently—that the IRA "owed" her something. She had been even more taciturn than usual since that revelation last night. All she would tell her friends was that she had once known a few IRA Volunteers and that she could get the Provos to come through for them. And here they were, trusting her on that basis. But in spite of not having many answers to her questions, Nuala knew instinctively that she could trust Igraine with her life—as she was about to do. The IRA, however—that was another matter.

"How long?" Heather had crept up behind them.

A glance over her shoulder showed Nuala that Fiona had remained at the other end of the alley, guarding their rear. Igraine didn't speak, so all Nuala could do was shrug in reply.

"It's freezing!" Heather shivered violently, as if to prove her point. Her gloved hands tugged her collar closer.

Without glancing back, Igraine spoke. "You'll want to be putting those gloves in your pockets. They're knit; your gun could slip."

Heather looked at her wool-covered fingers. "But the cold—"

"You'll forget it in an instant, believe me."

Heather looked to Nuala, who was looking at her own gloved hands. Without a word, Nuala took off her gloves and stuffed them in the pockets of her thick woolen coat. Heather followed suit, leaving her hands buried in her pockets.

"We're not going to kill anybody, right?" Heather asked. "Our guns'll be set only on stun?"

"*Ours* will," Igraine said. She pointed down the alley and whispered, "The gate."

The wire-mesh gate was being opened from the inside, and a moment later a truck came rumbling out—the same truck they had watched go into the *garda* compound nearly an hour before. It bounced a bit when a tire hit a pothole, then picked up speed and departed.

"Empty," Igraine murmured. "Wonder how much it was carrying?"

Heather took a hand from her pocket just long enough to push the cuff of her coat back for an instant. "It's nearly four o'clock. It'll be dark soon. Is it going to happen today or not? The demonstration's tomorrow."

"It'll happen," Igraine replied, shifting her weight, still intent on the fence and what she couldn't see behind it.

Nuala changed the subject. "I hope the Guerrillas got a shot of the unload—"

A deafening explosion rocked the pavement. Nuala and Heather jumped, but Igraine barely winced.

Smoke billowed up to the darkening sky from within the compound. Shouts rang out, then the sound of plasfire, several smaller explosions, and the staccato of ancient bullets.

Igraine had a smoke bomb in her left hand. She pulled another from her right pocket.

"I take it that was the signal?" Nuala said, ignoring the fact that her heart was trying to push its way out of her chest.

Igraine just nodded once, a sharp jerk of the head. "You know what to do." Then she was gone.

Nuala ran across the alley, flattened herself against the grimy brick wall, and stuck her head out, wondering as she did so if it was going to get shot off.

The first smoke bomb had gone off halfway to the fence; Igraine had rolled it along the pavement to her left, then rolled the other one, now smoking, to her right, laying down cover for Nuala and Heather. Just before Igraine disappeared into the smoke, Nuala saw plasfire hit the ground at her feet. Igraine rolled to the right, came up with her pistol in her hand, and opened fire. Then the smoke enveloped her.

"This is insane!" Nuala muttered, then pushed off and ran. Heather was right behind her.

They moved blindly through the smoke, listening to the sounds of a firefight directly ahead of them. No shots came anywhere near them; the *gardaí* must have been as blinded as they were.

The wire fence loomed up, directly in their path. Nuala stopped and fired her pistol at it. She thumbed the control to maximum plasfire, but it cut the fence too slowly. Heather's fire joined hers, and the two weapons sliced through the wire. Again plasfire scorched the pavement in front of them. Nuala felt the heat through her boots, but she continued working on the fence. A third time plasfire searched for them. Nuala winced as the heat took a swipe at her toes. The fence was almost cut through.

The smoke was clearing too fast; the cold breeze was more brisk than they had hoped it would be. Nuala could see the tower not a hundred meters away. The *garda* in it was bobbing in and out of sight in the smoke, looking in their direction. A grenade exploded somewhere behind him, punctuated by screams, but he didn't turn. Nuala's eyes darted from the *garda* in the tower to the almost-finished opening in the fence and back. She saw the *garda* straighten and bring his gun to bear. He had spotted them.

Heather dropped to one knee, her thumb hitting the control, and the pistol jumped up. She fired. The *garda* jerked as he was stunned, then fell backward. The two women forgot him as they finished cutting the fence.

A black van appeared behind them and slowed for an instant as Nuala and Heather jumped for the doors and held on, pressing tightly against the metal for protection. Nuala stuck her head through the van's window. Fiona floored the accelerator, and the truck punched its way through the hole in the fence. Nuala felt the still-sizzling wire ends scrape the back of her coat; then they were through.

The van screeched to a halt in front of a warehouse compartment. Nuala jumped from the van, almost landing on a blackened and smoking *garda* corpse. She felt her stomach clench, but hopped over the body and ran.

The firefight was going on across the compound half a block away; there were a dozen or more corpses scattered across the pavement like broken, uniformed dolls between the van and the fighting by the far fence. Nuala could see *gardaí* pinned down, out of her range and under steady IRA fire. None was too eager to step out of cover and come back and see what the three women were up to.

Fiona blasted the forcefield lock with a single shot. She and Heather stepped through and pushed, and the seamed metal door inside slid up and back. The warehouse compartment was stuffed with boxes and crates of all sizes.

Fiona and Heather grabbed a wooden crate and pulled. It toppled off several other crates and hit the ground on its side. The crate splintered, and the contents tumbled out.

"Plasma rifles!" Heather grabbed an armload, and Fiona followed suit. Nuala cast a final glance around, saw no one ominous in their vicinity, put her pistol in her pocket, and went to help. She grabbed a cardboard box labeled GRENADES and tried to hurry it to the van. It was no use; the box was too big, much too heavy, and she wasn't strong enough. She put it down, ripped open the top, and dumped out half the contents on the pavement. The grenades skittered in all directions. That was better; now she could lift it easily. She ran to the van and shoved the box in the back next to the pile of rifles that Heather and Fiona were building.

The fight continued on the far side of the compound. Nuala tried not to listen to the occasional screams of men dying. She tried not to think about what the IRA were doing or what they would do in the future with the grenades she was stealing. She concentrated on what she was doing and why, and on getting it done.

The ground under her bucked as another explosion shook the compound. The compartment four down from them had blown up. Nuala dived for the ground and covered her head. She felt shrapnel falling all around her.

Someone grabbed her shoulder. "I think it's time to leave now!" Fiona shouted the words, but Nuala had to read her lips; her ears didn't seem to be working.

She lurched to her feet and followed Fiona toward the van. They had almost made it when the world exploded.

Nuala was surrounded by fire. She whirled, but there was fire in every direction. Her nostrils were seared with the bitter odor of burning hair, burning wool, burning flesh. Her coat was on fire, her shoulder was—

Something hit her, hard, and she went down. Heather was hitting her, pounding on her shoulder. Fiona appeared behind Heather; Nuala saw her pistol fire, but she couldn't hear a thing.

Heather grabbed Nuala's arm, hauled her up, and then they were running through the flames.

Fiona kept firing as she ran backward, toward the van. Heather was shouting something, but Nuala couldn't hear her. She couldn't hear anything but a deafening roar in her head. She couldn't feel anything either, except her boots hitting the ground.

Fiona reached the van and scrambled in behind the wheel. Heather pulled Nuala to the back, where they dived in among the stolen weapons. Heather slammed the double doors behind them as the van charged forward.

They careened into a U-turn; Nuala and Heather were knocked across the van, rifles slamming against them, loose grenades swarming around their ankles. The van shuddered as it hit the gate at full speed, and then they were through and racing away.

Nuala slumped against the wall of the van, trying to shake the dizziness away, to dispel the roaring in her head. After a few moments, as they bounced along the street and down an alley, the roaring began to subside.

Heather was trying to keep her balance, her elbows braced on boxes, as she leaned over Nuala. The girl was so pale, horrified. She was talking, but Nuala couldn't understand her at first. Gradually the roaring ebbed away. Nuala caught the last two words: "—fire grenade." Heather was looking at Nuala's shoulder, tears in her eyes. Nuala looked down. Some kind of switch was thrown by the sight of her charred shoulder, and all the feeling came rushing back in a flood. Nuala heard herself scream.

The van finally ceased its agonizing bouncing and rolled to a stop. Nuala moaned, biting down on her lip—hard. She tasted blood. The pain was so intense she had trouble understanding what Heather was saying to her. Something about getting help, something else about Igraine, about the IRA. Her eyes squeezed shut as she moaned again.

The doors of the van opened and the cold night air rushed in. Nuala opened her eyes, lifted her head. That much movement made her gasp in agony; she felt another wave of nausea.

"Is she—" Fiona began.

"She needs a doctor!" Heather interrupted.

Fiona started to climb in the back, but the sound of a vehicle approaching changed her mind. Heather leaned over Nuala and spoke in a whisper, as if afraid her words would cause Nuala further pain. "We'll get help for you, Nuala. That must be Igraine and themselves now."

Nuala could only groan in reply, but forced her eyes open. She saw Heather take out her pistol gingerly and leave.

"Where's Nuala?"

It *was* Igraine, and Nuala heard Fiona reply, "In the back. A few of them got through. A rifle set off a fire grenade on the ground . . . Her shoulder's bad." There was a pause, then Fiona went on, her words vibrating with fury. "You! You bloody bastard! You set them off too soon! You could have killed us!"

"Now, now," a male voice said. "Nobody was killed—well, except their lot, of course. You have to expect a few injuries in war, don't you?"

"We destroyed every fucking compartment," another male voice gloated. "Half the weapons in Ulster—in one day! Fucking beautiful!"

"So, let's see what you got, then," the first man said.

"Later!" Heather snapped. "She needs a doctor *now*!"

"Right," Igraine said. "We'll meet up with you later, to give you your half, but right now—"

"Not later, now," the first man said, his voice curiously soothing. "And not half, love—we'll take the lot."

"What? You can't—" Heather began.

"The deal was for half," Fiona interrupted, her anger still boiling.

"The deal has changed," he replied, still cheerful.

"Now why don't you girls go back to playing with your dolls?" a third male voice said. "We'll take the weapons. Because *we* know what to do with them. This is *our* war, not yours."

"Put that gun away," Igraine demanded. "You're not going to betray me *twice*, Eoin. I'll not stand for it. And as you can see, I'm not unarmed this time."

"Ah, don't look at it that way, Igraine," Eoin said. "We've had our disagreements, you and I, true enough, but we had our share of good times, too; admit it."

"I admit nothing—except that you are a treacherous, self-serving, back-stabbing bastard I should *never* have trusted! And never will again."

"Up to you, love. But let's have the weapons, now, shall we? Any more delays, and I might have to shoot one of your darling friends here. We wouldn't want that now, would we?"

"I think . . . not," Nuala said, and pulled the trigger. She nearly fell out of the back of the van with the effort, but somehow she didn't miss. One of the three Provos crumpled as she shot him, astonishment on his face. The other two men, surprised, didn't move fast enough. Heather shot one, Igraine the other. They fell to the ground and lay motionless.

Igraine stood over the man she had stunned, hatred and revulsion twisting her face. "Should have killed him. Put him out of my misery."

Heather ran to the swaying Nuala as Fiona said, "Who the hell *is* he, Igraine? And why did you trust him at all?"

Igraine raised an eyebrow and sighed. "He's my husband."

Nuala shot a glance of astonishment at Igraine. She would have liked to hear more, but her pain picked that moment to catch up with her, and she passed out.

The night was a blur to Nuala; she was in and out of consciousness so many times she wouldn't have been able to count them had she been lucid. There had been more bouncing in the back of the van, each pothole stabbing a white-hot poker through her shoulder. She vomited more than once from the pain, and there were blurred memories of men screaming and dying, and of scorched corpses. Between all that there was Heather's frightened but soothing voice murmuring at her.

Then she was carried somewhere, and her coat and shirt were pried off, causing such agony that she mercifully fainted and didn't feel the doctor's ministrations.

More bouncing in the van brought her only halfway to consciousness; she was floating, oddly detached from her shoulder, from the vaguely remembered pain. Then she was carried again, until she sank into a soft cloud and drifted away.

She should have slept much longer than she had; the painkiller should have guaranteed it, but something woke her, some feeling of urgency. It took three tries before the room stopped spinning long enough for her to sit up. When she dared to try opening her eyes again, the room settled slowly into place.

Two narrow beds, one of which she was in, were covered with *báinín* knitted spreads and pale-blue flannel sheets. There was a mahogany press in the corner, an old-fashioned 2-D framed picture of someone on top of it. Next to the press was a chair with a red cushion. Nuala recognized her boots under the chair and her green canvas bag atop the cushion. On the wall above the press was a large poster of the Giant's Causeway in Antrim, and on the opposite wall hung three pictures of birds—

Audubon prints, perhaps. There was nothing else in the room. Nuala didn't recognize it; it was a new safe house, obviously. Were they still in Belfast? Had she missed the demonstration?

She tried to look at her watch, but her arm was so stiff she could barely move it. The agony of last night—was it last night?—came to her, but it was only a memory. Nuala plucked at her flannel nightgown—it was her own; someone had obviously dressed her in it while she was unconscious—and pulled it away from her throat. She tried to peer inside, to see what condition her shoulder was in. A light bandage covered her entire shoulder and her upper arm, and was taped to her left breast. She tried, gently, to move her arm, and was surprised when it obeyed without the remembered agony. There was only a curious deadened soreness under the bandage, not the mind-blotting pain of before. The skin under the bandage felt odd, not like skin at all, but stiff, hard, and the soreness seemed to be underneath the skin. Dermaclone, it had to be. As badly as she had been burned, the doctor would have applied dermaclone. She had read about the procedure, knew enough to know that she would have to be very careful with it until the new skin was completely grown. It should start to itch in a day or two, but if she tore it, there would not only be a great deal of pain involved, but scar tissue, as well. She would have to use a sling and exercise it gently on her own. Given her circumstances, a professional physical therapist was out of the question.

Suddenly remembering the demonstration, Nuala tried again to look at her watch: 8:30. It had to be morning because of the light streaming through the pale-blue curtains. But was it still Saturday? Or had she slept through it all and let everyone down?

Nuala carefully swung her legs out of bed and eased herself to her feet. She swayed for a moment, finally decided she wasn't going to fall, and wobbled to the door. As she turned the doorknob, it occurred to her to be grateful she was not left-handed.

Fiona and Heather were in the living room, drinking tea and watching a noiseless *teilifís*. Heather held her cup awkwardly, with just her fingers.

"Is it Saturday?" Nuala's voice cracked on the last word.

"Nuala!" Heather jumped to her feet, spilling her tea. She set the cup down and rushed over, frowning. "You should be in bed!"

"I'm all right. Is it Saturday? Have I missed the demonstration?"

"It's Saturday," Heather assured her, taking Nuala's right arm and leading her toward the sofa, where Fiona made room for her.

Fiona was peering at Nuala in concern. "You look like hell."

"I can't imagine why," Nuala replied, and allowed Heather to seat her on the sofa as carefully as if she were made of Waterford crystal. "Then I haven't missed it?"

"You haven't," Fiona confirmed.

"But you're going to." Heather raised her hands to stop Nuala's argument. But the words died in Nuala's throat at the sight of Heather's palms. They were an angry red underneath a hardened, transparent film. A memory flashed: Heather beating on Nuala's shoulder yesterday. She had put out the flames with her bare hands.

"Oh, *kidín*." Nuala couldn't speak further, and just stared at Heather's hands, wincing.

Heather blushed and dropped her hands. "It's nothing, really. Don't even need bandages if I'm careful. The doctor took off the blistered skin, which *looked* horrible, but it didn't hurt a bit, *really*, then he sprayed on this stuff—a biological bandage, he called it—that protects my hands while the new skin's growing, which it already is, and it really doesn't hurt, *really*, so don't worry about me at all, Nuala. I'm fine. Really."

Nuala could think of no reply that would adequately express the gratitude she felt for what Heather had done, or her pain that the girl had been hurt. What could she say? "Thank you" wasn't nearly enough. But then Igraine spoke, and the moment passed.

"You're up." She stood in the kitchen doorway. Nuala thought she looked older, somehow, than she had yesterday. Perhaps it was just the circles under her eyes; maybe those lines around her mouth and the crease between her eyes lining her forehead had always been there. "Will you live?"

"I believe I will, yes." Nuala wanted to ask about Igraine's husband, about what had happened the previous night after she had passed out. But that closed-off look was back in Igraine's eyes. It could wait. Maybe when they were alone . . .

"We're going, aren't we?" Nuala asked her.

"Yes," Igraine said, and "No," Heather said simultaneously. Nuala looked at Fiona. "And how do you vote?"

"Nuala, you can't—" Heather began.

"I'm asking Fiona," Nuala interrupted.

Fiona shook her head. "Yesterday was nearly suicidal. Today would be doubly suicidal. We may have destroyed most of their toys, but we also made them *very* angry. You should see the government reports they've been airing all morning."

"The Guerrillas have aired their version, as well," Igraine said, coming over to sit down. "They got some excellent shots of the stockpile, both long range to show the sheer numbers of the weapons and some nice close-ups of boxes of fire grenades. That should shake the complacency of a few loyal citizens."

"Got some shots of us, too," Fiona said. She included Heather, Nuala, and herself in one gesture. "Showed us breaking crates and you dumping grenades. And you on fire and Heather dragging you to safety. *Didn't* show us loading up, so it was carefully edited to make it seem we were trying to *destroy* the weapons, not steal them."

"But the government said we did," Igraine added. "So it depends on who the public believes. Are we the thieving, murdering terrorists the government painted us, or the daring weapons-destroyers the Guerrillas would prefer us to be?"

Nuala looked at her watch again, ignoring the stiffness in her shoulder. "The demonstration's in an hour. I wonder if anybody's going to show up."

"They will." Igraine was insistent. "I know they will. When they see the stockpile, when they realize what the government was planning—"

"They'll be scared to death," Fiona said.

"They'll be *angry*," Igraine countered. "And they'll come."

Nuala looked from Igraine to Fiona. "If *anybody* shows up, I have to. I said I'd be there. I said it to the entire country. To not show up would mean they'd scared me off. And not showing up would mean that yesterday was in vain, that we accomplished nothing."

"You should be in bed." But neither Heather's expression nor her tone were very adamant. When Nuala just looked at her, she shook her head and sighed. "If you're going, I'm going. But I still think it's stupid. You're in no shape to be doing anything dangerous at all."

"That's why I have you three to look out for me." Nuala tried to smile, but it felt false. She had to agree with Fiona and Heather: It was stupid and suicidal. But she had made that tape, told everyone she would be there. The *gardaí* would be expecting her—unless they thought her injuries too severe, or that she had died. But the people would be expecting her, too. All the people brave enough to turn out, those courageous enough to defy the tyrants in the face of certain violence. How could she do anything less?

"I'll get dressed," Nuala said. "We haven't much time."

Chapter 20

"IGRAINE WAS RIGHT!" Heather whispered as she and Nuala eased their way through the still-growing crowd. It was only nine thirty-five, almost a half hour before the protest was to start, and already the demonstrators numbered in the thousands.

Fiona and Igraine had gone to take up defensive positions, but Heather had refused to leave Nuala's side. Both Heather and Nuala were armed, but their pistols, two each, were hidden in the deep pockets of their voluminous tweed coats. They were disguised as men: Heather's long blond hair was tucked into her cap, and they wore mustaches and sideburns. Nuala wasn't sure how much good her disguise was; she thought she was the cause of several double takes from the people she passed. Was it her unsuccessful disguise or the fact that her arm was in a sling that parted the crowd so easily? She and Heather had no trouble working their way toward the center of the park across from Belfast City Hall.

The *gardaí* were out in force: Uniformed men ringed the crowd and stood in clumps on every corner. They were wearing combat vests and helmets, carrying rifles and brandishing batons. Hovercraft lingered over the crowd, men with cameras and rifles leaning from every window. But would they attack a crowd as massive as this one?

The streets leading to the park were clotted with people, all heading in the same direction. They carried tricolors that waved in the December breeze, and clung with determination to banners and signs that threatened to fly away. FREE SHANNON MACGREEVY some read, and others demanded FREEDOM NOW! The historian in Nuala smiled when she saw a sign proclaiming WE SHALL OVERCOME. So the revisionists had not succeeded—not completely.

Some of the people Nuala passed carried hurling and *camogie* sticks, and their faces were grim. Sticks would not be much use against rifles—unless the rifle could be knocked from a *garda*'s hands. Igraine had been right: The people had seen the Guerrillas' tape of the weapons, and they were angry. But if and when the shooting started, how long would the anger last before turning to panic?

"How's the shoulder?" someone said, and Nuala turned. A woman she had never seen before, tall and with a curly mop of dark hair, was smiling at her.

"Uh . . . fine."

"Good. I knew you'd be here if you were able."

"Take care, though," the red-bearded man behind her added. "They're looking everywhere for you." He motioned with his chin and Nuala looked in the direction he had indicated, to see a uniformed *garda* wading none too gently through the crowd, stopping occasionally to peer into faces or to pull off caps, sometimes tugging hair in the process. The baton in his other hand prevented retaliation by those who glared at him in open hatred, but his passage was blocked on all sides by people who either crowded so close together they seemingly couldn't move or who "accidentally" jostled him.

"Thanks for the warn—" But the couple had drifted away. Nuala and Heather eased their way through the crowd in the opposite direction from the *garda*.

The double takes increased as Nuala passed. She touched her mustache: Yes, it was still there. But it was evidently not much of a disguise, or perhaps she had simply become too famous. And everyone knew her shoulder had been wounded, so the sling was a dead give-away. People were smiling and nodding as they made way; Nuala was beginning to feel conspicuous.

A pipe and drum band at the top of the pavilion steps roared to life, startling Nuala. She glanced at her watch: almost time. She wondered who was going to start the official program. Éadaoin had merely said that the "local contingent" would handle it. A makeshift platform had been laid at the top of the pavilion, but who—

A woman Nuala thought she recognized climbed up onto the platform as the song ended. It took a moment before the name came to her: It was Maeve, the leader of that tiny group Máire had taken Nuala to meet her second night back in Ireland, the group that Igraine had belonged to. So Maeve had been recruited into the Network. Nuala wondered how many of the other women had also joined. If only Máire could see this.

"May I have your attention?" The tiny microphone in Maeve's hand was powerful enough to make her voice heard over the vibration of the hovercraft overhead. The people in the front of the crowd, nearest the speakers, had to cover their ears.

"Listen, please!"

After a few moments the massive throng began to quiet. Glancing back from the bottom step, Nuala could see that people had entirely filled the park and were still streaming in from all directions.

"Fáilte roimh!" Maeve called out into the microphone. "Welcome to all of you! By coming here today you have taken an irrevocable step forward toward Irish freedom. We *will* be free, and no one can stop us!"

A roar rose from the crowd. Tricolors of all sizes waved, and signs and banners pumped up and down in the air. The unintelligible yell gradually took shape into the word *saoirse*, freedom, and settled into a defiant chant.

The *gardaí* moved among the people, dodging the waving banners and flags, easing toward the sidelines. Nuala watched them go, wondering how much the demonstrators could get away with before the violence started. The crowd was so big, any attack by the *gardaí* could turn it into a full-scale riot in moments. Would the authorities be that stupid? Or that calculating?

Maeve raised her hands and eventually the chanting tapered off. "My name is Maeve Delahanty," she resumed. "I tell you that openly and I wear no mask, knowing full well what the consequences will most likely be to myself, for this reason: We can hide no more. As long as we censor ourselves out of fear, as long as we hide our identities, we will never—*can* never—be free. We will appear to be what the government claims we are: criminals. But if we speak out openly, claiming the protection of the Constitution, then we will show the *government* to be the criminals if they harass us for doing so. We must stop hiding. We are not criminals. We are Irish citizens who have every right to speak out openly in our demand for freedom. We will have no rights until we use them, so starting today, let us begin to live as if we were free. When enough of us have the courage to do so, then we *will* be free, and we need never accept slavery again, to Church or government!"

The crowd roared its agreement, and most of the balaclavas

being worn were slipped off, though hesitantly. Some were thrown toward the *gardaí* on the sidelines.

Maeve smiled and nodded. "Yes! That's it! Take the step toward freedom! They may learn our identities"—she pointed to the men armed with cameras in the hovercraft above—"and perhaps some of us will be arrested or disappeared. But they can't kill us all! The prisons aren't big enough to hold the entire population of the country. They cannot stop us, no matter how many weapons they possess. And as anybody with a *teilifís* knows, their weapons are far fewer today than they were yesterday!"

A triumphant shout resounded through the park. It was deafening; Nuala winced and instinctively ducked as she was assaulted by the waves of noise from all sides. Everyone was cheering—except for the *gardaí*, who were fidgeting at the edges of the crowd.

In their excitement, the people had surged forward and Nuala was prodded from behind farther up the steps. She and Heather would have been separated if Nuala hadn't grabbed Heather's arm and refused to give way. She glanced around, but Igraine and Fiona were nowhere to be seen. Nuala was hemmed in on all sides; a sudden rush of claustrophobia and a premonition of disaster threatened to drown her. This was a mistake—she should have listened to Heather and Fiona. She had to get out of there, push her way to the edge before she was trampled.

"If Nuala Dennehy were here," Maeve went on as the cheering subsided, "she would tell you that the *gardaí* had planned to use that hideous arsenal on *us*, here today. She would tell you that the *gardaí*—and the Church and the government—fear us. The government—which, as we all know, is run as much from the Vatican as from the *Dáil*—wants us to stay in the same subservient, submissive role of slave that we have known all of our lives. So when someone like Nuala Dennehy comes along and defies them, dares to fight back, what is their response? You saw it on the *teilifís* last night. She went to that munitions depot to destroy the weapons that were to be used against us here today, and what was the price she paid for her courage? They set her afire!"

Nuala winced. She wanted to get the hell out of this suffocating crowd, but how could she leave? She had promised she would be here; she would have to step forward—and quickly, before Maeve canonized her.

She nodded to Heather, who was looking very pale under her false mustache, and started forward, wondering if the government would be foolish enough to make her a martyr in public. Would the shot come from the hovercraft overhead, or from some *garda* on the sidelines?

"Because of her grave injuries, received in service to her country," Maeve was saying, "Nuala could not be here today. But if she were—"

"Maeve?" Nuala stepped around the last few people, tugging off her mustache and sideburns. She stuck them and then her cap in her pocket.

Maeve hadn't heard her, but turned, eyes narrowing, at the movement. When she saw who it was, she stared; then her face lit up with a grin. She held out the microphone. "I *knew* you'd find a way to make it!"

Nuala shrugged and took the tiny device. "Just can't stay out of trouble," she said to Maeve. Then she raised the microphone. "Actually I *am* here today, because I promised you I would be."

Before she could say another word, the crowd erupted in applause, cheers, and a frenzy of flag- and banner-waving.

Maeve was applauding, too, standing next to her, until Nuala leaned toward her and spoke in her ear. "You'd best step back a bit, just in case their sharpshooters miss."

When Maeve stared at her in dismay, Nuala tilted her head back and looked up at the hovercraft. The uniformed men were pointing rifles and cameras directly at her. Bracing herself for the shot, she waved up at them, thinking as she did so that this was the stupidest thing she had ever done in her life. She wished to hell she was back in nice, safe Edinburgh. Her wave to the men who would murder her set the crowd off even more. The cheering, applauding, and yelling increased.

Nuala looked back down at Maeve and raised her eyebrows. Maeve swallowed, nodding, then slowly climbed down from the platform and retreated to the steps, leaving Nuala alone at the top.

Every muscle tense, Nuala waited, looking out at the crowd, refusing to look up again. She saw Heather's terrified and ghostly pale face in a sea of strangers. She still couldn't find Fiona and Igraine, but she knew they must be somewhere nearby.

The furor continued for several minutes, so Nuala waited—waited for the noise to die or for the shot that would end it all, whichever came first. As the crowd began to quiet, she wondered what the *gardaí* were waiting for. Were they afraid shooting her would be too blatant even for them, in front of this many people? The hovercraft was still directly above her—she could hear its hum. And the rifles were still aimed at her; she could feel them. She took a deep breath—she hadn't realized she had been holding her breath—and began.

"I have been thinking a great deal lately about a woman named Rosa Parks. She was an African-American of the twentieth century, and she helped to start the Civil Rights movement in the United States with one simple, courageous act: She refused one day to move to the back of the bus where people of her race were required to sit. She had had a long, hard day, and she was tired—physically, yes, but also tired of being treated as a second-class citizen—and so she refused to get up to give a white person her seat. As Maeve said a few moments ago, we have no rights until we use them, and that's what Rosa Parks did that day in America: She exercised her right to be a free woman. She refused to be subservient any longer. Her brave act led to a bus boycott by African-Americans in her city, which started the Civil Rights movement. So you see: One action by one individual *can* make a difference.

"Shannon MacGreevy took action, by fighting back against the man who had been abusing her for years. She refused to be subservient any longer. She is not the criminal the government would brand her, she is a hero." Nuala tried to smile. "I hate the word heroine—it sounds like an unsavory drug. Shannon MacGreevy is a hero. And she should not spend one more *moment* in jail. Rather, she should be released *immediately*, and given a medal for her bravery!"

The crowd roared its agreement, the banners proclaiming FREE SHANNON MACGREEVY bobbing higher than all the rest.

Still no shot was fired. Nuala's sides were slick with perspiration in spite of the December wind; her throat felt like sandpaper, and her heart thundered in her chest. Were they going to shoot or not? Or try to push through the people to arrest her? What were they waiting for?

"We must become a nation of Shannon MacGreevys!" Nuala continued. "And we need several million people with the courage of Rosa Parks. We need to be reminded of the words of another courageous African-American of the last century, Malcolm X, who said, 'Any time you beg another man to set you free, you will never be free. Freedom is something you have to do for yourselves.' Isn't it time we did it for ourselves? Isn't it time we were free?"

The sea of people agreed; the noise was deafening. Nuala

looked out over the crowd that stretched as far as she could see. She had no idea how many thousands of people were here, how many thousands of voices were raised to cheer for her, for themselves, for the idea of freedom. How could they lose if this many people—

Nuala felt rather than heard something hit the wooden platform behind her. She turned, saw the end of a rope, and started to look up, but then, above the crowd's frenzied cacaphony, Heather screamed, "Nuala!"

A man had scrambled up the steps to the platform. He had a gun in his hand. The people around him saw it and some of them lunged forward, clawing at him. He went down, but not before pulling the trigger.

Before she could jump out of the way, something slammed into Nuala; blackness pounded into her skull. Rough hands seized her from above, but she blacked out before she could fight back.

Chapter 21

THE PAIN WOKE Nuala. The throbbing in her head and the stiffness in every joint were insignificant compared to the agony of her shoulder. She barely stifled the moan, and didn't open her eyes. Her cheek was pressed to a metal floor; the cold of the metal seeped into the bare skin of her right side. She tried to concentrate, through the pain, on what else she could feel. Cold. All of her was so cold. She had no clothes, but the bandage was still there; she could feel the tug of the tape that kept it in place. The pain: The dermaclone had been torn when—what?

She tried to breathe as normally as possible, knowing she was being watched. She could feel the eyes on her skin. Concentrate! What had happened? Where was she? The end of a rope falling onto the platform behind her. From the *garda* hovercraft above, had to have been. Heather's scream. The man with the gun. Plain clothes. *Garda?* Assassin? No, he hadn't missed, but she had only been stunned, then snatched. Had to have been a *garda* infiltrator. They had taken her the only way they could in a crowd that huge. By surprise. By air. Before anyone could stop them. Not murder, but "arrest," to make it look legal.

Jail. She was in a cell somewhere. Naked. Under surveillance. The photographs of Tríona Rafferty flashed before her closed eyes: Tríona's terrified face, Tríona's battered corpse.

And Máire. Had this happened to her? Were they going to do to her what they had done to Máire? Had Máire's madness begun in a place like this?

Don't move. Don't let that whimper of fear escape. She was already in pain, from her shoulder. There would be more. And degradation. Rape. Don't imagine it! There was little time. They probably knew she was awake, were giving her awhile to let the fear grow. Tactics. Their tactics. What would hers be? The pain, god, the pain. No. Ignore it! Survival. Only thing to think about now. Escape, if possible, later. But now, survival. The pain— deal with it. Control it now, while there's time to concentrate.

The abscessed tooth. Findhorn, the Scottish spiritual community she had visited out of skeptical curiosity in her postgraduate days. Because of the storm, no transportation in or out had been possible. No drugs allowed at Findhorn. Had to control the pain until the storm died. Self-hypnosis. It had worked. It really had worked. Concentrate, relax. Make the pain diminish. She had done it once, made it last over forty-eight hours, had even gone to sleep in the middle of it and woken with the self-induced anesthesia still half working. It had worked then. It could work now. It had to. Of course then she had merely been in pain, not terror, too. Concentrate!

Colored switches in the air. Pretty colors, all shades of the rainbow. Each one corresponding to a part of the body. Concentrate. Relax. Her feet: a yellow switch. Throw the switch. So light. Her feet were becoming so light they would float up off the floor in a moment. So light. Perfectly relaxed. Her feet could feel no pain, would feel no pain, no matter what they— . . . No! Concentrate. Her feet were so light, so relaxed. They were floating. Her legs: an orange switch. Throw the switch. Relax, concentrate. So light, no pain . . .

"Where would she have gotten any drugs? Who—"

"No one, Sergeant! There have been no drugs. She's been under constant surveillance since capture. I can't understand—"

"Then what the hell's wrong with her?"

Their voices weren't muffled, just far away. She knew they

were standing over her, inches away, but it didn't matter, really, because she wasn't there. Well, she was, of course, but she wasn't.

Irial, the Scottish woman who had taught her self-hypnosis at Findhorn, had been amazed at her ability. She couldn't be hypnotized by anyone else because her will was too strong—she was too stubborn, was how Irial had phrased it—but self-hypnosis was another matter, even when already in pain from that damned tooth. She hadn't tried it since—hadn't needed to. But it came back to her here, in this place.

"She winces when I hit the bandage—she feels *something*!"

"Whatever it is she's doing, she can't keep it up for long. Carry on."

"But we've been at it for almost ten hours and she hasn't—"

"I said carry on! Do you have a problem with that, Private?"

"No, sir!"

She felt a dull, numbed pain at the blow on her shoulder. Her shoulder: a violet switch. Throw the switch. Her shoulder was light, floating . . .

When Nuala awoke, they were gone. Her shoulder throbbed as if some tiny person were inside it beating a bass drum, but the pain was still controllable. Her mind wasn't detached from her body as it had been under full hypnosis, but there was still a certain distance involved; if her brain gave her body a command, it might take awhile for the message to be received. She felt the soreness, the stiffness in every muscle. The beating had been systematic, thorough. If she had believed in a deity, she would have thanked it for Irial and those lessons long ago.

It was impossible to tell what time of day it was, since there was no window. The light overhead was much too strong and was no doubt left on twenty-four hours a day; that was a torture tactic Nuala had read about. She could smell a toilet in the corner behind her. And a plate of food on the floor by the cell door, probably rancid or poisoned just enough to make her violently ill. She ignored it. In her half-drowsy state, hunger could be ignored as easily as pain. Of course she couldn't keep *that* up forever. She thought of Bobby Sands and the other nine hunger strikers who had starved to death so long ago. The body could last only so long.

Slowly she pushed herself to a sitting position just for a change of scenery. A soreness between her legs made itself known. The memory of several rapes, one after another, drifted back to her, but she swatted it away. Later, when she was able to handle it. She would think about it then. It couldn't have been much fun for them, raping a woman in that condition. Like raping a corpse. Well, they'd be back to do it again, to see if they could elicit the response they desired: humiliation, pain, fear. They wouldn't succeed.

Nuala scooted herself lethargically across the floor, stopping when she could lean against the wall. Let them see her awake and think they could get what they wanted from her now. All it would take at this point was a few silent suggestions to her mind and she would be gone again. Safe.

It was a game now. The only thing she could do to defeat them, to fight back. Detach and give them no satisfaction. If they killed her . . . Her father would grieve, her sister, Heather. Her death would cause the three of them real pain, but there was nothing she could do to change that now. Fiona and Igraine? Her death would make them more determined than ever to fight on. And the rest of the country? Would her death be forgotten in a day, a week? Would they just find someone else, a new voice to tell them what they needed to hear?

Heather had all but compared her to Pearse and Connolly. *Their* deaths had meant something, had rallied the people of Ireland to fight for freedom. Would her death accomplish anything at all? *She* was no Patrick Pearse, certainly no James Connolly. She was nothing. And she had failed. For all her arrogant speeches, what had she accomplished? A few rallies, demonstrations. So what? No doubt the authorities were already busy on the air, painting a portrait of her as a terrorist, claiming she confessed to who knows what. And many would no doubt believe them. Had her life been for naught, then?

A click at the door, then it swung open. Three large men in uniform strutted in, smiling. The second one was already undoing his fly.

"Well, look who's awake, finally."

Her lower body was a red switch. Throw the switch. Her legs, her thighs, her hips were relaxing, floating . . .

The next time Nuala awoke, the light was still too bright, her body still stiff and sore, her shoulder difficult to move at all, but the hazy lethargy of semihypnosis lingered to protect her.

After a few moments, she pushed herself laboriously to her knees and crawled to the stinking toilet. It took great concentration and effort, but she managed to climb up and sit on it. She imagined that she was emptying herself of all that had been forced into her, all that had been done to her. There was no toilet paper, of course, so she tried to ignore the wetness, the smell, what was dried and encrusted on her thighs.

Back on her knees—safer than trying to walk because there was less distance to fall—she crawled to the opposite side of the cell and leaned, her eyes closed against the painful light.

After an uncertain amount of time, the door clicked and opened again. But this time it was only one person in uniform, a woman, and she carried a plate of food. Nuala peered at her through squinted eyes. The woman wore dark glasses, making her eyes impossible to read, but at least she wasn't smiling at Nuala's condition.

The female guard walked over to her, stopping about five meters away, and squatted down to Nuala's eye level. She put the plate on the floor and nudged it forward.

"Don't try anything. Not that you could, in your condition. You should eat. You need to keep up your strength."

Nuala just stared at her, trying to read the tone of her voice. It was flat, certainly not friendly, but there was something there . . .

"I'm not an interrogator; you have no need to fear me. I won't hurt you."

Nuala studied the female guard, wondering what kind of woman would take this job. In her forties, Nuala guessed, she was built like a refrigerator, a small one, with broad shoulders and hips and a thick waist. The blue skirt of her uniform ended just above muscled calves, and her sturdy arms stretched the blue sleeves. But the face, what could be seen around the dark glasses, was not that of a gladiator or thug. The delicate features were a surprising contrast to the sturdy body. Nuala wished she could see the woman's eyes. So much was hidden behind the glasses.

"I mean it now, it's not just talk. I won't hurt you."

Nuala just continued her silent study, and the woman sighed. "Well, of course you have no reason to believe me, considering what they've done to you. But I am telling the truth."

But Nuala didn't move or speak, just watched her.

The squat was awkward, so the guard surprised Nuala by sitting down on the floor, her legs straight out before her, showing Nuala her thick-soled black shoes. Why was she so nonchalant with a potentially violent prisoner? Was she that sure of her own physical strength? She carried no weapon that Nuala could see. Or did Nuala look so bad, so helpless?

"They're at their tea now," the guard said, pointing at the tiny camera on the ceiling. "Only reason I'm in here, instead of just leaving the food. I wanted to meet you, you being so famous and all . . . Anyway, you're not being observed; you can relax."

Nuala just stared, squinting. The guard pretended not to notice the lack of response, and went on.

"Like I said, I wanted to meet you because, well, I can't believe that one woman could have caused what you have. It's amazing. So I thought it only fair that you know about some of it . . . Anyway, you've been here for three days, in case you've been wondering. It's the twelfth of December—about two weeks before Christmas, it'd be now. The Guerrillas have been showing the tape of the rally and your arrest several times a day since it happened, and rerunning your past tapes, as well. There've been protests all over the country, in every county, demanding your release. And in other countries, too. London had a bloody huge one; couple of hundred thousand people showed for that one, but then there's lots of Irish there. And Sydney, Edinburgh—you lived there, didn't you? Probably some of your friends were out for that one, then. Montreal, Copenhagen, Washington: They even mentioned you *there* in their own demonstrations. You're quite the celebrity, aren't you? I'd say you were the most important personage we've had inside these walls during my time, and I've worked here nearly twenty years."

She paused, but Nuala didn't respond, didn't even blink. The guard nodded. "Yeah, you're a strong one. I could see that right off. Women brought in here, no matter how tough they thought they were on the outside, it never lasts long in here. They break 'em soon enough." She paused. "And then they brag about it, especially to us. Women guards, I mean. They love to tell us how they break women." Her mouth twisted and the monotone turned bitter. "They place bets with each other on how soon they can get a woman to beg for mercy. And they laugh about it in front of us. It's plain on their faces they think we're no better than the inmates, because we're women, too."

The woman's sudden smile startled Nuala. "But you! You've got them so frustrated and confused they don't know what to do! Here they were so looking forward to getting their hands on you, blaming you for their tarnished reputation lately and especially for that attack on the depot, though it was clear it was IRA did the killing. Oh, they were so eager to get you in their clutches, and now they're in a complete dither." She laughed, her breasts bobbing. "They can't figure out how a mere *female* could ignore them and all their tricks. It's given *us* more than a wee bit of satisfaction, let me tell you."

Then all traces of the smile died, and her tone became grim. "But it'll be no good for you in the end. Since the usual isn't working, they're talking about stepping it up in ways they haven't had to use in years: drugs and electric—" She frowned; furrows appeared above the dark glasses. "I'd hate to see that happen, I really would. All of us agreed at least a bit with the things you've been saying, if not the tactics. I'd hate to see what was left of you when they finished. Couldn't you *act* a bit? Let them think they're succeeding? So they won't do something— worse? You'd know the truth, and we would—the women guards, I mean; we're no help to them—but the men would believe what they wanted to believe. Like they always do. Give them some small satisfaction, and it'll go easier on you. Tell them something of what they want, anything."

So that's why she was here. Nuala pretended to stop listening, leaning her head back against the wall, and closed her eyes. Good cop, bad cop. And of course the good cop would have to be a woman.

She heard the guard sigh. "It's not what you're thinking. I told you: I'm not an interrogator; women aren't given that job. I'm just a guard. It's not my job to get information out of you, or to persuade you to give any to them. I wouldn't even *be* here if they weren't all at their tea, and not watching the monitors. Tell them something to make them go easier on you, but hell, make it up, I don't care!"

Nuala opened her eyes, trying again to read the woman's expression. Could she possibly be telling the truth? Why would she?

"Take off your glasses."

The words came out scratchy, as Nuala hadn't spoken or had any water in three days, but the guard understood her. She hesitated in surprise, then complied. The glare made her squeeze her eyes shut, but she made a hood of one hand at her eyebrows and squinted over at Nuala.

Nuala leaned forward, staring into the guard's eyes. They were wary, nervous, but there *was* something there, something undefinable, but real. This woman was not evil, in spite of working here, and she was looking at Nuala as if she considered her a human being. That was something.

"I brought you food," said the woman to break the awkward silence. "You've got to keep your strength up, to survive. A lot of people are counting on you, and even if you never leave here, your just being alive will mean something to them."

"It's poisoned."

"No, I promise you it's not." When Nuala just continued to stare at her, the guard leaned forward and picked up a chunk of what looked like stewmeat. "See?" She plopped the meat in her mouth and chewed. "Not poisoned, and I brought you meat for the protein. Like I said, they're not watching."

"Could have taken an antidote."

The guard sighed and shrugged. "Could have, but didn't."

Nuala stared into the woman's eyes. She had been sincere in her dislike of the male interrogators, there was no doubt about that. But she was a guard; she worked for the same people. Could she be trusted at all?

Spots swam before Nuala's eyes. She was too weak; she needed food if she was going to survive this. Her only choices were hunger strike, which would mean either force-feeding or slow death, or to trust this woman. She didn't want to trust her; it was too dangerous. But she wasn't as strong or as brave as Bobby Sands and she didn't think she could face slow starvation.

Nuala pushed herself feebly from the wall and reached out with her good arm. The guard smiled and pushed the plate toward her.

"Good! I give you my word it's not poisoned. Besides, they want you in better shape than you'd be if you puked your guts out. But go slow and don't eat much at first, or you'll make yourself sick anyway."

The thick stew was cold and greasy, but Nuala forced it down, though chewing was almost too much of an effort. Before she was finished, the guard got up to leave, looking at her watch and slipping her glasses back on.

"They'll be back from their tea in a few minutes; I'd best go." She paused at the door. "Remember, tell them something—anything—to make them think they're getting to you. Not even you could take what they'd try next. And good luck."

"What's your name?"

The guard hesitated, as if afraid to trust her with the information. "Mary Bernadette Duffin . . . Benny."

"Thanks, Benny."

When the men returned some hours later, Nuala didn't hypnotize herself as deeply as before, so some of the gasps and winces were genuine and some were fake. Their smiles were triumphant and gloating when she pretended to weep and sobbed "please!" They asked for names again, and this time she supplied some—all fake. The men were so pleased they only raped her once apiece, then left her alone in the painfully lit cell.

Chapter 22

ALTHOUGH SHE COULDN'T tell night from day and had no way of knowing what time it was, Nuala began to perceive a pattern to the days she spent in the interrogation cell. The men came in what was probably the morning and spent several hours with her, slapping her, kicking her shoulder, using her torso as a punching bag, raping her. Occasionally they would demand information, names, but it was almost an afterthought; they enjoyed their work. Then they would leave and some time later Benny the guard would bring her unpoisoned food while the others were "at their tea." Benny would talk to her while she ate, mostly about how much she hated her job, or her ambivalence toward the man she was engaged to marry, but Nuala said little. The woman appeared sympathetic, but she was still a guard; Nuala couldn't allow herself to trust her. After Benny left, sometimes the men would return for another round, sometimes not. The days passed.

One day Benny came early; the men hadn't been there yet.

"They won't be in to you this morning," Benny said. "I'm to take you to get cleaned up; you're to have a visitor today."

"A visitor? But I'm on remand; I didn't think I was allowed—who is it?"

Benny shrugged. "Didn't see fit to tell me, did they? And you may be on remand, but you're too famous to suit the administration. Too many people wondering if you're all right. I imagine that's why this visit. Now come along; you smell fierce."

Benny led her down an empty corridor past other cells, but she couldn't see any of the occupants; the doors were solid metal like her own. And the change in lighting made it difficult to see much anyway. At the end of the corridor she paused, hearing a tapping sound.

"That's code," Benny explained. "Those that have been on the solitary wing long enough use it to communicate with each other. I expect you'll learn it eventually."

"How many women—"

"Mustn't ask questions," Benny interrupted. "Against regulations."

Nuala didn't say anything else, just followed Benny to the showers. They had the place to themselves. "Security reasons," Benny explained. "You're just too dangerous for any of the others to even see. Though they know you're here, right enough. They spread that news the minute you arrived."

Benny helped her remove the filthy bandage, and Nuala was relieved to see that the rips in the dermaclone hadn't become infected. Though the constant abuse kept the skin from healing properly, and she could see that she would have quite a large scarred area, it wasn't as bad as she had feared it would be.

Nuala washed herself with the vile-smelling liquid Benny gave her as thoroughly and rapidly as possible, so that she could spend the rest of the precious few minutes just standing under the hot water. She suspected Benny indulged her by letting her take more time than the minimum necessary.

There was a prison gown waiting for her. Nuala hesitated, thinking of Bobby Sands and the "blanket protest" of the 1980s. Political prisoners back then—some in this very jail, perhaps—had refused to wear prison garb because it branded them as common criminals, not the political prisoners they were. So their own clothes were forcibly taken, leaving them the hated prison clothes or a single blanket to cover their nakedness. They chose the blanket.

Nuala stared at the gown, to Benny's puzzlement. "What?" the guard asked. "It's the only clothes you've been allowed in a week. I should think you'd be eager to cover yourself. And you can't see your visitor naked, can you now? It's not allowed."

Nuala picked up the gown. "I'm no Bobby Sands, am I?"

"Who?"

Nuala sighed.

"Nuala!" Her lips moved, but no sound came out.

It was Kerry. She rushed to the security window and pressed her hands against it, trying to touch her sister.

The male guard shoved a chair into the back of Nuala's legs and pushed down on her shoulders, squeezing the left one deliberately. Nuala ignored him, didn't even wince. She leaned toward her sister as soon as he let go.

Tears streaming down her face, Kerry pushed the com button. "My God, Nuala! What have they done to you? I'll demand to see the administrator! They can't—"

Nuala pressed her own com button. "How are you, kid? Still a nun, I see."

Kerry's face was a war of emotions. She tried to smile, but she couldn't smile and cry at the same time. It took her a moment to get herself under control. "You ... You haven't been charged with anything yet. I checked."

Nuala shrugged. "Charges, trials. Mere formalities in a dictatorship. I'm not going anywhere—ever. Except to a different cell after the trial, perhaps. I wonder if I'll get Mairéad Farrell's cell. That would be poetic, wouldn't it?"

"Da's been phoning solicitors, trying to find someone who'll take your case."

"How is Da?" Nuala tried to keep the emotion out of her voice, her expression, because of the guard behind her and the surveillance cameras. But Kerry read her eyes.

"His condition is—no worse, praise God."

But Nuala read *her* eyes and knew she was lying.

"Tell him—" What? This might be the last message she ever got to her father. What could she say? "Tell him they won't break me." She knew the consequences that would bring, especially from the interrogator she thought of as Adolf. But her father was more important than Adolf's petty torments. "I'm strong because I'm *his* daughter. Tell him."

Kerry nodded tearfully. "I will. Is there anything I can do for you? Go see the prison officials—"

Nuala shook her head. "Please don't. I'm fine. But you could pray for me, I suppose." At Kerry's surprise, Nuala shrugged. "Well, it won't do any good, of course, but it can't hurt."

Kerry chuckled in spite of herself. "You never change, do you? No matter what."

"Well, of course not. I am constant as the morning star. If I wasn't I wouldn't be the success I am today."

Kerry smiled again, but it was brief. "Did you hear about the violence after your—arrest?"

"Violence?" Nuala shook her head again. "My subscription to

the morning *Times* has been curiously held up lately. What violence?"

Kerry glanced at the guard behind Nuala, then said, "After your—after they took you, the crowd was so enraged that they rioted. They killed the man who shot you, beat him to death. He was a *garda*, and two other *gardaí* were killed, and eleven protestors. They tried to storm City Hall, they burned the pavilion in the park, and destroyed several *garda* vehicles. They even burned down half the Europa Hotel. There were scores of injuries. The worst rioting in nearly a hundred years, the Evening News said."

"Really?" Nuala had to struggle to keep her face emotionless. "All that because of little old me? How extraordinary."

"I've been saying novenas for the dead," Kerry said.

"Good of you," Nuala replied. How could she pretend this meant nothing to her? Fourteen people dead, because she had been arrested! She wasn't worth the lives of fourteen people! The bastards! They would pay. They would pay dearly for this.

"Time's up," the guard behind Nuala said, and pulled on her chair.

"It can't be!" Kerry cried. "We only just—"

But she stopped at the look of Nuala's face. She wouldn't give them the satisfaction, and neither must Kerry.

"See you around, kid," Nuala said, and stood up.

"I—I love you, Nuala." Kerry tried not to cry, but failed.

Nuala gritted her teeth and blinked hard. "Well, of course you do. I'm your sister." She said it with her eyes, then turned at the guard's touch and left the room.

Nuala was still seething with rage and pain when Adolf and his two fellow Gestapo entered her cell soon after Benny had strip-searched her and had taken her gown away again.

"Have a nice wee visit with your sister the holy bitch?" Adolf said, grinning the death's-head grin he always wore. Nuala ignored the comment. She was too angry to visualize the colored switches. Fourteen people dead! Because the government and bastards like these petty little monsters were too afraid of losing their grip on power to allow harmless people like herself to speak the truth! Fourteen people!

Adolf crossed his arms and studied her with anticipation. "We've just been playing up to now, softening you up and having a bit of fun. But now it's time to get serious. You're going to tell us the name of your leader, right? Tell us what man is se-

cretly in charge of all this nonsense, and we'll let you off easy.
If you don't, well . . . that just means more fun for us, and more
misery for yourself. Which is fine with us, right, lads?"

The other two goons—Fritz and Hans, as Nuala thought of
them, when she thought of them at all—chuckled. Fritz, as
usual, started to undo his fly. He was so predictable.

Nuala stared at Adolf. They thought a man was in charge. Of
course they would. It wouldn't occur to them that three women
like Éadaoin, Brigid, and Dana could ever be the force behind a
revolutionary movement. Not three *women*. She could give them
a fake male name, but their reaction when they had discovered
the phoniness of the last names had been particularly unpleasant.
But she would die before giving up Éadaoin or Brigid or Dana.
Die. As Wolfe Tone had died in his cell, cutting his own throat
before the British could execute him.

Adolf took a step closer. "So let's have it, love. The name.
Who is he?"

"Wolfe Tone," Nuala said. "My leader is Wolfe Tone."

"Eh?" Adolf stopped, puzzled at how easy it had been. "And
just where could we find this lad Tone?"

Hans cleared his throat, apparently embarrassed at Adolf's ig-
norance. Nuala smiled. "Uh—" Hans said. Adolf turned to him.
"He's out of history," Hans explained. "Some fellow led an uprising or other."

Adolf turned back to Nuala, his face turning purple.

"The Father of Irish Republicanism," Nuala said, smiling.
"Seventeen ninety-eight. You really should have known that,
you ignorant arsehole."

Adolf swung at her, but somehow she dodged the blow.
"Missed," she said, too angry to care how furious she was mak-
ing him. "Would you like some more names? How about Patrick
Pearse? James Connolly. Robert Emmet. Bernadette Devlin
McAliskey. Red Hugh O'Donnell. Gerry Adams. Constance
Markievicz. Joe Doherty."

The next punch landed, and Nuala was knocked backward.
She fell against the toilet, stunned for a moment.

Adolf loomed over her, and before she could raise an arm to
ward off the blow he had slapped her right ear, knocking her
head sideways.

"You want the leader?" she yelled before he could land another. "You bloody damn fools, you think it's a man? A *man*?
Well, it's a *woman*, and you're looking at her! *I'm* the leader,
you pus-filled pissants!" Let them think it was her, and look no

farther. "Myself, and no other! You stupid bollixes! You've had me an entire week and you didn't *know* that? The whole of the country knows it, but you lot don't, because you're too dim-witted to figure it out!"

Instead of hitting her, Adolf leaned over to grab her. Something fell out of his uniform pocket and hit Nuala's thigh. He didn't notice and she didn't have time to look at it, but whatever it was, it might prove useful. Twisting sideways as if to avoid his grasp, Nuala batted the small object behind the toilet, screaming insults at him to cover the sound. Then Adolf got a hold on her still-painful left shoulder and squeezed. Roaring in pain and uncontrolled rage, Nuala twisted back again and kicked up as hard as she could. Her foot landed squarely on Adolf's testicles. He screamed and fell backward, landing on his knees. Hans and Fritz, taken by surprise, stared at their comrade. Nuala stared at him, too, panting from exertion and grim satisfaction. "I bet that hurt," she said as he vomited.

She tried to conjure up the colored switches, but it was difficult without preparation time to slow down her pulse and her breathing. She had no time to relax because of what they were doing to her. Before she could achieve self-hypnosis, she had passed out from the pain.

When Nuala awoke, she was alone. She tried to move, but gasped and lay still. They had outdone themselves this time. It would do little good to sit up, because it would be too painful to sit in any position. She saw that her thighs were slick with blood. It hadn't completely dried yet; she was probably still bleeding.

The door clicked, and Nuala frantically tried to visualize the colored switches. But it was only Benny with her supper. Nuala slumped in relief.

Benny stared at her, horrified. Then she put the plate of food on the floor and left quickly. Nuala hadn't moved by the time she returned with a wet towel.

Benny gently wiped Nuala's thighs and buttocks, wincing at Nuala's gasps as she touched bruised and torn membranes. "You need a doctor!" Benny muttered, her fury contrasting with the gentleness of her touch. "No excuse for *this* ... Bloody bastards, think they can do whatever they like ..." Nuala didn't even try to reply; she had no energy for it and was in too much pain. When Benny was done with her ministrations, she brought the plate over, in spite of Nuala's mute protest. "Now, now, you need your strength, and I wouldn't be allowed to bring more later."

Benny, the burly prison guard, held Nuala across her lap and patiently fed her every bite, murmuring to her the entire time about what a strong woman she was, and how she would survive this and come out of it even stronger. When the food was gone, Benny laid her back on the floor.

"Now, then. I'm sending for the doctor, whether it costs me a reprimand or not. And because I'll make it an official request, they can't come back to you tonight. Don't worry."

"Thanks, Benny," Nuala mumbled through bruised and swollen lips.

After the visit by the doctor, a grim and somber man who didn't even raise an eyebrow at the nature or extent of her injuries and treated them none too gently with antiseptic, Nuala crawled to the toilet and made a pretense of vomiting. Meanwhile, her hand was searching for the small object Adolf had dropped. Finally grasping it, she hid it in her hand and pulled it close, pretending to clutch her ribs in pain. Then she crawled to the corner farthest from the camera and lay on her side facing away from it, hiding the object from view. Curling herself into a fetal position, she opened her hand.

The rectangle was small, perhaps eight centimeters by five, with a heavy coating of plastic. No words were printed on it, but Nuala knew what it was: a cardkey! This little card unlocked her cell door and who knew which others in this hellhole. Since it had fallen from Adolf's pocket, that meant it was imprinted with his own bioscan. All employees would have their own cardkeys, imprinted with their bioscans; she knew that much about security.

Nuala ran her fingers over the card. It felt completely smooth. She knew the circuitry pattern was inside, but she couldn't trace it with her fingers. And the card was just solid black; she couldn't—Wait! Something glinted in the strong light of the cell. She tilted the card. There! An iridescent holo pattern shone against the black background of the card. It *was* visible—because of the abnormally bright light.

She knew that on all cardkeys the pattern of the circuitry was overlaid with the individual's bioscan pattern, but she didn't know enough about the technology to know which was which; the two patterns were interwoven and mingled like a braid. Braid. Yes, it did vaguely resemble an ancient Celtic braid/knot design, like the ones the nuns had taught them to draw in art class.

Nuala was careful to remain hunched over and apparently motionless as she studied the pattern. They were watching. She couldn't just get up—even if she were able to stand—open the door, and walk out of the jail naked. And even if Adolf somehow hadn't missed his cardkey yet—or hadn't figured out where he had lost it—he surely would by morning. So she had little time. She had the key to her cell door, but what . . . The key. Dev. Lincoln Prison. Michael Collins, the Big Fellow. Her father's favorite story.

If she could draw—her father would know; he would remember the story. And he knew how to contact Éadaoin's people; they had been working with him, asking his advice about setting up hedge schools like the one he had begun in Falarragh. But even if they somehow managed to translate her attempt at a drawing into the real thing and make an exact duplicate and got it to her—somehow—what good would it do? Surely keys today didn't open *every* door in a prison. And so Adolf's bioscan would work only on whichever doors he was authorized to open. It would be all computerized, of course, all on some database somewhere.

Database. Éadaoin's people had infiltrated other government databases; could they get into this one? Éadaoin's husband, Piaras, designed software; perhaps he would know how to analyze and duplicate the pattern combination. But if Adolf's bioscan pattern wasn't authorized to open other doors, could Piaras change that? The cooking class. Some woman had said that her nephew had a new job in the Department of Corrections. Could *he* infiltrate the database? Or help Piaras to do so? Could Adolf's bioscan pattern be combined with other circuitry patterns? Would Piaras know which pattern was which? With the help of that nephew, could he make changes without being caught? Probably not; the very thought was crazy.

Nuala didn't know if any of these wild ideas were even remotely plausible. She stared at the card's patterns. It could even be a trap. Had Adolf intentionally dropped his cardkey? She had no way of knowing, of being certain about anything. But it was a chance, if a very remote one—it *was* a chance. She had to take it, to try. After that, it was up to her father and Éadaoin or Piaras. She had to put her life in their hands.

She had only one night, if she was that lucky, to memorize the design in every detail, and to figure out how to incorporate every minor twist and turn of the pattern—because she didn't know which ones were essential—into a Celtic braid. It was her only chance.

Chapter 23

"THEY WON'T BOTHER you today," Benny said when she brought breakfast: dry toast and tea. "The doctor told them to hold off."

"Did you get in any trouble for calling him?" Nuala asked after taking a sip of tepid tea. She was leaning against the wall; it hurt too much to sit up straight.

Benny shrugged. "A few insults is all. I pointed out to the supervisor that in case your sister dropped by for another visit, you'd better be able to go see her. Last thing the administration needs is a nun crying abuse. Wouldn't look good."

Nuala smiled and took a bite of toast. She wanted to launch into her plan, pour out her request, and plead with Benny. But of course she couldn't—it might ruin everything. It had to be done properly. She let Benny chat on about some prisoner in another wing who was due to have a baby any day, and how all the guards had a pool on when it would arrive, while she finished her toast and tea.

As Benny collected the plate and cup, Nuala finally spoke. "Benny?"

"Hm?"

"You've been very good to me, and I'd never do anything to cause you trouble. I just want you to know that."

"Right," Benny said, but waited for the rest of it.

"So I wouldn't ask any favors that would cause you trouble, I mean."

"Why do I get the feeling you're about to, then?" Benny looked distinctly uncomfortable; she glanced over at the camera and winced in spite of the dark glasses.

"It's my father." Nuala hurried on, hoping desperately that Benny wouldn't refuse to hear any more. "He's dying—and I'm not making that up for sympathy; it's true. He's the reason I came back from Scotland in the first place. He *is* dying, and he's too ill to come visit. Since it's not likely I'll be getting out of here to go visit him, it looks like I'll never see him again. I have no idea how much time he has left, but I know it isn't much. I just—I just wanted to write him a letter, that's all. Even convicts are allowed that much, aren't they?"

Benny fidgeted. "You're not a convict yet; you're just on remand. Special privileges are not—"

"Don't quote rules at me, Benny, please! My da's dying!" Nuala hoped the desperation in her voice was the right amount, but not too much. Benny *had* to believe her. She took a deep breath and made a show of calming down. "I'm not asking you to smuggle anything out; I just told you I wouldn't want to cause you any trouble. You could show the bloody thing to the prison censors, I don't care. I just—I just want to be able to tell my da that I love him, one last time. Is that so terrible? And it would make the administration look good, right? For the same reason they allowed my sister to visit me. To show that I'm being treated fairly. Just a harmless Christmas card . . . Or did Christmas pass and I missed it?"

Benny shook her head, still frowning. "It's three days before Christmas. And all prisoners are required to attend Mass on the day. Even you, I should imagine."

"Then it's not too late for me to make a Christmas card for me da?" She let the pleading show on her face now, shamelessly trying to manipulate the woman's soft heart.

Finally Benny sighed. "I can't promise. But I'll see what I can do." She turned to go.

"God bless you for the trying, Benny."

The guard just grumbled as she let herself out.

Not ten minutes later she returned, but the expression on her face chilled Nuala.

"If you've lied to me—"

"What? What are you talking about?" How could she know what Nuala was planning? She hadn't done it yet.

Benny stared at her, frowning and uncertain. "He's lost something, and if you've got it—"

"Who? Got what? What is it?"

"Higgins. He lost it, probably when he was—when he was here yesterday."

"Who the hell's Higgins?"

"One of the—the tall one, with the bushy mustache. One that does most of the talking."

"Oh, Adolf. What's *he* lost, besides his mind and any shred of humanity his mother gave him?"

Benny was still studying her carefully. Nuala felt the perspiration in her armpits in spite of the cool temperature of the cell. She had never been any good at lying. If Benny found her out . . .

"It's not as if you could use it undetected . . . or had anywhere to hide it," Benny murmured, as if to herself.

"Hide what?"

Benny looked around the cell. There was nothing in the room except the toilet and Nuala. No bed, no blanket, nothing.

"Stand up."

Nuala groaned. "For god's sake, Benny, not another cavity search. Didn't the doctor treat every crevice on me yesterday? If I was hiding something on me, wouldn't he have found whatever the hell it is you're looking for?"

Benny frowned again. Obviously she hadn't thought about the doctor. She glanced around the cell again, focusing on the toilet. She crossed to it. Meanwhile, Nuala forced herself to her feet, grumbling, but making a show of obeying.

Benny looked in the toilet bowl, in the open tank, around the base, and finally behind the base. Then she tensed like a hunting dog on point and shot a suspicious glance at Nuala, who was leaning against the wall as if she were going to collapse at any moment.

Benny got down on her knees and reached behind the toilet, coming up with the cardkey.

"What's that?" Nuala asked, breathing hard from the pain and the effort of standing up.

Benny studied her for a moment, then slipped the cardkey in her pocket. "Nothing important."

"Well, are you still going to search me or can I sit down?"

"How would it have . . ." Benny looked back at the toilet.

"Adolf lost something behind the toilet?" Nuala asked. "Could have happened when I kicked him to his knees, I suppose. We were in that vicinity."

"You kicked him?" This was news to Benny, and not unpleasant news from the look on her face.

"In the balls," Nuala confirmed. "Square kick, dead on. He felt it, he did. Love to do it again, too."

Benny squelched a smile. "Wait until I spread *that* about." She frowned suddenly. "So that's why they, uh—"

"Yeah," Nuala said. "That's why they, *uh*. Can I sit down or do I have to bend over and spread 'em?"

Benny waved at her. "Sit, sit. I found it. It was his own damn fault, and you didn't even know it was here ... Right?" She squinted at Nuala, still a little suspicious.

"Right. Whatever you say." Nuala slid slowly down the wall, her pain not an act. Benny, headed for the door, shot Nuala one last look before leaving. Nuala sighed in the most profound relief she had ever experienced and leaned back against the wall, exhausted.

Perhaps an hour later Benny returned again, a piece of green paper and a pencil in her hands. She looked embarrassed as she handed them to Nuala. "The argument about fair treatment for the public's consumption worked."

"Oh, Benny! Thank you! *Go raibh míle maith agat!*"

Benny brushed aside the thanks. "But it will have to go past the censors, of course, so remember that."

"I will; no problem. *Thank* you!"

"Yeah, yeah. You'll be watched, you know, to make sure you don't try to harm yourself with them."

"With a pencil and paper?" Nuala raised her eyebrows. "How ever could I—"

"Regulations. I'll pick them up when I bring your supper. You have until then ... Oh, and sorry about—before. About not believing you, I mean."

An apology? Nuala almost felt guilty about lying to her. Almost. "That's all right. Occupational hazard, I should think."

Benny muttered something that sounded like "hmph" as she left.

Nuala folded the paper, put it on the floor, and leaned over it, pencil clutched in her hand. She closed her eyes and conjured up the memory of the bioscan/circuitry pattern she had spent all night memorizing. Her hand trembled slightly as she began to draw.

Benny stared at the card. "Didn't know you were an artist."

"Hardly," Nuala said, watching the guard. Would she spot it? Was it too obvious? "A few Celtic border designs and a bit of calligraphy is all I ever learned from the nuns in art class. I couldn't draw a real picture if my life depended on it." Which it did.

Benny shrugged. "Looks good to me—I can't draw at all. What's this Big Fellow business? You call your own da that?"

Nuala smiled the most desperate smile of her life. "It's an old nickname. He got called Big Fellow when he was young, because he wasn't. Big, that is. Still isn't. The name stuck."

"Hm," Benny said. "And Dev Lincoln?"

"Da's best friend. They were inseparable. Until Uncle Dev—that's what I called him—died, almost twenty years ago now. We had some good times, the three of us. I just wanted Da to remember our good times."

Benny stared at her. Nuala fought to keep the smile on her face. She was the world's worst liar; surely Benny could see that.

But Benny just nodded and slipped the card and the pencil in her pocket. "Assuming it gets past the censors, I'll mail it tonight myself. Should get to Donegal by Christmas Eve."

"Thanks again, Benny. I appreciate it more than you know."

The next few days were agony, but at least not the physical sort. Adolf and his friends made no appearance, without any explanation from Benny, who was the only person Nuala saw.

So Nuala sat or leaned, whichever was the least uncomfortable, and waited, wondering. Wondering whether the three men would arrive to torture her again. Wondering if the card had arrived at her father's house—Benny had told her she had mailed it. Wondering whether the drawing of the pattern hidden in the braid border had slipped by the censors or whether they knew what it was and were going to catch her father with it somehow. Wondering if her father would know what to look for. Would he understand the references to Éamonn de Valera's escape from Lincoln Prison with the help of Michael Collins, the Big Fellow, and the picture of the cell-door key Dev had drawn on a Christmas card? How could Da not understand it? It was himself who had taught her that story. But was he too sick to do anything about it? Surely he was being watched, even with his outlaw daughter locked up. Could he get it to Éadaoin's people? And what would they do with it? And was her drawing accurate enough? And how could she possibly get away with using it if she *did* get a duplicate cardkey? Nuala had no answers, and the uncertainty was agony.

The cell door clicked. Nuala automatically braced herself, but it was Benny.

"Merry Christmas."

"Is it today?"

"It is," Benny replied. "And I'm taking you to the showers."

"Really?" Nuala pushed herself up eagerly. A shower suddenly seemed like the best Christmas present she had ever received. She couldn't help but grin; she was so happy at the thought of being clean.

"Yeah." Benny smiled, too, though she tried to hide it. "I was supposed to take you later, to clean you up for Mass, but you're to have a visitor, so it's to the showers now."

"A visitor?" Nuala didn't dare hope. "My da? But I thought he was too—"

"I don't know who it is!" Benny snapped. "They don't tell me, remember?"

"Oh, right. I'm sorry, Benny. I forgot."

"Well, come on, then."

Nuala followed Benny into the corridor. It was so dark Nuala felt blind; she stumbled over nothing. Benny took her arm.

"This is normal lighting," Benny said, an odd note in her voice. "If they keep you in there much longer . . ." But she left it unspoken.

Nuala batted aside the sudden fear of blindness. She concentrated on the prospect of a shower.

After they had walked down half the corridor, Benny spoke quietly. "The protests for your release are increasing. The Scottish Prime Minister paid a call to Dublin to discuss the matter with the *Taoiseach*."

Nuala was astounded. "She did? You're kidding!"

"Keep your voice down!" Benny whispered. "I shouldn't be telling you this, but I thought you should know the world hasn't forgotten you. Things can't continue with nothing being done— but whatever they might do, it won't necessarily be good news."

Killed while trying to escape flitted across Nuala's mind. Her throat constricted; she swallowed.

"You're walking better," Benny remarked.

"Yeah, I don't hurt near as much. I keep expecting Higgins and company to pop in just to undo whatever healing has been going on."

Benny was silent for a moment, then began to whisper. "They were told to lay off until after Christmas, because the administration wanted you looking all right for a possible Christmas visit and especially for Mass, when a priest and several nuns will have a look at you. Don't want any bad publicity, you know . . . I wasn't allowed to tell you before."

"I understand. Psychological torture, my fearing their imminent arrival. I know you wanted no part of that; it's okay, Benny."

By the time they got to the showers, Nuala's vision had improved enough for her to see what she was doing. She recognized the prison gown waiting for her after her shower, and hesitated only a moment before slipping it over her head.

"You again. Hi, kid." Nuala smiled at her sister. Of course it had been irrational to hope that Da had come; he was sick, after all.

"You're looking better," Kerry said, the relief plain on her face and in her voice.

"Must be all that lounging about the pool I've been doing."

Kerry smiled. There was a certain tenseness in the way she sat; or was it Nuala's imagination? After all, how well did she know Kerry? But there was something . . .

"Merry Christmas."

"Bah, humbug."

Kerry chuckled. "You always pretended you didn't like Christmas, but I know better. Remember when we used to go to confession on Christmas Day when I was little? You'd hold my hand all the way to the chapel, and let me go in first, then you'd be next in to talk to the priest."

Nuala blinked. What the hell was Kerry talking about? By the time of Kerry's First Communion, Nuala had long since refused to go to confession—ever—and she had left for Scotland not long after. What was Kerry trying to tell her?

"Remember old Father Collins?"

Who? Collins? As in Michael Collins? Had Da told her—
"Sure, I remember him. Sour old bag of bilge."

Kerry shook her head, smiling. "An apt description, if an unkind one."

"How's Da?" Stop dancing around it, Kerry.

Kerry smiled again, a genuine smile with no hidden shadings. "Better. *Much* better. Your card perked up his spirits so, he's ten years younger, I swear! Leave it to you to remind him of all those happy memories of Uncle Dev."

So. The message had gotten through, and Kerry knew about it.

"I'm glad," Nuala said. "I wish there was more I could do for him."

"You might yet, you never know." Kerry's eyes were saying

things her mouth didn't dare. "And he wishes he could do something for you, of course. But as he can't at the moment, he told me to tell you to look to your soul."

"My soul?" What the—

"Yes," Kerry said, the intensity of her gaze urging Nuala to read her mind. "Since you've been off in heathen Scotland for so long, he doesn't doubt that it's been a long time since you were last at confession."

Confession again.

"It has, hasn't it?" Kerry shook an admonishing finger. "Admit it."

"Well, I suppose—"

"I knew it. Well, I've checked, and I'm told that there will be a Christmas Mass here today, with opportunity for confession before. And you'll be allowed to participate in both; I was assured by the supervisor himself. So now you've no excuse."

Confession? What did that—

"Da told me to tell you to go to confession *today*, no more delays. You will find everything your soul yearns for in the confessional: God's love and forgiveness, His sure help and steady Hand."

Nuala blinked and almost shrugged, but remembered the cameras. She smiled. "Well, like I said before, it can't help, but it couldn't hurt."

Kerry smiled back. "Seek the Lord's help, Nuala, and you will find it."

Nuala certainly hoped so.

"Time," the guard said. Another over-before-you-know-it visit. But this time Kerry didn't protest at all. She was smiling.

"Shall I tell Da you promise you'll go to confession today? It'll make him so happy."

"All right, all right," Nuala said as she stood up. "Stop nagging, will you? I'll go see the blasted priest." Message received, Kerry. Whatever it means.

"Good. I'll come again soon, then. Take care."

Nuala followed Benny into the sparse, depressing prison chapel. No stained glass windows here, and no statues. Just a huge crucifix above the plain altar and several candles. And only one surveillance camera, in the back.

Benny left Nuala in the back of the chapel, waving her forward. She went over to the corner to chat with other female guards.

Nuala walked up the center of the room, aware that hundreds of inmates, every one who did not have her head bowed in prayer, were staring at her. They *all* recognized her? She felt conspicuous in the thin, faded-blue gown. She hadn't seen a mirror in weeks; she wondered how many bruises were still visible.

There was a line of women sitting in the pew next to the confessional. Eight women ahead of her. Would there be time before the Mass started? What if there wasn't? Would it be too late? Would the priest leave, or would he delay Mass until they all got their chance? What was in that blasted confessional? And when could she use it if it was what she hoped? Which doors would it unlock? And how would she get to them?

Nuala sat, every muscle tense, pretending to contemplate her sins, as the women ahead of her filed in and took forever to find forgiveness.

"I'm sorry you got caught."

Nuala jumped and turned. The woman ahead of her in line, a thin, bedraggled woman with dead eyes, was staring at her.

"Excuse me?"

"I heard about what you were doing," the woman said. "We hear things, even in here. It was the first thing in a long time gave me any hope. But then you got caught." She sighed, the sound seeming to come up from her toes. "Figures. Knew it was no use."

"I—" Nuala began, but the woman turned away and then got up to take her turn in the confessional.

Nuala sat, not sure how or what to feel. She felt eyes on her and turned around; half the women in the room were still staring at her. Did they feel the way that woman did? Without hope? And she had something to do with that? It was a responsibility she didn't want. But she had no time to think of that now; she had to be ready. But ready for what?

In a surprisingly short time, the woman exited the confessional, looking every bit as hopeless as when she had entered. She didn't glance at Nuala.

Stepping into the dark booth, Nuala was blinded when she pulled the heavy curtain shut. It had been difficult enough to see in the dimly lit chapel, but in here it was impossible. Immediately her hands began to search the tiny compartment. She couldn't see a bloody thing!

"Yes, my child?" a male voice said softly—in her ear, it seemed.

Nuala jumped, then felt foolish. She had almost forgotten the priest in her eager search. Of course she couldn't see him; he would be on the other side of the screen. She found that with her hand.

"Uh, right," she said. She would have to stall while her hands groped blindly. "Forgive me, Father, for I have sinned," she recited. "It's been about . . . uh . . . hell, I don't know, twenty-five years or more since my last confession."

She was surprised to hear humor in the response. "You really shouldn't say 'hell' in the confessional, my child. Unless referring to the actual place, of course."

"Oh, right. Sorry."

"I forgive you."

Nuala's hands continued their fruitless search.

"What is your first name, child?"

What? Wait a minute, names weren't a part of this drill. Nuala considered this, then played along. "Nuala."

"I thought so. And it's about time."

"What?"

"It's under the seat."

"What?" Was this a trap?

"Éadaoin sends her regards," the man whispered.

Nuala was speechless. Éadaoin? Then this man was—

"Are you really a priest?"

He chuckled. "Of course not. And this confessional isn't bugged; I checked. Have you found it yet? It's under the seat cushion on the right side."

In wonder, Nuala's fingers pried up the cushion and slid under it. There it was! Her hand closed around a slim, plastic-coated card. *You did it, Da!*

"Well?"

"Got it!" Nuala whispered. "Who the hell—"

"You may not need it," the phony priest interrupted. "Let's hope not. It's really just Plan B."

"There's a Plan A?"

"Yes—listen. When you leave the confessional, go sit in the front row on the right side. There will be three other inmates we've persuaded to sit there who have a similar build to yourself and short, reddish hair. From the back, you will all look much the same. Then, toward the end of the Mass, two of my 'nuns' will cause a commotion in the back of the chapel with some of the inmates, and the third 'nun' will block the camera's view— accidentally, of course. Don't look back at them; look up at me. When the guards are all distracted, I'll nod. You will *immedi-*

ately run forward and slip into the sacristy. You'll find a nun's habit on the bottom shelf of the press. Put it on quickly and hide in the closet with our coats. I'll finish up the Mass as fast as I can, and then you'll walk out with the rest of us."

"Are you kidding? That will never work!"

"It's the best we could do on such short notice! And besides, we'll be gone before they have time to count heads."

Nuala shook her head, but he couldn't see her. "This may be my only chance. If you're anything remotely resembling a priest, say a few prayers for success."

"I will. And don't lose the cardkey, just in case. There was no time to make more than the one, and of course no way to test it, but Piaras believes it will work without tipping off security . . . We've been trying for years to break into the prison network, but passwords and such never worked. It required a pattern-recognition sequence, and we never could get our hands on the correct pattern or even figure out just what kind of pattern was needed. But your drawing, crude as it was, did the trick. Piaras isolated all the elements—well, I won't go into it now, but the point is, it worked. We got into the database and changed—look, it doesn't matter, and there's no time. Let's just hope you don't have to test the duplicate we made. Good luck with Plan A. Now go in peace, my child, and wait for my nod."

Nuala slipped from the booth and could see again—almost. She shot a glance at the back of the chapel. Benny was busy in conversation, her back turned.

Nuala went straight to the front pew. There they were: three women with short auburn hair. Without looking up from their silent prayer, the women slid down to make room for her.

"Good luck!" one of them whispered.

Nuala smiled. How many of them were in on this? And how could it possibly work?

The Mass droned on and on and on. For a fake priest, the pious-looking fellow with the blond hair was every bit as long-winded as the real thing. Nuala kept her eyes glued to him, afraid to miss the signal. Her heart was pounding so fiercely, she was sure Benny could hear it in the back of the chapel. Benny. What would happen to her if this worked? Would she be blamed? Nuala couldn't think about that now.

The distraction, when it finally happened, startled Nuala so much she nearly jumped to her feet prematurely. There was a crash in the back of the chapel, and then loud voices. Nuala stared, eyes wide, at the fake priest. After an agonizing eternity,

as more voices joined in the argument behind her, the priest's
eyes finally darted to Nuala and gave her a curt nod.

She was on her feet and running. She pushed through the
door, then caught it before it could hit the wall. Closing it
quickly but gently, she listened for some cry of alarm at her actions. But the argument was continuing; apparently no one had
noticed her.

She ran to the clothes press and ripped the doors open. There
it was: a nun's habit and guimpe. She slipped the habit over her
head and was adjusting the guimpe when she found the closet.
She started in, ran back to the counter to pick up a heavy candlestick, darted into the closet, and closed the door. Blind again.

Holding the candlestick between her knees, Nuala eased the
guimpe into place and pushed every lock of hair under it. Then
she seized the candlestick in her two hands and waited, panting,
her nerves taut.

An eternity passed. She could hear nothing in the closet,
could see nothing.

Finally footsteps, hesitant ones. But only one pair of feet.

The door was opened and light stabbed her eyes; Nuala still
couldn't see.

"I thought so," a familiar voice said. "You know I can't allow
this; think what would happen to me."

"Let me go, Benny," Nuala pleaded, as some vision returned
to her. "I consider you a friend, but I won't hesitate to kill you
if you try to stop me. I mean it. I won't be raped again."

She raised the candlestick and stared at Benny. Benny stared
back at her, an unreadable expression on her face.

"I'm tired of this job," Benny said, sighing, as she slowly
turned her back. "But I've no desire to end up an inmate myself,
so it can't look as if I helped you. Just don't hit me too hard."

Nuala gasped in disbelief; she found herself inexplicably near
tears. "Thanks, Benny," she said for the last time, and brought
the candlestick down.

When footsteps came again, there were several pairs of feet,
and they were in a hurry. Again the door was pulled open, and
again Nuala was blinded by the sudden light. She swung the
candlestick, but someone caught it. "Hey, it's ourselves! Let's
go!"

Nuala stepped over the unconscious Benny as the others
grabbed for their coats. One of the nuns looked at the guard. "Is
she—"

"Still breathing!" Nuala snapped. "Let's move!"

The guards they passed at every internal security gate nodded respectfully to them, not seeming to notice an extra nun. Nuala kept her head down. They were almost out.

"Two more," the priest murmured as they were buzzed through another wire mesh security gate. Then: "One more."

They were almost to the last gate when a claxon sounded, making Nuala's heart stop momentarily.

"Hold it!" The guard on the other side of the wire mesh gate held up his hand. "Sorry, Father, but I'll have to find out what's going on before I pass you through."

But before he could activate the 'phone, Nuala pulled Benny's pistol from her habit and stunned him.

"What are we going to do?" one of the nuns asked. "We haven't time to cut through the wire, and that pistol might just melt the lock—"

"Try it anyway!" another nun pleaded.

"No!" Nuala tossed the pistol to the priest and clawed the habit up and out of her way, digging in the pocket of the prison smock she wore underneath.

"The drawing was exact; my memory was accurate; Piaras knew what he was doing," she breathed to herself as she fit the cardkey, hand trembling, into the gate's lock. She passed it through and pulled. No click. Nothing happened.

"No! Come on!"

Nuala tried it again, more slowly.

The lock clicked. She pulled the gate open and ran the last few meters to the opening door to the outside, the others behind her.

The priest pushed Nuala aside and stunned the guard who was entering before he knew what was happening. Nuala jumped over the unconscious man and hit the door, kicking it open, then sped out into the cold night. Damn it, she was blind again! There wasn't enough light! Her companions grabbed her arms and pulled her along.

A vehicle roared up, spraying gravel.

"Stop!" a man shouted from above them. The whine of plasfire sounded very close.

"Get in!" the priest yelled, and pulled her inside so that she landed in a heap on top of him.

"Go, go!" one of the nuns shouted.

Plasfire hit the outside of the van, but then they were off.

Nuala lay, huddled in the midst of fake nuns and priest, as they bounced along at top speed. The van hit something but barely slowed. There was a lot of firing and shouting; they swerved violently several times. Nuala could see nothing, but heard sirens. They sounded close, right on the van's tail, but incredibly, the sirens fell behind and eventually—after a long, full-speed, tires-squealing chase—died out.

After an eternity of bouncing across all kinds of terrain, during which Nuala and the others were thrown all over the back of the van, they finally slowed, then stopped. The interior light came on, and Nuala's vision slowly came back to her. The nuns and priest were arranging themselves, getting up off the floor and taking seats, removing habits and collar and looking out the van's windows when Nuala saw a blurred shape climb back to them from the driver's seat. It bent over her.

"Long time no see," Fiona said, grinning.

"I should've known it was you," Nuala replied. "Only maniacs and Fiona drive like that."

Someone laughed, and suddenly there was a babble of voices: the former nuns and priest were congratulating each other and Fiona, their relief ringing with joyous victory. Fiona continued to grin at her. "Welcome back."

Nuala smiled back, shivering violently from the tumult of emotions, then surprised herself by suddenly bursting into tears.

"I'll drive," the defrocked priest said as Fiona pulled Nuala into her arms.

Chapter 24

"THE RUMORS YOU may have heard are true," Nuala said as she looked into the camera. "I did indeed escape from prison this evening, less than two hours ago."

It was a familiar scene: another safe house, three Guerrillas she hadn't met before with a tiny camera and bedsheet backdrop, and her three friends out of camera range, watching. A familiar scene, but the familiarity seemed unreal to Nuala, as if it were all a dream and she would wake at any moment back in the interrogation cell. She had been fighting back exhaustion since her rescuers had dropped her and Fiona off here and had hurried away to ditch the van and disappear. But exhaustion wasn't the only thing Nuala had been fighting to keep at bay. She was struggling to remain in control. A whirlwind of urges had been swirling inside her head: She wanted to scream at the top of her lungs, to let out her pain and rage; she wanted to weep until there were no more tears left; she wanted to destroy something—anything—with her bare hands; she wanted Adolf in her gunsights; she wanted to open the prison doors and watch every woman run out into the free air, then set off the biggest series of orgiastic explosions she had ever seen and watch the prison's every brick, every chunk of concrete and steel shatter and blow apart, never to be reassembled again. But mostly she wanted to collapse into a soft, warm bed with clean sheets and a downy pillow, to sleep for a week or perhaps a month. This had to be done first, though. Before the bruises and the purple blotches under her eyes faded. The worse she looked, the better the propaganda value. There was a war on.

"They had me at their mercy for two and a half weeks," Nuala continued. "Two and a half weeks of hell. For there is no such thing in this country as civil liberties or the rights of the accused. At no time did I see an attorney; I was never advised of my rights—as a matter of fact, I was told that I *had* no rights, that they could do to me whatever they wanted, and they proved that. They proved it several times a day, every day."

She had to pause. It was still difficult to breathe. She had noticed it first in the van, after their pursuers had fallen safely behind: She couldn't seem to catch her breath. Her ribs hurt no worse than before, but every breath was a gasp, a struggle to continue.

"I've been told that the authorities are making claims that I confessed to all manner of crimes while I was being 'questioned.' I hope you know that that is not true. I confessed to nothing; I told them nothing, in spite of almost continuous torture. I am not a criminal. They know I'm not. But they are afraid. They are afraid of the truth, so they try to silence it. They want to silence me and they tried to force me to name names, to tell them who else knows the truth and works to pass it on. They tried to make me inform on my friends." She paused. "This is what they did to me."

Nuala stood up and opened the front of the robe, letting it fall to the floor. She stared at the camera while the Guerrilla behind it zoomed in for a close-up. He did exactly as she had instructed him: starting at her ankles, lingering on every still-purple or now-yellow bruise, he slowly moved up her naked body. She had chosen not to wear any sort of underwear, not only because it would hide many of the worst bruises, especially those on her breasts, but also because she knew the effect it would create. No naked body had ever been seen on Irish television or at the cinema. Distributing pornography or anything resembling it was one of the worst, most severely punished of crimes, and therefore such material was virtually nonexistent in Ireland. So she would bring the sight of a naked female body into their homes, their living rooms. The authorities, especially the Church, would be hysterical; they would use this as evidence of her depravity or even of insanity. But the image would remain. The people would see her bruises, and they would picture in their own minds how the injuries had been inflicted. Their imaginations would be a powerful weapon on her side. It was not an image they would easily forget.

The camera lingered on her shoulder, which was really quite painful to look at: bruises on top of unhealed, burned skin, cracked dermaclone revealing scar tissue beneath. Since the bruises on her face were minimal, the camera didn't linger there; Nuala turned around and let it glide over her back and buttocks, down her thighs. She avoided looking at Heather, who had tears in her eyes—had since Nuala had returned. Nor did she look at Igraine, who had been curiously withdrawn. She looked instead at Fiona while this was going on, ignoring the pain on her friend's face, waiting for her to relay the signal from the Guerrilla that he was done. When Fiona nodded, Nuala turned back. In no hurry, she picked up the robe, slipped it on, and held it closed as she reseated herself and looked into the camera again.

"The bruises," she resumed, "are only the visible signs of injury. The worst of what they did to me cannot be seen by anyone else. I carry those marks in my memory. They raped me, you see—three men who enjoyed the pain and degradation they were inflicting. Raped and sodomized me on a daily basis, taking turns. Two would hold me down while the third defiled me. I cannot remember the number of times they violated me." The gasping breath made her shudder, but she managed to keep her expression impassive as she went on. It was almost as if she were describing something that had happened to someone else. Almost.

"They picked this method of torture because I am a woman, and what more effective way for a man to demonstrate to a woman that he has complete power over her than to violate her body, to rape her? It's a method that men have used for thousands of years to subjugate women, to make us surrender to their will and to obey, in desperate hope that they won't rape us again." She paused to breathe, another painful shudder, and Adolf's face flashed before her eyes. Her jaw clenched, her eyes narrowed in rage and hatred. "But it didn't work! I told them nothing they could use to hurt anyone else, and they have not stopped me. I will never cease fighting back. They have accomplished nothing with their torture except to ensure that I will *never* surrender. I will go on fighting them, through every means available or necessary, until I see this country free, or until I die, whichever comes first. But I warn you, Mr. *Taoiseach*, members of the *Dáil*, the Church, and especially the *gardaí*, I warn you: It won't be so easy to kill me. There will be no more announced public appearances; I've learned that much. You won't know where I'll be, and you won't see me coming. But I'll be there. Wherever you least expect me, I'll be there. And you won't shut me up; you won't silence me. You cannot silence the truth. It's like a virus: It spreads of its own accord, from one person to the next. And no amount of violence or persecution can stop it; there is no vaccine. We will not be silenced, we will not be stopped. We will be free."

She glared into the camera for a long, silent moment, then nodded. The red light went off and the Guerrilla lowered the camera, but then he didn't move. He just stared at Nuala, pain and respect mingling in his eyes. Nuala glanced away, embarrassed. She didn't get up, and no one else moved or spoke. After another few painful gasps, Nuala suddenly looked back up at the cameraman.

"Could I—could you turn it on again? I need to—I'd like to add something."

"Of course," he said, eager to help her in some way, the best way he could. She acknowledged this with a grateful smile, then took as deep a breath as possible, preparing for the camera again. The red light came on.

"I just wanted," she said, her voice cracking, "to add something personal to my father." She had to pause, searching for the words, knowing that several million people would see this.

"Da . . . I wish that I could see you in person, look into your eyes as I speak to you, but you know they won't allow that. It'd be too dangerous for both of us. Even though you've never broken a law in your life, seeing your own daughter face to face would be enough excuse for the bastards to arrest you, to lock us both up. So I'll have to speak to you this way. I just wanted—" Her voice cracked again, and she grimaced in irritation. She cleared her throat. "I just wanted to tell you how grateful I am to you for raising me to love Ireland and to love the truth. It was those stories you taught me as a child that kept me sane in that hell. I didn't think of myself and my own fear; I remembered the bravery of Bobby Sands, Mairéad Farrell, Wolfe Tone, Jeremiah O'Donovan Rossa, and all the others you told me about who were imprisoned for Ireland's sake. Some of them died in prison, some escaped, some were released. But every one of them made a difference. I knew I could never be as brave as any of themselves—" Her voice cracked again, and the tears were coming too fast to blink back. "But it was their inspiration and your teachings and your love that kept me going." She had to pause again; the veneer of her control was dangerously thin. But she had to fight it. After swallowing hard a few times and swiping at her eyes, she went on.

"I just wanted you to know, if I never get the chance to tell you in person, that I am proud—" Another swallow and shuddering gasp. "I am proud to be the daughter of Séamus Dennehy, the finest man I've ever known. And as long as I live, those stories you taught me will continue to be told. The past will live, an inspiration for the future.

"I love you, Da. So much. Thank you for your help, for everything." He would know she meant the escape.

She could no longer see because of the tears, so she signaled the cameraman with a raised hand. The red light went off.

Nuala buried her face in her hands, trying to breathe, trying not to cry. No one was saying anything. After a moment gentle hands found her. "Come on, Nuala," Heather whispered. "I'll help you." Nuala let the girl lead her out of the room.

Nuala was at a doctor's office, the same one who had first treated her burned shoulder. He had grimaced in anger at the extent of her injuries—the cracked ribs, the contusions, especially the damage to the shoulder he had treated.

"I could remove the damaged skin and reapply dermaclone. That's the only way to avoid scarring," he said as he peered closely at the scar tissue that had begun to form.

"I don't care what it looks like," Nuala replied. "I just want it to heal—and quickly. It slows me down."

The doctor smiled at her. "I wouldn't think it was possible to slow you down. But it would take longer, of course, to remove the skin and—"

"Then forget it," Nuala interrupted. "As long as it won't restrict movement, leave the scar. Just do whatever it takes to heal it quickly. Please."

The doctor nodded and picked up a small plastic bottle from his tray. "This shouldn't hurt much." He sprayed the entire shoulder with a liquid that smelled like raw potatoes and dried almost instantly—but not without first making Nuala think that fire ants were burrowing into her skin through the cracks in the dermaclone. She winced and gripped the edge of the padded examining table. The pain quickly faded, leaving a prickling sensation behind.

"There," the doctor said. "Mind the shoulder, nothing strenuous, if you can avoid it, for about a week, and it should be right again. I'll give you some stretching exercises—*gentle* stretching—that you can begin straightaway. Now, then. Let's have a look at those eyes."

The prognosis, when he was finished, wasn't as bad as Nuala had feared. Laser therapy would be necessary to repair the damage done to the retinas, but when finished and given a few days to heal, her vision would be as good as new—almost. "Bright light will always be painful," he explained, "so avoid it. And your night vision won't be quite as good as it once was. But nearly so—nothing to worry about. I can do the therapy now, if you like. No sense waiting, and it won't take but a few moments."

It seemed to take less time than that, because soon after the soft hiss of the injection, she was asleep. When she woke up he had some bad news waiting for her, and probably a grave expression to match his tone, but there were bandages over her eyes, so she couldn't see him.

"I did the pelvic examination and some tests while you were asleep," he said. "To make it easier on you emotionally. I've treated rape victims before, so I know how traumatic the examination can be. I . . ."

He paused—reluctant, obviously, to say something. If Nuala hadn't been so drowsy from the sedative, she might have been alarmed.

"What is it?" she asked, fingering the bandages over her eyes.

"I'm afraid—I'm afraid you're pregnant. I'm sorry."

Nuala froze, then slowly lowered the hand to her side. "Are you certain?" Her voice didn't sound like her own.

"No mistake. I don't suppose there's a chance it could have happened before—"

"No."

"You haven't—I mean, there's been no one—"

"Not in six—seven—years. No, it was one of *them*." Though she could see nothing but blackness, faces appeared before her: Adolf, Hans, Fritz, all leering at her. "No!"

She must have yelled it, because she heard the door open and someone rush in. "Nuala! What is it? What's wrong?" Heather, sounding scared and angry. "What have you done to her? I *knew* I should have stayed with her!"

"He's done nothing," Nuala assured her. She felt the girl grip her hand protectively. "It wasn't *him*."

"What, then?" Fiona asked.

"I'm pregnant." The words seemed to echo, to hang in the air. It still didn't sound like her own voice.

"Oh, god," Fiona murmured.

Heather's grip on her hand tightened. Nuala felt the long hair brush her cheek as Heather leaned over her, speaking gently. "What do you want to do, Nuala? Do you want an abortion?"

"Now, wait a moment!" the doctor protested. "I can't—I could be charged with murder!"

"You're already breaking the law by treating her at all," Fiona reminded him.

"But I can't—"

"You know how, don't you?" Heather interrupted him.

"Well, yes," he replied. "I trained in London, so of course I know *how*, but—"

"Get rid of it," Nuala heard the strange voice that was her own say. "I'll not have *this* inflicted on me by those bastards, too. Get rid of it *now*."

"For all I don't agree with the government," the doctor said, sounding more frantic, "I am still a Catholic, I couldn't—"

"You can," Igraine said, speaking for the first time from across the room, her voice flat and cold, "and you will. Or I'll shoot you myself."

"Shoot me? You can't be serious!"

"Does this look like a joke?" Igraine must have pulled a pistol.

"Doctor," Nuala said. "Please. You can't honestly want me to suffer any further than I already have at the hands of those—"

"Of course I don't," he interrupted. "But what you're asking is—not easy for me."

"Do you think it's easy for *herself*?" There was irritation in Heather's voice, but when she spoke again, it was gone; she tried a reasonable tone. "You've done so much for us already, and we are truly grateful. We are only asking this one more thing. You can't leave her in this condition. You *must* help her, Doctor; it's the decent and compassionate thing to do." Heather didn't sound at all like the unsure young girl Nuala had met only a few months before.

"And, Doctor," Igraine added, her voice all the more dangerous for her calm tone, "mind you do a good job. If she has any complications whatsoever at all—"

"Igraine, I'm sure threats aren't necessary," Fiona interrupted. "The doctor is our friend, our ally. He *will* help us, because as Heather said, it's the compassionate thing to do. And he is a compassionate man. Aren't you, Doctor?"

The doctor sighed. "All right. All right, I'll do it. I never meant to refuse, I just—my conscience is my own to deal with. I'll help you, of course."

"There's a good lad," Igraine murmured. Nuala wondered if she had put her gun away.

"Stay with me?" Nuala said, and Heather squeezed her hand again.

"Of course we will."

"We'll be right here," Fiona assured her.

"Watching his every move," Igraine added.

Nuala wasn't sure what she felt about this, or *how* to feel; it was all so—detached, and only partly because of the lingering effects of the sedative. She finally decided it would be easier to be *completely* detached, so she conjured up the colored switches in her mind once again—the colored switches that had protected her from Adolf and his two accomplices. They would serve her one more time, and when it was over, she would be free of what Adolf or perhaps Hans or Fritz had left inside her as a grotesque souvenir. Then, when her injuries and her bruises healed, the only trace left of the three men would be in her mind.

Chapter 25

"THE PROTEST TURNED violent when *gardaí* opened fire on the demonstrators," the Guerrilla was saying, "and the crowd, instead of fleeing in panic, retaliated. In the end, the *garda* station was set afire, and the officers were forced to flee for their lives. Three demonstrators and two *gardaí* were killed, scores more were wounded. No arrests were made successfully, as demonstrators outnumbered and overpowered the security forces, rescuing those who had been stunned or restrained. The *gardaí* were forced to flee to the next village, leaving Ballygar without any police 'protection' at all. But, contrary to the lies you've been hearing on the official news, there was no looting, no fights in the streets, no crime wave. Instead there was a solemn wake for the dead, followed by a townwide victory celebration. When *garda* reinforcements roll in, there is certain to be resistance. The citizens of Ballygar are not likely to give up their first taste of freedom so easily."

As the Guerrilla paused, Heather began to speak. "It's the side of a building. It's been painted to say 'You are now entering Free Ballygar.'"

Nuala smiled. Although she couldn't see the *teilifís* because of the bandages, she could picture that painted sign. She remembered the old photographs of a similar sign in Derry, painted almost a century before she was born.

The Guerrilla went on. "As usual, the official government response has been to blame Nuala Dennehy. They seem to think that she is a one-woman terrorist organization, responsible for everything they find unpleasant. Having met Ms. Dennehy, I'm sure she is flattered by the government's appraisal of her influence." The four women chuckled. "However, I can tell you that she was nowhere near Ballygar yesterday. She was still in Belfast. Where she is today . . . is anybody's guess. We at Guerrilla TV wish her a speedy recovery from her injuries.

"And to the people of Ballygar: Congratulations and good

luck. You are an inspiration to the entire country. Ballygar *abú*! . . . This is Guerrilla TV, signing off from somewhere in Mayo."

Someone clicked off the *teilifís*. Right on cue, Heather asked, "Do you want something to eat? Some tea?"

Nuala smiled, but Fiona spoke before she could. "Gods, girl! You're forever pushing food down her throat. Maybe she's not hungry."

"But she's lost so much weight!" Heather argued. "Look how thin she is! She's got to get her strength back."

"Thank you, Heather, but Fiona's right; I'm not hungry," Nuala said. "I think I'll take a nap in the other room. I'm still so bloody tired."

"I'll help you."

"No, no. You stay and argue with Fiona. Igraine, would you mind?"

There was a momentary pause. "Sure," Igraine said, sounding surprised.

Nuala took Igraine's elbow and was led into the bedroom of the Ardee safe house.

"Could you close the door and stay a moment?"

Again a pause; then the door closed. Nuala heard a mattress squeak as Igraine sat on the other bed. The other woman said nothing, waiting for Nuala.

"You've never been much of a blatherskite," Nuala said. "Not one to run off at the mouth. But ever since I came back, you've been unusually taciturn, even for yourself. I like quiet people as a rule; there's no need to hold up one end of a conversation that doesn't exist. Very restful. But something's wrong. You can tell me to butt out if you like, but I'm concerned. What is it, *mo chara*?"

"*Mo chara*," Igraine murmured. "Nobody's called me 'friend' in a very long while." She fell silent, but Nuala just waited, giving her time. Finally Igraine sighed, and the sound of it was wretched. "If you hadn't listened to me—we should never have gone to that damned protest rally. It was stupid! The *gardaí* knew you'd be there—"

"Hold on!" Nuala interrupted, leaning toward Igraine. It was so frustrating not to be able to see her. "You're blaming yourself because I was—That's crazy! It wasn't your fault!"

"I talked you into going—"

"The hell you did. Nobody talks me into anything. It was my own damned arrogance to blame, and nothing and nobody else. I told myself that I had made a promise and that everyone would

be disappointed if I didn't show up." Nuala grimaced; the words
tasted bitter on her tongue. "What conceit!" She sighed. "It's
just as well there'll be no more public rallies for me. I'm
ashamed to admit that the rush of power was becoming too
strong, stronger than my common sense. As if *I* was the only
voice they needed to hear. How stupid ... I shouldn't have
gone, no, but it wasn't your fault I did; it was my own."

"That's generous of you."

"Generous, hell. It's the truth, and you know it. Now stop
blaming yourself."

"Or what, you'll thrash me?" There was relief in Igraine's
voice, though she tried to hide it behind sarcasm.

"I might." Nuala played along.

"You couldn't find me; you're blind as a bat."

"Then I'd use my sonar."

Igraine chuckled and they let it drop, the air cleared. A few
companionably silent moments passed. "Are you sleeping any
better?" Igraine asked.

Nuala was surprised. She shared the bedroom with Heather;
how could Igraine be sure she was awakened half a dozen times
a night by visions of horror?

"Uh, not really."

"Yeah. It'll be like that for a while. Months, probably. Then
the nightmares will grow fewer. Eventually you'll sleep through
the night again, but it won't be soon."

Nuala hadn't realized until the last two days how much she
relied on facial expressions to relay what she felt without having
to say it. Now she couldn't see, couldn't meet Igraine's eyes to
tell her with a look that she understood from her friend's tone
that she was speaking from personal experience, and that she
was sorry that Igraine had suffered so. She had to say it aloud,
and it was damned awkward.

"I ... is that the reason you don't want to return to Kerry?"

"Yeah. One of them." She fell silent for a moment. "If I ever
saw them again—the *gardaí* who—I'd kill them. No matter the
consequences. I'd kill the bastards."

Nuala nodded. "I see their faces all the time—especially since
I can't see anything else at the moment. I want them dead. Men
like that don't deserve to be taking up space on the planet. I
wanted to describe them on that tape I made, so that
someone—I don't know who, anyone—would kill them for me.
I almost did, but—as much as I want them dead, I can't ask any-

one to commit murder for me; I haven't the right. But I still want them dead."

Igraine said nothing, but Nuala felt her agreement. She was suddenly overwhelmed with relief. Somebody understood, really understood, not just sympathized. Then, just as suddenly, the relief was replaced with a wave of sorrow, for Igraine and for herself. The tears crowded her bandaged eyes. Her breath shuddered in.

"Yeah, that, too." Igraine's voice was soft but matter of fact. "Your emotions'll be a rollercoaster. Depression, grief, self-loathing, hatred, relief that you're out of that place. And the shortness of breath, and the exhaustion: It's all part of it."

"How long—" It was all she could say; the tears were too close to the surface.

"Give yourself a week or so longer just to rest; don't even try to do anything. Then you'll be so bored with doing nothing that you'll need to get off your arse, depression or no."

Nuala nodded and took several slow, deep breaths. Gradually the emotional havoc subsided. Igraine just waited.

"Were you in the IRA, then? In Kerry, with your husband?"

Igraine didn't respond right away. Then one quiet word: "Aye."

"How did you—I mean, when—"

"I met him when I was sixteen," Igraine said, sounding as tired as Nuala felt. "After I was thrown out of boarding school for being a troublemaker. My family didn't want me back because I refused to say I'd lied when I accused my uncle Des of molesting my younger sister, as he had myself when I was her age. Anyway, I was on my own. This was before the God Patrols and the like, and I was Protestant—well, atheist, but not Catholic, you know? Same thing. So I wasn't rounded up as I would be today."

"You were on your own at sixteen? What did you do?"

"Whatever I could: washed dishes in a restaurant when their mechanical dishwashers broke down, sorted recyclables, worked at a seafarm until I smelled like dead seaweed. I even pumped ethanol for a time. Then I met Eoin." She sighed, the sound of it painful and wretched. "What can I say? I was just a kid, terribly alone. He was handsome—or so I thought then—and dashing, because he was a rebel, a nonconformist. And he showed real interest in me, not just the leering sexual interest other men had, but interest in what I had to say. Of course I was too young and inexperienced to realize that he was conning me, manipulating me. If it was just sex he wanted, I would have figured that out soon enough and booted him out of my life."

"What *was* he after, then?"

"A cover, a meal ticket, a wife who couldn't testify against him in court." Igraine's short laugh was harsh, bitter. "Is there any creature more foolish than a young girl who's infatuated?"

"Was he in the IRA then? Already?"

"Oh, aye, he was 'RA, all right. But him and his mates only listened to the High Command when it suited them. They had their own agenda going: petty extortion and theft, blackmail. They were a sweet bunch, they were. The Provos threatened them time and again, ordered them to clean up their act and not make other Volunteers look bad with their example. They'd behave for a while, but then they'd go back to their true nature. It's a wonder the High Command didn't kill them in the beginning, but I suppose the IRA is so small now, they needed everyone they could get, even if tainted."

"And so you joined?"

Igraine sighed and hesitated before she answered. "Eoin convinced me—he could convince me of anything in the beginning—to fight for freedom, for Ireland. I was all for it. I started out just passing messages, but that was how I found out that Eoin and his mates weren't following orders. We'd been married about two months when I saw the *real* Eoin, when he dropped the pretense of being a patriot fighting with the IRA for his country. He was out for himself, and no one else. He followed orders only often enough to keep himself in the 'RA's good graces, and what could *I* do about it? By then it was too late; we were married. I couldn't exactly divorce him, could I? I couldn't tell the authorities—not that I *would* have, *those* bastards—what he was up to, and if I tried to inform on him to the High Command, Eoin would probably have killed me before they got to him. He kept a close watch on me."

Nuala could think of nothing to say. After all this time, Igraine was finally opening up to her, and what could she offer in return?

"So I danced on a tightrope between them for several years," Igraine went on. "I passed messages—some from the High Command to other units in Kerry, bypassing Eoin altogether when I could. I believed in what the 'RA were doing, still struggling for a free Ireland when so few supported them, but did they appreciate or respect me in return? Hell, no, I was just somebody's wife, and a troublemaker's wife at that."

"What happened? What changed?" Nuala asked quietly, half afraid Igraine would quit the story in disgust at the memories.

"What happened? Eoin and his worthless arsehole friends tried to rob a betting shop, the damned fools! They killed two people! But they got away, though without any money. Next thing I know, *I'm* being picked up because someone thought they had recognized Eoin's voice during the robbery."

"But you couldn't testify—"

"Not in court, no, but that didn't stop the *gardaí* from trying to get information out of me." Igraine paused. Nuala wanted to rip off the bandages so she could see her friend's face.

"They kept me for three months," Igraine went on, her voice cold and trembling with hatred. "I don't have to tell you what they did to me . . . But I told them *nothing*. Not out of loyalty to that piece of shit I was married to, I can assure you. But if I had informed on him, the IRA—the lads who really *were* fighting for Ireland—might have been dragged into it. So I kept my mouth shut until they finally cut me loose."

Nuala tried to keep the emotion out of her voice; somehow she thought Igraine would be embarrassed if she expressed her sympathy. "And Eoin?"

"Never did a day's time for it, the bastard. No real proof. He was living underground, though, on the run from both the *gardaí* and the Provos, who'd finally had enough of him and his petty terrorisms. But he found me when I got out. That's when I learned he'd framed some other poor saps for the holdup and the killings. He thought that made everything all right between us; he claimed he'd done the frame to get *me* out of jail!"

"You didn't stay with him, surely?"

"I did, actually," Igraine replied, a curious note of satisfaction in her tone. "I played along, pretending to be grateful he had assured my release, and we went back to the way things had been before."

"Whatever for?" Nuala said. "You must've had a reason."

"Didn't I, though? . . . Eoin was keeping an eye on me just to be sure I was truly as grateful to him as I seemed; we were in hiding because the Provos were still looking for him. It took almost six months of that before I got the chance to get the word to them where he was. I wanted him to pay for what he'd done to those two men in the betting shop who'd been killed, and those that he framed, and for what had been done to me."

"They obviously didn't kill him, the IRA."

"No, they did not." The bitterness in Igraine's tone increased.

"Eoin did them a major favor—I won't bore you with the details; suffice to say it involved disabling an entire fleet of *garda* vehicles before a big 'RA operation—and they forgave all, the bastards. Three months I'd done in hell and another six living with Eoin after, him getting drunk and threatening me on a regular basis, and for what? *They* decide he's more valuable to them alive. All they did was threaten him, force him to promise he'd pull no more jobs on his own. Bastards! And after what I did for them! Did they care what had happened to me? I could've talked in jail, I could've—" Igraine took a deep breath, cleared her throat. "So I got even in my own way."

"How?"

The note of satisfaction was back in Igraine's voice. "I waited, biding my time, until he came home blazing drunk one night. He finished off whatever was in the house and finally passed out on the bed. So then I took a needle and thread, and I sewed him inside the sheet."

"What?" Nuala wasn't sure she had heard right. "Sewed him inside—the sheet?"

"I did," Igraine said, sounding quite pleased with herself. "Then I packed everything I owned that I wanted to keep. When he woke up, I was waiting with a hurling stick."

Nuala wasn't sure whether to gasp or laugh. "You—"

"Beat the bastard to within an inch of his life with it, I did." Nuala could hear the grim pleasure in Igraine's voice. "And him roaring that *he* was going to kill *me*! The bastard. All I put up with from him: the lies, the betrayals, the drunken beatings, forcing sex on me, using me for his own ends, and then leaving me to rot in jail for three months . . . A good thrashing was letting him off easy. If I'd been more like himself, I would've murdered him. But I settled for the beating, and then I left."

"Remind me never to make you angry, right?" Nuala said. She was surprised at what Igraine had done, but she felt a certain amused admiration for her friend, too. "And then? After you left?"

"Oh, well, not much to tell. I worked for the Provos occasionally, nothing desperate, but I learned a few things. And I ran into Eoin a couple of times. He almost got me killed once, accidentally on purpose—but that's another story. I don't want to talk about him any more."

"But why did you call him when we—"

"I didn't. I called the local 'RA unit. The bastard was obviously in town and must've volunteered when he heard it was me. I didn't know he was involved until we were in the middle of it." She paused, then sighed again. "And then I passed up *another* chance to kill him. Sometimes I wish murder was an option . . . Well, anyway, that's enough of my life story. You need to get some rest."

"Wait," Nuala said. "You've worked off and on with the IRA for years, then, right?"

"Aye."

"Good. Then you've no doubt a great deal of experience and information that we're going to need."

"Oh? Have I?"

"Yes. Teach me, Igraine. Teach me everything you know."

"About what?"

"Well, let's start with explosives."

The bandages came off after another very long day, and Nuala could see again. Just in case, they kept the lights in the safe house dim for another day to let her eyes adjust.

She slept a great deal, more than she ever had in her life, and woke each time from a nightmare. Heather was always there for her, and in the middle of the night, when it was most difficult, Nuala didn't object to Heather holding her, though she would have been embarrassed if Fiona or Igraine had seen.

When she grew bored with sitting, she did the stretching exercises the doctor had given her. They weren't too different from the yoga she had learned years ago at Findhorn, so she blended the two together. That made her feel so much better, physically at least, that she moved on to Tai Chi. It took awhile to remember all the moves, but they came back to her. The other three women watched, fascinated; then Heather asked Nuala to teach her. Igraine and Fiona weren't interested in learning it until Nuala demonstrated how Tai Chi could be used defensively. After that, all four women practiced daily.

In the evenings, while Nuala exercised with the three-pound weights that Fiona had procured somewhere, Igraine taught them about explosives, sabotage, and computer network infiltration. The *teilifís* was constantly on, the sound usually turned down, to catch any Guerrilla broadcasts. It was because of the Guerrillas and Fiona's frequent calls to Éadaoin that they knew how the revolution was progressing.

And revolution it was, finally. The authorities, especially the Church, were frantic. The unrest that had simmered for years had finally boiled over. Women all over the country were joining in and dropping out. Social services that were performed primarily by unpaid, compulsory "volunteers"—married women—were stalled because these women no longer showed up to work. Attendance at Mass had dropped dramatically. Public transportation companies were losing alarming amounts of money because no one was riding the buses; graffiti such as ROSA PARKS WAS RIGHT! were being painted on the sides of buses by vandals. Government 'phone lines were jammed; with no one to answer them, offices couldn't function. Even single women who worked for money had stopped coming in. Hydroponics farms and seafarms, too, fell behind in production and harvest. Recycling plants were quickly overflowing with recyclables that were not being sorted, long lines formed at stores that suddenly had few clerks. Work was not getting done, because every day more and more women were calling in sick.

Bishops condemned these actions, priests scolded, God Patrols made frequent visits, but to no avail. When appeals to the women themselves accomplished nothing, pressure was put on husbands or fathers. Emergency clinics all over the country saw more beaten and injured women than ever before—and men, too, when the women fought back. But in spite of the violence, for the most part the women held fast.

In the weeks that followed, Éadaoin reported small victories in local politics: Men who were sympathetic to the movement—some secretly and some openly—were now coming forward to announce their candidacy for public office as city councillors or even county councillors on a platform of "compassionate reform." Perhaps the people themselves, they campaigned, could work out the country's problems together, rather than just look to the Church for the answers.

Nuala watched the news and listened to Fiona report what Éadaoin had told her, but she felt more worry than satisfaction. It wasn't going to be this easy. The government backlash would come, and things were going to get ugly. Thanks to Igraine's teaching and her increasing strength, she would be ready.

When the Church's sermons on its broadcast network turned ominous, subtly threatening people—especially women—to conform or face the unspecified consequences, Nuala knew it was time. They couldn't allow the people to be frightened off by the power of the Church. The Church had to be shown to be vulnerable. They had to strike.

* * *

"You're sure this will work?" Heather whispered. Nuala could barely see her, dressed all in black as she was. The night was overcast, no moon visible, and Nuala's night vision was not, as the doctor had promised, nearly as good as new. She could see very little at all, but there was the occasional glint from someone's eyes, and her joke to Igraine about sonar wasn't too far off.

"My part will," Igraine replied. "One at each leg, and one halfway up the tower. Grenades'll do the work inside."

Nuala turned to look behind her. Several indistinct images crowded there, waiting. "You ready?"

"Right," one of the Guerrillas said; she easily recognized his voice as belonging to a man named Barry. "We'll have a clear view of the explosions from here."

"And I'm ready when you are," said a voice she knew to belong to another cameraman, this one named Hugh.

"Okay," Nuala said. She looked around at the shadows dressed in black. "Everybody knows what to do?" There must have been nods, but Nuala couldn't see them. "Then, Fiona, you're off first."

"Right. Good luck." The shadow that was Fiona melted into the night, heading back to the van.

"Okay, let's go."

The door wasn't locked. Igraine led the way in, Nuala behind her, then Heather; Hugh brought up the rear with his camera. They walked past the empty lobby, their pistols in their hands, past the dark reception area, down first one hall and then another, tiptoeing, and not running into anyone. At 2 A.M. the station looked deserted. But they knew it wasn't—not completely.

Finally they found the metal box marked PHONES on the wall, somewhere in the bowels of the station. Igraine opened it, and they all winced at the creaking of the metal hinge. But no one came to investigate. Nuala held the flashlight while Igraine found the right chip and pried it out with a pair of pliers from her coat pocket. "There," she said when it was out and in her her hand. "Incommunicado." She put the pliers and the chip in her pocket and closed the metal box. It creaked just as loudly, but still no one came. So far, so good.

Farther into the station they came upon hallways where the lights were on. Nuala could see clearly again, to her relief. They searched every room in the building, and the closets, too. No one. Finally they were certain that the only people in the station would be together, in one place. They headed for it.

There were only two men in the booth. Nuala peered through

the glass window in the door at them. One seemed to be asleep, leaning back in his chair, his arms crossed over his stomach. The other was nearly asleep: His head was propped on one hand, and he was yawning.

Nuala held a finger to her lips and her three companions nodded. She eased the door open and stepped into the booth.

"Psst!"

The sleeping man never opened his eyes, but the other jerked upright at the sound and turned. Igraine's shot knocked him back in his chair. Heather shot his sleeping companion so he wouldn't wake up before they were through. As the women put the stunned men's hands behind their backs and slipped plastic restraints around their wrists, Hugh ripped two pieces of wide tape from the roll he carried and taped the sleeping broadcasters' mouths shut. Then they were rolled, slumped on their chairs, to a corner of the booth and out of the way.

While they were doing all this, the priest in the studio had his head bowed, eyes closed in fervent broadcast prayer. Hugh pressed a button on the board, and the priest's words assaulted them.

"—through your guidance, our most Heavenly Father. Give us your strength and your wisdom to root out this evil from among us, that good, Christian women will remember their true vocation as children of God and will return to the bosoms of their families, seeking once again the instruction of their husbands and fathers—"

Hugh hit the button again, cutting the noise off. At a nod from Nuala, the big man in the balaclava pressed a few more buttons on the board and the red light above the broadcast booth went out.

"Off the air," he said, and lifted his own camera. Its red light went on. Nuala slipped off her balaclava.

"This is Nuala Dennehy, speaking to you from the broadcast station of the Church's own network, TF-PRAY. We have come here to expose this network for what it really is and what it does. And to put an end to its lies."

Igraine, pistol in hand, opened the studio door for Nuala. She walked in, followed by Hugh and his camera. Igraine and Heather stayed in the booth, on alert in case any unexpected visitors showed up.

"—for these misguided daughters of Eve—"

"Excuse me."

The priest jumped, his eyes flying open. He stared at Nuala and the masked cameraman behind her.

"You! What—" He turned to the booth for help, but two more women in black balaclavas were all he saw. Heather waved at him.

"You're on Guerrilla TV," Nuala said. "Quite a different venue from the one you're used to. I have a few questions."

"How did you—this is preposterous! Get out!"

"Well, that's not very friendly," Nuala said. Hugh moved, getting a better shot of Nuala and the priest together.

"I should strike you down for the evil—"

"As I said, I'd like to ask a few questions," Nuala interrupted. "And please don't try anything violent. This is a gun; I'm sure you recognize it as such. But I would prefer not to use it."

The priest turned to the studio camera. "Please! Anyone watching, this station has been seized by terrorists! Call the *gardaí* immediately!"

Nuala whistled, a nonchalant tweet, to get his attention. "That's turned off. The only camera working here is this one, ours; it's only tape, not live. And if you think anybody's going to notice your station's off the air, who do you imagine would *watch* this crap at two in the bloody A.M.? But," she conceded, shrugging, "just in case somebody does, we'll be out of here in a moment. But first, a few questions. What's your name?"

"I refuse to cooperate with terrorists!" the priest blustered.

"Fine, don't tell me your name," Nuala said. "I'll call you George, then. So George, isn't it true that the Church's Sunday call-in program, 'Irish Christian Aid,' raises thousands of pounds from phoned-in donations every week?"

"What? Well, yes, but what—"

"And isn't it true that you tell the viewers that the money they donate goes to various charities, to help people all over Ireland?"

"Yes," the priest said, still angry, but confused as to where this was leading, and more than a bit frightened. "The Church gives substantial amounts—"

"But isn't it in fact true that not one penny of the money raised by this program or by this station actually goes to those charities?" The anger was apparent in Nuala's tone now, and she made no effort to hide it.

"No!" the priest said. "All the money goes—"

"Into the coffers of the Church!" Nuala took a step toward him. The look on her face made him back up. "The money raised by donations given by generous, caring people to help those poorer than themselves—the Travellers, or unwed mothers who are cast out by their families because of intolerant Church policies, or women who are fired from their jobs when they reach the age of fifty, still unmarried—all of that money that is supposed to help these people instead goes to line the pockets of the Bishops, the Cardinals, the Vatican itself! *Isn't that true?*"

"No! That is a lie!" The priest's tone was hollow, not very convincing, as he took another step back. The camera followed him relentlessly. "The money goes to the charities we—"

"That's not what I hear from my sources in your accounting department," Nuala interrupted.

"What? You're—I don't know what you're talking about!"

"Counting the checks that come in the mail, adding them up," said Nuala, "that's unpaid 'volunteer' work, isn't it? Married women who give you their time and effort and get nothing back for it. They know where the money gets sent, into whose personal accounts it gets deposited, because they're the ones who do all that menial, clerical work. For instance, on Sunday, the seventh of February, the 'Irish Christian Aid' program raised twenty-seven thousand, eight hundred and fifty pounds and seventy-six pence. Two days later, on the ninth of February, six thousand pounds was deposited into the *personal* account of Cardinal Eoin Turlough, five thousand pounds was deposited into the *personal* account of Bishop Declan Murphy, four thousand pounds went into Bishop Mícheál Sullivan's, and so on. The women in the accounting department know all this. And now we know."

The priest stared at her, uncertain how to respond. Hugh saw this, and his camera captured the twitch under the priest's right eye. Remembering the camera, the priest tried to bluff his way out of it.

"You are lying!" He pointed a condemning finger at Nuala, who merely stared at him, boredom and disgust on her face. "You made it all up. Everything that comes out of your mouth is a lie! You—"

"That's enough, I think," Nuala cut him off. She waved at Hugh, who swung the camera around to close in on her, leaving the priest out of the picture.

"I have never lied to you," Nuala said to the camera, "and I've no intention of starting now. It is true that all the money this network raises goes, not to charity as they claim, but to the

Church, one of the richest institutions on this planet. You have been bilked out of hundreds of thousands of pounds—"

"That is a lie!" the priest roared. "The Church would never—"

"And furthermore," Nuala went on, ignoring him, "besides robbing you blind, the Machiavellian ministers of propaganda who use this station do so to further their own cause, the cause of the Church and its puppet, the Irish government. They would have you believe that freedom is slavery and slavery is freedom, that to control one's own destiny and conscience is to lose one's soul. Well, I've had enough of this nonsense. It's time somebody put an end to it. And that's what I'm here to do."

She nodded and the red light went off. Hugh lowered his camera. "Got it all. Perfect."

"Good," Nuala said. She turned back to the priest, raising her pistol. His eyes widened at the sight of it. "Okay, George, let's move out." She waved the pistol toward the door. "Move it."

"I will not cooperate with—"

"Move your arse or get it shot off! I've run out of patience with you!"

The pistol was set on stun, but the priest couldn't see that, and the look on Nuala's face gave him no reassurance for his own safety. He hurried toward the door.

Back in the booth, Igraine and Heather had pushed the chairs with the two stunned men on them out into the hall.

"No reason you should have to do all the work," Nuala said. "George, give 'em a hand." The priest started to argue, then thought better of it when she threatened him with the pistol. He pushed one chair, Hugh the other. In a few moments they were outside the station, shivering in the cold February night.

Nuala blinked her flashlight twice, then three times, and the van appeared from behind the trees and came roaring across the parking lot. Hugh and the outraged priest loaded the two unconscious broadcasters inside.

"Hands behind your back." Nuala waved her pistol at the priest. "Come on, there's a good lad."

He didn't try to argue, but stood, unmoving and defiant. Hugh and Igraine grabbed him and put the restraints on his wrists. Hugh was smiling when he slapped some tape across the man's mouth. "Always wanted to do that to a priest."

"In," Nuala said, pointing to the van. The priest, eyes wide, obeyed once Hugh made a move toward him.

Nuala squinted off to where the other Guerrillas waited in the darkness. She couldn't see them, but knew they could see her. She waved at them to start taping.

"Okay, let's do it." Igraine pulled a box of grenades from the van.

"You watch him," Nuala said to Fiona, pointing at the priest.

"He won't be any trouble," Fiona assured her.

Nuala, Heather, and Hugh grabbed three grenades each and ran back inside. Igraine took the rest and ran around to the garage where all the mobile broadcasting units were parked.

The explosions didn't look like much from the front of the building, until some windows were blown out and flames started to reach into the night. But the cameraman, Barry, got a truly spectacular shot later on. The van stopped about a kilometer away, almost on the outskirts of town, so they could pile out to watch. Barry turned on his camera and pointed it at the ancient broadcast tower. They were too far away to make out the small satellite dish on top.

"Now?" Igraine asked, holding the transmitter.

"Why not?" Nuala said.

Igraine pushed the button, and five explosions shattered the night simultaneously. The flames lit up the tower, so Barry got an excellent shot of what was left of it falling over as if in slow motion, landing on top of the burning station, and breaking apart.

The Guerrillas, Heather, and Fiona cheered. Igraine just watched, smiling in grim satisfaction. Nuala stared at the flames, mesmerized. She had a brief fantasy that it was the prison burning, and that Adolf, Hans, and Fritz were trapped inside.

A moment later, distant sirens jarred her out of it.

"Out!" Fiona ordered, pointing her pistol inside. The priest emerged, unintelligible complaints and rage locked in by the tape. The Guerrillas unloaded the two still-unconscious broadcasters and laid them by the side of the road.

"Sit," Nuala said, and pointed toward the unconscious men. Hatred in his eyes, the priest sat on the frozen ground next to them.

"Won't they freeze out here if we leave them?" Heather asked.

"Don't worry," Nuala replied, "help's already on the way." She pointed toward the town, to the approaching headlights and the sound of sirens. "All George here has to do is step out into the road to get their attention."

"Let's go." Fiona was already behind the wheel.

Nuala took a last look at the burning *teilifís* station. "No more propaganda from that lot—not until they rebuild or buy new mobile units, anyway." She shared a smile with Igraine as they all climbed inside.

In a moment, the van had disappeared into the night.

Chapter 26

"I CAN'T BELIEVE how fast this has escalated," Fiona said, staring at the *teilifís* as she passed the plate of sandwiches.

"People are angry." Igraine took a sandwich and passed them on.

"They've been angry as long as I can remember," Heather said. "But they've never taken to the streets like this . . . Nuala? Nuala, do you want a sandwich?"

Nuala heard her name and tore her eyes from the vidscreen and the scenes of rioting in Dublin. "What?"

"Food," Heather said. "Eat something, please; you're still too thin."

Nuala started to reach for the plate, belatedly remembering the ten-pound weight in her hand. She used them constantly, whenever sitting or standing, especially when watching the *teilifís*. Never again would she be as weak as when Adolf and his fellow thugs had had her in their power. If there was a next time—and her conscious mind refused to picture that, leaving it to her dreams—she would be stronger. Her body would be ready to face them, even if her mind was reluctant to think about it.

She put down the weight in her right hand and took a sandwich, but her left arm continued its rhythmic pumping.

"The riots that have gone on sporadically all week," the Guerrilla on the *teilifís* continued, "were not confined to the major cities of Dublin, Belfast, and Derry, but have spread around the country. 'Rebel Cork' has rewon its ancient nickname with its courageous occupation of government buildings in Cork City, Cobh, Kinsale, and Youghal. *Garda* barracks have been burned to the ground in nearly every county. And members of the

Dáil—most of them, anyway—are finding it harder and harder to get to work."

The scene changed to the *Dáil* building and a shot of the persistent demonstrators and their signs, which read RULE FROM IRELAND, NOT THE VATICAN, IRELAND FOR THE IRISH, NOT THE POPE, FREEDOM MEANS WE MAKE OUR OWN CHOICES, and GARDAÍ OUT. The camera zoomed in on a squad of four *gardaí*, pistols drawn, who trotted down the steps toward the protestors. It was a bad tactical move, even with weapons. The demonstrators outnumbered them at least ten to one and were determined not to be chased off. Even as the *gardaí* approached, the demonstrators formed a tight circle to face them, signs now ready to swing. At a shout from off-camera, the *gardaí* froze. The camera swung about to show a man in a suit and sash, carrying a briefcase.

'This is Representative O'Hanlon of Donegal," the Guerrilla said, "who has surprisingly become sympathetic to the Movement. Some say he's merely trying to get reelected by saying what the people want to hear. Others point out that he hails from Gortahork, the home of martyr Tríona Rafferty. In any case, Representative O'Hanlon has, in the past two weeks, entered two bills for discussion in the *Dáil*: the first a general amnesty for all political prisoners currently being held, and the second, that there be an official *Dáil* investigation into the charges made by Nuala Dennehy three weeks ago that the Church broadcast network—whose transmitter and mobile units she helped to blow up, putting the Church out of the broadcasting business for the time being—was not using any of the money it raised from weekly call-in pledges to help various charities, but was in fact keeping all the money for private use by Church officials. The archbishop's office in Armagh has denied the charges, of course, but because of the public outcry, the *Dáil* is, for the first time in this reporter's memory, not willing merely to accept the Church's word for it."

The demonstrators on the steps of the *Dáil* parted for the man in the government sash, some of them nodding at him in respect. The four *gardaí*, who had not attacked because of his order, escorted him inside the building.

The Guerrilla went on as the picture changed to another picket line, this one around a cathedral in Armagh. "In other news, the Church is under attack from all sides. Our sources report that attendance at Mass has plummeted, except in a few isolated cases of parishes of the so-called Liberation Theology priests. Those few—very few—priests who have come out in favor of separating the Church from the state have seen their congregations increase dramatically. Whether this is a trend that will survive Church censure or not remains to be seen."

"Fat chance," Igraine muttered as she opened a bottle of Guinness.

"In today's Nuala Watch," the Guerrilla's voice continued, a smile evident in his tone as the scene changed again, this time to a familiar community center, "we have news of the sixth spotting of Ms. Dennehy since her dramatic escape from prison almost two months ago. It was here, at the Toomevara Community Centre in Toomevara, Tipperary, that Ms. Dennehy made another surprise appearance three days ago."

"Notice they never mention us?" Fiona said to Igraine. "Hardly fair that herself gets all the publicity."

"A tragic injustice," Igraine agreed, and took a sip of Guinness. Nuala just smiled and ignored them.

"Ms. Dennehy had been hiding out somewhere in the vicinity," the Guerrilla went on, "and apparently heard of the Toomevara Married Women's Guild's meeting to discuss the housework stoppage that had been suggested at their last meeting. The purpose of this strike by the married women of Toomevara was to persuade their husbands to support them in their demand of the Toomevara City Council that housework be paid for, as it is a necessary and important job that deserves a wage, and a decent one, at that. Ms. Dennehy and two or three companions—"

"That's us," Heather said. "See, we aren't forgotten."

"Just unnamed," Igraine pointed out.

"—attended the meeting, apparently to merely listen. But upon being recognized, Ms. Dennehy was prevailed upon to speak. Shortly after she began, however, a *garda* squad car appeared outside the building. It is still not known if the *gardaí* were even aware of Ms. Dennehy's presence and were seeking her arrest—"

"They weren't," Igraine said to the *teilifís*. "They couldn't find their arses with both hands."

"—or whether they were simply investigating—which means, of course, harassing—the women's meeting. In any event, the women had been carrying mops, buckets, and recycling bin lids as a sort of symbol of their jobs as homemakers, and turned the tables on the very surprised *gardaí* by advancing upon them, brandishing these weapons. Under cover of this, Ms. Dennehy and her companions stole out the back to where a van was waiting—"

"That would be myself." Fiona raised her hand.

"—and escaped quite easily."

"It wasn't as easy as all that," Fiona objected mildly. "It took a bit of fancy driving."

"Which you could do in your sleep," Igraine said.

"Do you mind?" Nuala smiled. "I'm trying to listen."

"Sh!" Heather scolded the other two, shaking a finger at them. "Herself is trying to listen."

"Oh, sorry," Igraine said.

"So sorry, do forgive us," Fiona added. Nuala laughed at their clowning, which she knew was for her benefit, and threw some potato crisps in their direction.

"And finally," the Guerrilla said, "the international news." The vidscreen showed them more demonstrations, one after another. "The Freedom Movement—or Freedom from Religion Movement, as some have called it—continues to spread from Ireland to other countries. This weekend antigovernment, antifundamentalist demonstrations were held across the United States, in many of the major cities, including Washington, and in Cascadia, the nation comprised of the former western coastal areas of the United States and Canada. As always, since the beginning of this movement, a majority of the protestors were female, and many of their demands they defined as 'feminist,' not antireligion."

"Same thing, if they have any sense," Igraine muttered.

The camera scanned a massive crowd near the Lincoln Memorial. "Among their demands were: a reinstatement of the original First Amendment to the American Constitution, which would guarantee a free press once again; overturning the laws that make homosexuality a crime; and, of course, as in every American demonstration of this sort, a return to legal abortion, which the Americans have been arguing over for almost a century."

The scene turned violent: Water cannons were turned on the crowd by the police, who also used clubs, stun pistols, and sonic weapons to make arrests. "Across the United States, over two thousand arrests were made on Saturday and Sunday, but the protestors say they are determined to continue." The *teilifís* showed a close-up of an angry African-American woman with a bloody bandage tied around her head. "Give up? We're fighting for our *lives*, here! Hell, no, we ain't gonna give up! They're crazy if they think so!"

"Tell 'em," Igraine muttered.

"Similar demonstrations occurred in Santiago, Mexico City, Cairo, St. Petersburg, Nairobi, Warsaw, Calcutta, and Singapore. We at Guerrilla TV insist these demonstrations are not—as the various governments would have you believe—isolated, internal problems. We believe they are all part of a worldwide demand for freedom. There may be individual issues being debated or fought for in each country, but the similarities are far more abundant than the differences. In every case, in each of these countries, basic human rights have been consistently denied and are now being fought for. These rights include freedom of speech, freedom of or from religion, free elections, separation of religion from government, and equal rights for all citizens. And in every country, can it be a coincidence that women have surged to the forefront, taking positions within the movement that they are denied in their own societies?"

The vidscreen closed in on women, arms linked, marching in some unnamed city. The signs in the crowd were in Spanish. The Guerrilla went on.

"Freedom for all people means freedom for *all people*. Women should not be denied the freedoms that men claim as their right. These freedoms are fundamental and should be universal. As is guaranteed in some nations, but nowhere as specifically stated and enforced as in the Fleet."

"The Fleet!" Heather whispered, and leaned forward, her eyes wide. The vidscreen showed a shot of Fleet Headquarters in Geneva, then cut to a woman in a silver uniform, enough braid on her forearm to prove her high rank.

"Of course we are sympathetic to the democracy movements in the various countries," she was saying to a reporter in a EuroNet blazer. She had a southwestern United States drawl. "Before joining the Fleet, many of us in Command were citizens of the countries embroiled in these struggles today. And for most, if not all, people who join the Fleet, the main attraction for joining is the guarantee of those basic human rights by the Fleet Charter." She frowned at the camera. "But as we must keep telling everyone who asks the Fleet to use our military capabilities to intervene in these struggles, we cannot take sides in the internal struggles of any nation. To do so would violate our most important directive: noninterference. Just as we do not intervene in the internal affairs of any of the inhabited planets of the Unity or others we come into contact with, so, too, must we refuse to interfere here, on our own planet." She sighed. "I believe there is not one of us who is not sorry that we cannot help those seeking freedom. I wish that we could. But it is up to the citizens of every nation to fight their own battles—"

The knock at the door startled the four women. Nuala dropped the weights and lunged for the pistol on the table near her hand. Heather hit the *teilifís* switch, silencing the room. Fiona and Igraine ran to the door, pistols ready, and took up positions on either side. They were ready before the sequence of knocks was completed: three raps, then two, then four.

"Éadaoin," Fiona said, but not one of the four women lowered her pistol.

"*Cé atá ann?*" Fiona called, trying to sound nonchalant.

"Brigid and Dana" came Brigid's reply, to the women's surprise. Fiona unlocked the door and opened it a crack, then opened it wide, lowering her pistol. Nuala waited until the two women were all the way in and the door was closed before lowering her own pistol.

"We were in the neighborhood," Dana explained.

"Hello," Brigid said. "Sorry if we startled you."

"Well, well," said Fiona, waving them over to the couch. "Have a seat."

"Should I wet some tea?" Heather asked.

"It's good to see you again, Nuala," Brigid said with that same motherly smile that Nuala remembered. "I can't believe it's been only a few months since you were in Rathcoole. So much has happened since then."

"And so much *is* happening," Dana added. She sipped her second cup of tea and took another sugar biscuit when Heather offered them. "Thank you, my dear. And how have *you* been?"

"Me?" Heather asked, surprised. "I'm fine. Never better."

"You look—older, somehow," Dana observed.

"Really?" Heather was delighted. "Do I?"

Dana chuckled. "When you get to be my age, Heather, you won't be so happy at that prospect."

Heather blushed and suddenly looked nineteen again. Nuala stared at her for a moment. She had forgotten just how young the girl really was.

"How's your cat?" Igraine asked Dana.

"Despondent. He barely speaks to me since you left. You know, once all this unpleasantness is over and women have true choices at last, you really ought to become a veterinarian. Your rapport with animals is quite remarkable."

"I'll consider it," Igraine said, smiling.

"And you?" Brigid asked Nuala. "How are you doing?"

Nuala shrugged and used Heather's line: "Never better." But no one in the room believed that, least of all Nuala herself. Uncomfortable with Brigid's concerned scrutiny, she picked up one of the weights to give her hands something to do. "I'm fine," she insisted when Brigid continued to study her.

"Of course you are," Brigid murmured, and took a sip of tea.

"So what brings you two to Banteer?" Fiona asked. "Just thought you'd pop in since we were in Cork and so close by?"

"Yes, as a matter of fact," Brigid said. "What with all that's been happening in the country, we wanted to see for ourselves just how all of you were holding up." But it was Nuala she was looking at.

"And to thank you, Nuala," Dana added, putting down her teacup.

"Thank me?" Nuala said. "Whatever for?"

Brigid put down her cup too and laid a gentle hand on Nuala's arm. Her expression was so grave, so worried, that Nuala knew what was coming.

"We know what was done to you in that horrible place." Nuala looked away from Brigid's compassion, embarrassed by it, but the older woman went on. "We know what they did to you to make you name names. But no *gardaí* showed up at our doors to arrest us. You didn't tell them."

"Of course not!" How could they think she would have betrayed them? "I would never—"

"We know," Brigid hastened to reassure her. "We know you would never inform on any of us. We trusted you instinctively from the beginning, and that trust has only been strengthened by your courage."

Courage? Nuala's collar felt tight. She tugged at it. They could never know how terrified she had been, still was every night when her nightmares jolted her awake, covered with sweat, her heart pounding. They thought her brave?

Brigid was looking at her as if she could read Nuala's every thought. She smiled, the compassion still glistening in her eyes. "You were our unanimous choice, Nuala. We knew that you could speak for us, that you would have the courage and strength—"

"Right, we're all agreed that I'm a bloody hero," Nuala interrupted, the joke betrayed by the sarcasm of her tone. "Can we move on to a new subject now?"

"Only if you agree to accept our thanks," Brigid insisted gently.

"You exceeded our expectations, child," Dana said. Child? Well, Dana was twice her age, but still. Nuala raised an eyebrow at the term. Dana pretended not to notice. "You have spoken brilliantly on our behalf, you have roused the people as no one of us could ever have done, and you protected us in the face of horrible—"

"You're welcome!" Nuala tugged at her turtleneck again. It was very warm in the room. "Can we move along now?"

Dana and Brigid exchanged a knowing smile.

"So where's Éadaoin?" Igraine asked, and Nuala shot her friend a grateful glance at the change of subject.

"She'll be along," Brigid answered, picking up her teacup again. "She had to make a call."

"We have news," Dana said. "We wanted to tell you about it in person."

"Yes." Brigid smiled. "Good news."

"That's a change," Fiona said.

"A welcome one," Brigid agreed.

"The pressure is building," Dana said. "People all over the country have been demanding new elections, pressuring their councillors, flooding the offices of *Dáil* members to call for a General Election."

"And it's becoming obvious that the *Taoiseach* is on his way out," Brigid said. "He couldn't survive a confidence vote."

"But he'd just be replaced by one of the other fools," Igraine said. "Every leader of every party is hand-picked by the Church."

"That's why we need a new party." Brigid's smile gave it away: This was the good news.

"A new party?" Nuala put down the weight and leaned forward, her hands gripping her knees. "But surely the Church would never allow—"

"The people would no longer stand for such interference," Dana interrupted. "Not this time."

"We've got people in position," Brigid said. "Even some junior members of the *Dáil* are on our side, ready to abandon their parties and run on a new ticket."

"And those new faces who have been popping up on the news, talking about 'compassionate reform'?" Dana smiled, triumphant. "Ours. All ours. Ready to declare for the new party, as soon as it's announced."

"And we want you to announce it," Brigid added.

"Me?" Nuala said. "I don't know anything about it."

"That's why we're here," Dana explained. "To tell you all about it, so you can make an informed, persuasive tape."

"We need you, Nuala." Brigid nodded for emphasis. "Yes, again. Still. You are the one the people listen to. Soon there will be others, once the campaign truly gets under way. But for now, you are the voice we need."

Nuala looked from Brigid to Dana and back. "And you really think there's a chance this will work? This new party? The Church and the present form of government have over half a century in power behind them. They're entrenched; it'd take explosives to blast them out. I'm not sure it's possible yet. It sure as hell won't be easy."

"Nothing ever is," Brigid said. "But, yes, I think there's a very good chance this will work. Even if all our people aren't elected, those who are reelected will have to compromise to keep their jobs. The tide has finally turned. It's too late to go back—every small victory ensures that. So it's time we offered the people something new, a real *choice* of politicians for the first time in their lives. And *now*, before the Church comes up with more lies that sound like the truth."

Nuala considered this. Finally she sighed and nodded. "Well, if I'm going to be telling people who to vote for, then I'd better approve of them myself first. I hope you know I won't endorse anyone on just your say-so. I'll have to look them over myself."

"Of course," Dana agreed. "We've got a full background on every man who's agreed to run—"

"Man?" Igraine interrupted. "I thought you said this was a *new* party. What's new about male politicians?"

"Yeah," Heather agreed. "Where are the women? I think *Nuala* should run for leader of the new party. That way, *she'd* get to be *Taoiseach*."

To Nuala's dismay, no one laughed. "Now wait a moment—"

"Not a bad idea," Brigid interrupted, "and one we certainly considered. But somehow we thought Nuala wouldn't want the job. But if you—"

"Hell, no!" Had they all lost their minds?

"It would be a bit difficult to campaign with a *garda* under every bush, just waiting to nab her," Dana pointed out.

"Well, that has nothing to do with it," Nuala reluctantly admitted. "Bobby Sands was elected to Parliament while on hunger strike in Long Kesh. You don't have to be free to—but I don't want the job. And it's ridiculous to even consider me—"

"No, it's not," Heather argued. "You'd be grand. You could—"

"She said she doesn't want the job," Igraine interrupted. "And it is *her* decision, isn't it, now?"

"Well, yeah, but—" Heather began.

"Thank you," Nuala said to Igraine. She turned to Brigid. "So what's this new party to be called? And some of those running *are* women, aren't they? You'd better have some, if you want my help."

"Yes, some are," Brigid assured her. "In the less conservative districts: the larger cities. And the party is to be called '*Saoirse na Héireann*, or '*Saoirse*' for short."

" 'The Freedom of Ireland Party,' " Nuala repeated, smiling. "It has a ring to it, doesn't it?"

"But the Church," Fiona said. "Surely they'll try to stop this before it's started."

"That's the other piece of good news," Dana said. "The grip of the Church is weaker now than it's been in generations. You've heard on the Guerrilla TV that Mass attendance is still dropping steadily."

"Right," Brigid said. "And the God Patrols are proving to be quite ineffective; the loathing the people have always felt for them is now out in the open."

"Did you hear that a Patrol was attacked by a group of teen-age girls in Galway?" Dana asked. "They threw buckets of sour milk on them from a second-story window. Fairly drenched the bastards." She smiled at Heather. "Your generation, my dear. And I don't doubt for a moment that the pamphlet you wrote had a hand in it. It's been copied and passed around in every school in the country, I should think."

"You don't mean it! Mine?" Heather was shocked and pleased at the same time. "I hadn't heard—"

"Well, you've been a bit busy lately." Dana patted her knee in a grandmotherly way.

"Any student caught with it is immediately expelled," Brigid told the girl. "That's how afraid of it the Church is."

"But that isn't stopping the kids," Dana said. "That pamphlet has been read by more students than any textbook. And now they're writing their own."

Heather was speechless, but the grin that lit up her face said it all.

"Congratulations, kid," Fiona said. "We told you it was good."

"Heather *abú*," Igraine said, and raised her teacup in salute. The others repeated the war cry and raised their own cups. Heather's face was by now bright red. She looked at Nuala, her eyes shining.

Nuala smiled, feeling an embarrassingly warm rush of affection for the girl. "I always knew you could do it. Since that day I first saw you with your cuffs rolled back."

Heather's blush increased, and tears glistened in her eyes. The raw emotion on her face as she smiled at Nuala was powerful enough to embarrass both of them.

"So you were saying about the Church?" Igraine covered the awkward moment with her usual diversionary tactic.

"Oh, yes," Dana said. "The rebels within the Church—and I use the term rebel advisedly—are speaking out. At least somewhat; they're *beginning* to speak out, let's say."

"Rebels?" Heather asked, confused. "In the Church?"

"Even the most totalitarian of organizations will spawn rebels, my dear," Dana told her. "Perhaps I should say *especially* the most totalitarian."

"People who are committed to spirituality, but not to the dominant form it takes in society," Brigid explained. "There has always been a tiny group of priests and nuns and brothers who prefer to break away from the Vatican and form a separate Irish Celtic Church."

"Like in the old days?" Nuala asked. "Hundreds of years ago, before the Italian Church grew powerful enough to dominate the others?"

"Precisely." Brigid nodded.

"So what?" Igraine said. She leaned back in her chair and crossed her legs. "Of course I believe that people have the right to whatever religion they want, but I can't say that one flavor of Christianity is much of an improvement over another—not in *my* opinion, at least. They all taste like swill to me."

Nuala smiled. Once again Igraine had voiced her own thoughts for her.

"But imagine a Church without a Pope," Dana said. "With the Virgin back at the top of the pyramid, so to speak. After all, it's not such a large step from worshipping the Virgin Mary to worshipping the Goddess she was before Christianity arrived on these shores."

When that thought sank in, the women began to smile. Even Igraine.

"So the stronger these rebel voices become," Brigid went on with her explanation, "the more divided and distracted the Church, and therefore weaker. Which is to our advantage."

"Your sister, by the way," Dana said to Nuala, "is definitely one of those rebel voices."

"What?" Kerry had never said anything of the kind to Nuala. "Are you sure?"

Brigid smiled and nodded. "Being your sister of course means she's watched very carefully, so she uses discretion. And her Mother Superior has always been one of the rebels and is quite fond of Kerry. She protects her as best she can."

Nuala didn't know how to respond. She didn't know Kerry— her own sister—at all. And she apparently knew less about nuns that she had thought.

"So all of this works to our advantage, as I said," Brigid continued. "We are infiltrating every facet of society with our contagious message of freedom. Even into the very structure of our enemies: the Church and the government."

"Yes," Dana agreed. "That's really why we wanted to come see you four in person. To tell you that we are indeed gaining ground and that we owe a great deal of the success to you. Our scheming behind the scenes could never have succeeded without your distracting attention from us and your courage in taking the risks. We are very grateful to all of you."

The four women looked at each other, none of them sure what to say.

Was it really true? Nuala wondered. Could it be true that they might actually win—and herself live to see it? If only Máire—

Another knock at the door made them all jump. The four fugitives grabbed their pistols, and Nuala and Fiona started to hurry Brigid and Dana toward the back door. Then the knock was completed: It was the secret "password."

"It's just Éadaoin." Brigid turned back. "She's finally caught up to us."

It was Éadaoin. She hurried inside, barely glancing at her mother or the others, and came directly over to Nuala, a frightening expression on her face. Something gripped Nuala's heart and squeezed.

"Nuala, it's your da," Éadaoin said, confirming Nuala's premonition. "I'm afraid he's taken a turn for the worse. He—he hasn't much time left at all. I'm sorry."

Nuala found herself sitting. She didn't remember finding the chair. They were staring at her, compassion written on every face.

"I have to go to him," she said, her voice thick with tears.

"But they'll be lying in wait; you know that," Éadaoin said.

"I don't care! I have to. I cannot let my father die without—without—"

"I'll go with you," Heather said. She knelt by the chair and put her arm around Nuala. There were tears in her eyes. "We'll get you there, and we'll get you out. Won't we?" The question was a challenge to Fiona and Igraine. For the moment the other three women didn't exist.

"We'll get you to him, Nuala," Igraine promised.

"I'll drive, of course," Fiona said, and tried to smile.

Brigid, Éadaoin, and Dana exchanged a somber look. Then Brigid nodded. "All right. We owe you that much. But don't go off halfcocked. We'll arrange a safe way to get you to him."

"Fine," Igraine said. "We'll accept your help, but let's figure it out *now*. It sounds like we haven't much time."

"Da," Nuala murmured. "Please wait for me."

Chapter 27

"THERE GOES ANOTHER one."

Heather peered through the slit of the barely open door, watching a *garda* patrol the hospital corridor. Nuala hung back in the dimly lit stairwell, her pistol in her hand. Both she and Heather were wearing the white habits of the Church's nursing order, but Nuala's face was by now recognizable to everyone in the country; the disguise would be of little use at close range. And so she kept her pistol in her hand. When they entered the corridor she would put it away, but not until then.

Heather glanced at her watch. "Almost time. They should be switching to the tape any moment now."

Nuala just nodded. She knew she should feel guilty about risking so many people, but they had all volunteered to help get her to her father; it had been their choice to risk their freedom and possibly their lives for a dying man they had never met. What extraordinary people they were—she owed them so much. But she couldn't think about that now.

"There's our man!" Heather whispered. Nuala moved up beside her to peer through the narrow opening. Aidan Donlon, a thirtyish blond man who was one of Éadaoin's people, was sauntering down the corridor toward them, wearing a *garda* uniform. He glanced in their direction and idly rubbed his nose.

"They've done it!" Heather whispered. "I hope to god Security doesn't notice the switch."

Nuala didn't reply. Whether Security caught on or not, there was no turning back now. Her father was just down the corridor, a few meters away, and nothing was going to keep her from saying good-bye to him.

Donlon turned the corner in the middle of the corridor, following the sign that said INTENSIVE CARE UNIT, and disappeared. Nuala and Heather waited, every muscle tense, for the sound of plasfire or shouts or anything else that would tell them that Donlon had been caught. But they heard nothing but the usual hospital sounds: signal tones and the soft female voice paging someone on the com system.

After a few anxious moments, the two women saw another *garda* leave the ICU. A young man, barely in his twenties, he rubbed an apparently stiff neck as he walked quickly to the lift and pressed the button. As he stood waiting, he rolled first one shoulder and then the other, grimacing. The two women watched him from their hiding place, not daring to leave until he had gone. The fewer *gardaí* they had to pass, the better. Finally the doors opened, but all the man did was take a step forward, then stop, scowling. He didn't get on the lift; it must have been full. The doors closed. He hit the button with his fist.

"Come *on*," Heather murmured.

After an impatient wait of but a few seconds, the *garda* pushed back his uniform sleeve and looked at his watch. That seemed to anger him; his lips moved in what was most likely an oath. Then he glanced around, turned, and headed right for them.

"He's coming this way!" Heather whispered, as they jumped back from the door. "Did he see us?"

Nuala shook her head. "Just wants the stairs." She hoped she was right. "Come on; let's go."

"Right past—" Heather dropped her protest when Nuala tucked her pistol in the voluminous pocket of her habit and reached for the doorknob.

"No! Let me go first!" Heather pushed her aside with one hand, put her pistol away, and reached for the door. It was shoved open, almost hitting her.

The *garda* stopped abruptly, surprised. He stared at them.

"Goodness!" Heather pressed a hand to her chest. "You could have hit us with that door. You should be more careful, Officer."

"Sorry, Sister," he muttered, then stepped back into the corridor and motioned for them to pass.

Nuala walked past him, following Heather, keeping her head down.

"Wait!" the *garda* said, and Nuala froze. Her hand squeezed the pistol in her pocket. She didn't look up.

"Do you know where the nursery is? I'm supposed to meet my brother there to have a look at his new son, and I'm late, because my damned—uh, I mean—my replacement was late."

"Second floor, east wing," Nuala murmured.

"Thanks." The *garda* hurried toward the stairs.

Nuala and Heather each took a shaky breath and started down the corridor.

"I thought the floor plan said the nursery was in the *west* wing of the second floor," Heather whispered.

"East wing; I'm sure of it," Nuala replied. "This way."

Turning the corner, they saw a *garda* sitting on a chair just outside the doors that led to intensive care. Keeping her head down, Nuala followed directly behind Heather. They walked as slowly as they dared. Where was Donlon?

Just as the officer looked up from his magazine at them, the doors slid open with a quiet *whoosh*, and Donlon appeared.

"Why don't you take that break, now that I'm here?" he said to the seated *garda*, a man in his forties, with the beginnings of a paunch. "I can cover for you. And bring me some coffee, will you?"

"As soon as I—" The *garda* pulled the datalink out from under his magazine, looking at Heather.

"I'll do that," Donlon said, as Heather retrieved an ID chip from around her neck. "You go along."

The other man shrugged, bored, and handed the datalink to Donlon. Nuala eased unobtrusively behind Heather as the man passed. She started to remove her ID chip, but Donlon, watching the *garda* leave, raised a hand to stop her.

"Thank you, Sisters," he said, loud enough for the *garda* to hear him from where he was probably waiting for the lift around the corner. "Now that you've checked in, this won't be necessary again; I'll remember your faces. Thank you for your cooperation." He dropped his voice to a whisper. "Third door on your right. Private room. There's a nun in with him. Couldn't see her face, but she's not a nurse—she's in black. The shift changes again in three hours, but they've been doing spot checks. Don't take too long."

Nuala nodded and stepped through the doorway, Heather behind her.

Intensive care was quiet; two nurses occupied the station in the center of the floor. One was typing notes into a computer while the other took patient chart chips out of a very full in-box. At the far end of the floor, under the *AMACH*/Exit sign, sat another *garda*, reading a paperback book. The chair in front of the third door on the right was vacant; Donlon would have been sitting there if he hadn't been covering for the *garda* at the ICU entrance.

Nuala glanced at Heather, who nodded and headed for the nurses' station. Nuala ducked into the first room on her right.

A very old woman lay asleep in the bed near the door. A red light pulsed on the Vital Signs Board on the wall above her head and an EKG line blipped in sync with it. A constant stream of blue numbers ran across the VSB, another line of green numbers under it. Curtains were drawn around all the cubicles, so Nuala couldn't see any other patients. She waited just inside the door, listening.

An instant later she heard the distraction.

"Oh, I'm sorry! Let me help you!" Heather's voice could be heard above the clatter. Nuala waited until she had counted to five, then eased open the door.

The box of patient chart chips had fallen, showering chips all over the floor. Both the nurses and Heather were kneeling, picking them up. The *garda* at the exit watched them for a moment, then sighed and looked back down at his book. Nuala stepped out into the hallway on noiseless crepe soles and crept the few steps to the third room. The *garda* never looked up, nor did the nurses as Heather prattled on, dropping nearly every chip she picked up. Nuala slipped into her father's room.

Kerry sat in the chair next to the bed, eyes closed, head

bowed in prayer, fingers worrying the rosary in her lap. Séamus
Dennehy was asleep, his face nearly as white as the sheets.
Nuala stared at him, her eyes flooding, her throat constricting.
The VSB over his head monitored his weak pulse. She didn't
know what the blue or green numbers meant, but it couldn't be
good. The tears threatened to drown her. She sniffed, and Kerry's eyes flew open.

"Nuala!" Kerry jumped to her feet, ran to her sister. But instead of embracing her, she grabbed Nuala's arm. "You
shouldn't be here! The camera!" She pointed to the tiny
vidcamera high up on the wall opposite their father's bed.
"They'll see you!"

"Relax." Nuala stared at her still-sleeping father. "Right now
the lads in Security are watching a tape of Da sleeping yesterday
afternoon. They'll never suspect a thing—if you were here yesterday, too."

"What? Yes, I was, but how did you—"

"I have very clever friends." Nuala stepped around her sister
and went to her father's side. "How—" Her voice broke. "How
is he?"

Kerry came up behind her, stood very close. Her voice was as
sad as Nuala felt, but strong. "He's in and out of consciousness.
The drugs ease his coughing, but they make him so groggy, it's
difficult for him to speak." She paused. When she spoke again
her voice wavered for just a moment, then strengthened. "I
thank God for the miracle every time he wakes up. He could slip
away at any time. The doctors are surprised he's lasted this long
. . . but I suspect he's been waiting for you. He asks after you
every time he wakes."

Nuala heard the chair as Kerry pushed it closer. When it
touched the back of Nuala's legs, she sat down, still staring at
her father's ravaged face, the tears flowing at the stark whiteness
of the skin under the gray stubble.

Kerry leaned over her father and stroked his forehead. "Da?
Da, can you hear me?" Her voice was soft but firm. "Da, please
wake up. Nuala's here at last."

Séamus's hand lay on top of the white sheets. Nuala stared at
the purple veins that bulged out of the slack white skin. She remembered suddenly the day of her dog's funeral when she was
six.

Parnell had been her best friend in the world, an Irish terrier
who possessed the most noble of souls. When he had been killed
by a drunk driver, her father had made Parnell a coffin, fash-

ioned lovingly with those strong hands. And a tombstone with
the words "Parnell, Beloved Friend" burned painstakingly into
the wood. She had watched her father's hands lower Parnell's
coffin into the ground, shovel the earth over him, then pound the
tombstone into place. He had held her in those strong arms until
it was too dark to read Parnell's name, then lifted her and carried her into the house.

Kerry was still speaking to Séamus, urging him to wake up.
Nuala's arms seemed to weigh a ton as she reached for her father's hand, but she made the effort and grasped the frail hand
that had once been the strongest thing in the world to her. She
squeezed, willing him to wake up, to look at her.

Séamus's eyes fluttered, opened. Kerry, still leaning over him,
smiled. "Da," she said, "look who's here." She turned to look at
her sister and he followed her gaze.

Nuala forced herself to smile through her tears. She suddenly
couldn't think of a thing to say.

Séamus's sunken eyes crinkled at the corners. His voice was
raspy, his words slurred, but Nuala understood him.

"Having *one* nun in the family is sufficient holiness to get me
into heaven. You needn't have joined up on *my* account, *cushla*."

The smile was no effort this time. "I look ridiculous, don't I?
But it worked to get me in to you."

Séamus frowned. "D-dangerous." His voice was so weak it
frightened Nuala.

"No, no, I'm quite safe," she hastened to assure him, squeezing his hand. "The Guerrillas have tricked Security with a tape,
and I've several friends outside keeping watch. There's nothing
to worry about."

But Séamus continued to frown. "Don't want you to get
caught . . . again . . . Hurt you . . . before."

"I'm fine, Da," Nuala said. "And they won't catch me again.
They can't take me out so easily. I'm in this until it's over, until
we win. I'm the daughter of Séamus Dennehy. They tried locking me up before, didn't they? But you got me out." She smiled,
her pride in him shining in her eyes. "I escaped because of all
those stories you taught me. You gave me the knowledge I
needed to draw that card, like Dev did, and you supplied the
key. You saved me."

Séamus managed another weak smile. "The tyrants can't beat
. . . the resourcefulness of the people . . . Dev and Collins proved
that."

"And so did we." Nuala held onto his hand as she once had as a child, with both of her own.

"Ireland . . . will be free," Séamus murmured, his eyes smiling at her. Then his body was racked by a wrenching cough. When it stopped he was gasping for breath, but Kerry was ready with an oxygen cone. Séamus took a few deep, ragged breaths, then nodded, and Kerry removed the cone from over his face.

It took a moment before he could speak again. "Ireland . . . I taught you to worship Ireland. I—I should have given you more, Nuala."

"What? And isn't it more than most people have?" Nuala argued. "I have never wanted more. You gave me Ireland's past, and now I'm going to help build her future. Could there *be* anything grander than that?"

"Love," Séamus said. "Someone to love. That's what I want for you."

"And haven't I always had that?" Nuala's voice was soft; it almost cracked on the last word. She squeezed his hand again to tell him who she meant.

Séamus's eyes were now as damp as hers. He acknowledged her squeeze with one of his own. It was so weak it broke her heart.

"I—" Séamus attempted. "I gave you . . . my ambitions . . . along with my love. I hope I did you . . . no injustice." Nuala opened her mouth to argue, but he shook his head, the slightest of movements, and she fell silent, waiting. He breathed raggedly for a moment before trying to continue. "The past is easy to love. The present is more difficult to live in. I am afraid . . . that my own sense of failure has . . . pushed you onto the path you've chosen."

"I make my own choices, Da," Nuala told him, her voice strong and steady now. The *last* thing she wanted for him to feel before he died was guilt. "That's what life is about, isn't it? Choices. And the right to make them. That's what freedom is. You taught me to cherish freedom and to fight for it. People who are raised in slavery don't know what freedom is, but I know. Because you gave me the past. It lives in me; it breathes in me. And as long as I live, and if I pass it on to someone else as you passed it to me, then it will never die."

The worry was still there in his eyes, but she saw the pride warring with it. "Connolly . . . James Connolly said . . . 'in Ireland the worship of the past is often engaged in . . . simply as an escape from the mediocrity of the present.' Perhaps that's why I sought the refuge of others' past deeds . . . because I accomplished none of my own. And now, of course, it's too late—"

"And Patrick Pearse said," Nuala interrupted, raising her voice in determination, " 'if you strike us down we will rise again and renew the fight. You cannot conquer Ireland. You cannot extinguish the Irish passion for freedom. If our deed has not been sufficient to win freedom, then our *children* shall win it by a better deed.' " She forced a smile. "Don't bandy quotes with me, Da. I've a bloody Ph.D. in the subject, haven't I?" His smile was her encouragement. "You taught me, right? That was your deed. And I've gone on Guerrilla TV and repeated what you taught me, and now there's an entire *revolution* flourishing out there! And all because of yourself. So I'll have none of this 'I haven't accomplished anything' nonsense. You have . . . you *have*. And I'm damned lucky—" Her voice betrayed her, cracking as her throat constricted. "I'm lucky to have you for a father."

She couldn't talk after that; the tears refused to be held back. They streamed down Séamus's face as well. A loud sniff reminded Nuala that Kerry was about to lose a father, too. Séamus turned his head to look at his younger daughter. He tried to raise his free hand, and Kerry circled the bed, pulled the other chair close, and took his hand in her own. Séamus smiled at them both. His eyes were drooping in exhaustion; his speech was more slurred than before.

"Such daughters I have . . . finer than ten sons." He fought to keep his eyes open. "I love you . . . both. Kerry, you have . . . your God. And Nuala . . . you have your country. But try . . . try to find something—someone—not so . . . abstract . . . to love. I had Ireland . . . but I had your mother, too. And yourselves." He was tiring so quickly it terrified Nuala.

"Da, please; you've got to rest!"

"No, I've done with that now," he fought to say. "I know you can't . . . come back . . . so there's no more need for me—" He dragged a ragged breath into his lungs. "Promise me—" He coughed, and Kerry leapt up and grabbed the oxygen cone, placed it over his mouth and nose. He gasped for a few moments, then nodded. Kerry removed the cone, frowning. Séamus smiled his love at her. "Promise me . . . that you'll be happy. You'll allow yourself—selves—to be happy."

"Of course, Da," Kerry murmured through her tears.

"And you," he said to Nuala. "You promise me you'll let someone love you."

Nuala nodded, crying. She would have promised him anything at that moment, even something as unlikely as that.

"Good." Séamus's voice could barely be heard. He stared into Nuala's eyes. "I love—" His words broke off, and he seemed to collapse into himself. He continued to stare as the alarm on the VSB shrieked.

"Da? Da!" Nuala clutched his hand. "No! Da!"

Kerry cried out, falling forward and beginning to keen, her face on the bed near his hand.

The door to the room burst open and people in white began to pour in. They swarmed around Séamus's bed; someone was barking commands. Nuala and Kerry were pushed out of the way, and lost their grip on their father's hands.

Someone grabbed Nuala from behind. "We've got to go!" Heather said in her ear.

"No, my da—"

"Now, Nuala! The gardaí!"

"Go," Kerry said, and came to hug her sister in one brief, fierce embrace. "Go, now. Be safe. I'll stay with him. Go, Nuala!"

Heather dragged her backward. She couldn't see her father's face because of the crisis team.

Then she was out in the corridor. Heather had her by the hand and was pulling her along.

"What's going on in—" a male voice began. "You! Halt or I'll—" The garda never finished the sentence. Pistol fire buzzed past Nuala's ear.

"Let's go!" Donlon said, his gun in his hand. He grabbed Nuala's other arm, and they ran past the garda he had stunned.

The escape was a blur to Nuala. She followed Heather and Donlon, her body remembering what she was supposed to do, while her mind was back in that hospital room. She ran down stairs, down corridors, up stairs, doubling back, past Éadaoin's people, some in garda uniform and some in white habits, all with pistols, then down more stairs; she had her pistol in her hand somehow, and she used it. There was shouting, plasfire, then the van, and Igraine laying down covering fire from the back long enough for them to pile in. Then Fiona took off.

Racing away, bouncing along at top speed, Nuala saw only her father's face, heard his last two words: "I love—" Tears streamed down her face, but she made no sound.

* * *

"Séamus Dennehy, the father of the terrorist Nuala Dennehy, lies near death tonight in St. Emmanuel Hospital in Falcarragh, Donegal," the RTE2 announcer was saying. "He nearly died earlier today, when his heart failed, but the swift intervention of the hospital staff averted his death."

Nuala stared at the *teilifís*. The pretty blond woman in the green blazer was lying; she had seen her father die. But—

"Bastards!" Igraine stepped in front of the vidscreen. "Don't listen to this crap, Nuala. It's a trick, to get you to come back."

"Are you sure?" Heather asked. "I mean, if there's a chance—"

"They're lying!" Igraine insisted.

"Turn the sound down," Fiona said, "and let's wait to see if the Guerrillas will tell us anything."

"Can you call Éadaoin?" Heather asked as Igraine hit the volume button, silencing the announcer. "Maybe she knows—"

"I'll go as soon as it's dark," Fiona said.

But they didn't have to wait that long. About an hour later, the familiar Guerrilla logo appeared. The Guerrilla announcer was wearing the usual black balaclava, but sorrow was evident in his tone, if not his face.

"Séamus Emmet Dennehy has died."

Nuala gasped and her eyes closed; her chin sank to her chest as the tears returned. She had known the truth, but irrational hope had lingered. She felt Heather put her arms around her, but she didn't move or open her eyes as the Guerrilla went on.

"Earlier today you heard an RTE anchor tell you that the father of Nuala Dennehy had been pulled back from the brink of death. But that, I am sorry to say, was a lie. Séamus Dennehy—a visionary, historian, and the man who fostered the patriotism and love of freedom that motivates Nuala Dennehy, one of the foremost leaders of this revolution—did in fact die today, during a clandestine visit from his daughter. I am pleased to tell you that Nuala escaped from the *garda* trap set at the hospital in Falcarragh. The *gardaí* were using her father's condition as a lure to ensnare her, and the lie told previously about his recovery was more bait to lure her back so they could try it again, with better results. But we cannot allow that to happen. We will not allow those animals to use the love Nuala feels for her father to ensnare her. Nuala, if you are listening, I am truly sorry. I share your pain, and all of Ireland grieves with you." He paused, but Nuala didn't look up.

"Now it can be told," the Guerrilla went on, "now that no one can harm Séamus Dennehy, that he helped his daughter escape from Maghaberry some months ago. While she was in jail, Nuala communicated with her father, reminding him through code of how Éamonn de Valera escaped from prison in 1918. Being an amateur historian himself, Séamus Dennehy immediately recognized what his daughter was trying to tell him, and came to her aid with the assistance of members of the underground. Without his courage, and especially the knowledge and love of Ireland's past that he passed on to his daughter, Nuala would still be in jail today.

"Though he was not a famous man during his lifetime, Séamus Dennehy was truly an Irish hero, a hero who should not be forgotten. His funeral will be day after tomorrow in Falcarragh. I urge all people who love Ireland to turn out to show their respect for this man, this hero: Séamus Emmet Dennehy. And Nuala, our hearts are with you . . . This is Guerrilla TV, signing off."

Nuala stood up, wobbling slightly, and left the room. Her three friends let her go, saying nothing. But from the bedroom she heard Heather ask, "How much more can she take? She still hasn't recovered from what those bastards did to her. And now this. I'm frightened for her."

"I suppose she'll insist on going to the funeral," Fiona said.

"Of course," Igraine replied. "Wouldn't you, if it was your da?"

"It's suicide," Fiona pointed out.

"Right," Igraine agreed.

"But we're going," Heather said.

"Sooner or later," Fiona said, sighing, "our luck is going to run out."

Chapter 28

"THIS IS . . . INCREDIBLE!"

Heather voiced what Nuala had been thinking for the past half hour, ever since they had been forced to abandon the van and join the ocean of pedestrians that blocked the road.

They were still more than a mile from the cemetery, and the road was a writhing wave of people, hundreds or thousands of them carrying flowers or tricolors in the light mist of cool rain, speaking quietly in accents from all over Ireland, or trudging in silence, mourning a man they couldn't have known. Those few that looked around in bewilderment and spoke in a Donegal accent might have known her father, especially those she saw wiping away tears or not bothering to, and Nuala ached to stop them, to speak to them, to ask "Did you know him? Did you *really* know the man he was? Were you his friend?" But the *gardaí* were everywhere: lining the road with rifles ready, armored vehicles at every crossroads, men with cameras leaning out of hovercraft vibrating overhead. Even though Nuala and her three friends were dressed in male camouflage, she had been taped in such a disguise before; the *gardaí* might recognize her if she called attention to herself. So Nuala kept her head down; all the men overhead would see was the top of her tweed cap and the slope of her shoulders.

She was fighting back tears at the wonder of this crowd, wishing desperately that her father could have seen this, when a deep male voice murmured near her, *"Ba fear iontach é."* Nuala started in surprise, but the hovercraft was too close; she didn't dare look up. So she tilted her head and peered up from the corner of her eye. Cuan Mulcahy, whom she hadn't seen in over a decade and a half, smiled mournfully at her. He hadn't changed; he was even wearing that same tan corduroy cap with the chocolate-brown patch on the left side of it. She remembered teasing him about buying a new cap almost sixteen years ago at the pub, on his birthday. He had just beaten Séamus at chess—again—and so he bought her father a pint and herself a cup of tea, gracious at winning, as always. The memory brought a sheen of tears to her eyes and a tremulous smile. Seeing this, Heather took her hand off the pistol in her pocket and eased back a step to let the man get closer.

"I said, in case you've forgotten your Irish, that he was a wonderful fellow entirely."

Nuala nodded. "I haven't forgotten a thing. And you're right; a finer man there never was."

Cuan nodded in somber agreement. They walked together in silent memory for a time; as the hovercraft moved ahead of them and they could relax somewhat, he went on. "He was so terribly proud of you. He'd bring every letter from Scotland to the pub, to read me bits of it. I'll wager I knew everything you were up to over there as well as he did himself."

"Really? He did?"

"Oh, aye. I remember in a few letters you mentioned some fellow name of Kenneally, in the Irish history department with you. Your da had some hope there for a bit that you'd found somebody, so you wouldn't be alone." Cuan glanced sideways at her. "But then you stopped mentioning the lad. What happened at all?"

Nuala couldn't answer for a moment, surprised that Cuan would be thinking of such a thing. Seán Kenneally. She hadn't thought of him in years. It had been but a brief flirtation, the last time she had felt even a glimmer of attraction for a man, and she had put him out of her mind almost as quickly as she had banished him from her heart. What had she said to her father about Kenneally to make him think—she couldn't remember.

"Him?" she said, dismissing the memory with a flick of her hand. "He had only a few faults, but he made the most of the ones he had."

Cuan laughed, the sound incongruous in this somber but defiant crowd. "Well, I must admit it's relieved I am to hear it. I suppose you don't remember, but it's myself you promised to marry." When Nuala shot him a look of astonishment, he laughed again. "You were all of four years old at the time."

Nuala chuckled, her mind flooding with memories of Séamus and Cuan and all the times in her childhood when she was allowed to tag along when they went fishing, or to tend Cuan's illegal *poitín* still, or to the pub, where they argued politics endlessly. When the stinging of tears threatened again, she smiled and said, "And how's Mrs. Kinsella?" Nuala and Séamus had been the only two people in Falcarragh who knew about the decades-long but extremely careful affair between Cuan and the handsome wife of the vicious, usually drunken postal carrier.

Cuan smiled, his eyes lighting up. "The old bugger finally did us the favor of falling into a ditch and breaking his neck, the Devil take him. As soon as Sláine's six months of mourning are up, we'll be married—finally."

"Oh, Cuan, that's grand! I'm happy for you. And it's about bloody time."

Cuan blushed; he suddenly looked younger than his fifty-some years. "At least what we've been doing for the past thirty-two years won't be illegal any longer." His smile faded. "But it'll be a sad day for me, too: Your da won't be standing with me."

Nuala squeezed Cuan's arm. "He'll be there. And he'll be smiling."

Cuan sniffed and returned her smile. He patted her hand. "Let's hope the lads with the guns don't spot me arm in arm with a fellow in a mustache. They'd arrest the pair of us, wouldn't they?"

Nuala dropped her hand. "Sorry. I forget sometimes." She fingered her mustache, then looked ahead. They were coming to another crossroads; men with rifles would be scrutinizing every face they could see. "You'd best go on ahead, Cuan. If they spot me and arrest you, Mrs. Kinsella will miss that wedding day she's been waiting so long for."

Cuan got a stubborn look on his face, but before he could argue, she smiled at him. "Please. Being near me endangers everyone I care about. I need to know that you'll be safe and happy with your new bride."

Cuan stared into her eyes for a moment, a struggle going on inside him, then finally sighed and nodded. "It makes me feel a coward, but Sláine has no one else—"

"You're no coward," Nuala assured him. "And Sláine Kinsella is a lucky woman."

Cuan blushed again at the compliment. "She's behind us somewhere. I left her when I recognized you; I had to come see you."

"And I'm glad you did. But it's at her side you belong now, not my own."

Cuan raised a hand to her cheek, then remembered and dropped it, glancing around. "Well, all right, then. I'll go. But my thoughts and prayers will be with you—and with Séamus—always."

Nuala sniffed and nodded, blinking back tears.

"Dennehy *abú*." Cuan started to go, then turned back, smiling. "By the by, I always knew that he let me win at chess just so I'd have to buy the Guinness." He chuckled at the memory, his own eyes as damp as Nuala's. "Crafty lad, your da. And a better friend no one ever had."

Nuala swallowed with difficulty. "Did I really say I'd marry you, Cuan Mulcahy?"

"That you did, and you were quite serious, for four."

"Well," Nuala said, smiling, "I don't want to have to fight Mrs. Kinsella for you, so I'll concede gracefully."

Cuan chuckled. "I'll tell her that. Considering your fearsome reputation of late, I'm sure she'll be quite relieved." He looked into her eyes for one last, long moment. "Be happy, Nuala. And give 'em hell." Then he was gone into the crowd.

Her eyes blinded by tears, Nuala stumbled, but Heather caught her arm. She felt rather than saw Igraine at her left side and Fiona behind her. She had protection on every side but the front. She went forward.

Men and women in balaclavas, one after another, got up on the platform by the coffin to speak for Séamus, though none of them had ever met him. The *gardaí* hung back, apparently not interested in the ringing appeals for freedom, or in the urging of the crowd—which must have numbered in the tens of thousands, to Nuala's unending astonishment—to fight in whatever way necessary to achieve freedom and a genuine democracy.

People from Falcarragh, including Cuan, also stepped forward, to speak not of revolution but of the quiet and noble man they had known. So many of them came forward to share memories of her father that it broke Nuala's heart. Even the parish priest, a youngish man Nuala had never seen before, praised Séamus. From the warm but spirited debates he related, obviously he had known him well, and had liked him.

The casket was draped in a tricolor, a custom restricted by law to the funerals of politicians and *gardaí*. But the armed men ignored this, too. They were waiting for her, Nuala knew. But this time she wouldn't fall for it. They wouldn't descend upon her from the sky and snatch her back to hell. She would stay hidden in the safety of the crowd. What she had needed to say to and about her father she had already said, both to him in the hospital and on the *teilifís*, thanks to the Guerrillas. She didn't need to make a speech here today, and she doubted she would have had the strength to do so anyway. Let others make the speeches for once; she was struggling hard enough to endure her grief.

Kerry stood by the coffin, where Nuala longed to be, her head bowed while all the eulogies were given and the fiery exhortations made. Finally the priest finished saying his bit and then he introduced Kerry.

Nuala was standing a hundred meters or so away, between two hoisted tricolors, trying to use the banners' folds as cover. She could clearly see her sister, her father's coffin, and the front of the crowd. The people were not moving, except for shifting from one foot to the other occasionally. So the man easing his way through them caught Nuala's attention. Her heart caught in her throat; she couldn't breathe.

It was Adolf.

He wasn't in uniform, so no one paid him any mind, except for a glare or grimace of irritation if he peered too closely at them as he passed. He was searching for her, looking beyond mustaches or nun's habits or any of the disguises she was known to have used. And who better to recognize her? Hadn't he and his accomplices been—intimate—with her for weeks? And didn't he have a grudge against her for her using *his* cardkey to escape? That must have caused him no end of trouble.

As Kerry began to speak, another movement caught Nuala's eye: Hans, moving as slowly through the crowd as Adolf. That meant Fritz was most likely there, too—perhaps behind her. Nuala turned, vaguely aware that her teeth were chattering.

"What is it?" Fiona murmured, taking the one step forward that had separated them. Nuala motioned toward Adolf with a sharp jerk of her chin.

"*Garda?*" Heather whispered at Nuala's side. "The one moving through the crowd?"

"Adolf." She barely got the second syllable out; her voice cracked and her jaw wouldn't stop quivering. The memories crowded in, suffocating her. When she spotted Fritz off to the side, a roaring began in her head. "All—all three. There—" She pointed them out, her hand trembling. "And there. And that one."

"Jesus!" Heather's pistol was in her hand. She stabbed Adolf with her glare of hatred, her knuckles white on the gun.

"If we move, they'll spot us," Igraine whispered, keeping an eye on Hans.

"So we keep our heads down," Fiona whispered back, watching Fritz.

"And if they spot us anyway—" Igraine began.

"We kill the bastards!" Heather spat out. Several people in front of them turned, glancing back. One of them, a woman, did a double take at the sight of Nuala, stared, then whispered to the man next to her. He turned to look at her, then whispered to the man next to him.

"Fucking great!" Igraine muttered.

"My sister could not be here today," Kerry was saying into the microphone, "for reasons you are all aware of. Of course she would want to be, because she and our father were very close. Very close."

Nuala's eyes darted from Adolf, to Hans, to Fritz, her head jumping back and forth as if she were watching a tennis match. Every muscle in her was trembling, and the roaring in her head was growing so loud that she could barely hear what her sister was saying. The three men she saw every evening in her night-mares moved inexorably closer.

"... My father died before he could see his dream of a dem-ocratic Ireland brought forth, but he passed that dream on to us—my sister Nuala and myself. Each of us has her own idea of how that dream should be brought to fruition, but in spite of our differences, we are both dedicated to that dream of a free coun-try, a free Celtic Church, a free people."

Kerry's words barely registered. Nuala's eyes were locked onto Adolf, who was now as close to her as she was to her fa-ther's casket. He ignored everyone his own height or taller, but stooped to peer into the faces of everyone else. The roaring in her head was drowning her.

"Shit!"

At Heather's curse, Nuala jumped and looked back. Hans was staring at her, frowning in uncertainty. For a split second he froze as their eyes met, then he plowed forward, pushing people out of the way. "There!" he bellowed. "Between the flags!"

"No." Nuala moaned, freeing her pistol from her pocket. Plasfire buzzed by her ear, and one of the tricolors fluttered to the ground as the man holding it went down. There were screams all around her, and then the crowd boiled and surged into a stampede.

Another man near her fell as plasfire hit him, his coat smok-ing, and Nuala whirled. Adolf was standing his ground as peo-ple, screaming and running, fought to get out of the line of fire. He was trying to take aim again, leaning this way and that, twisting to see over the heads bobbing around him.

Nuala ignored the roaring in her head, the screams and jos-tling of the crowd. She thumbed the pistol's control from stun to plasfire and took aim at his forehead.

"Come on, Nuala!" Heather yelled, and grabbed her arm, throwing off her aim. Nuala's pistol fired, but the shot went past Adolf's ear. He flinched. Then his face turned purple with fury, and he took aim at her again.

"Come on!" Heather dragged her backward, into the stampede. Igraine was at her other side; Fiona had been separated from them, but was only a few meters away.

Plasfire came from above, toppling people like bowling pins. The *gardaí* in the hovercraft were shooting into the crowd.

Plasfire whined past Nuala from all sides. Heather let go of her when she stumbled over an unconscious woman. Not seeing any way to run to safety, Nuala turned back to face Adolf. If she was going to be shot, it would not be in the back. She was deafened by the tumult around her and in her own head. There was no safe direction to flee. He was going to kill her unless she shot him first.

She saw the pistol glow as Adolf fired. A woman running past her screamed, her coat smoking, and fell. The image of Máire falling facedown, dead, into the gutter flashed before Nuala's eyes. She took aim.

Plasfire singed her hair, but she didn't flinch. She pulled the trigger. Adolf was knocked backward by the blast. He didn't get up. He didn't move. His coat was burned, as Máire's had been.

Heather roared in fury and defiance next to her, and fired to the left. Hans was in the open; he jerked as he was hit, and went down. The crowd swerved and surged over and around him, hiding him from view. But Nuala had seen the smoke. The *gardaí*'s guns weren't set on stun. Neither was Heather's.

"There!" Igraine yelled. Both she and Fiona aimed. Fritz pushed a woman out of his way and pointed his pistol at Nuala. The two women waited a split second while a man dodged away, then shot at the same time. Fritz was hit twice before he could fire and disappeared under the waves of the panicked crowd.

Two steady, parallel streams of plasfire scorched the ground, digging up furrows in the dirt and charring tombstones as they headed straight for Nuala, fired from a hovercraft no longer hovering, but diving in her direction.

"Run, Nuala!" Heather screamed, but Nuala didn't run. The chaos around her faded, disappeared, as she raised her pistol and took aim at the monster swooping out of the sky. Silence enveloped her; the hovercraft seemed to soar in slow motion as she stood, tiny weapon raised, waiting.

Clods of flying dirt struck her as the plasfire streams sliced the ground on either side of her. Her upraised arm followed it: up, overhead, back. She turned in a singular, smooth motion, following the flying predator, her aim never faltering. She squeezed the trigger.

Sparks flew, and a moment later smoke billowed out of the armored bird's tail. It started down, but the flight was almost smooth; they would land, not crash. A brief pang of regret was overwhelmed by relief, then Nuala was jarred back into the pandemonium around her.

"Come on!" Heather grabbed her again.

"That way!" Fiona yelled, waving her pistol toward the too-distant trees. They would never make it across the entire cemetery to the relative safety of the trees. But they had no choice.

The armored vehicles that had been parked at every crossroads had arrived; *gardaí* poured out, shooting as they came. Everyone who was not already dead or unconscious was running—most still screaming—or crouched behind tombstones.

The four women ran.

The tricolor covering Séamus's coffin was singed; a thick black stripe marred the white. As Nuala passed it she saw the priest and Kerry crouching there. Cuan and a woman—she recognized Sláine Kinsella—cowered near Kerry, Cuan trying to shield both women with his own body.

"*Behind* the coffin, Cuan!" Nuala yelled as she ran. "Into the grave!" She saw the four people scramble in that direction, and then she was past them.

Igraine was firing behind herself when she was shot in the side. There was no smoke, but she went down. Fiona caught her, and Nuala and Heather ran to help. Then pistol fire found Heather, and she fell.

"No!" Nuala roared.

Fiona was shot half a second before something smacked into Nuala and she, too, fell, hearing distant screams before she blacked out.

Chapter 29

WHEN NUALA AWOKE, the jackhammer in her skull told her she had been stunned. She groaned and tried to move. Every muscle protested, and the pain in her head increased; she gave up, slumping back onto the bed.

Bed? Her eyes flew open, and the brief hope vanished. No, she hadn't managed to escape somehow. This was no safe house.

Nuala looked around the cell in despair; her worst nightmare had come true. She had sworn to herself after her escape that she would die before allowing herself to be captured and raped again. Her heart raced and she found herself panting. This could not happen again—it just couldn't! She took a deep breath; she had to calm down, keep from panicking. That would only make it worse.

She was lying on a cot, not a real bed, and it was bolted to the wall. On the floor next to it was a folded, clean blanket. Across the cell was the toilet. She couldn't smell it, so perhaps it was clean, too. Near the door was a fauxwood chair and on its seat was a small *teilifís*, turned off. The puzzlement of this distracted her—somewhat—from her despair. She pushed herself up slowly, wincing and suppressing the moans that tried to escape, and made it to a sitting position. It took a moment for the other incongruity to sink in.

Nuala stared down at her black denim pants, the forest-green sweater, tan corduroy coat, and black boots. They hadn't taken her clothes. She felt her upper lip: the fake mustache was gone, and a quick glance around proved that her cap was nowhere to be seen. Why had they left her her clothes? Why wasn't she in an interrogation cell like the last one? And why the *teilifís*?

As if in telepathic response, the *teilifís* suddenly came to life. So they were watching her. Yes, there was the tiny vidcamera, high up in the corner, out of reach. So why was this *teilifís* not out of reach?

"A funeral in Donegal turned into a bloodbath yesterday when IRA terrorists attacked the mourners . . ."

Nuala stared, mesmerized, at the scenes of *garda* violence. The cameras didn't show the sources of the plasfire—the *gardaí*; they only showed innocent people screaming in terror and running, far too many of them falling and not getting up.

There she was. Nuala stared at herself, watched herself take aim at Adolf—whose hands and therefore her gun were not visible—and shoot. She saw him jerk, his coat smoking, and fall backward.

". . . Terrorist Nuala Dennehy, whom you can plainly see in

this shot, murdered an innocent, unarmed man in cold blood during this vicious assault."

Nuala turned away in disgust. How many people did they think they could fool with this nonsense? No one believed the official news reports anymore; everyone knew that only the Guerrillas were to be believed.

"Justice did triumph in the end, however," the announcer went on, "when Nuala Dennehy and three of her accomplices were killed by the *gardaí*."

Killed? Nuala turned back to the *teilifís*. She winced, crossing her arms and hugging herself in pain as she watched first Igraine, then Heather, then Fiona, and finally herself shot. Her friends. Were they—

There was no smoke. When a plasfire weapon was set on maximum, it scorched its target as it killed; there was always smoke. But not here, in this taped scene. On none of her three friends and certainly not on herself was there a charred, smoking blotch. So they were alive—they hadn't been killed, any more than she had. They were alive. Just stunned, like herself. Igraine, Fiona, and Heather were alive.

Nuala's relief was short-lived. If her friends were still alive, then they were undoubtedly in the same predicament as herself. Arrested. At the mercy of men like Adolf. And all because she had insisted on going to her father's funeral. Fiona's words came back to her: "Sooner or later our luck is going to run out." It was her fault. Her fault her friends had been captured. And the deaths—all those people killed, those innocent people who had come to honor *her* father. That was her fault, too.

"At the end of this tragic day," the announcer was saying as the camera panned the cemetery that looked like a battlefield, with scorched bodies sprawled in every direction, "twenty-seven people had been killed."

A moan escaped Nuala. She stared at the *teilifís* in shock and horror for a moment, then curled her head down to her knees, her arms wrapped around herself in misery.

"This was a day of infamy that Ireland will not soon forget."

The sound ended, but Nuala did not look up. Her fault. Her fault. It was bad enough that they were going to torture her again. How could she live with the knowledge that twenty-seven people were dead because of her? Instead of subsiding, the pounding in her head increased, every thud an accusation.

The *teilifís* came on three more times that day—or perhaps it was night, Nuala couldn't tell. Each time the same scenes were repeated. Each time the number of deaths was emphasized. The second time Nuala gave up wondering where the Guerrillas were. Even if they had tried to break in, the *teilifís* would have been turned off; they wouldn't let her see the truth—whatever that might be. The third time she refused to look, covering her ears and trying not to hear what she had done, what she had been responsible for. She remained on her bunk, curled into a fetal position. So many people—innocent people, good people who had come to that cemetery because of her—dead. All her fault.

The fourth time the *teilifís* blared its tragic accusations, Nuala uncurled herself from the cot and crossed the room on unsteady feet.

The *teilifís* was just sitting on the chair; it wasn't bolted down. It was just a monitor, without controls. Why had they left it there, exposed and within reach? Were they merely taunting her? Mind games this time, in place of the violence? Or a prelude to violence? She should defy them by ignoring it; Nuala knew that, but she couldn't take any more. Let them think they had won the first round—she didn't care.

The *teilifís* was small, lightweight, and she lifted it easily. When she hurled it against the concrete wall, it made a satisfying explosion. Bits of plastic ricocheted in all directions; something struck her cheek. It stung, and when she touched the spot, her fingers came away with a few drops of blood. She stared at her fingers for a moment, then wobbled back to her cot.

Hours later she was awakened from an agonizing dream in which she mowed down rows of people with a rifle. They each fell backward into individual, newly dug and waiting graves. It was the click of the door's lock that jolted her awake, panting and drenched in sweat.

The female guard didn't even look at her. She simply placed the tray of food on the chair, swept the bits of broken *teilifís* into a dustbin, and left.

Nuala ignored the food. Eating it would have been cooperating. The only way she could fight back was to refuse to eat; it was the only weapon she had.

The despair and guilt and terror were devouring her. How could she survive this a second time? They wouldn't let her escape again. And if everyone thought her dead, who would help her? Would she have the courage to refuse to divulge names? She doubted it. She doubted herself. Despair was not a feeling she was accustomed to, but the memories, the pain, the degradation—she just didn't have the strength anymore. She was afraid she couldn't do it again.

Eventually she fell into an exhausted sleep.

For the next two days—at least it seemed that long—Nuala was left alone. No one came to question or torture her; no one came at all, except the female guard, who, unlike Benny, was not inclined to talk. She merely took the untouched trays of food, replacing them with new meals, and then left without a word.

Nuala clung to her determination not to eat, not to cooperate. The lack of food, however, was making her even weaker. She had not been interested in food since Éadaoin had come that night to tell her her father was dying, so she hadn't had a decent meal for days before being locked up here. And worse than her hunger pangs, the physical weakness was exacerbating the tenuous control she still had over her mind, her emotions. The grief, fear, and despair were harder and harder to keep at bay. She was deteriorating rapidly.

The light in the cell was not painfully bright, as it had been in that other cell; this time they were using new tactics. Perhaps they thought that isolation and her own guilt would break her.

If that was their plan, it wasn't far from working. Nuala was not the person she had been when Adolf and his friends had used violence against her in an attempt to get what they wanted. She had had little time to recover from the emotional wounds they had inflicted. And then Da ... And then all those innocent people cut down in cold blood just because she had foolishly insisted on going to her father's funeral. What had she done? Almost as soon as she had returned to Ireland, the killing had started, beginning with Máire.

Máire. What would her troubled friend think of the mess she had made of everything? Máire had urged her to avoid violence. If only she had listened ...

The door clicked, then swung open. A tall, powerfully built male guard strutted in. At the sight of him, Nuala's muscles involuntarily began to quiver; the roaring in her head began.

The colored switches. Have to imagine—the colored—the—

Each thought shattered almost as soon as it formed. She couldn't concentrate. But she had to. Had to slow the racing of her heart, her frantic breathing. Mustn't hyperventilate. The colored—

The guard stopped just inside the door, staring at her through heavy-lidded eyes, and took a step to the right. A second guard appeared behind him, carrying a small *teilifís*, a twin to the one she had smashed. She stared at it, bewildered. Weren't they here to—

The second guard placed the *teilifís* on the chair. He took a remote control from his pocket and pressed a button. Then he took up a position on the right side of the chair. The first guard stepped closer and took his position on the left side of the chair.

They weren't here to attack her; they were here to protect the *teilifís* from her. An insane giggle almost escaped Nuala at the absurdity. But she couldn't stop trembling. And the roaring in her head made it difficult to hear the RTE1 announcer.

"Thousands of arrests were made today, for the third straight day, as *gardaí* continued to infiltrate and close in on the IRA network of terrorists, criminals, and sympathizers."

The *teilifís* showed over a dozen women being herded at rifle point toward an armored transport. Nuala winced when she recognized Bébhinn, one of the women who had sheltered her and her friends in a safe house. Some of the arrested women were weeping in terror, while some spat at the armed men in defiance and contempt and were shoved or struck in retaliation. Bébhinn betrayed no emotion; she walked with her head held high, the orange handkerchief Nuala remembered still sticking up jauntily from the pocket of her black sweater.

The scene changed to that of another arrest, another group of women. "Bishop Doheny explained the large number of *women* being arrested by telling RTE that Irish women had been led astray by the terrorist Nuala Dennehy and others like her, who made them false promises of 'equality,' convincing them that the elevated status of women under Catholicism was in fact some form of debasement that they should aspire to rise above. These women had been confused, the Bishop said, by clever lies and malicious duplicity. But now that Nuala Dennehy is dead and the IRA movement crushed, this evil campaign will be brought to a swift end. What is needed now, he said, is firm guidance, reeducation, and Christian forgiveness. Bishop Doheny has spoken to the *Taoiseach*, urging compassion in the sentencing of the almost three thousand women arrested so far and also for those who will be arrested in the days to come, as the rest of the misguided women are rounded up. 'Ireland should not be torn apart by this tragedy,' he said, 'but must be made whole again, and only Catholic judgment tempered with compassion can accomplish this end.' "

A fifth scene of women being herded into transports ended,

and the female announcer's face appeared. "We will continue to bring you updates on the arrests as they occur. And we at RTE would like to remind our viewers that these arrests should be seen as a cleansing action, as the Bishop called it later in the same press conference. He urged everyone in Ireland who loves peace and justice to pray for the souls of these misguided women as the long reign of terror, confusion, and lies is brought to an end. Stay tuned to RTE—"

The picture vanished. The shorter guard put the remote back in his pocket and turned to stare, expressionlessly, at Nuala.

"Your wee 'revolution' is finished," the tall guard said, contempt dripping from every syllable. "Every friend you ever had, every sympathizer, every woman who hasn't been behaving herself lately or showing sufficient respect is being rounded up. Some we'll just have a bit of fun with, to teach them a lesson and scare them into proper behavior, but as for the others . . ." He smiled, the expression an obscene rictus. ". . . the others we'll never let out of here."

Nuala stared at him, trying not to think of Maeve or Éadaoin or Sorcha or Brigid or all the others, all the brave women she had met. Had they been arrested, too? Betrayed? By whom? If just one person broke under torture, it could all collapse. Or had that already happened? Was it really all over? No, that's just what they wanted her to think. There were too many of those courageous women, all over Ireland. Maybe *her* role was finished, but not the revolution. It was bigger than she was—bigger than even Éadaoin and Brigid and Dana. It wasn't over. It couldn't be.

She pushed all thoughts from her mind and stared blankly at the big man.

"We've been ordered to keep our hands off you for now," he went on, frowning in obvious disappointment, "to let you—think things over, so you can come to the correct decision about cooperating. But we'll get our chance if you make the wrong decision." He took a sudden step forward, towering over her. "And I promise you, it won't be pleasant. Because *I'll* be in charge, and I won't be so easy on you as Higgins and his lads were."

Higgins? Oh. Adolf. Nuala kept her face carefully blank, trying to keep the tremors hidden.

"So you be giving the matter careful thought," the guard said as his companion picked up the *teilifís* and headed for the door. "Because I'll be back, and so often that you'll begin to see this face every time you close your eyes." He paused at the door, again displaying that obscene grin. "And don't even think about escaping again. As far as the outside world is concerned, you're dead. There's no one to help you now. You're ours. Oh, and by the way, your three friends are already enjoying my company. The two old biddies aren't much fun, but that young blond girlie—now *she's* juicy."

Every muscle in Nuala's body was fighting, urging her up off the cot, ready to launch herself at the smiling monster. Her fingers dug into her thighs as she forced herself not to react.

"Yeah," he said, smiling, "my wife's been complaining that I'm neglecting her, but after a full day with that feisty kitten, I just haven't the energy, you know?"

Something must have given her away, because he laughed, delighted, before closing the door behind him.

Heather!

Nuala wanted to hurl herself at the door, tear it from its hinges, find Heather. But there was nothing she could do. She was helpless.

She curled back into a ball on her cot. Her first glimpse of Heather, looking so very young in her school uniform with her cuffs rolled back, flashed before her squeezed-shut eyes, taunting her. And the adoration in those blue eyes when Heather looked at her. And other memories. The time Heather had stripped that stunned *garda* in the alley and thrown his clothes up onto the fire escape. Heather, beating out the flames on Nuala's shoulder with her bare hands. Heather, holding her in the middle of the night when her nightmares woke her. Heather, dressed in a nurse's habit, risking her life to sneak into the hospital with her. Heather, who surprised the three of them daily with her courage and determination and her astonishing skill with a pistol. Heather, who used that skill to kill Hans because of what he had done to Nuala, and what he was trying to do. *Heather.*

A moan escaped Nuala. She should have taken the time to teach the girl self-hypnosis. But she had been too self-absorbed, too involved with her own pain. She should have taught her—she should *not* have gone to that school in the first place, should not have interfered with Heather's life, ruined that life. Before Nuala, all Heather did to defy anyone was to roll back her cuffs. She had been safe. It was all Nuala's fault. And there was nothing she could do now for the girl. Heather would have to be strong—as strong as she had proved herself to be, countless times. Now it was up to her to remain strong, not to give in and talk, no matter what they did to her. I'm sorry, *kidín*, Nuala thought, wishing she could project the words telepathically to whatever portion of hell had claimed her young friend. Fight them in whatever way you can. Be strong. And I'm sorry I got you into this.

Nuala's misery and her three—or was it four? She couldn't remember—days on hunger strike caught up with her. She was so weak. She began to drift in and out of consciousness, images swirling together in her mind: Da, telling his stories of Irish heroes; old photographs of Patrick Pearse reading the Proclamation and Jim Larkin inflaming crowds of workers; an old video of Bernadette Devlin McAliskey elected to British Parliament for Ulster at the age of twenty-one; Heather, beating out the flames with her bare hands; Igraine, admitting that the IRA man she had just shot was her husband; Fiona bending over her after the escape, smiling; a video of the funeral of Bobby Sands in 1981.

That image kept returning, that scene from over a hundred years ago. It dominated all the others. Bobby Sands had died on hunger strike, and had inspired a nation, had moved the world.

It was the only card she had left to play, all she could do for Ireland, for all the others out there who believed in the revolution: don't talk, don't let them break her, and serve her country in the only way that remained to her.

She wondered vaguely, when semicoherent thoughts managed to form, where she would end up after she was dead. Where did atheists go? Would she see Mam and Da there? And Parnell? Did dogs go there, too, wherever it was? Maybe she'd get the chance to apologize to Máire for bollixing up her rosy vision of a bloodless revolution. Maybe she would meet Bobby Sands. If she did, she would ask him, "Did I do all right, Bobby? And was it really worth it, dying for Ireland?"

The images, the voices continued to swirl around her head as she grew weaker. The curious thing was, once she stopped toying with the notion of how far to carry the hunger strike and made up her mind to endure it to its inevitable conclusion, her doubts about having the courage and strength to do so melted away. All her life she had made her own choices, and it was fitting that she should decide how to end that life. If dying was the only thing left she could do for Ireland, then she would make that choice.

An image of Máire flickered in her mind: Máire's half-crazed ramblings about Nuala fulfilling her "destiny." Surely this was not what Máire had had in mind.

A fragment of a quote from an American, William Jennings Bryan, drowned out Máire's ravings: "Destiny is not a matter of chance; it is a matter of choice."

Nuala smiled as she lay huddled on the prison cot. Some-

one—she couldn't remember who, but it no longer mattered—
had once said "The only true revolutionary is the person who
has nothing to lose."

So she could still win after all, still beat them at their own
game. It was her choice.

Chapter 30

SEVERAL TIMES OVER the next few days the guards returned
with the *teilifís*, but Nuala paid no attention to it, didn't even
open her eyes until it was turned off. This must have annoyed
them, because the tall one's insults increased; he demanded she
watch, threatening her with all manner of painful consequences
if she refused. It took more physical effort than she would have
imagined possible to smile at him in reply. This so enraged the
fellow that he raised his fist, but his comrade caught his arm and
murmured something, Nuala couldn't hear what. She wondered
how long the new policy of not hurting her was going to last before they figured out it wouldn't work either.

The tall man pulled his arm from the other man's grasp, but
let it fall to his side. Nuala watched him through barely open
eyes. He bent over her.

"You'd best eat your dinner today like a good little bitch, or
we'll cram it down your throat. And *drink* something, damn you!"

Nuala closed her eyes, tuning him out, and he stomped from
the room. She worried for a moment about force-feeding. She
had read about the procedure used in the days of hunger strikes
past, long ago, and knew how painful and degrading it had been.
She wondered if that was what they had in mind for her, but that
part of it worried her less than the notion that it might work.
Would they take her only weapon from her? But it took too
much effort to worry. And there was nothing she could do about
it, anyway. She slipped back into unconsciousness.

She was awakened by something sharp being jabbed into the
back of her hand. A man in white bent over her as he attached

the IV tube. Nuala didn't move; she knew she was too weak to fight him, but she tried to focus her incoherent thoughts, wondering when she had been transferred to the hospital ward and where her clothes were. Why hadn't she awakened when they moved her? How far gone was she?

The tall guard hovered behind the doctor. "Can't you slip some *useful* drugs into that thing? To get her to babble?"

"Those are not my orders and you know it, Lavery," the doctor replied. "I was told just to stop her from killing herself, and to treat her well enough so that she might be inclined to cooperate. They need her healthy—and as soon as possible."

"I knew it wouldn't work," Nuala heard the second guard say. He sounded a little farther away than Lavery. Or was that just herself fading out again? "Passing her off as killed? Not bloody likely, not with those fucking Guerrillas around."

"We've got to get her to talk, Doctor!" Lavery insisted, his frustration evident. "I can't touch the bitch, but they still expect results. It could mean my job."

But Nuala wasn't listening to Lavery; she had heard the other guard. The Guerrillas were still at work, then; they hadn't been stopped! And everyone knew she was alive? A tiny flame of hope flickered in her.

"She's their leader," Lavery went on. "If we can prove she's turned on them, it would break the backs of all—"

"Not my problem," the doctor interrupted, sounding bored as he fastened the straps around Nuala's wrists, pinioning her to the bed. "I have my orders." He finished with the restraints, then bent over her and pushed back one of her eyelids, peering at her. She watched him with the one open eye. He was looking right through her; she wasn't a person to him, just a body he had to keep breathing. When he released the eyelid, she didn't bother struggling to open her eyes again; they were too heavy.

"She's been on hunger strike for over a week," the doctor went on. "She'll be no use to you for a few days at least, so why don't you give it up for now, Lavery?"

"Higgins was a friend of mine, and she—"

"Higgins was a savage who *enjoyed* hurting women," the doctor snapped. "It's no loss to the world, his death. And you're every bit the ignorant sadist he was, aren't you, Lavery?" The doctor hated this guard; Nuala could hear it in the furious tremor of his voice. "It's just eating you up that you haven't been allowed to touch any of them, isn't it?"

Any of them? Nuala's eyes would have shot open if she'd had the strength. Did that mean that he hadn't—was Heather unharmed? But why?

"You don't have to care for me, Doc; I don't give a Prod's knackers. You just get her in shape. I'll get my chance, once they come to their senses and see that mercy doesn't work."

"Don't tell me my job." The doctor moved to the end of the bed. "I've got to get a catheter into her; you two get the hell out of my hospital and give us the room to work."

Nuala must have faded out momentarily; she didn't hear the footsteps walking away, but then she felt hands on her bare legs. Unconsciousness was welcome this time.

The next time Nuala awoke she felt a little stronger, after a moment or two of disorientation and blinking to get rid of the spots in front of her eyes. She was still in the hospital ward, but curtains were drawn all around her bed; she could see nothing but her own little area, and there was nothing in it worth seeing.

The restraints still held her wrists securely. She looked up and saw the bottle that dripped life back into her. At least they hadn't resorted to force-feeding; that was some small comfort.

But why was it so important that she live? Were they afraid of making her a martyr? Which was exactly what she had been trying to do, of course. Lavery had said something about her turning on "them" and how this would break their backs. They expected her to turn traitor? But why would she, if torture hadn't worked? Were they holding off torturing the others to use that threat against her?

Was her confusion just a side effect of the hunger strike? She couldn't make sense of any of this. She wished her head would clear.

Voices murmured, growing nearer. Someone—two people?— were coming. Nuala closed her eyes as the curtain rustled.

"Can't you wake her up, Doctor? The *Taoiseach* is expecting my report this afternoon—"

Nuala opened her eyes at that. He was a short little man, round-faced, double-chinned, with a government sash over his expensive three-piece suit. Stopping in midsentence he stared back at her for a moment, then cleared his throat.

"My name is Declan Haughey, Miss Dennehy."

She just continued to stare at him, pretending supreme disinterest. He flushed, annoyed.

"Deputy Minister for the Interior? Surely you've heard of me."

When she merely blinked, he flushed again, shooting a glance at the doctor to see if his embarrassment had been noticed. But the doctor was busy checking the IV. Minister Haughey straightened his shoulders—trying to make himself taller? Nuala wondered—and cleared his throat again.

"You have committed grave crimes against the state," he intoned, "including cold-blooded murder."

Nuala raised a contemptuous eyebrow at that; this little government weasel knew damn well it had been self-defense in each case.

"And you will be tried for your crimes." Haughey's tone demanded that she fear him. Nuala yawned. His eyes narrowed, but he went on. "The *Taoiseach*, in his generosity and compassion, however, has decided that extenuating circumstances could be taken into consideration—in exchange for your cooperation."

A deal.

Nuala blinked, trying to hide her surprise. The government wanted to make a deal with her. What in the hell was going on? Lavery and others like him had been forbidden to torture her—and possibly anyone else, if she had heard correctly—they would not allow her to starve herself to death, and now they wanted to deal? What did they want that they thought they couldn't get by force? What had them running scared? Or were they? She wished she were not still so weak, that she could think straight.

"Did you hear what I said?"

Nuala stared at him, studying him. She had heard of Haughey: He was an obsequious, ineffectual little man, with no political clout of his own. He was a political joke, continually reelected without challenge simply because he was the *Taoiseach*'s brother-in-law. And this was the man they had chosen to deal with her?

But she nodded anyway, curious to hear more.

He smiled, as pleased as if he had won some minor victory over her. "Good," he said. "But first you have to agree to stop this childish hunger strike."

Nuala just stared at him. She wondered if her contempt showed.

It must have; Haughey flushed yet again. Nuala thought idly that politics would be a difficult career for a man who couldn't hide his feelings or his own lack of self-esteem; they were all too obvious by the frequent reddening of his face.

"Before we can discuss your cooperation, you must promise you'll be alive to cooperate, right?"

Nuala continued to stare, not helping him. He tried again, obviously hating the fact that he had to.

"You claimed in all those outrageous and illegal speeches you made that you 'loved' your country. Well, if there is any truth to that at all, then you'll want to help Ireland overcome the chaos that *you* created. To get the country back on an even keel, to stop the riots."

Chaos? Riots? Nuala barely managed to hide her smile. Lavery had been lying to her about everything. Maybe people were being arrested—if that RTE report was to be believed—but the revolution was obviously far from over. And the government was worried. They had to be worried, or they wouldn't have sent this odious little rat to cut a deal with her.

"You do want to help Ireland, as you claimed?"

Nuala hid her elation and nodded, once. Haughey smiled again.

"Good. Then you'll agree to end this hunger strike of yours?"

Nuala shook her head, and Haughey frowned, both angry and worried. She wondered what kind of trouble he would be in if he failed to win her cooperation.

"What do you mean you won't—"

Nuala tried to speak, but her throat wouldn't work; all that came out was a weak squawk.

The doctor had been checking her vital signs on the VSB. "Just a moment," he murmured, and left. Haughey looked after him in bewildered annoyance.

It was more than a moment, but finally a nurse appeared, without the doctor but with a plastic glass, a straw sticking out of it. She raised the head of Nuala's bed about a foot, then leaned toward her, pressing the straw to her lips.

Nuala didn't hesitate before drinking. It was only a little liquid that she needed in order to speak. Theoretically she had not yet abandoned the hunger strike.

A few sips later her attempt to speak succeeded, though her voice was very weak and scratchy. "Conditions," she said.

"Eh?" Haughey frowned in suspicion. "What are you talking about? You are in no position to dictate—"

"I have . . . nothing left to lose," Nuala interrupted him. Her voice was so weak he had to move closer, which he obviously didn't want to do. His nose wrinkled in distaste. Nuala wondered what she must smell like after a week.

"You had better cooperate, Miss Dennehy, or—"

"Or what? You'll kill me?" Nuala made a sorry attempt at a chuckle. Haughey glowered at her. Nuala went on. "If *you* haven't the authority—"

"Of course I have!" he snapped. "I am a deputy minister. What conditions? And mind—I may choose not to grant them."

Petty little tyrant, Nuala thought. Just as well; he might be easier to manipulate.

"General population," she said, then had to accept the straw again before she could elaborate. "No more solitary. Move me into the general population or no deal." She had to find out what was going on, and she wouldn't as long as she was kept apart from everyone else.

"That's impossible!" Haughey puffed himself up like a bantam rooster. "You have no right to request anything; you have committed capital crimes—treason, murder—"

"Then fuck off." Nuala closed her eyes. She was so exhausted that she had the sensation of falling into the pillow. The few words she had managed to say had depleted her tiny store of energy.

"I'm afraid you'll have to leave now, sir," the nurse said. "The patient is in no condition—"

"The 'patient' is a criminal!" Haughey spluttered at her, infuriated. "And I am—"

"My responsibility is to my patient, sir," the nurse interrupted. It was a good voice: strong, self-assured, mature. Nuala would have liked to study the face of the woman in the white nun's habit, but she hadn't the strength at the moment to open her eyes.

"Perhaps you could return tomorrow, sir."

After a moment of silence, through which Nuala could hear the man puff in outrage, Haughey spoke. "Miss Dennehy, I advise you to accept the government's terms, and do not attempt to demand *any*thing. I will return tomorrow—for the last time, I warn you—to give you another chance."

Nuala didn't open her eyes; after a moment she heard him mutter, "Keep me informed on *any* change in her condition," and then he stomped away.

"I'll leave the water within reach," the nurse said. Nuala heard a soft *whir* and felt her bed raised further. When it stopped she felt some small object placed next to her right palm. "Just press this and someone will come straightaway . . . And remember, you can have a meal any time you request it."

Nuala ignored the nurse, keeping her eyes closed. She felt the woman lean over her and straighten her pillow. She heard the faint whisper: "Don't give up. There's many who admire your courage." Then, with a rustle of cloth, the nurse was gone.

Nuala tried to fight off the exhaustion, to remain conscious so she could think.

The government wanted her alive, and badly enough to offer some sort of deal. That meant they needed something from her. And that must mean that the revolution had caused—was still causing?—enough damage to worry the *Dáil*. So it meant there was still hope; it wasn't over. Maybe death—martyrdom—was not the best or only thing she could do for Ireland. But they had to believe she was serious in her attempt to kill herself, or they might not deal.

Nuala couldn't be sure of her own reasoning; she might not be thinking clearly in her weakened state. But it seemed to make sense. They had to believe her. She knew what she had to do, but she didn't have the energy right now. Maybe if she got some sleep . . .

When Nuala awoke again the lights were dim; it was night. She saw the glass sitting on the tiny tray over the bed. It was so close. All she had to do was lean forward and she could take a sip.

The thought of the cool water gliding down her throat tortured her, but she glanced away from it. She remembered what she had to do.

Only her eyes moved as she looked around the small curtained alcove. Yes, there it was. High up on the ceiling was a tiny vidcam, pointed directly at her. Her eyes immediately slid away: If they were watching her, she didn't want them to know she had noticed the camera.

She lay still for several minutes, gathering her strength. It would have to be done quickly, in case they *were* watching.

Finally she was as ready as she was going to be this night.

Nuala leaned forward from the almost-sitting position the raised bed allowed her and bent her head toward the glass. But she didn't fasten her lips to the tantalizing straw; she lowered her head farther and nudged the table with the side of her head. Not hard enough—it barely moved. She nudged it again, and the table glided a few feet from the bed on its smooth wheels.

Panting from the exertion, Nuala leaned farther, until her forehead touched her right arm. Her head was so heavy!

Finally her mouth found the back of her hand. Her lips fumbled with the IV tape. After a few nibbles she got hold of the tape with her teeth and pulled. She knew it would hurt less if she did it quickly, so after bracing herself for a second, she pulled with all the strength she could muster.

The needle came free of her hand, and she dropped the tape, wincing but making no sound. She considered trying to undo the wrist straps with her teeth, but she hadn't the strength, and what good would it to, anyway? This was supposed to look like a suicide attempt, not an escape.

Nuala pushed her upper body back until she could fall against the raised bed. She wondered how long it would take them to notice if no one had been watching.

She passed out from exhaustion.

Nuala felt the needle go back in, and murmured an incoherent protest for effect. She had no idea how long it had been since she had pulled it out. She drifted back off to sleep.

When Haughey made his reappearance the next day, he was not a happy man. Did the *Taoiseach* blame his brother-in-law for her "suicide attempt"? Nuala didn't smile at the thought. She had to look determined, which she was, and perilously near death, which she wasn't. Though physically she was nearly as weak as she had been yesterday, emotionally she was making a rapid recovery. The government needed something from her—*needed* it, whatever it was—so she held at least a few cards. It wasn't time to give up and go out a political martyr after all.

"I have been authorized by the *Taoiseach*," Haughey was saying, reluctance and resentment heavy in every syllable, "to grant your request. You are to be moved in with the general population of prisoners—as soon as you end your strike and begin eating."

Nuala saw the glint in his eye. Did he think she was a fool?

She shook her head and looked at the nurse, who was ready with the straw.

"What do you mean, no?" Haughey demanded. "The *Taoiseach* has been more than generous. He didn't have to agree to your request; he didn't have to show you any mercy at all—"

"It wasn't a request," Nuala interrupted. "It was a condition. I get moved in with the general population, out of solitary, *then* I break my fast. And not until then."

Haughey glared at her, but she deflected his hatred with a nonchalantly raised eyebrow.

"Take it or leave it, Declan. If you want me alive, I have to have a *reason* to live. And I won't believe a bloody word *you* tell me. Put me in with my own kind, then I'll consider cooperating. Not until then."

Haughey looked as if he wanted to strangle her with his bare hands, but apparently he had his orders. After turning and walking away as if there was a poker in his spine, he disappeared behind the curtain. Nuala accepted another sip from the straw while she waited.

Their voices weren't close, but Nuala caught most of it.

"She shouldn't be moved! I will not be held responsible—"

"She won't stop the hunger strike until she's moved. The decision is not up to you, Doctor. Now, I'm sure you can manage something. Perhaps one of the nurses could stay—"

"One of my nurses, stay in a cell?"

Nuala's eyes found the nurse's. The woman in white, her back to the vidcam, winked.

The argument continued for a few more minutes, but Nuala knew she had won. She closed her eyes to rest.

They wheeled her on an old-fashioned gurney; the prison apparently couldn't afford antigrav props or thought them an unnecessary expense. But Nuala didn't mind the jostling. The nurse had raised the head of the gurney a bit so she could see where she was going.

They passed through endless gates, guard after guard staring at her as she went by. An armed guard preceded the gurney and another one followed. Nuala smiled at this. What did they think she was going to do, jump up and make a run for it? She was too weak even to stand up on her own.

She knew when they had reached the last gate because she heard the voices: hundreds of female voices, a drone of conversation.

Down one more corridor after the gate and around a corner.

The common area was large; Nuala could imagine several hundred prisoners gathering there under normal circumstances. But the recent arrests had made the circumstances anything but normal. Thousands of women, hundreds in prison gowns but most in their regular clothes, jammed the room. The noise of their conversations was deafening; it reverberated off the concrete and made Nuala's ears buzz. The guard in front had to shout and shove a few of them to get their attention.

The ones who were pushed aside turned, their faces twisted in anger until they saw Nuala. Then they stared. A few of them winced. Did she look that bad?

She heard her name murmured on all sides as the gurney started forward, and then silence began to spread like a rippling wave over the sea of women.

They parted for the gurney, ignoring the armed men, staring at Nuala as she passed. The conversations had died out completely.

Nuala felt more than a little conspicuous. And filthy. She hadn't bathed since—since the morning of her father's funeral. That seemed a century ago. But why were they staring so? She smiled awkwardly at those closest to her; they instantly smiled back, but the others just stared.

Passage through the crowd was not difficult, but slow. They were not quite to the center of the room when the noise began.

The guards glanced around, their eyes darting up to their comrades on the catwalks above, sweat beginning to bead on their faces as they gripped their Armalites.

The clapping seemed to be coming from a few women in the far corner to the right, but then women on the left joined in: slow, rhythmic, steady. It spread as quickly as the silence had; within moments every one of the thousands of women was clapping in unison. The noise was thunderous.

Nuala continued to smile at the women she passed, but it was an awkward grimace. What did they expect from her, a papal wave? She wished they would just stop. But the clapping continued even after the orderlies had guided her gurney out of the room and down another corridor.

Nuala sighed in relief when they rounded a corner. She didn't want to be in solitary, but she didn't want to put up with *that*, either. The clapping died out, and a now-excited buzz of conversations resumed.

Finally the guard in front stopped and turned around. The gurney wheeled to the right and through the open door of a cell.

There were only two cots, but several thin mattresses and blankets were folded and piled up on them.

"Which one?" the orderly behind her asked.

"Well, this one, I think," the nurse who had been walking behind Nuala replied. "Give us a hand." She moved to the right bunk and began moving the folded mattresses. The orderly in front of Nuala helped her. Then the attendant behind pushed the gurney forward, alongside the bunk, and her blanket was whipped off her by his partner. Together the two of them lifted her from gurney to bunk. The nurse helped her sit up, leaning against the wall. The two men made for the door with the gur-

ney, their job done, but the nurse unfurled the blanket in the air
and let it settle around Nuala, tucking it under her legs.

"My clothes?" Nuala said to her. "This hospital gown's a bit
drafty."

The nurse shrugged. "I'm not sure what's become of them; I
wasn't on duty when you were brought in, but I'll check. If
nothing else, they'll scrounge up a gown for you—if there's any
to be found. I think they ran out days ago. I'll see what I can
do, though."

"Thanks."

The nurse just nodded and finished fussing with the blanket.
"Now then," she said, "you're not to move, do you hear? One
of the guards is supposed to be on her way here with a hot meal.
And you're going to eat every bit of it, right?"

Nuala started to nod, then asked, "I'm not going to be alone
in here, am I?"

One of the guards who lingered in the doorway snorted. The
nurse smiled at Nuala. "What with all the arrests lately, we're
greatly overcrowded. You'll find yourself with more than
enough company, believe me."

"Oh," Nuala said. "That's good—I think."

"Here we are," a voice said, and the nurse moved aside. A female guard entered the cell, a covered dish on a tray in her
hands.

"Ah, at last," the nurse said. She took the tray from the guard,
but the woman didn't leave; she just stood, watching.

The nurse set the tray down by the bunk and uncovered the
plate. Steam rose from the scrambled eggs and the bowl of oat-
meal. The smell of the fresh bread nearly made Nuala swoon.
And there were two pitchers of juice, apple and grape, and a pot
of tea.

"You won't be able to swallow easily," the nurse said as she
poured some apple juice. "You'll need a sip with every bite,
nearly, to wash it down."

The three guards were still staring at her. They were concerned she still wouldn't eat? Is that why they were still here?

The nurse picked up the plate and stuck a fork into the fra-
grant eggs. "I'd best help," she said. "You're still shaky; you'd
probably just spill everything."

She held a forkful of scrambled eggs up in front of Nuala,
who looked at the food, then up at the one female and two male
guards. All three of them were watching her, waiting.

Nuala smiled and opened her mouth. The eggs slid in and

melted on her tongue. She moaned in appreciation and smiled at the nurse as she chewed.

That must have been the signal. All three guards left, one of them saying "Here, move along!" as he went. Nuala saw two prisoners peering in the door at her, but they left at the guard's command.

Other prisoners walked by as Nuala ate, drifting slowly over to stare at her as they passed. A woman came into the cell, pushed the mattresses on the other bunk aside, and sat down. She was about twenty-five, a brunette, and dressed in prison blue. She watched Nuala eat. After a while two others in blue showed up together. They each took a mattress and spread it on the floor. Then they, too, watched Nuala eat. She felt conspicuous again, as if she were giving a performance. Did they approve of the way she chewed and sipped? She wished they would stop staring. Feeling uncomfortable at their scrutiny, she began to chew with her eyes closed.

"Give you a hand with that?" a familiar voice said, making Nuala's eyes fly open again.

Fiona knelt next to the bunk and took the apple juice glass from the nurse, holding it up so Nuala could grasp it with a trembling hand and take a sip.

"Hey, roomie," Fiona said. "Where the blazes you been, then?"

Chapter 31

"WHAT'S THAT NOISE?" Nuala murmured, and forced her eyes open. The faint tapping sound had been continuous since her arrival in the cell, but she had been too preoccupied really to notice it before.

"Code," Fiona said. She had been sitting on the floor next to the pitcher of juice the nurse had brought, leaning against Nuala's bunk.

"Code," Nuala repeated. She cleared her throat and tried to sit up. Fiona had to help her.

"For communicating between wings," Fiona explained, "or between cells during lockdown."

Nuala nodded. She remembered Benny telling her about that. She nodded again, noticing that her head was not as heavy as it had seemed before. Was she already stronger, after only one meal?

"How long was I out?"

"A few hours. Have some juice." Fiona poured a glass; it turned out to be apple, Nuala's favorite kind. "How are you feeling?"

"Besides foolish, for giving up so easily?"

Fiona shook her head. "It was a way to fight back; hell, Nuala, everybody knows that. Now how *are* you feeling, really?"

Nuala was grateful for her friend's seemingly automatic support. She considered the question of her physical condition as she took a swallow of the juice. Her vision was clear again; no more spots danced in front of her eyes. She raised her hand and made a fist to see how much strength she had reacquired. It was a pitiful attempt, but she smiled. "Better."

"Going to be awake for a while?" Fiona asked. When Nuala nodded, she called over to one of the women in prison blue who were playing cards near the door. "Banbh, go ahead, if you're still wanting to."

The woman who had arrived first after Nuala had been brought in nodded and tossed in her cards, saying "Fold."

Nuala watched as Banbh picked up a tin whistle from the floor beside her, and smiled when a reel began to enliven the cell. Banbh's fingers flew on the instrument. After a few moments a faint echo of harmony drifted in through the small barred window in the metal door; someone in another cell was playing along.

"Quite the musician, our Banbh," Fiona said softly as Nuala finished the juice. "She's in for a robbery a few years back, and the other two are Teresa and Úna, petty theft and embezzlement respectively. We don't know if the cell was bugged before, but now that you're here, we have to assume it is, just to be on the safe side."

"Is that what the music's for?" Nuala whispered. "To act as cover—"

"The music's because we like it," Fiona said, her voice still low. "If the cell is bugged, the bug's most likely under your bunk or somewhere close. The music probably won't drown us out, but it might help a bit."

"If it worked too well, they'd just confiscate the whistle," Nuala pointed out.

"Yeah," Fiona agreed. "So Banbh won't play too often, just in case."

"I have a thousand questions. Heather and Igraine—" Nuala was still whispering, but when Fiona spoke, it was at a normal level.

"Our two friends are well. They're in another wing, so I haven't seen them, but word on the pipeline says they're unharmed."

So Lavery had been lying.

"I had a visit from a wee deputy minister," Nuala said, hoping the bastards were listening. "A noxious little toad name of Haughey."

"The *Taoiseach*'s brother-in-law?" Fiona chuckled. "Must've been the highlight of your day, that."

"He was trying to offer me some sort of government deal, but he gave no details. I've been wondering why the government would want to deal with me. They've got me where they want me, so why—"

"Oh, I imagine they're a wee bit concerned, is why," Fiona began to explain. "What with the riots, the general strike, the fact that the *Dáil* itself is under siege ..."

"Siege?" Nuala sat up straighter, not needing Fiona's help. "Literally?"

"In a manner of speaking. Surrounded, it is." Fiona's smile was grim. "As is the Holy See in Armagh, and at least half the *garda* stations in the country."

Nuala stared at her, afraid to believe what she was hearing.

Fiona went on. "The people began to appear in the streets within an hour after the Guerrillas showed them what *really* happened at your da's funeral. Once they realized they'd been lied to again—once they knew who had actually committed the murders, and why—I guess they decided they'd had enough. So they've surrounded a great many government buildings, and not just in Dublin. As I said, *garda* stations all over the country are under siege. As well as this prison. The pipeline says there's been a huge crowd at the entrance for days: they won't leave, or maybe they send in reinforcements, I don't know. They know you're in here—along with a few thousand other women rounded up in the last week or so."

"Only women?"

"Oh, some men have been arrested, too, to be sure, but the vast majority are women ... Stupid bollixes. They think such heavy-handed tactics are going to scare us back to the kitchen?"

"Has anyone been hurt?"

"Of course. But they're standing firm; it hasn't chased the people off." Fiona got up off the floor and sat on the edge of the other bunk, leaning toward Nuala, her elbows on her knees. She was wearing a shapeless prison gown at least two sizes too big for her.

"I think the government realizes it's in *serious* trouble this time. No one's listening to the RTE or government spokesmen. They're not even listening to the Church any longer, and you know that's always been the way to get the people to obey the government: Threaten to excommunicate them. But it's not working any longer." Fiona smiled in grim satisfaction. "I think the *Taoiseach* realizes how deep he's in it this time and that the backstroke will no longer work."

It was hard to believe. Fiona made it sound like they were one step away from winning. Was that for the benefit of who-ever might be listening in, or was it really true?

"But these arrests—"

"A stupid move." Fiona's tone was bitter. "They seem to think they can lock up the entire country."

How long would the people hold out against indiscriminate murder—as at the funeral—and mass arrests? How deep was their anger? Nuala wanted to ask if Fiona had any news from Éadaoin, but of course she couldn't just blurt that out, in case of electronic infestation.

"How did you say our three friends were?" Nuala stared at Fiona, willing her to understand, to notice the word.

Fiona blinked, then smiled. "They're unharmed, as I said. They have a lot of friends in here, and word travels easily on the pipeline."

"They're still hopeful, then?"

Fiona nodded, her eyes saying she knew exactly what Nuala was asking. "They haven't given up. In fact, they're even more confident than usual."

The revolution was gaining momentum? Is that what Fiona meant? Nuala shook her head in wondrous disbelief. A few days ago all had seemed lost. She had thought she had no future, that all she could do was offer herself up as some sort of sacrifice, hoping her death would be sufficient to make up for the deaths she had caused. A wave of shame washed over her: She had had so little faith in the people for whom she had been ready to die. Had her terror at the prospect of being raped again, her mind-numbing grief over her father, her guilt at the deaths of twenty-seven people blinded her that completely? She had been so wrapped up in herself and her own pain that she had given little thought to the hundreds or perhaps thousands of people in the Movement who knew what they were risking, but chose the risk anyway. People like Bébhinn, who had been arrested—but not because of Nuala. It was arrogant to think that *she* had been the instigator. Bébhinn had chosen to become involved, to fight for a dream of freedom. She was a courageous woman, and Nuala felt privileged to have known her. Her and all the others. They would survive and they would win; she would just have to trust them to succeed—with or without her. She deserved neither the credit nor the blame.

"Hey, you okay?" Fiona whispered, leaning closer, frowning in concern.

"Some leader I am." Nuala felt her cheeks flush with her shame.

"Oh, is that it, then?" Fiona sighed. "Just you beating yourself up again, is it?"

"What?"

"That's a very annoying habit, you know?" Fiona said as the music ended. "Nobody expects you to be a superhero except yourself. Give it up, can't you?"

Banbh walked over to them. "You want to play?" She held the tin whistle out to Fiona.

"Not just now, thanks."

"You play?" Nuala asked in surprise.

"Several instruments, actually. Bit of a child prodigy on the pipes, flute, tin whistle I was. Years of lessons—until I realized that music scholarships only went to boys, that there was no future for me as a professional musician. Gave it up completely as a teenager out of anger. But I came back to it purely for my own enjoyment later on. Just never had the opportunity when we were on the run."

"Really? I didn't know—"

"Sh!" Banbh interrupted, holding up a hand to silence them. "There's another for you."

"What?" Nuala asked. But Banbh motioned for her to be quiet and walked over to the corner where the toilet sat. The tapping was louder over there where the pipes were.

"It's repeating now," Banbh said, and slowly translated the coded message. "Nuala: The food is lousy . . . but please eat it anyway . . . We need you . . . Love from—*Kidín*?—and the Kerrywoman . . . Nuala *abú* . . . That's it; it's repeating again."

Nuala and Fiona shared a smile. "Can you reply?" Nuala asked Banbh.

"Sure, what do you want to say?"

"Well, I—"

A clanging noise reverberated in the cell and was echoed outside. An instant later the cell door slid open.

"Suppertime," Úna said, gathering up the cards. "Our wing's turn at the trough."

"I'll send the message later; I'm starved." Banbh's eyes widened as she realized what she had said. She stared at Nuala, blushing. "I didn't mean—"

"Forget it." Nuala smiled at her. "It's just a word, right?" She swung her legs out from under the blanket.

"And just where do you think you're going?" Fiona asked.

"To supper, of course." Nuala took a deep breath and prepared to attempt the launch.

"Don't be silly." Fiona put a restraining hand on Nuala's shoulder. "You'll fall right over on your nose."

"Probably," Nuala agreed. "But then you'll pick me up, won't you?"

"I'm sure they'll have one of us bring a tray back for you," Teresa said. "There's no need—"

"Yes, there is," Nuala interrupted. "Foolish pride dictates it."

Fiona sighed, shaking her head. "Banbh, grab an arm."

"You're not going to try to talk her out of it?"

"Ha! Talking Nuala Dennehy out of or into anything is about as likely as the Pope getting pregnant. Grab an arm; I can't carry her myself."

So Banbh took Nuala's left arm, Fiona took her right, and they hauled her to her feet. Nuala felt the breeze in the back.

"Bloody hospital gown," she muttered.

"I'll tie it tighter," Teresa offered, and the women helped turn Nuala around so she could do so.

Nuala swayed on her feet, but her cellmates supported her, and she began the laborious journey with as much dignity as she could muster.

That first trip had been a foolish mistake; Nuala nearly passed out more than once before getting there. A nurse with a wheelchair showed up not long after Nuala had sat down to what everyone else considered an unappetizing supper. She ate as much of it as she could, then allowed the nurse to wheel her back to her cell. Later trips were easier, as long as she didn't try to hurry.

The next few days were quiet; other than the once-a-day visit from the nurse, Nuala was ignored by the authorities. Even the guards just watched her, not speaking.

She finally got a shower, which made her feel human again. Her cellmates were no doubt grateful for that shower, too, but they tactfully didn't mention it. And she was allowed to replace the hospital gown with a blue prison gown. Again she thought of Bobby Sands—his memory had been haunting her since she had first chosen the hunger strike—and of his blanket protest. But she thought Bobby would understand if she wore prison clothes. At least for now, when she still didn't have a clue as to what the government wanted from her. A blanket protest could always be used later, if it was needed.

Nuala's physical strength rapidly increased, now that she was determined to continue fighting. The terror and despair she had felt in the first days of the hunger strike only came to her in her nightmares now. Lavery's face would fuse into Adolf's in her dreams, but fortunately she always jolted awake just as he/they began to rape her.

Whenever she joined the others in the common area—with Fiona at her elbow in case she got dizzy—the stares were unremitting. Some of the women said hello, most at least nodded in greeting, some just stared—but the only women who really made her uncomfortable were the ones who gushed at her, telling her how much they admired her. Even the few who asked to speak to her in private and then offered up moving stories of how she inspired them to become involved made her wish she could escape; she never knew how to respond to such talk.

The chatter on the pipeline never ceased. Through Banbh, Nuala was able to converse with both Heather and Igraine, who were in a wing that didn't connect with Nuala's. Her friends were really all right, they assured her. Other than a few slightly intimidating but not physical interrogation sessions, the guards had left her alone, oddly enough. Coded messages were even relayed from Éadaoin herself, though she was never named, of course. Nuala had no idea how Éadaoin—who, along with Brigid and Dana, was safe in Rathcoole—got word into the prison, but she did. The revolution continued, though the arrests had dealt it a serious blow, especially the number that were the result of spies, infiltrators. Everyone in the Movement was jumpy these days, but they were encouraged, too, by the solid, to-be-believed rumors that a general election would be called soon. It was only a matter of time. The advice from Éadaoin was: Stand firm, be strong; victory will be ours.

So Nuala passed several days, growing stronger, putting back on a few of the pounds she had lost. She played cards with her cellmates, was entertained by Banbh and Fiona's delightful tin whistle playing, or talked on the pipeline with the help of the three women who had been here for years. As hard as it was being there, considering how close she had come to death it wasn't so bad. But she wondered when they would come for her.

They finally did, of course, after nearly a week. Two male guards appeared at the open door just as Nuala's hand of two pair was beaten by Úna's flush.

"Come with us," the blond of the pair said. He didn't bother to say why or where.

Nuala had already decided that she wouldn't refuse when the time came; it would do no good, and it would be so undignified to be dragged out. And she didn't want to endanger her cellmates.

So she got to her feet and straightened her gown. "See you soon," she said to her friends, looking at Fiona. She hoped it was true.

The conversations in the common area died as the two armed men escorted Nuala through, one man gripping each arm. The women stared.

"Where are you taking her?" someone called out, and the dark-haired guard on Nuala's right tightened his grip. Neither man replied.

The women moved closer, ignoring the guards with rifles who were watching from the catwalks above.

Nuala could feel the tension of the guards, saw the hostile frowns of the women surrounding her. She had to dampen the fuse before it could be lit.

"It's all right!" she called out. The blond guard started in surprise, and squeezed her arm tighter; she knew she'd have a bruise there.

"Someone just wants a brief chat with me about my trial. I'll be back soon enough."

The women were still not happy about it, but they didn't interfere, stepping back to let them pass easily. The guards relaxed a little bit, but only after turning the corner that separated them from the staring women.

Nuala wondered, as they led her along, whom she was going to see: Haughey or Lavery? Just in case, she visualized the colored switches as she walked.

"We have kept our end of the bargain," Haughey said, leaning over the table at her. "Now it's time for payback."

Lavery stood at the closed door of the tiny room, watching her with cold, dead eyes. He hadn't said a word to her, but his presence was threat enough.

Nuala had been seated in a chair behind a table, the table then pushed in, pinioning her against the wall. It didn't quite touch her, but it would if she leaned forward even an inch. She gazed up at Haughey impassively.

"I'm sure I don't know what you mean," she said. "The only deal I agreed to was to go off hunger strike if I was put in with the others. I was, so I did. End of deal. Anything else will have to be renegotiated."

Haughey began to shout. "You are in no position—"

"What does the government want from me, Declan?" Nuala interrupted, which further insulted him. He turned purple, spluttering. She sighed impatiently. "Let's stop all this posturing, shall we? Just tell me what you want, and I'll consider it."

Haughey clenched his fists and struggled to control his temper. "You will refer to me as Deputy Minister and show me the proper respect." The words were forced out between gritted teeth.

"Sure, whatever," Nuala replied. "So what's the government want?"

Haughey squinted at her, still seething. He shot a glance at Lavery, but the tall guard ignored him. The Deputy Minister was inspiring respect in no one today. But surely he was used to that, Nuala thought.

Haughey cleared his throat and straightened his waistcoat with a sharp tug. "You will make a tape for the *teilifís*, urging the citizens to return to their homes and to their jobs. You will persuade them to renounce violence and to obey the law."

Nuala laughed, a mirthless sound that further irritated the officious little man. But he continued. "In exchange for making this tape, certain extenuating circumstances will be taken into con—"

"No."

Haughey blinked. "What?"

"I said no." Nuala shook her head at Haughey, to emphasize the point. "Telling people to quit when they're so close to winning would be the act of a fool. I am no fool."

Haughey leaned closer. "You can be persuaded, but it won't be pleasant for you."

But Nuala just sighed. "Oh, Declan. Didn't anybody tell you that torture got nothing from me the last time? It doesn't work."

"I understand you have a young friend," Haughey said, switching tactics quickly. "One Heather Lonnegan?"

But Nuala had had time in the past week to deal with that brand of guilt, too, due to Heather's tapped-out reassurances that she would be all right, no matter what. "Threatening to harm anyone I care about won't work either, Declan. They wouldn't thank me for sparing them by betraying what they believe in. Your threats won't work."

Haughey straightened up and glared at her, but he wasn't surprised. "You will regret not cooperating. Sergeant Lavery here will see to that." He strutted to the door, and Lavery stepped aside, opening it for him.

Haughey turned back. "I will return tomorrow to see if you have changed your mind."

"Violence and threats won't work, Declan," Nuala assured him. "Negotiation is always a better plan."

"We shall see." Haughey turned on his heel and disappeared.

Lavery closed the door and smiled at Nuala. "I've been waiting for this. And I don't intend to share it; I want you all to myself."

Nuala's muscles began to tremble, but she stilled them. She expected the roaring in her head to start, but it didn't. The overwhelming terror, the panic that had nearly broken her the last time she had been alone in the room with this man did not return. She was surprised to realize that they were gone for good: The act of choosing death had banished many of her ghosts. Never again would she let this man or any other terrify her. Except in her nightmares.

Lavery moved toward her leisurely, in no hurry. He was a very tall man, and the table was relatively low.

She waited until he was but an inch or so from the table, just reaching for it to move it and get at her. Her hands were holding the edge of it, and she pushed as hard as she could. The corner of the table slammed into Lavery, catching him in the genitals. He doubled over, his face turning purple, his mouth open.

Nuala used the few minutes she had bought herself to conjure up the switches that waited in her mind to protect her.

The beating, when Lavery had recovered enough to deliver it, was savage. But Nuala barely noticed it. It was happening to someone else, far away.

"Go to hell, Declan," Nuala muttered. She didn't bother to open her eyes again. She had spent the night in the hospital ward, where they had taped her cracked ribs. It hurt to breathe. But he had spared her face, so she could talk, at least.

"As I said ..." Haughey raised his voice in irritation. "I would prefer to avoid another—incident—like yesterday's."

"Oh, I'd definitely avoid it, if I were you," Nuala said, her eyes still closed. "You wouldn't enjoy it at all."

There was a moment of silence. Was Haughey exercising his tiny brain to come up with a new tactic? Maybe she shouldn't antagonize him too much. As long as he was here, talking, Lavery couldn't get at her again. He hadn't raped her yesterday because he had been far too furious, too eager to beat her to death—which he might have done, if two other guards hadn't appeared finally to call him off. But some of his rage would have subsided by today. And even though she was in hospital and therefore theoretically off limits, she couldn't trust him to obey the rules.

"I am prepared," Haughey said, reluctance obvious in his tone, "to renegotiate."

Nuala's eyes opened. She sorely missed the Guerrilla News. She wondered if something new had happened yesterday or last night to persuade Haughey or his puppetmasters to try a new tack with her. Had the riots grown worse? Had the general election been called?

"I'm listening," Nuala said.

"The government—we—want the violence to end," Haughey began.

"Then the government should stop committing it," Nuala replied.

It was obvious how much Haughey hated this job, hated her. He glared at her, his eyes narrowed.

"You are being offered a choice," he said tightly. "You will plead guilty to treason. You will publicly state that this civil unrest should cease at once. You will persuade the people to obey the laws and to effect change, if that is what they want, by peaceful means: by voting. If you do so, and the people obey, the other four thousand women and men arrested so far will be released immediately. You will serve ten years in prison, and then you will be released. You must admit that this is a *very* generous offer, far more generous than you deserve."

"And if I refuse?"

"If you refuse," Haughey said, smiling in grim satisfaction at the prospect, "you will be found guilty anyway, and sentenced to planetary exile."

Nuala betrayed no emotion in either expression or tone. Planetary exile! Ireland had never sentenced anyone to such a fate. In centuries past the British regime had sentenced Irish people to "transportation" to Australia, but off the planet! She tried not to let the image take root in her mind; it would have shown on her face.

"In addition to that, *all* the other prisoners will be tried for treason, and I can guarantee that the sentences will not be lenient."

He couldn't be saying— "You can't sentence four thousand people to exile," Nuala protested. "That would be suicidal for any government."

"I'm sure the majority would only get prison terms," Haughey said, dismissing the idea as unimportant. But he took a step closer to the bed. Nuala was reminded by his hatred that she was helpless; as a supposedly dangerous prisoner, her wrists were again strapped down.

"I'm tired of playing games with you." Haughey lowered his voice. Somehow that made it more ominous. "If this government is truly on the way out," he said, barely loud enough for her to hear, "then we will take as many of those responsible as we can down with us."

"A new government would overturn the convictions, pardon those convicted," Nuala argued.

"They might," he agreed, "but that would only help those in prison here. Those unlucky ones—like yourself—who had been sent away to exile would never be retrieved, and you know it. Ireland has no space fleet, nor the resources to fund a rescue mission. You'd be taken by the *U.S.* Space Command, and they *never* go after convicts. Exile is a one-way ticket. Once you're gone, you're gone."

Nuala fought to keep her face blank, her tone calm. "The Fleet would certainly—"

"Would it? That would be interfering in the internal matters of a sovereign nation. The Fleet has sworn never to do that,"

Haughey reminded her with a sadistic smile. He had her there, and he knew it. He savored the moment.

"Each person should be allowed to choose for herself—"

"*Your* choice," Haughey interrupted. "Only yours. You're their bloody 'leader.' You call off this uprising, or you personally will guarantee planetary exile for—who knows how many people?"

Nuala studied him, wondering if he was bluffing. Would the government really go that far? Surely every member of the *Dáil* knew someone who had been arrested: a daughter, a sister—

"I'm not making this up out of whole cloth," Haughey interrupted her thoughts. "Your friends the Guerrillas reported just last night that the United States has begun to deal with its similar internal problems in such a manner as this."

"What?" Nuala hoped he was lying, but he seemed far too pleased with himself.

"Oh, yes. And one could even assume that it was your fault, couldn't one? After all, tapes of your speeches have been shown extensively by pirate broadcasters in the States and Canada, and God knows where else. Some even say that it was Ireland's— *your*—'inspiration' that caused the American women to revolt, and in all those other countries, too." He smiled at whatever he imagined he saw in her eyes. "Yes, the United States has already begun the trials, already made arrangements for an exile mission. As a matter of fact, that was what gave us the idea. Nice turnabout, don't you think? Quid pro quo."

Nuala couldn't think of a reply; she was too shocked that any government would inflict such a punishment, normally reserved for serial murderers, the criminally insane, or the like, on women who only wanted—

"You can't help them," Haughey interrupted her thoughts again. "It's too late for the American women. But it's not too late for Irish women." His eyes glittered, and Nuala thought of a shark scenting blood. Maybe he wasn't just ineffectual and pathetic. Maybe he was mad.

"You can save them, Nuala. Every one of them would be released." He nodded. "That's right; they would all go home. All you have to do is tell everyone to go back to work and mind their manners, obey the law. They can vote in a new government at some future time, but for right now, they call this off."

Nuala stared at him, wishing he would back off, shut up, let her think.

"If you don't," he said, "you'll be sentencing hundreds—

perhaps thousands—of people to be marooned on some godfor-
saken, uncolonized planet, never to see Ireland—to see Earth—
again. Never. It's up to you."

Nuala wanted to tell him to go to hell again, but she knew
from the triumphant look on his face that he would just laugh at
her.

Having responsibility for her own fate was one thing, but—

"You have until tomorrow to decide." Haughey turned to go.

"Wait!" Nuala said. "I want to go back to my cell, with the
others."

Haughey smiled. "I don't give a damn what you want." Then
he walked away.

Nuala was left strapped to her bed, her mind whirling. What
was she going to do?

Yes, everyone involved had made her own choice when she
joined up, but that didn't change the fact that Nuala had all their
lives in her hands. She could send them all home to fight another day, or—

If they were released and if the present momentum was
slowed—it would not be stopped in its tracks at mere word from
her, Nuala knew now; it was too powerful for that—there was
still the possibility for another try, and soon.

But even if she *did* ask them to call it off, would they, even
temporarily? If the people were angry enough to have laid siege
to government buildings all over the country for over two
weeks, why should they want to stop now? Maybe they would
just ignore her, and the government would carry out Haughey's
threat anyway.

And how could she say it had been a mistake, an
overreaction, which seemed to be what the government wanted
her to say? Who would believe she meant the words even as she
said them?

Nuala's thoughts continued to tumble long after the lights
were dimmed for the night.

Plead guilty? Sure, no problem: She *was* guilty—of breaking
their immoral laws. So was everyone else who chose to join the
revolution. But did that mean they deserved planetary exile? Did
it mean they wouldn't mind if she chose that for them? Some
wouldn't, Nuala knew. Heather, Fiona, Igraine: They would like
it no better than herself, but they wouldn't blame her for it. But
the others, people she didn't even know? Did she have the right
to decide their fate?

Choices, choices. Everyone had the right to make her own

choices, Nuala had always believed. But when they were not given the opportunity to choose for themselves? When somebody else—namely herself—was told to choose for them, how could that be ethical, moral? How could it be right?

But how could she betray everything she had ever believed in by saying that the revolution was over when they were so close to winning, even for the sake of all those people?

But how could she not send them home?

But even if she did as the government asked, how could she believe it would keep its word?

Nuala lay wide awake, strapped to the hospital bed, going over and over it in her mind. It was her choice. No matter how immoral that she should have to choose for others, it was, in the end, her choice.

Sometime around dawn she made up her mind. She could only hope that someday she would be forgiven.

Chapter 32

"I HAVE BEEN asked to speak to you," Nuala said, looking into the camera, "about the recent unrest. But first, I would like to assure you that I am fine. As you can see, I am in good health, and I have been treated well."

The dress they had given her had long sleeves and a high neck. The bruises on her body wouldn't show, and Lavery had carefully, even in his rage, followed orders and avoided hitting her face. Although she hadn't seen a mirror in quite some time, Nuala supposed she looked well enough. Maybe no one would notice how stiffly erect she was sitting, or the fact that she took only shallow breaths.

Haughey watched from the taping booth, but Nuala ignored him. Likewise she ignored the armed guards who were covering all the exits, out of camera range.

"I am truly sorry," Nuala went on, "about the injuries and most especially the deaths that have occurred in the last few weeks. I share a certain measure of responsibility for the deaths of the twenty-seven people killed at my father's funeral in Falcarragh. If I had not been there, they would not have died."

The red light on the camera went out, and Haughey's voice filled the studio. "Enough of that! Get on with it."

Nuala's eyes narrowed, but she only nodded in acquiescence. The red light came back on.

"And I think it's time that the violence ended." Nuala paused, going over what she had planned to say in her mind. Her fists were clenched in her lap.

"I understand that you have taken the law into your own hands. You've destroyed *garda* stations, stoned the *Dáil* itself, and have gone out on general strike, bringing this sad nation of ours to a standstill. This cannot go on. This must not. A solution must be found." She paused again, taking a few short breaths.

"I have always spoken what I believed to be the truth," she said. "I *have* made mistakes in my life, but I have always tried to do what was right. And so when this revolution began, I was elated to see how many people agreed with me and were willing to risk their lives and their liberty in their struggle for freedom. But then the killing started, and I was forced to ask myself, is it worth it? And when the mass arrests began, I asked myself again, is it truly worth it? Wouldn't it be better for people to stay home and simply vote for whichever politician promised to do the least amount of harm? And after much considering of this matter, giving it a great deal of thought, I was reminded of the words of James Connolly: 'Our demands most moderate are, we only want the earth.' And I was further reminded of the words of a great American, Thomas Jefferson: 'A society that will trade a little liberty for a little order will lose both, and deserve neither.' And that gave me my answer.

"It is time the violence was ended by those who have caused it, by those who have committed it. Has it been worth the deaths, the arrests, the threats of exile? Yes, it has. A nation's freedom is worth any price, and now it is time for the violence to end by calling a general election—"

The red light finally went out. Nuala was surprised she had fooled Haughey that long; that he had believed she would turn it around at the last moment, as she had promised him. She looked up at him. He glared down at her, the hatred palpable through the glass.

"You'll regret this wee trick, you bitch."

Nuala shrugged and sighed. "You gave me the choice and the

chance, Declan. I took it. I couldn't have done anything less and lived with myself."

"We'll see how long you have the *chance* to live with yourself," Haughey snapped, "once the others learn what you've sentenced them to."

"It's been announced, about the sentence of general exile," Lavery said as Nuala was marched down the prison corridor, her hands cuffed behind her back. "They were rather quiet at first. Now they're angry." He chuckled. "I'm sure they'll be *terribly* glad to see you, since it was yourself that earned it for them."

Nuala stumbled, and Lavery chuckled again.

The aborted attempt at taping had been yesterday. Immediately afterward Haughey had ordered the tape destroyed so it wouldn't fall into Guerrilla hands. But the Guerrillas, as Nuala had counted on, were everywhere. One of the broadcast technicians in the booth that day disappeared into the underground on his way home from the taping, and later that night the tape appeared on every *teilifís* in Ireland.

Nuala only knew this because she heard one guard tell another. Not long afterward, Lavery had appeared in the interrogation cell. She had just enough time to hypnotize herself before he began.

They had apparently decided they would get nothing helpful out of her, but Lavery had been rewarded for his earlier restraint with free rein to do to her what he liked—short of murder. He had been thorough, taking his time, and he had enjoyed it. Now she was being returned to the general population. Lavery seemed to be looking forward to it; he kept chuckling in anticipation.

At the last gate he looked down at her, smiling. "I'd enjoy doing it myself, of course, but the psychological effect if your own do it for me will be much greater."

The gate was opened and Lavery motioned her inside with mocking gallantry. Her cuffs were removed when the gate had closed. Lavery pushed her from behind, nearly knocking her off her feet.

"Well, go on. Aren't you eager to be with your friends again? Or are you afraid they're going to save us the trouble of a trial?"

He laughed again, but Nuala didn't wait around to listen. She went forward.

Keeping her face unmarked was no longer important after the fiasco of the taping, so Lavery had done his job thoroughly. One of her eyes was swollen shut; she could only imagine what she looked like. Her ribs were killing her, and she was so sore from the rapes that she could barely walk.

But she forgot about any of that as she neared the corner. What would their reaction be? Did they blame her? How could they not? Nuala turned the corner, toward the roar of thousands of voices.

The common area was jammed with women, just as it had been the first time she had seen it. She paused uncertainly, turning her head to see out of her still-open eye. She saw a few women she recognized, but didn't approach them; at the moment she just wanted to find her cell and collapse.

As she came closer, first one woman then another saw her. They gasped and stared. And then, just as on that first day, the conversations died and silence spread.

They stared as she moved among them. She saw anger and accusation on many faces, but something stopped them from making a move against her. Had Lavery won her their grudging pity by leaving her in this condition? If so, she was sure he would not be pleased. He hadn't followed her, so he must be watching from one of the catwalks. She didn't look up.

Nuala eased her way through the crowd, trying to walk without limping, trying to hold her head up. It would simply not do to pass out now; she had to make it to the cell.

It was eerie, the way no one spoke to her. No accusation, no welcome, no greeting. Were they still in shock over their fate? Did they hate her too much to speak to her?

She started when she heard the murmur. "Welcome back, Nuala." A young red-haired woman no more than Heather's age smiled at her.

"Go raibh maith agat, a Shinéad," Nuala replied in thanks. Her swollen lips made her mumble, but her voice itself was clear and steady.

That seemed to break the spell; suddenly she was being greeted left and right, by nearly everyone she passed. But there were some who turned away from her, their faces filled with hatred.

Because of her pain, it seemed to take forever to cross the crowded room. Banbh had appeared at some point to walk beside her, not touching, but there if needed. Nuala smiled her thanks.

As she was leaving the common area, Nuala finally looked up at the catwalk. Lavery glared down at her, furious she hadn't been torn apart by an angry lynch mob. She smiled at him and left the room.

When she stumbled, Banbh caught her elbow, helping her along the corridor toward the sound of a tin whistle. "The news has been all over the pipeline," she said. "Everybody's scared to death that the general election won't be called in time to save the lot of you."

"Any word on the election?" Nuala asked through swollen lips.

"It's being discussed in the *Dáil*," Banbh replied, "but it's not been brought to a vote yet."

"What are the bastards waiting for—as if I didn't know," Nuala muttered. "They want to see us sent away, out of sheer spite and hatred."

"Here we are," Banbh said, and helped Nuala limp into the cell. Fiona's reel stopped in midnote. She jumped to her feet, dropping the tin whistle on Banbh's bunk, and ran to Nuala.

"I had no choice," Nuala said to her friend. "I mean, I did, but I couldn't tell them to give up, could I?"

Fiona took her free arm and she and Banbh helped her to the bunk Úna once again vacated.

"Could I?" Nuala repeated.

Fiona put the pillow under Nuala's head. "Of course not. If you had done anything else, you would have betrayed us; you wouldn't have been Nuala. And you would have kept the four of us awake at night, I suppose, defending yourself to the phantoms of Connolly and Pearse and—"

"Bobby Sands," Úna added.

"Right," Fiona agreed. "Especially himself."

"So you're not—angry?" Nuala said, feeling foolish that she needed to hear it.

Fiona chuckled and shook her head. "Is it delirious you are, then? Angry!"

"Banbh, get on the pipeline," Fiona said as Teresa pulled the blanket up over Nuala. "Tell everyone she's back, if they don't already know, and that if they come to take her again, we're going to stop them."

"What? No." Nuala tried to sit up, but her ribs stabbed her and she collapsed on the bunk. "I don't want anybody more to be hurt because of—"

"Shut up, Nuala," Fiona said affectionately. "And get some sleep; you look like hell."

* * *

They didn't come for her, to Nuala's surprise. Perhaps there really was nothing more they wanted from her, since nothing they had tried had worked. Or maybe they were simply too busy to exact revenge. The number of prisoners increased daily, as more and more arrests were being made. There was no more room left in the cells, and mattresses had to be thrown down in the common area.

The pipeline kept them informed: The riots were increasing, as was the pressure on the *Dáil*. The Archbishop had been summoned to Rome; God Patrols didn't dare leave their monasteries unless they were in mufti. *Gardaí* could travel only in armored vehicles, and even then they weren't safe: The civilians may not have had guns, but Molotov cocktails weren't difficult to make. The violence increased.

With every report Nuala worried more. So many people were being hurt! Why wouldn't the *Dáil* give in and allow a general election to be called? Were they that blind or that arrogant, that unfeeling? When would it be over?

Even international news trickled in over the pipeline. Over two hundred women from the United States had been sentenced to planetary exile so far. Mexico had just sentenced her first handful of women to the same fate, and Chile's trials were to start any day. Fleet Command expressed concern and disapproval, but that was all it could do. When the Ghizhbassan ambassador expressed doubts about the wisdom of having allowed Earth to join the Unity, the Fleet diplomatic corps had its hands full. They had to convince the Ghizhbassans and other members of the Unity that Terrans were not all barbarians, that not all Earth nations were ruled by despots.

Nuala stayed in her cell except for meals and showers. The fear of planetary exile had been of something abstract and perhaps not likely—until the news of the American and Mexican women's sentence. If Americans and Mexicans could be banished from Earth, so could the Irish. Nuala felt the stress of hatred stabbing her in the back at every meal, heard the occasional shouted threats, but other women always shouted the few down and surrounded Nuala. Fiona never left her side. They would both have felt safer if Igraine and Heather had been there. It helped a little to converse with them on the pipeline.

It was Heather who asked, in a series of taps, for Nuala to repeat the story of how Red Hugh O'Donnell had escaped from Dublin Castle in 1594. It was one of her favorites of the stories Nuala had told when they had been on the run. Nuala didn't want to tie up the pipeline that long, but Banbh told her that that was partly what it was for: education as well as communication. So Nuala told the story, in a simplified version, and Banbh tapped it out with her tin whistle on the pipe. After that it was a different story each night. Banbh explained to Nuala how the taps were repeated at relay points, so that the stories went all over the prison. Even some of the guards remarked at how quiet things got at a certain time every evening. So Nuala told her stories as her audience continued to grow.

One day a somewhat familiar face appeared at the cell door. The young woman greeted Nuala with a smile. "Remember me?"

"Uh, possibly," Nuala replied, trying to place her.

"Noreen O'Mahony," the woman said. "From the travelport in Belfast?"

"Great Dagda!" Nuala smiled and waved her into the cell. "The first person I met when I returned to Ireland. When was that, a thousand years ago?"

"About." Noreen sat down at the end of Úna's bunk, which Úna had insisted Nuala keep until she was completely recovered from her injuries.

"Fiona," Nuala said, "this is the woman who helped your friend Rose—" She stopped. They had never determined whether the cell was indeed bugged or not, but there was no point in adding to the evidence against Noreen, just in case.

"Right," Fiona said. "Nice to meet you, and thanks, for Rose's sake."

"It was my pleasure," Noreen assured her. "I've always found it a virtue to help my friends, and their friends. Especially our three southern friends."

Noreen looked from Fiona to Nuala, waiting to see if they understood the reference. It dawned on Nuala a split second before Fiona: Rathcoole was in the south of Ireland, so the three friends had to be Éadaoin, Brigid, and Dana.

Nuala smiled. "How long have you known themselves?"

"Several years, actually," Noreen said. "I'm always doing—was doing—them wee favors."

"I should have known," Nuala said. It certainly explained how Noreen had managed what she had.

"How long have you been here?" Fiona asked.

"Only since yesterday. I'm sleeping out there." Noreen pointed in the direction of the common area.

"Were you in Belfast recently, then?" At Noreen's nod, Fiona added, "What's happening there?"

Noreen leaned forward and lowered her voice. The other women gathered around. "The entire city has stopped functioning—well, not entirely; some shops stay open, because people need to make a living, and others need to buy food and such. But the government has all but shut down." She shrugged, smiling. "After all, no office can run without clerical help."

The women smiled back. "Do you think it'll end any time soon?" Teresa asked.

"Not that it will help *us*," Úna explained to Noreen. "We were here long before the revolution started."

"But we care, too," Teresa added, and Úna nodded.

"Sh!" Banbh said, startling them. She was walking toward the pipe, listening intently to the incessant tapping. Finally she turned and looked at Nuala, her face pale. "Your trial. It starts tomorrow."

"I haven't even been charged with anything yet," Nuala said. "I haven't seen an attorney." She laughed bitterly. "Or perhaps they've dispensed with those formalities, too. The result is a foregone conclusion, after all."

"But with the attention of the international media—" Noreen began.

"Oh, they'll be barred from the courtroom," Nuala interrupted. "Definitely. So the government can say whatever it likes about what a 'fair' trial I'm getting. It'll be like the old days of the PTA."

"The what?" Úna asked.

"Prevention of Terrorism Act," Nuala explained. "Before Reunification, back in the late twentieth century, the British passed the PTA, which in effect gave them permission to suspend anyone's civil rights in any part of the old U.K., including the north of Ireland, in order to convict them on broad charges of 'terrorism.' Juries were banned, informers—called 'supergrasses'—were paid to lie, the judges were all handpicked for their political beliefs. It worked quite well: The conviction rate soared in the Diplock courts. Anyone accused of terrorism—often simply because they were nationalists, Catholics—didn't stand a chance, whether they had actually done anything or not. I expect it'll be the same for these trials, too, for us."

The women fell silent, contemplating a frightening future.

"Nuala," Noreen finally said. "Remember the last thing I said to you as you were leaving the travelport that day?"

"Well . . . no, actually," Nuala admitted.

Noreen smiled. "You asked me why I had helped you, and I said I had a hunch about you, that maybe someday I'd brag about it." She put a hand on Nuala's shoulder. "I was right. Whatever happens, I'll always be proud I helped you."

The emotion Nuala felt at the simple statement embarrassed her; she felt her cheeks redden.

"So it will be a foregone conclusion, as you said," Fiona said to Nuala. Her tone was bleak. "Our only hope, to save us from exile, is that the general election will be called in time."

Nuala had been prescient about the nature of her trial and the others that followed. The *Dáil* passed emergency legislation—a new version of the ancient PTA—that assured convictions. Juries were banned, for the same old reason: so they wouldn't be swayed by threats to themselves or their families by "terrorists." The judges acted in teams of three, and all were priests or Brothers, and therefore not at all sympathetic to the defendants, or even impartial. Most of the attorneys were appointed by the court, and even when defendants hired their own attorneys, the judges had little patience for listening to them. And the international media, as Nuala had predicted, were banned from the courtroom. After a few outraged reports on EuroNet about this ban, reporters began to be held up at customs; problems developed with their passports.

It was all unfolding as Nuala had feared it would: a foregone conclusion, and she was first.

She tried to speak at her own trial, and was immediately gagged and cuffed to her chair. There were no spectators, no reporters to tell that no witnesses were called on her behalf; only prosecution witnesses were called to the stand. They were *gardaí*, most of them, but a great many men she had never seen before, too: men who described to the three dour priests how their wives or daughters had listened to this terrorist, this unnatural woman, and had become surly and finally uncontrollable. Nuala didn't know if the men were paid supergrasses who had memorized their lines, or whether there was any truth to their stories. She hoped they were true; they were the only part of the ordeal she enjoyed.

The trial took only a few days, as her own court-appointed attorney offered little in the way of a defense. The verdict took less than an hour, and the sentence was hardly a surprise: planetary exile, as soon as possible.

The news had spread before she was returned to prison. As the van approached Maghaberry, she heard the pandemonium. She couldn't see out; there were no windows, but she heard the crowd.

The shouting was incoherent, but Nuala heard her name and the rage in the voices. The four guards in the back with her gripped their Armalites, knuckles white on the barrels, and avoided her eyes as the van was assaulted by what sounded like rocks or possibly bricks. The van slowed, almost stopped, and Nuala was afraid for a moment that the crowd would try to free her. Enough people had died because of her; she couldn't bear the thought of any more deaths on her conscience. But then the van sped up again, and she heard plasfire and screams. It was over quickly. The gates shut behind the van and she had been returned to prison. She wondered how many people had been hurt or killed.

Nuala's trial was only the first one, and the longest. After her conviction the process went more smoothly and the accused were shipped along the judicial assembly line in courtrooms all over the country. Within a week of Nuala's conviction, Igraine, Heather, Fiona, and almost a hundred other women shared her sentence of planetary exile.

Since the media were banned, the Guerrillas had no tape to steal from them, and didn't manage to sneak any cameras in themselves, but they reported what little they had been able to find out. None of the defendants was allowed to speak on her own behalf, which the Guerrillas noted and soundly criticized. This was picked up by the international nets, which joined the Guerrillas in their condemnation of the trials. Questions were asked, answers demanded, about why all the *women* were being tried first. But the government ignored the Guerrillas, ignored the international condemnation, ignored the demonstrations both home and abroad—ignored everything. It was digging itself into a deeper and deeper hole. But the *Dáil* didn't seem to care.

The trials continued, with no end in sight.

"The election! It's been called!"

Nuala was playing poker with her four cellmates when she heard the words shouted from cell to cell. The women dropped their cards and crowded around the closed metal door. Banbh ran to the pipe, her tin whistle ready to tap out questions at the first break. She leaned close to hear and decipher the code.

"The general election's been called!" a voice, muffled by distance and closed doors, shouted. That was the entire message, apparently; the same sentence was yelled from cell to cell, all the way down the wing. Faint cheering started up a few moments later.

Nuala and Fiona looked at each other, afraid to hope.

"Isn't it wonderful!" Teresa exulted. "You'll be out of here in no time; they can't exile you if the new government pardons you, and it will!"

Nuala sighed. "Yes, it is wonderful—for the country. But for us?" She shrugged.

"Why not?" Úna asked, frowning in confusion. "You can't *not* be pardoned, right? A new government will have to, to end the riots."

"If we're still here," Fiona said.

"Remember what Haughey told me about taking as many of us down with them as they could," Nuala reminded them. "I'll believe in my own freedom the day it happens."

"Oh, don't be so negative!" Teresa scolded her. "It'll happen; you'll see. You have to think positive, that's all."

Úna wasn't so sure now. "Think positive? And where has that ever gotten us? You've been here two years, right? And I've been here three."

Teresa shrugged. "Not for being heroes. *They*'ll be pardoned. I know they will. I think we should celebrate."

"I'd hold off," Banbh said, and the others turned. Her grave expression made Nuala's stomach lurch. "The election's been called, all right, but for next month."

"When next month?" Fiona asked, her voice flat, knowing the answer wouldn't be good.

"On the twentieth."

"That gives them more than six weeks." Fiona exchanged a somber look with Nuala. "You think they've made the arrangements yet?"

Nuala nodded. "I think they started preparing it before Haughey even told me about it. They've had plenty of time."

The faint cheering began to die out as the pipeline carried the news of how much time remained for the government to act. The five women listened to the fading victory cheers.

"Teresa," Nuala said, startling the others out of their fearful reverie, "do you have any of those chocolates left that your mother brought you?"

"Yeah." Teresa brought the box over, prying off the lid. "Five left. One for each of us."

"Good." Nuala reached into the box. "Everybody take one."

Puzzled, the other women each took a chocolate cream. Teresa tossed the empty box onto Banbh's bunk.

Nuala held her candy up in the air. "We don't have champagne—which is fine with me, as I don't drink—so these will have to do."

Fiona smiled and raised her chocolate. The other three women followed.

"This *is* a victory," Nuala said. "It was our goal to bring down this totalitarian government, and we have succeeded: It is on its last legs. We should dwell now not on our own fears, but on what we have gained, so . . . to the future and a free Ireland."

"The future and a free Ireland," the others echoed, smiling, and popped the candies in their mouths.

"And may we be here to see it," Fiona murmured.

Chapter 33

"YOU HAVE VISITORS."

Nuala and Fiona looked up from their card game. In the cell doorway stood one of the guards, a not very friendly woman named Mullavey—she claimed her first name was not the business of any convict.

"Which one of us?" Nuala asked.

"Maguire."

"Really?" Fiona got up. "Since when are we allowed—"

"Do you want to see them or not?"

"All right, all right." Fiona shrugged at Nuala and followed Mullavey out.

When she returned some time later, her eyes were red-rimmed, and she sat down in a corner by herself. Teresa started to speak to her, but Nuala waved to get Teresa's attention and shook her head.

At suppertime, almost an hour later, Fiona said she wasn't hungry and looked at Nuala. Nuala told their cellmates to go on without them.

When they had gone, Nuala came over and sat down by Fiona, waiting silently.

"It was—my parents." Fiona's voice was heavy with tears. "And Gormfhlaith . . . They—they came to say good-bye."

"Good-bye?" There was a sinking feeling in the pit of Nuala's stomach.

"Aye." Fiona sniffed and wiped her nose with the back of her hand. "They were informed"—she swallowed—"that I will be shipped out next week."

"Next week." Nuala repeated the words in a stunned monotone. There had been no word of this on the pipeline. If there had been a general announcement on the *teilifís*, they would have heard by now.

"They were told only this morning," Fiona explained, as if reading Nuala's thoughts. "The families are allowed one last visit, to say good-bye." She sniffed and had to clear her throat. "It was—so hard—"

Nuala rarely touched anyone by choice; it made her uncomfortable. But she put her arm around Fiona now and squeezed. She tried not to think of anything at the moment, to banish her own fears and concentrate on her friend's pain.

"Gormfhlaith—she's just a kid, barely thirteen . . . She was trying so hard not to cry." Fiona broke down and Nuala just waited, her own eyes beginning to fill as she remembered the eager young rebel she had met that day in the park.

"She said—" Fiona swallowed and took a deep breath. "Gormfhlaith said she was proud of me, no matter what Mam and Da said; she was proud to be my sister. And not to worry, that she would remember everything I ever taught her. She said she would never stop being a rebel . . . and that she planned to write a book."

"A book?" Nuala repeated.

"Yeah." Fiona sniffed again and then smiled through her tears. "*The History of the Revolution and Its Leaders* by Gormfhlaith Maguire. Or *My Sister Fiona and the Revolution* by Gormfhlaith Maguire. She hasn't decided on the title yet."

Nuala laughed. "Good for her . . . Remember when she wanted to cut my hair with those tiny wee scissors?"

Fiona chuckled, nodding.

"Quite a kid," Nuala said. "I liked her straight off."

"So did I," Fiona said, starting to cry again. "From the moment she was born . . . And now I'll never get to tell her—"

"Tell her what?"

"That—" It was a moment before Fiona could get the words out; her tears were choking her. "She's not really my sister."

"She isn't?" Nuala was baffled. "What do you—"

"She's—" Fiona interrupted. "She's—my daughter."

Nuala was stunned; all words fled her. Gormfhlaith was—The age difference had seemed a bit odd for sisters, but not all that improbable. And the resemblance between them—well, sisters could certainly look that much alike. Nuala had never imagined—Fiona, Igraine, and Heather were her closest friends, but this proved—again—how little she really knew them.

"I wasn't married, of course," Fiona said, her voice still quavering. "And you know what happens to 'illegitimate' children and their mothers in this country . . . The only way to prevent my baby from being taken from me for adoption and me being sent to a convent was to . . . hide the pregnancy. So my mother pretended to be pregnant, wearing the right amount of padding as time went on, and I . . . took a leave of absence, claiming family illness, and went away to Sligo, where relatives took me in. I pretended to be just widowed. I'm sure the locals knew better, but they were so kind, no one told on me . . . And when it was time, Mam came 'for a visit' and stayed until Gormfhlaith was born. No one was ever told the truth—not even Gormfhlaith herself. We had to—protect—"

Fiona broke down again.

"Of course you did," Nuala murmured, holding her friend more tightly. What could she say to ease such pain? It was hard enough, losing a sister—she forced Kerry's image from her mind—but to lose a daughter!

"And now . . ." Fiona said, the words barely audible, "now I won't get to see her grow up."

"But she *will* grow up," Nuala said. "And in a free country. You've seen to that. And she'll help ensure that it stays free. You taught her well."

Fiona nodded. "But I'll miss—" She couldn't go on, and Nuala held her.

They had been listening to the pipeline all morning. Since Fiona's news the day before, Nuala had been waiting—hoping—to hear that she would get the chance to see Kerry before she was sent away forever. But she wouldn't put it past them to deny her that one small comfort. So she tried not to think about it, listening to Banbh's translation of the taps.

"Riots increasing in Dublin," Banbh was saying now. "People

demanding that sentence of exile be commuted ... Counter-demonstrations ... urging end to violence now that election called ... Father Colm MacManus announces establishment of ... Independent Celtic Church ... severs ties with Rome."

"Dennehy."

The women jumped at the voice. Mullavey stood in the doorway. "Visitor."

Nuala got up from the bunk, but Úna grabbed her arm. "It could be a trick! That bastard Lavery—"

"Yeah, it could be," Nuala said, extricating her arm from Úna's grasp. "But I have to take the chance, don't I?"

It was no trick. Kerry waited for her on the other side of the security window. Nuala sat down to face her. She knew they wouldn't have much time.

Kerry pressed her com button. "You look ... thin. Have you been eating?"

Naula smiled and pressed her button. "Three times a day, don't worry. And yourself? Are you well?"

Kerry nodded. "I'm fine, Nuala. I—" She started to choke up but got herself quickly under control. "I know we don't have much time, so I wanted you to know about the marker on Da's grave."

Nuala frowned in confusion. "What about it? I thought Cuan—"

"Yes, Cuan bought one, the best he could afford, but—did you know that people have been coming to Falcarragh from all over Ireland?"

"Coming? Why?" Nuala wasn't following.

"To visit Da's grave," Kerry said, smiling, her eyes damp. "And they often stay over for at least a night. The O'Donnell Mórs have turned their house into a bed and breakfast ... Anyway, the visitors stop in at the pub, MacIvar's—you know, the one Da always—"

"Of course," Nuala said. "I know it well."

"Right. Well, so many of them remarked on how small Da's marker was, so Mr. MacIvar told Cuan, and the two of them have set up a fund there in the pub to buy a more fitting one—a grand one, Cuan says—and all the visitors have been contributing. They've raised quite a bit already."

Nuala couldn't believe it. "Strangers have been—"

"Oh, and the locals, too." Kerry smiled. "It's going to be grand, Nuala. A big stone Celtic cross, with a marble slab underneath. Cuan's going to hire a fellow to carve a tricolor on it and

Da's name and dates. What do you think of 'Séamus Dennehy, Irish hero, father of Nuala and Kerry'? Cuan said to ask you what to add to that. He said you'd have a fitting quote."

"He did?" Nuala's mind was blank; she couldn't think of a single quote.

"Something from Pearse or Connolly or somebody," Kerry said. "To 'tell everyone who sees it that a patriot lies here.' That's what Cuan said. So, can you suggest something?"

"Well . . ." Nuala suddenly realized that she would never see the marker, never visit her father's grave. *A patriot lies here.* Buried in the land he loved so much, while she—

"Yes," she said. "Of course I have a quote. Isn't that my profession, knowing things like that? Tell Cuan this: 'Life springs from death and from the graves of patriot men and women spring living nations.' Patrick Pearse."

Kerry smiled. "Perfect. I knew you'd know just the thing—Da would love it. Tell it to me again so I won't forget."

Nuala repeated it twice, and Kerry memorized it. Then an awkward silence fell. There was so much to say, so much that Nuala had never had or taken the chance to say. And now that time was running out for them, she didn't know where to begin.

"I wanted to give you something to take with you," Kerry began, her voice wavering, "but I don't own anything, except perhaps—" She fumbled with her rosary, but Nuala stopped her with a soft word.

"They won't let us take anything personal with us," she said. "We've already been told."

"Oh." Kerry's mouth trembled. "Then I can't—"

"Do you have any hair under that thing?"

The incongruity of Nuala's question made Kerry blink in surprise, and then smile. "Do I—well, of course I do. It's short, but I—why do you ask?"

"Could I see it?"

"What? Nuala, why?"

"Please," Nuala said. "I know it sounds bizarre, but humor me?"

Kerry must have thought her mad, but after a glance at the bored guard who couldn't have cared less, she reached up and in a moment the guimpe had been removed. Her hair was dark, almost Nuala's natural color, with a chestnut sheen. It was only a few inches long, but it fit her head like a sleek cap.

Nuala smiled. "Thank you. That's much better. *That*'s the way

I'll remember you: a beautiful, strong woman with very pretty hair."

That made Kerry sniff, and touch her hair self-consciously. Nuala fought back her own tears. "Do you know anything about this Independent Celtic Church?"

Kerry had to clear her throat before answering. "Well, yes, actually I know quite a bit about it. You'd be surprised how much."

Nuala smiled back. "I thought so. Good. So listen: Here's your chance, right? This thing's just starting up, so you can get in on the ground floor, so to speak, help make some of the rules—if there *must* be rules."

"Like what?" Kerry smiled in anticipation.

"Like nuns—you are going to have nuns, I suppose?"

"Of course."

"Of course. Well then, nuns can wear whatever they want to, no more medieval uniforms hiding themselves or their hair. And no more ridiculous vows of obedience. And nuns—and priests, for that matter—can marry if they want to and have children."

Kerry chuckled. "Somehow I can't imagine—"

"Well, if you can't imagine it, it won't happen. So imagine it, okay? Somebody has to. Gods, Kerry! You're a Dennehy—you can accomplish anything you set your mind to!"

Kerry stared at her sister. She was trying to smile.

"Now's the time," Nuala said. "Everything will be new. New government, new church, new society, if you want it badly enough. And you can help build it. You can build it for me, since I won't be here."

That brought the tears Kerry could keep back no longer, but she nodded firmly. "I will," she managed to say. "I *will*; I promise."

"Then it'll be okay." Nuala's voice was breaking. "You'll be okay, and I won't worry. I'll know the Dennehys are still fighting for Ireland."

"Time," the forgotten guard said.

"No!" Kerry pressed her hand to the window. "Nuala—"

"I'll be fine, Kerry," Nuala said, barely able to talk. She forced a smile to her face and held it there by force of will. "You be happy. And I meant it about nuns marrying and having kids. Name one of them Séamus, okay?"

"Me? . . . Well, actually there is this ex-priest I—" Kerry knew there was no time, so she didn't finish the thought. "Yes, *if* I have children, I'll name one Séamus and one Nuala. And I'll teach them all those stories Da told us, and about you—"

"Let's go," the guard said.

"Everything's going to be okay," Nuala promised her little sister. "The future is going to be grand."

Kerry mouthed the words *I love you* because she was too overcome to speak. Nuala nodded, then turned to go. At the door she looked back.

Kerry had picked up the guimpe. She was staring at Nuala, still crying. Then she looked down at the cloth in her hand. In one determined motion, she tossed the guimpe aside, letting it fall to the floor. Then she crossed her arms and smiled at Nuala.

Nuala smiled back, her eyes shining with tears and pride. She took one last, long look at her sister, then turned and left her behind.

"Trials suspended!" Banbh said five days later, a little before lights out. She was translating the frantic tapping.

"What?" Teresa said. They all crowded around the pipe.

Nuala and Fiona had been feeling numb since seeing their families for the last time. There had been a great deal of weeping coming from the cells around them, and the atmosphere in the common area was somber, depressed. Several days earlier there had been talk of rioting, of taking over the prison, but that had been abandoned when one of the guards mentioned that such an action would ensure a life sentence for every "regular" convict—those there on criminal charges before the revolution began. Some of the "regulars" were willing to go along with the riot anyway, but too many were not, and as desperate as the exiles were, they couldn't risk their fellow inmates. So the fear and the lethargy spread.

"No more trials," Banbh translated slowly. "Further judicial proceedings on hold . . . pending outcome of election."

Nuala sighed in relief and shared a tired smile with Fiona. "At least some of them will go free."

"Yeah," Fiona said, "Noreen and Bébhinn among them. They haven't been tried yet."

"In exchange . . ." Banbh continued, frowning in concentration, "for cessation of demonstrations and . . . attacks on *gardaí*." She listened for a moment longer. "It's repeating."

"Think they'll go for that?" Fiona asked.

Nuala shrugged. "Depends on how angry they are, I suppose.

I guess I hope they do. As much as I appreciate the support, I'd like to see as many of us get out of this as possible and go free."

"Yeah." Fiona sighed as she ran her fingers through her hair. "Six hundred of us is *more* than bloody enough. The bastards—"

"Sh!" Banbh hushed them, leaning near the pipe. The others saw the color drain from her face. They moved even closer, watching in silence.

Finally Banbh looked over at Nuala and Fiona. "A and B Wing exiles are being shipped out. You're leaving!"

"In the middle of the night!" Úna said. "The bloody cowards!"

Nuala thought her heart had stopped, but then she felt it sledgehammering in her chest. She and Fiona stared at each other.

"Here!" Banbh grabbed her tin whistle from her bunk and held it out to Fiona. "Take this with you!"

Fiona tried to smile. "Thank you, Banbh, but you know they won't let us—"

"You could hide it!" Banbh cried.

"Even if they *don't* do a cavity search," Fiona said, "I'm afraid it's a bit large . . ."

That made them all laugh. Banbh shrugged and started to put it away under her mattress, but Nuala stopped her.

"Play us something jaunty," she said. "A jig or a reel. And keep playing until—well, as long as you can."

"Aye," Fiona said. "Please, Banbh?"

Banbh smiled and sat down on her bunk. The other women sat down, too. Nuala and Fiona weren't allowed to take anything with them, so they didn't bother to gather up the few cheap prison-issue toiletry articles that were the only things they owned. They just sat, trying not to think, and listened to the music.

Banbh was still playing when the door finally slid open. A male guard with an Armalite in his hands stood silhouetted in the doorway.

"Dennehy and Maguire! Out!"

Their cellmates stood up along with Nuala and Fiona. The good-bye hugs were quick but fierce; the three women being left behind had tears in their eyes.

"Move it!" the guard barked.

"Keep playing," Nuala said to Banbh. "Play us out."

Banbh nodded. As Nuala and Fiona stepped out into the corridor to join the stream of pale, frightened exiles, the strains of "O'Sullivan's March" followed them.

Chapter 34

IT TOOK A while to load the three hundred women from Maghaberry onto the short-hop shuttles; by the time they had flown across Ireland to the Shannon travelport, the night was nearly gone. There was no explanation of why they were leaving from Shannon and not Belfast, but perhaps it was a diversionary tactic. The guards kept a tight grip on their Armalites, even while in flight. Nuala wondered if they were expecting a rescue mission. She tried not to hope for something that foolish and suicidal.

Upon arrival at a nearly deserted Shannon, they were jammed into an empty hangar. They huddled together to keep warm. At least a hundred armed guards and *gardaí* surrounded the hangar, both inside and out.

Nuala and Fiona's group arrived nearly an hour before Igraine and Heather's. They had a brief reunion; there wasn't much to say, as each of them was weighed down by her own thoughts. But at least they were together. Heather stayed very close to Nuala, practically in her pocket, Nuala thought, but she didn't mind; she found it comforting, and it was warmer that way.

A couple of *gardaí* were pushing a set of movable stairs at the front of the hangar, turning it around. When it was in position, one of them climbed up the stairs, with a short fellow in a shiny green government sash following him.

"Attention!" the *garda* on the stairs shouted, unnecessarily. The women were all watching him, wondering what was going on. "Quiet!" he barked.

When they had quieted enough to suit him, the *garda* and the man in the sash changed places. The *garda* handed the other fellow the microphone.

Nuala recognized him the minute he opened his mouth: It was Haughey.

"You have been found guilty of—"

"We know why we're here, ya stupid bollix!" a loud female voice interrupted Haughey.

Laughter rippled through the crowd and the mood shifted a little; defiance had tempered some of the fear.

Haughey glared at them, then tried again. "In accordance with the law, you are to be transported from Ireland to the United States of America, to the Canaveral Space Depot, from where you will be launched to the Mercury Space Station. There you will await transfer to an American vessel, which will then remove you from this solar system and take you to an as-yet-unspecified, uncolonized planet. You will be supplied with sufficient material to establish a colony . . . and there you will spend the rest of your natural lives." He paused for a moment. Nuala couldn't see him well, but from his posture and his tone, she could tell he was taking enormous satisfaction from this.

"May God have mercy on your souls," Haughey finished.

"And may the hearthstone of hell be your bed rest forever!" someone yelled, calling down the ancient curse against informers and traitors.

Haughey glanced nervously around the crowd, then turned and hurried down the stairs to an accompanying chorus of boos and obscenities.

"He's out of a job soon," Fiona muttered. "Along with his bleeding cancer of a brother-in-law."

The song started somewhere in the back, as soon as Haughey had slipped out the door. It was the Irish national anthem, "A Soldier's Song," and the singing quickly spread through the crowd.

Nuala and her three friends joined in, though Nuala sang it softly, more to herself.

As soon as the anthem ended, another ancient song of freedom began somewhere and was taken up by the exiles. Nuala couldn't join in at first; grief constricted her throat. She swallowed a few times, took some deep breaths, and was able to murmur the last verse:

> Well, they fought for poor old Ireland
> And full bitter was their fate.
> (Oh, what glorious pride and sorrow
> Fill the name of Ninety-eight!)
> Yet, thank God, e'en still are beating
> Hearts in humanity's burning noon,

Who would follow in their footsteps,
At the rising of the moon.

As the song died, Nuala heard soft weeping, shaky breathing, and noses blowing all around her. They were trying so hard to be brave, these women who had fought for freedom; she felt proud to be standing with them, even as the grief overwhelmed her.

Ireland had been her entire life, everything to her. The history, legends, folklore, the stories of heroes and villains, and the long, tragic battle for freedom. And now she was losing it forever. What would she have left?

"Nuala?" someone murmured at her elbow. An unfamiliar blond woman in her forties stood there in prison blue.

"Yes?"

"My name is Mairéad," the woman said, smiling. "I have a message from Éadaoin and Brigid and Dana."

Nuala glanced around, but the guards were against the walls and she and her friends stood in the center of a singing crowd; they couldn't be overheard.

"Actually," Mairéad went on, "the words are Brigid's, but the sentiment is from all three."

Nuala didn't bother to ask how the message had been delivered, but just nodded.

"The message is: 'We are sorry we could not risk a rescue attempt; the price in lives lost would have been too high. But do not consider this a defeat. What you have lost you have gained for millions. What you leave behind will be entrusted to and nurtured by future generations in freedom, which you by your sacrifice have granted them. Your deeds and your memory will never be forgotten. Thank you.' "

Mairéad smiled at the four women. "That's the official message, and it was for all four of you."

When Nuala had no immediate reply, Mairéad smiled again. "Éadaoin and her mother had a bet with Dana that you'd not be at a loss for words, even at that. I guess Dana won, eh?" Nuala and her friends chuckled. "The unofficial message," Mairéad went on, "is that the election is in the bag. The new party has the votes, and the leader of the party is one of ours: He's the husband of one of Brigid's oldest friends, and a feminist himself. He's our next *Taoiseach*."

"Then we've really won?" Heather asked.

"Aye," Mairéad replied, nodding somberly. "And the victory

was gained by every one of the three hundred women in this room and the other three hundred at the Dublin travelport. We won, all right."

The doors to the hangar rolled open, letting in the cold morning air. The women had already been shivering in their thin prison gowns; now their teeth began to chatter in earnest.

"All right! Move out four abreast!" a guard barked.

"I've got to get back to my friends," Mairéad said. "See you—well, later, I suppose."

Nuala nodded. "Thanks for the message."

Mairéad pushed back through the crowd that was slowly moving forward.

When Nuala got to the door, hunching her shoulders in the cold, she was not prepared for what she saw.

At the edge of the tarmac, to the left of the hangar, people stood watching, ignoring the hundred lethal Armalites pointing at them. The attempt to sneak the women out before the country was up and about hadn't worked. The people knew. And they came.

Some were weeping in silence; some called out names and heartbroken farewells. Nearly all of them carried candles. Not flashlights or glowlamps, but candles—hundreds of candles that lit the cold predawn night.

Nuala left the hanger with Heather on her left and Fiona and Igraine on her right. They followed the four women in front of them toward the InterContinental Suborbital Transport that squatted on the tarmac, waiting.

They weren't marching, but Nuala felt as if they were in a kind of parade nevertheless as they walked, eyes left, watching the people watching them.

A few hundred meters from the ICST, Nuala saw a man holding a tricolor in the crowd. Her heart jolted for a moment: She thought it was her father. But of course it wasn't. It was just a man about his age in a corduroy coat like the one Séamus used to wear.

"Thank you!" the man called out every few moments, as line after line of women started up the ICST steps. *"Go raibh maith agaibh!"*

Nuala looked straight at him, but she couldn't be sure he met her eyes; it was still too dark to tell.

It took over an hour to get the three hundred women strapped in and secured for suborbital transport. Heather took the window seat, Nuala next to her, then Fiona, then Igraine. They weren't talking any more than anyone else around them; they were in no mood for chatter.

Finally the engine noise increased.

Heather squeezed Nuala's arm and pointed at the window, tears in her eyes. Nuala leaned that way.

It was daylight now. A blanket of mist enveloped the green land and the surface of the River Shannon. Still the people stood, watching, waiting until the last moment.

But it wasn't the people, or even the few distant tricolors, that Nuala watched through tear-filled eyes as the ICST lifted. She stared at the land, the fields, the rivers, the mountains in the distance: Ireland.

" 'Yet I have no choice but to leave, to leave/And yet there is nowhere I more yearn to live/Than in my own wild countryside/Backside to the wind,' " she murmured, watching her country grow small beneath her.

"Slán," she whispered as Ireland disappeared. "Good-bye."

Nuala leaned back in her seat and closed her eyes, tears slipping from the corners. Except for the sounds of weeping and the roar of the engines, the cabin was quiet; no one was able to speak.

A silent half hour later, Nuala heard Heather speak beside her. "I wonder where we're going." Nuala opened her eyes, blinking. To a *land of shimmering green stones*? she wondered, seeing Máire's face in her mind. Had Máire truly foreseen something? Had she known that Nuala would be leaving Ireland forever? Had she known where they were going? To a *land where women are free and proud*?

"I always wanted to join the Fleet," Heather said quietly. "I always wanted to see space . . . And now I will."

"That you will," Igraine said, smiling fondly at her.

"What do you suppose it'll be like, this place we're going?" Heather asked.

"Magical and wondrous," Fiona said, then shrugged at Igraine's raised eyebrow. "Well, why not? It's as good a guess as any, isn't it?"

Igraine chuckled. "I suppose it is, at that."

"What do *you* imagine it'll be like, Nuala?" Heather asked.

Nuala looked at her young friend's hopeful face and took a deep breath. "Whatever we choose to make it," she said, and smiled.

Irish Pronunciation Guide

CONSONANTS

Consonants are pronounced roughly as in English, except:

bh, *mh* before *a*, *o*, *u* = *w*
bh, *mh* before *e*, *i* = *v*
(but usually silent in the middle of words)

c is always hard like a *k*, never soft like an *s*

ch as in German *Bach* or Scottish *loch* (a kh sound)

fh is silent

s before or after *e*, *i* = *sh*: Séamus (SHAY-mus), *teilifís* (TELL-ih-feesh)

sh, *th* pronounced as *h*: *thraipisí* (HRAP-ih-shee)

t before *e*, *i* sometimes sounds like *ch* in English: *fáilte* (FAWL-chuh)

VOWELS

If they are short (without an accent mark), they are pronounced roughly as in English.

If long (with an accent):

á = *aw* as in thaw: *tá* (taw), *fáilte* (FAWL-chuh)

é = *ay* as in say: Séamus (SHAY-mus)

í = *ee* as in see: *sí* (shee), *teilifís* (TELL-ih-feesh)

ó = *oh* as in toe: *nós* (nohs)

ú = *oo* as in too: Úna (OO-nuh), *tú* (too)

aoi sounds like *ee*: *saoirse* (SEER-shuh), *Taoiseach* (TEE-shakh)

ACCENT

Accent is usually (but not always) on the first syllable unless there's an accented vowel in another syllable.

Irish Glossary

abú forever. Used in war cries, as in *O'Donnell abú!*
agus and
Agus cad is ainm duitse? And what is your name?
agus suigí and sit (plural command form).
An bhfuil siad leat? Are they with you?

Ba fear iontach é. He was a wonderful man.
Bandia duit. Goddess with you. (Variation on the standard Irish greeting, *Dia duit,* or, God with you.)
báinín the cream-colored yarn that "Irish fisherman" sweaters are made of
Bean agus cara. A woman and a friend.
Beir bua! Seize victory!
Bua agus saoirse! Victory and freedom!
Buíochas le Dia. Thank God, or, Thanks be to God.
bunscoil primary school

camogie an ancient Irish game somewhat similar to field hockey, played by girls and women
cara friend
Cé atá ann? Who's there?
Ceart go leor. Right enough, or, Right entirely.
céilí party, social gathering, dance
Cuir do thraipisí go léir ar an mbord agus siúil tríd an scanóir. Put/ Place all your belongings on the table and step through the scanner.
cushla heartbeat, pulse. An endearment, as in "You are the pulse of my heart."

Dáil Irish Parliament
Dia duit. God with you. Standard Irish greeting.

Dia is Muire duit/daoibh. God and Mary with you (singular/plural). Standard greeting response.

Fáilte romhat/roimh. You (singular/plural) are welcome, or, Welcome to you.
Fanaigí. Wait (plural command form).
Fanaigí go fóill. Wait a minute/awhile.

garda/gardaí police officer/the police
Go raibh maith agat/agaibh. Thank you (singular/plural).
Go raibh míle maith agat. A thousand thank yous (singular).

IRA Irish Republican Army. Freedom fighters or terrorists, depending on your point of view.
_____ *is ainm dom.* _____ is my name. (*Is* is always pronounced iss, not iz.)
Is mise. I am.
Isteach anseo, le do thoil. In here, please.

kidín A made-up endearment. *-ín* is the Irish diminutive ending.

Lean an riabh uaine. Follow the green stripe.

meánscoil secondary school
mo chara my friend
Molaim sibh. I praise you (plural).

poitín illegal home-brewed alcohol, "moonshine"

RUC Royal Ulster Constabulary. The police force of Northern Ireland, or state-sanctioned thugs, depending on your point of view.

Samhain 1 November, Celtic New Year, pagan holy day
saoirse freedom
Saoirse na hÉireann Freedom of Ireland
saoránaigh citizens
sean nós literally "old style," refers to Irish "folk" or traditional music
Sinn Féin literally "Ourselves" or "Ourselves Alone." A legitimate, nationalistic political party of nineteenth- and twentieth-century Ireland. In the late twentieth century it has been censored by the government by being banned from the broadcast media and by being dismissed and ignored as the "political wing of the IRA."

siopadóir shopkeeper

Slán. Farewell, good-bye.

Stad anseo. Stop here.

Tá. Is. Used as "yes" in answering some questions.

Tá a fhios agam. I know.

Tá an ceart agat/aici. You are/She is right.

Tá sé go hálainn. It's beautiful.

Tagaigí isteach. Come in (plural command form).

Taig derogatory slang term for a Catholic/Irish nationalist/Gaelic person

Taoiseach Irish Prime Minister

teilifís television

uillean literally, "elbow." Irish bagpipes are filled with air, then squeezed with an elbow to play, unlike Scottish pipes, which are blown into as they are played.

DEL REY DISCOVERY

Experience the wonder of discovery
with Del Rey's newest authors!

... Because something new is
always worth the risk!

TURN THE PAGE FOR AN EXCERPT FROM
THE NEXT *DEL REY DISCOVERY*:

Chimera
by Mary Rosenblum

"Mr. Ishigito." Jewel bowed as she entered the small man's virtual office. He was wearing a classic business Self: bland smile, not-too-tilted dark eyes, hair knotted into a sleek club that couldn't possibly stay so smooth in the flesh. Don't think about that. She bit her lip, let go quickly and forced her lips to relax. "I appreciate the time you could spare me from your busy schedule."

"Please be seated, Ms. Martina." Ishigito bowed formally. "How may I be of service to you?"

Be cool. Jewel seated herself in a chair of polished teak, aware of sleek wood beneath her thighs. In actual, she was sitting on a plastic chair in her bedroom ... The knowledge intruded and she shoved it away. The room was very Japanese, all clean, uncluttered spaces, with a single branch of cherry blossoms in an earthenware jar. Custom designed and expensive, because Ishigito was very inside. Very big. Jewel tried to relax, hoping that the body-language edit in her office was projecting a Self full of seamless confidence. If Ishigito read her nervousness, he might figure that her package contained a hidden risk, and he'd pass. She struggled for calm, but it eluded her. Beyond the unreal walls of this office lay the corridors of Erebus Complex, and beyond that, the freezing desert of Antarctica. Mr. Ishigito might be short and fat, with a pimple on his chin. He might be sitting in a public VR cubicle outside a bus station in Duluth. The image intruded, and Jewel struggled with a terrible urge to giggle.

She was blowing it, and she knew it. Before she'd even made her pitch. With a sinking feeling, Jewel studied the faint aura that shimmered around Ishigito: soft magenta. Her office was interpreting his edited body language as moderately positive, but her office was a cheap model and probably couldn't read his editing for shit. "I am honored that you could spare me this time." Jewel touched the crimson wax seal that lay on her desk.

"This Secure File represents a package that should provide a healthy margin of profit for Epyxx." And had cost her a lot of expensive Net time to set up. Don't think about that either. Jewel leaned back, struggling to keep her body language relaxed.

"I may be interested." Ishigito inclined his head a fraction of an inch, cleared his throat. "I can spare you a few minutes, Ms. Martina."

Steady magenta. Still reading positive. Was this damn cheap office worth *anything*? "I received an advance report on the latest ozone survey from the Zurich Center for Environmental Control. It will be released in two days, and will reveal that the melanoma risk factor for the northeastern United States has risen by nearly one percent in the past six months. The demand for high-quality sunscreen will certainly increase." Jewel snapped her fingers and a large white screen appeared in the air beside her desk. "If you will look at the figures, you will see that projected sales of high-end cosmetic-grade sunscreen in the region exceed the immediately available local supply."

This was the moment, the hook. Jewel felt herself sweating and struggled for a smile that projected seamless confidence. "A Thai phamaceutical company is overstocked with the required base at the moment. Labor costs are quite low in Thailand since last year's revolution. Projected leasing costs for necessary manufacturing hardware and soft support fall well within market norms. The manufacturing can be done there. The political situation is stable enough for sound short-term investment." She tapped the virtual screen and numbers appeared, scrolling slowly down the white surface. "The first product could reach northeastern cosmetic companies within thirty-six hours. A profit margin of seven percent is a conservative estimate. I have already optioned the necessary hard and soft support."

It was a nice, tight, custom-manufacture package; small-scale, but profitable. She sat back, hands folded, remembering not to hold her breath. She was sweating under her skinthins, but her office would edit that out. Her Self—a blonde, slightly Scandinavian model—would be smiling at him, sure of herself . . . sure enough that his office couldn't see her sweat? Stop *thinking* about it. Jewel let her breath out slowly, but the tension didn't go away. Mr. Ishigito was a mid-level node in the Epyxx corporate web. If he bought her information package—if this deal worked and she made him money—it was an entrance.

You needed an entrance in the universe of global brokering.

There were plenty of brokers, all hungry to put together packages for the big corporate webs. Here is the market niche, there is the raw-material source, and over here is the best deal on hardware and labor, all optioned and ready to sign. Take it and run, and I get fifteen percent, thank you. Newcomers were an unknown quantity, a risk in a game that carried enough risks already. And she was a raw newcomer, pushing in on her own instead of slipping in as some broker's carefully groomed protegé.

And she'd damn well do it on her own, thank you. She'd gotten this far. Jewel realized that her smile had grown stiff. *Relax!* She stretched her lips, feeling as if her face was about to crack.

The node frowned at the blob of crimson wax, but made no move to touch it. "Your numbers interest me, Ms. Martina." Ishigito nodded at the screen. "You have a sound premise, but upon considering the margin of profit involved, and the absolute numbers, I must apologetically decline." He got to his feet, still smiling, and bowed. "I'm sure that you will find a client for this particular package. Perhaps we will have the opportunity to do business at another time."

"Perhaps we shall." She returned his bow, her smile plastered to her face—so what, if it was stiff? So *what*? "Thank you for your time, Mr. Ishigito. I know you are very busy."

He ushered her through the door of his office with more polite, meaningless words. No, they weren't meaningless. They translated to *Don't bother me, amateur.* His door closed firmly behind her, and Jewel stood in her own cheap off-the-rack office again. "Shit!" She clenched her fists, tears and anger struggling in her throat. "I was so *close.*" And if she didn't sell this sucker, it was going to mean a big hole in her account. It had taken expensive hours of net time to put together—never mind the cost of the security certification. That ozone tip had been so *hot.* The Worldweb, a mosaic of a million small companies, formed, broke apart, and reformed with the shifting winds of demand and supply. You either rode the crest of those winds, guiding those patterns, pitting your information and guesses against those of other nodes . . . or you worked for somebody else. You belonged to them. As she belonged to Alcourt. "That bastard." Her voice trembled. "Exit office . . ."

Water! Jewel gasped in terror as blue ocean closed over her head. Ice stalactites speared down from a frozen ceiling, and a gray-green seal slid by. Cold . . . freezing . . . she was trapped in a subsea ice cave. Jewel's chest spasmed, her trachea clenching tight in a drowning reflex. For one agonized moment of panic, she clawed for that distant white ceiling of ice, terror a beating wing in her head. Then sanity caught up with her and she grabbed for her virtual lenses. The seal had swum close and it metamorphosed suddenly, became a red fox perched on a thick lump of bottom ice, green eyes glinting like gems, grinning at her. Jewel ripped off her lenses.

White light made her blink and she gasped in a breath of blessed air. She was in her room, of course, facing the futon sofa where she slept, the tipped-over chair prodding her calves. No water to drown her, no ice ceiling to trap her. Breathing hard, Jewel dropped onto her sofa. For a moment, she had been drowning in an icy sea—her body had thought so, anyway. She pushed sweaty hair out of her eyes and shivered. The cold had been illusion, but her flesh had believed it. She rubbed her arms, anger tight in her belly, goosebumps ridging her arms.

Someone had done this to her on purpose—the green-eyed fox. He—or she, or it—had crashed her office and had diverted her into another virtual. That fox had laughed at her terror. Jewel clenched both fists, swallowing down the hard lump of her rage. The most likely culprit was one of the infinitely spoiled children who lived in this place. They *lived* in virtual, and the trick had a childish feel to it. A prank.

If one of the children here had played it, there was nothing *Jewel* could do about it. She swallowed bitterness. She was not an employee here, not a resident.

Not yet.

"Jewel?" The voice came over her audio implant, brusque and impatient. *"I'm awake."*

The boss. Harmon Alcourt. "I'm coming," Jewel said, stifling her sigh because he might be listening in. He usually slept longer than this. If the little fox bastard hadn't dumped her into his freezing ocean, she might have had time to try another Web contact.

But none of them were as inside as Ishigito. She had blown her big chance. Jewel slapped the palm lock on the inside door of her tiny apartment, folding her anger like a piece of cloth, tucking it away in the deep places of her mind. Anger was a privilege of wealth. And of poverty. On the tough road from one to the other, you couldn't afford it. Jewel folded her gloves and lenses, stuffing them into her uniform pocket. The rear door of her apartment took her directly into a hallway by the Alcourt complex. It closed behind her, locked tight by Security. Only Security could unlock it—because this was, after all, the Antarctic

Preserve. Only the centermost nodes in the Worldwebs lived here, the men and women who shaped the economic structure of the whole planet. They took no chances. None.

Jewel straightened her uniform as she hurried down the corridor, smoothing the red medical-aide patch on her coverall. It was the key that had let her enter at all into this world of power and wealth buried beneath the frozen skin of Mt. Erebus. But she would get no farther unless she opened a door to the Worldweb, and that didn't seem very likely at the moment. Jewel smoothed her short, thick hair back from her face, wincing at the cost of the wasted virtual time. Her skinthins—a cheap model—itched beneath her uniform coverall. Alcourt kept his rooms warm, perhaps because it was so cold outside. Harmon Alcourt was one of the most central nodes in AllThings Web, so he could live however he wished. Jewel unsealed the front of the skinthins and tucked the neck down out of sight beneath her uniform.

He napped in the solarium, so she took a shortcut through a leisure room. Empty sofas, recliners, and floor cushions clustered artfully amid flowering bougainvillas. A housekeeper skittered across the floor, silently lifting dirt from the handwoven carpet with a localized electrostatic charge. It had been designed to look like a giant blue beetle. Jewel sidestepped it and walked into the midst of a bougainvilla. Even after a whole year here, she still flinched when she walked into a holo.

Alcourt liked illusion. He had even hired a live-in virtual artist named David Chen to design and redesign his complex. Whole rooms were nothing but holograms projected into recessed doorways that led nowhere. Jewel ran her fingers through a tumbling fountain of unreal crystal water. Did Alcourt do it simply to watch strangers bang their noses on invisible walls, or walk around a bush that was nothing more than a smear of colored light on the air? Perhaps he simply enjoyed manipulating people, as the web he belonged to shaped and manipulated the economies of a hundred nations.

"*Jewel? Where are you?*"

Alcourt sounded petulant, in a bad mood. Jewel hurried down the hall beyond the living room, past the grand dining room with its immense table and dozen chairs—holo—and the library, thick and claustrophobic with dark furniture and walls of expensive, leather-bound, press-printed books—real, and he never opened the books. The next doorway displayed a holoed garden.

It was new, and Jewel paused for a quick glance. Yesterday,

massed clumps of flowers had bloomed between brick paths. Today, textured stones, ochre sand, and cactus filled the space. A rattlesnake basked on a rock and a small lizard perched on a dead branch of sage. It flicked its tongue out at her and streaked away, almost too fast to see. Jewel shivered suddenly, shaken by an unexpected memory of heat, sand, and dust that coated her throat and made her cry. Then it was gone. *I never went into the desert,* Jewel thought. But she had remembered . . . something, and the memory had shaken her. Uneasy, she walked the last meters to the solarium's wide door. The memory had had a childish feel to it. As if she had been very young. Jewel slapped the door open, angry at this brief bit of intrusion, and, beneath that anger, a little afraid. The past was dangerous. Jewel looked over her shoulder as the door whispered closed behind her, as if something might be following her from that holoed desert.

David Chen sat down on a thick ledge of virtual ice and propped his chin on his fist. The vast ice-cave arched meters above his head, its farthest reaches lost in shadow. Thick spires and buttresses of clear blue ice jutted from the walls, polished to a wet sheen, carved into fantastic whorls and arches. A thin slick of water puddled on the smooth floor, and the metronome tick of dripping water rang through the cavern. David shivered in the chill, although the cold was only suggestion, an electrical tickle of modulated frequencies and amperage changes transmitted by his intradermal net. Because he was sitting in an ice-cave, he felt cold. If he'd been sitting in the desert scene he was designing for Alcourt, he would be sweating, his flesh fooled into reaction by the visuals.

It was pretty damned easy to fool the flesh, if you got right down to it. And not only in virtual.

David sighed and ran his finger along the ragged gouge that zig-zagged across a graceful curtain of ice. This piece hadn't been out on the Net long; only a few people had stumbled onto it yet. Chips of broken ice lay on the floor, beside a virtual hammer and chisel. More tools lay on the ice beside him: hammers, an ice pick, a wire brush, rasps. Whoever had gouged the ice curtain had smashed one leg of a fragile arch and hammered cracks into some of the buttresses.

The damage swirled rage across the surface of the ice like oil rainbowed across a puddle. David tilted his head, surveying the effect. It changed the direction of the piece. He got to his feet, tugging at the long braid of his hair. *Try this . . .* With one finger he smoothed away the small cracks that radiated from the gouge. Better. It gave the damage more impact. He wandered through the cave, softening or erasing some of the chips and cracks, deepening others, leaving some untouched. Carefully, he enhanced the edges of the shattered arch so that the broken pieces gleamed like icy daggers in the muted, directionless light.

Perhaps a human figure or two, frozen into the ice ... He reached into the largest of the buttresses and began to shape a face. It took on form: a man trapped in the ice, frozen in an eternal struggle to scream. Yes, this piece was taking a dark and angry turn. Because of his unknown collaborator? Or was some of that anger seeping up from inside him? He withdrew his hand from the cold grip of the ice, staring into the face of the trapped, frozen man. Yeah, some of it was his own. He reached into the ice again ...